THE
TRAITOR'S
SONG

ELIZABETH BAXTER

VINCI
BOOKS

By Elizabeth Baxter

The Songmaker

The Last Priestess
The King's Mage
The Traitor's Song

Vinci Books

vinci-books.com

Published by Vinci Books Ltd in 2025

1

A CIP catalogue record for this book is available from the British Library.
Paperback ISBN: 9781036708481

The EU GPSR authorised representative is Logos Europe, 9 rue Nicolas Poussion, 17000 La Rochelle, France
contact@logoseurope.eu

Chapter One

Maegwin de Romily pinched the bridge of her nose, fighting back a headache that was slowly drilling through her skull.

The wind on the hilltop swirled, sending her hair whipping out behind her and squeezing tears from the corners of her eyes. She squinted into the biting breeze at the darkening landscape below. By the light of the setting sun she saw grassland spreading out in an undulating map all the way to the horizon.

This was the land of the Shinnar, a prairie bordered by the forest of Roamsford Edge on one side and the distant Sunbiter Sea on the other. A landscape of gullies and hidden valleys, of a million different places that might hide an enemy.

Oh, how she hated it.

Footsteps thumped to a halt behind her. After a moment, General Shallon, the commander Leo had assigned to her, cleared his throat.

"High priestess, the scout has returned. We're ready."

Ready? she thought. *Do you think so?*

Maegwin turned to stare at the general. Somewhere in his middle years, he had the physique of a blacksmith and blunt, almost homely features. He wore a black uniform with a silver breastplate over the top and a helmet tucked under one arm. Although his tone was always carefully respectful, Maegwin knew he didn't like her one bit. That was fine with her. She didn't like him either. Shallon was Leo's man and served Maegwin only because Leo had ordered him to. Shallon wasn't the only one in the army who resented Maegwin's sudden rise.

Her eyes flicked to the Shinnar scout kneeling at General Shallon's side. A dark tattoo on his shoulder marked him as a member of the Bison Clan, the only Shinnar clan to have gone over to Leo's side.

"Tratek. I hope you bring me good news."

A quick look of triumph flashed in the young man's eyes. "Yes, mistress. We've found them. There's a small ravine about five miles east where they've made camp. We can take them now if we move quickly."

Maegwin's heart thumped. At last. After all these weeks of tracking, after all the failed missions, she might be able to capture Leo's prize and redeem herself in his eyes.

"General Shallon, ready your men. Tratek, lead the way."

They moved quietly and swiftly through the gathering dusk. Maegwin walked up front with Tratek and the general whilst their troops, a strike force of thirty elite soldiers, spread out around them. Nobody spoke.

The grass was so high it came almost to Maegwin's waist. In the breeze the grass shimmered and hissed.

Traitor, the voice of the prairie seemed to whisper. *You are not welcome here.*

2

Gritting her teeth, Maegwin strode on. It was not the first time she had heard such voices in her mind and she doubted it would be the last. But they were not important, only figments of her past coming to haunt her. If she achieved her goal tonight she hoped those voices would be silenced forever.

General Shallon suddenly paused and dropped onto his haunches, signaling for Maegwin and the other soldiers to do the same. Maegwin went to her knees in the long grass and waited. There was no sound except the whisper of the wind. The smell of grass and the pungent yellow wild-flowers that dotted the prairie filled her nostrils. A large black beetle crawled over her knee. Maegwin sat motionless.

A whisper ran through the soldiers and they pressed themselves flat into the grass. Carried on the wind, Maegwin thought she heard a drum of hooves. They approached her hiding place and then receded into the distance. General Shallon let out a long slow breath.

"That was close," he muttered. "Too close."

"The Eagle Clan?" Maegwin asked.

Shallon shook his head. "Impossible to say. Whoever they were, they were traveling in a hurry, messengers possibly. They didn't see us, luckily, otherwise we could kiss goodbye to any hope of completing our mission tonight."

He poked his head above the tall grass and turned his head slowly to right and left, trying to locate their scouts. He nodded. "It's clear. Safe to move on."

When he paused, Maegwin realized he was waiting for her command. Even after all these weeks of having the soldiers do her bidding, it still felt alien to be the one in charge. Well, she'd better get used to it.

"Very good, general. Lead the way."

They moved more slowly as they approached the Eagle

camp, pausing regularly to flatten themselves into the grass whilst the scouts checked for any enemy pickets. Maegwin bit back her impatience. She'd waited weeks to get this opportunity, a few more minutes would make no difference. She chewed her lip.

A damned book, she thought. *All of this for one damned book.*

After the fall of Tyrvanan, in flame and smoke, Leo had gone a little crazy. He'd disappeared for days and left Maegwin in charge of securing the ruins of Tyrvanan and marshaling their forces. He left a company of a hundred soldiers with her, an excessive force to Maegwin's mind, as the only things left behind were Leo's instruments, some old documents, and his library. These Maegwin had collected into a series of wooden chests, locked them in one of Tyrvanan's remaining cellars and set a guard on the door, all in line with Leo's instructions.

So she'd been utterly unprepared when she was woken in the middle of the night by the bellowing and shrieking of soldiers. A Shinnar raiding party had approached in the dark hours before sunrise and caught Maegwin's force unawares.

At first Maegwin assumed they'd come for her, to take revenge against the woman who'd betrayed them. Or perhaps they had merely seen an opportunity for a quick strike with Leo gone. But it wasn't until Maegwin's men had fought off their attackers that the dawn light had revealed the Shinnar's true goal.

The door to the cellar had been broken open, the guards killed, the chests scattered across the floor and one of Leo's precious books stolen.

The raid had been a feint, a diversion, yet Maegwin didn't understand it. Why risk lives to steal a journal? What could possibly interest the Shinnar in that book? From what

4

she remembered, it had been filled with Leo's ramblings. Why did the Shinnar want it?

Leo had returned the next day and been incandescent with rage at the theft. He wanted that book recovered at all costs. At all costs.

And that's why she was here, crawling through the grass toward the camp of the Eagle Clan. To steal back what they had stolen.

A book. All this for a damned book!

Ahead, the ground began to rise until she saw a sharp escarpment cutting through the landscape. Shallon ordered the soldiers to take cover behind a large rock outcropping. Maegwin pressed herself against the hard stone and carefully peered out. The escarpment had been scoured by the wind until all the covering vegetation had been removed. It stood out of the grassland like a backbone. Cut through it, almost invisible unless you knew what to look for, Maegwin saw the deeper shadow of a defile.

"This is as far as stealth will take us, my lady," said Shallon. "I recommend we attack quickly, take out the guard at the entrance and then pour through the defile in force, sweeping away any of their defenders, and if the Lady is with us, catching them unprepared."

Maegwin peered at the defile. From her position it looked like a dark tunnel leading to who knows what. "How do we know this isn't a trap?"

The general shrugged. "We don't. It's a risk we have to take. The Songmaker's instructions were clear. He said to retrieve what they stole—"

"Yes, I remember," Maegwin snapped. She sighed. "Fine. Order the attack."

The general nodded tightly then gave silent orders to his men through a series of curt hand gestures. They burst from their hiding places and sprinted toward the defile, keeping low to the ground and into the shadows. Maegwin was swept along in their rushing advance. As she ran, heart pumping, breath laboring, exhilaration washed through her. Action! At last!

Tonight there would be bloodshed. Tonight her mistress would be pleased.

Close to the entrance, two Shinnar warriors suddenly stood up from the grass. They took one look at the force pelting toward them and then turned tail and sprinted back through the defile. Maegwin's men saw them and, like hounds spotting their quarry, increased their pace, swords clutched in their fists.

Maegwin passed into the defile. Darkness flashed by on either side. Her skin prickled. This was the perfect place for an ambush. Up ahead, a tumult ran through her soldiers as they reached the end of the defile. Maegwin tensed, expecting to hear the clash of weapons, the cries of struggling men. There was nothing but the pounding of her feet and the labor of her breathing.

With Shallon beside her, she burst from the ravine, holding her knife high, and dropping into a fighting crouch, anticipating attack. But what she found was a broad basin ringed on all sides by sheer walls. A fire burned in a pit in the center of the basin, surrounded by several sleeping figures. Of the fleeing guards, there was no sign.

What was this? Frowning, she straightened then nodded to Shallon. He and four others crept toward the fire, weapons ready. When they were only a few feet away they paused for a moment and then rushed forward, stabbing at the slumbering forms.

Who didn't even flinch.

"Hold!" Shallon cried and his men froze, blades held

high. The general crouched and pulled away the blanket of the nearest figure. "Curse it!"

Maegwin stared. A tumbled heap of sacks lay beneath, arranged carefully to appear like a sleeping person. As the rest of the blankets were removed, they revealed the same.

"Quickly," Maegwin barked, "five of you go back through the defile and guard the entrance. Give warning if you see anyone approaching. The rest of you spread out and check every inch of this place. I want to know who was here and what direction they took."

And why they went to the trouble of this ruse, she thought uneasily.

"We won't find anything," General Shallon said, sheathing his sword as he returned to her side. "They're long gone."

"Really? Then who were the guards we saw? And where did they go?"

The old soldier frowned but didn't answer. Maegwin stalked toward the fire and kicked the embers over the grass in a fit of rage. Sparks flew into the sacking which began to burn steadily. Good. Let it. The whole prairie could burn for all she cared.

Fury and frustration made her giddy. The goddess-damned Eagle Clan had thwarted her again. Curse them. Curse every last one of them. She would have to return to Leo's camp empty handed. Again. She glanced around the shadow-filled bowl and wondered. Why would the Shinnar dupe her so? Why not just attack? What were they up to?

————————

Rovann flinched as Maegwin's gaze passed over his hiding

place and moved on. Beside him, Kandar whistled under his breath.

"By the World Mother's sagging tits, it worked. She can't see us."

"No," Rovann agreed. "She can't."

He went to his haunches, placing one palm flat against the stony ground. He and the Eagle shaman crouched atop the high cliffs surrounding the basin, both cocooned in a shield of Aethyr. Below, Maegwin's soldiers were milling in confusion.

"Dranvey and Preyen escaped?" Rovann asked, thinking of the two warriors who had volunteered to act as lures.

The old man snorted then grabbed one of the bones tied in his hair and yanked it savagely. "Yes. We left a rope ladder attached to the far side of the cliff. They pulled it up after them." He cackled suddenly. "Curse my behind but it feels good to pull one over on the bitch, doesn't it?"

Rovann didn't answer. This was the first time he'd seen Maegwin since she'd betrayed him in Tyrvanan. During the intervening weeks he'd returned to Tyrlindon and mobilized its defense. He'd rallied the Council of Mages, visited Silverport, Mandrake and Mallyn to oversee their garrisons. He'd deployed a circle of mages to each of the major cities to guard against a surprise attack by the Songmaker.

Together with Prince Owen, Mage Syrie and Captain Tyan, he'd set up an elite strike force whose job was to gather intelligence and hunt down any rebel mages at large in the countryside. He'd talked Tanyaka, a Dragon of Fire, into helping with the defense of Tyrlindon and right now she was patrolling the skies above the capital, keeping Lord Cedric Hounsey's besieging army at bay.

The last few weeks were a blur, a haze of activity that

bled one day into the next and as he'd worked, done his duty as King's Mage of Amaury, Maegwin had grown and grown and grown in his mind until she'd become some kind of monster. A cruel, dark-hearted woman who couldn't possibly bear any resemblance to the Maegwin he had known. But now, as he watched her quietly talking to her men, he realized she looked no different. No different at all.

Rovann startled at a sudden cracking noise and glanced down to see that he had inadvertently curled his hand into a fist and in that fist was a rock that he had squeezed so tightly it had shattered into dust.

Kandar crouched beside him. The old shaman rested his elbows on his bony knees and watched Rovann with hard black eyes as keen as a hawk's. That knowing gaze flicked toward Maegwin and back again.

"We should kill her now and be done with it."

He said it casually, with no emotion. To Kandar she was now merely an enemy, just like any other enemy of the Eagle Clan. For Kandar, it was as simple as that. Rovann wished it were as simple for him.

He shook his head. "No. We must discover where the Songmaker is and what he's planning. We might not get another chance to follow her. Besides," he added dropping the shattered remains of the rock onto the ground by his foot, "I'm not sure we would find killing Maegwin so easy. She's the Songmaker's creature now, remember? She's protected by his powers as well as her own."

The old man's tanned face scrunched up into a frown and he spat out a stream of brown phlegm. "That's what I think of the Songmaker's powers! Haven't we been beating the bastard? If it wasn't for the Shinnar he'd be halfway to Tyrlindon by now!"

Angry pride flared in the old man's eyes and Rovann placed a hand on his shoulder.

"Peace, friend. Your people have done more than I could ever have wished but the fact remains: we must discover the Songmaker's plans. Both he and Maegwin have eluded our scouting parties until now."

He didn't bother to add that the only reason the Songmaker had not yet swept aside the Shinnar resistance and marched into Amaury was because of his desperation to recover the book Rovann had stolen from him. Right now that book lay under close guard in the Shinnar camp miles away, far away from where it might fall into Maegwin's hands.

It was another reason why he had to follow through with this plan. The book was a mystery that must be solved. To Rovann it appeared to be nothing more than a logbook of Leo's travels as a minstrel. It was full of maps, poetry, diary entries. None of which seemed overly important despite all the hours Rovann had spent poring over them.

It had been Prince Owen who had alerted him to the importance of the book. He had been Leo's prisoner for many weeks in the tower at the top of Tyrvanan. During that time, before he'd been tortured into blindness, he'd seen Leo sitting by the fire reading this book hour after hour and having his servants bring in other books and maps that he would cross reference with his own before tossing them away in anger.

Yes, definitely a mystery.

Dusting off his hands, Rovann rose. Down in the bowl, Maegwin's soldiers had finished checking the perimeter and had found no trace of anyone. Even from this distance Rovann could see the fury in Maegwin from the harsh set of her shoulders. She snapped something at her soldiers who sheathed their weapons and marched toward the defile.

"Kandar, it's time. Is everything ready?"

The old shaman nodded. *Although I can't say if this will work. Pluck my eyes out, but I've never heard of any human surviving such a thing. I would tell you you're insane, but I'm sure you know that already.*

Rovann smiled wryly. "I must be, Kandar. Who but a madman would put up with you and your ridiculous sense of humor?"

"Ha! Charming!" He straightened, leaning forward to get a better look into the valley. "She's moving. Ready yourself. It will be any moment now."

Rovann nodded. Maegwin had sent soldiers on ahead of her and now, alone in the valley, she spread her arms wide and began to walk forward. On the edges of his perception Rovann sensed her power flare and something draw close in response. The air around her began to rip as though a set of claws had raked through a sheet of fabric. Through the tear, darkness bled. And into that darkness, Maegwin stepped.

Something tugged, deep in his belly, as the trace that he and Kandar had placed on Maegwin took effect. Around him the air shimmered as if reality was beginning to melt. Then he was yanked violently forward. Kandar, the bowl, the prairie, all disappeared as Rovann was pulled into the realm of Chaos.

Rallack, the college's resident mage of Chaos, had postulated that traveling through Chaos would be much like traveling through the Eorthe. It wasn't. There was no sense of movement or the passage of time. Instead there was an infinite moment where Rovann's mind and body were stretched and mangled beyond all recognition. He felt as though he was being flayed. An alien, violent force took him and shook him, trying to find its way into his very soul.

When he opened his eyes he was surprised to find the night sky above him. Surprised to find that his body was still whole. Surprised to find that he was still alive.

Every bit of him hurt. Blinding pain twisted his muscles, forcing him onto his side where he retched into the dirt. He lay insensate, feeling as though he'd been turned inside out and put back together incorrectly. Finally, he opened his eyes and forced his screaming body to its knees.

Rows of neat white tents surrounded him. Guards patrolled between the rows, weapons gleaming at their hips. Rovann gulped and reached for Aethyr then choked out a gasp of relief when he realized the shield he and Kandar had woven had held, even through the fury of Chaos.

Thank you, angels, he thought. *Thank you.*

Nevertheless, he went as still as a statue as a pair of guards strolled by. They were arguing in loud voices about a dice game. They walked right by without seeing him.

He blew out a breath and scrubbed a hand through his hair. Directly before him rose the pristine white walls of a large pavilion. The trace Kandar had woven was locked onto Maegwin so he guessed she must be inside.

Get up, he told himself. *Get moving.*

With a groan, he clambered to his feet. He was going to kill Rallack. Next time anyone needed to travel through Chaos, *he* would to be the one to do it.

Bracing his legs wide to steady himself, Rovann closed his eyes and sent his senses questing outward. He detected thousands of lives, clustered together within two square miles. The space where he stood was at the center of the camp.

He allowed himself a small smile of satisfaction. So far, so good. The trace had brought him to the Songmaker's camp. Closing his eyes, Rovann slowed his breathing and heart rate then focused his consciousness inside. He floated out of his body and up onto the astral plane. He moved warily, cautious that there might be enemy mages patrolling the astral plane. Until now, the danger of discovery should he walk the astral had been too great. Now he'd found the Songmaker's camp, the risk was worth taking. The Shinnar needed all the intelligence they could get. Floating gently on the astral tides, he looked down on the landscape below.

The Songmaker's army sprawled in a natural enclosure made by a line of low hills. It lay within Shinnar lands but close to the border with Amaury. A couple of miles to the east of the encampment spread the dark, brooding mass of the great forest of Roamsford Edge.

Rovann turned slowly, fixing every detail of the enemy's deployment in his mind. Brennan, the chief of the Eagle Clan, would want every scrap of information he could gather.

Satisfied, he dropped back into his body and opened his eyes. After a quick glance to left and right to check for guards, he pulled out his belt knife and silently slit a hole in the tent wall. Slipping through, he found himself in a large space, sectioned into smaller rooms by canvas hangings. He went very still, listening, but no sound came to him.

He stepped noiselessly forward, weaving his way between the hangings until he reached the center of the tent and crouched out of sight behind a chest. Carefully, he peered around the chest into the large, circular space beyond. This was unadorned but for a large rug covering the floor. A figure sat cross-legged in the middle of the rug, murmuring in a low voice.

In the dim light it took Rovann a moment to recognize Maegwin. He tensed, his hands balling into fists. She was only a few meters away and completely unaware of his presence.

I will kill them all, he had promised Tanyaka. He should start with Maegwin right here, right now. After all, he owed her precisely nothing. Not anymore.

But before he could complete the thought, Maegwin glanced up suddenly and her hair billowed in a wind that gusted through the tent, strong enough to send the walls sagging outwards. When it subsided, it revealed a person seated opposite Maegwin. A gangly young man with red hair, green eyes and freckled skin.

Leo March. The Songmaker.

The youth grinned at Maegwin. "Ah! You are a sight for sore eyes! It was very cruel of you to leave me with our Shinnar friends. Not an ounce of humor among them. I've seen more life in a bowl of withered prunes!"

Maegwin didn't bother with greetings. "Leo, you are the one who left, remember? How go our plans?"

Leo's grin faded. "Oh, don't tell me you're going to be as bad as they are! All business and no pleasure will turn us all into bores! Tell you what, I'll sing us a song, shall I? I've been working on it for weeks. I call it, "The fall of Tyrvanan." Ah! It will make you weep!"

"Why have you been gone so long?" Maegwin asked, ignoring his question. "And why didn't you answer my messages? The Eagle Clan has been causing problems."

Leo tapped his nose and winked conspiratorially. "Ah yes! Very vicious fighters, the Shinnar! Now can you understand why I had so much trouble taming them? Even when I was their Lord Shaman the buggers would thwart me at every turn. Yes, certainly an entertaining contest!"

"This isn't funny," Maegwin grated. "They've killed many of my soldiers and made me look a complete fool!"

"Oh, I wouldn't worry about that," Leo waved a hand graciously, "if I worried every time someone thought me a fool, I'd never have left my house. And where would I be now? Well, still in my house, obviously. But you see my point."

Maegwin shifted uncomfortably. "Leo, I—"

The minstrel held up a finger. "I know what you're going to say."

"You do?"

"Of course. You're going to tell me you failed to retrieve my book from the Eagle Clan. Again."

The blood drained from Maegwin's face. "How did you know?"

Leo stared at her and suddenly his sharp gaze seemed full of menace. "I'm the Songmaker, Maegwin. I have my ways. You would do well to remember that."

"I've never forgotten!"

Leo raised a hand and scratched his arm pit. "Yes, I was right. You are in quite the crabby mood today, Maegwin, my dear. Are you sure you don't want to hear a song? It might cheer you up."

Maegwin placed her hands in her lap. She looked ready to throttle him. When she spoke, her words were barely above a whisper. "Leo. You have been gone for weeks. In your absence I have fought the Eagle, Wolf and Lynx clans at every turn. I have done my best to protect our supplies and baggage train from their guerrilla attacks. I have led raids on Eagle Clan camps to try to recover your cursed book and now you sit there grinning like it's all some damned game!" Her last words ended in a shriek.

Leo flinched, ducking as if she would hit him. "Whoa! Remind me never to get on your bad side, Maegwin! All right, all right. Calm down. I'll tell you everything."

She crossed her arms. "Go on."

A wide grin split Leo's face. "I'm not concerned with the book anymore. Oh, my life would be easier if we recovered it, but it no longer matters. Let Rovann have it. He'll never understand it, anyway. You see, I've found it."

"Found it? Found what? The book?"

"Not the book. Something better. Something I thought I couldn't find without the book. But I did. All on my own. Aren't I clever?"

Maegwin shook her head, exasperation making her voice sharp. "What are you talking about?"

"I've been scouting. That's why I've been absent. I've been searching for what I need to complete my plans and give us a way to topple Tyrlindon. And I've found it."

In his hiding place behind the chest, Rovann tensed. What was this? He leaned forward, determined to memorize every word.

Leo rubbed his hands together. "A place. A very special place. Called Near Point. It's close to the mountain passes in the north, just within the border of Amaury. This is where we will gather our forces, Maegwin. It is from this place that we'll launch our attack."

"Why Near Point? I've never heard of it."

Leo nodded, a smug grin on his face. "Not many have. My mages wait for us there and their ranks grow by the day. When we're ready we'll move swiftly on Tyrlindon from the north and hit them so quickly they won't have time to prepare. Hounsey's army is already besieging the capital from the south. We'll have the city surrounded."

Maegwin said nothing for a moment. Finally, she asked, "And what of Rovann?"

Leo's eyes flashed. "What of him?"

"You're sure he doesn't suspect your plans?"

"He doesn't suspect. Why would he? With Hounsey's forces marching on Tyrlindon and your attacks on the Shinnar here, his attention must be consumed. He's already fighting a war on two fronts. He won't expect us to bring a third."

Maegwin nodded although she appeared distracted. Leo leaned forward, peering at her.

"What is it?"

"Nothing."

"You've got that look on your face again."

"What look?"

"The look you get whenever you think about him."

She straightened. "I don't know what you're talking about."

Leo rested nonchalantly on one elbow. "Really? Shall I tell you what's going through your head right now? You're wondering if he hates you. You're wondering if he'll ever forgive you. You're hoping that you'll never have to face him in battle because you're not sure what you'll do. Am I right?"

Maegwin glared at him.

Leo sighed. "How many times must we go through this? We gave him a choice didn't we? He could have joined us. He could have served Sho-La, but he walked away. He left you with no choice. You couldn't abandon your goddess for him."

Leo's voice was smooth and charming. Utterly reasonable. How could anyone argue with such slick persuasion? He made it all sound so simple.

"From the start, you were my creature, never forget that."

He leaned forward suddenly and gripped her chin, forcing her to look at him. "You have darkness in you, Maegwin de Romily. You may have played at being the good little girl for a while but you have been walking my path since the day you were born."

An unreadable expression passed across Maegwin's face. Rage? Horror? Or was it acceptance?

"Have you practiced the Song Spell I taught you?" Leo asked.

"Yes," she sighed, throwing up her hands. "But I still haven't mastered it."

Leo nodded. "I'd be surprised if you had. It took me months to get it right. Let's try it now."

Rovann tensed as Leo reached behind him to pull his lute from where it had been strapped against his back. The minstrel set it into the crook of his arm and began to play. A bawdy, cheerful tune rang out. It was a tavern song you might hear anywhere. Nothing special. Nothing out of the ordinary.

Except, at the sound, the hairs on the back of Rovann's neck stood on end. Power bled out from those notes, charging the air like lightning. After a moment Maegwin began to sing.

> *Long years and memories,*
> *A life of sweat and toil,*
> *I am the one who waits for you,*
> *A seed growing in the soil.*

Energy rippled out in a warm wave, stirring the curtains. Maegwin's words seemed to gather the notes from Leo's lute and weave them together into something new. Something *other*.

"I can't do it!" she cried suddenly, slumping forward as if exhausted.

Leo stopped playing and the manifestation evaporated. He seemed frustrated, annoyed and something else. Worried?

"It doesn't matter," he said eventually. "It will come in time. This is how it should go."

Plucking the string of his lute forcefully, Leo sent the tune spiraling into the air once more and now he sang as well, the same words that Maegwin had. Only this time the words and the notes melded together seamlessly, forming a complex Song Spell that made Rovann's stomach twist with dread.

Somewhere deep within the Realms, Rovann sensed something stir. Something with a vast regard turned its attention on the tent.

"Sho-La," Maegwin murmured.

Aethyr suddenly flowered in Rovann's mind. The voices of angels cried, *we cannot protect you from Her! Flee now! Before She sees you!*

Rovann spun, making no sound as he wove through the tent to the hole he'd cut. He ducked through it and ran. He felt tendrils of a dark presence following him, reaching out like tentacles.

Run! She is almost upon you!

Rovann fled, pelting through the camp as fast as his shaking legs could carry him. He reached the camp's edge, burst through the pickets and out into the dark prairie. Gradually the presence faded. Finally, miles from the Songmaker's camp, he came to a halt, heart laboring, breath a ragged saw burning his lungs. He threw himself into the grass to catch his breath.

What was that? he thought.

He was surprised when a voice answered him from the Aethyr. *That, Warrior of the Realms, was Shel-Masa the Destroyer.*

Chapter Two

Maegwin sucked in a deep breath. With it came...peace. Contentment. The song of Sho-La shimmered in the air like mist, rocking her as though she were a sleepy child. She'd been frustrated at her lack of progress with Leo's Song Spell but now that dissipated. She swayed gently, humming softly along with Leo's music.

But he suddenly fell silent and Sho-La's presence vanished abruptly. Maegwin opened her eyes, gasping at the sudden absence. Leo's eyes were narrowed, staring at something behind her.

"What is it?" She twisted, scanning the tent.

Leo shook his head. "Nothing. It's nothing." He grinned suddenly and gripped her hands. His touch was like ice. It was all she could do to stop herself flinching. "Things are coming together nicely, my dear, don't you think? Things are falling into place. Soon we'll have everything we've been fighting for! I can feel it in my bones!"

Maegwin pursed her lips. "So you say. But we haven't

yet achieved our aims here, Leo. The Shinnar are still a problem."

Leo waved a hand dismissively. "Oh, forget the Eagle Clan! General Shallon can take care of them."

Maegwin stared at him. "What? After all they've done to me? Are you mad?"

Leo shrugged. "That depends on your point of view, doesn't it? Does a madman see that he's mad? If he realized, it would prove he wasn't mad, wouldn't it? Only someone who believes he's sane can be truly mad."

Maegwin crossed her arms and arched an eyebrow at Leo. The youth frowned as though confused by his own words then threw up his hands.

"Anyway, that's beside the point. What I mean, my dear, is that I have a different task for you."

"Which is?"

He stared at her for a long time and Maegwin got the uneasy impression that he was assessing her. At last he nodded. "I know you think I overreacted about the theft of my journal. And I know you reckon I wasted too many of our resources guarding my library in Tyrvanan. But, as I hope you'll soon agree, there can be huge power in the written word."

Somewhere outside a coyote barked. The tramp of guards moved past the tent. Maegwin waited, saying nothing. She had learned that silence was often the best way to get Leo to come to the point.

"I have a gift for you, Maegwin."

He sang a note and she sensed an emanation of Air. The space before Leo shimmered and when it cleared, he was holding a book in his hands. He held out the thick, leather-bound tome toward her. "Here."

Maegwin took the book hesitantly. It was much heavier than she expected. "What is it?"

"Take a look."

Maegwin unclasped the two golden locks that kept the book shut and carefully opened the cover. As she read the title she gasped and glanced at Leo sharply.

"Where did you get this?"

He grinned, enormously pleased with himself. "What did I tell you? Books, my dear, are far mightier than any blade. It is in knowledge that we find true power."

With trembling fingers, Maegwin lightly touched the page, hardly daring to believe it was real. The pages were brittle and yellow with age. The faded script was written in a language that had been dead for centuries. Even so, Maegwin could read it. Any priestess of Sho-La could read it. Four words. That was all.

The Canticle of Darkness.

The lost chapter of the Book of Sho-La. The chapter that had been banned, along with worship of the Dark Goddess. As far as she knew, nobody within living memory had ever read what she was holding in her hands now. Except Leo, it seemed.

"Why didn't you tell me you had this?" she asked, breathless and a little fearful.

"I'm telling you now," he shrugged. "You weren't ready. But now? Now it's rightfully yours. Read it. Study it. You're going to need it."

"Need it? For what?"

Leo tapped his nose and winked. "All in good time, Maegwin. All in good time." He stood abruptly and brushed down his garish shirt. "Now, I'll leave you to get acquainted with my gift. We'll leave for Near Point in the morning. I think you'll like it there." A huge smile showed his big square teeth. "In fact, I'm sure you'll love it there."

He was being evasive again, dropping hints that he wouldn't explain. There was more to this, Maegwin suspected. There was something he wasn't telling her.

"I'll be ready," she murmured.

"Excellent!" Leo clapped his hands together. "Well, until the morrow, my dear!" He turned with a flourish, flinging his cloak over his shoulder in a swirl of yellow material, and strode from the tent.

Maegwin was left alone. The sounds of the camp reached her: people talking, the braying of horses, the tramp of many booted feet. Yet it seemed distant, unimportant. She gazed down at the *Canticle*. Slowly, hesitantly, she reached out and ran her fingers along the title. A shiver slid down her back. In sudden fear, she dropped the book on the floor and scooted backward a few paces. She stared at the book as though it was a viper that might bite her.

"Fool," she muttered to herself. "What do you think will happen? It's just words."

But she didn't approach. Instead, she rose and made her way over to her traveling trunk. She took out another book and returned to the rug, seating herself cross-legged once more. This book was smaller, less grand. Opening it, she read the words on the title.

The Canticle of Healing.

This was the most studied of the chapters of the Book of Sho-La, a goddess of peace and forgiveness. It was the chapter closest to Maegwin's heart. She opened the book to the page she needed and set it on the rug in front of her.

With her left hand she reached up, grabbed the collar of her tunic and yanked it over her head. Sudden pain shot through her shoulder and she grunted, biting her lip to keep from crying out. She set aside the tunic and sat only in her under-vest. The cool air sent goose bumps riding up her skin.

Squinting, she studied her right arm. There had been no improvement. The skin from hand to elbow was blackened and burned. Her fingers were useless and curled in on themselves so that her hand appeared more like some shriveled claw. She may have survived the fall of Tyrvanan but she hadn't survived unscathed. Nothing helped. She had tried every potion Leo's people could offer her. She had tried every healing trick she knew. It made no difference.

Pulling the *Canticle of Healing* closer, she scanned the words on the page and softly began to sing. As usual, nothing happened. Once, long ago it seemed now, she had been healed by a Sentinel. In turn, she had used that power to heal Rovann. But something had changed. She suspected that the *Canticle of Healing* used the energy of Aethyr, the Realm of the angels.

And they no longer answered her.

Sudden tears pricked her eyes and she blinked them away ruthlessly. With a cry of exasperation she snapped shut the *Canticle of Healing*.

Instead, she reached for the *Canticle of Darkness*.

Rovann walked all night. When he judged he was a safe distance from the Songmaker's camp, he let the cloak of Aethyr slip and was grateful for the sudden burst of energy. Holding a cloak of Aethyr was exhausting. He marched roughly south, hoping he was heading in the right direction.

Even though he'd spent the last few weeks living with the Shinnar, Rovann was still surprised at how silently they could move. One moment he was treading warily through the darkened prairie, the next he was surrounded by armed men who rose from the grassland like dark, silent ghosts.

He recognized Dranvey, the Eagle warrior who had apprehended him and Maegwin the first time they'd entered Shinnar lands. Realms, it seemed like a life-time ago. The young man approached Rovann, shaking his head and grinning.

"I don't believe it. You're still alive!"

Rovann frowned. "I'm not sure whether to be pleased or offended by that statement. Clearly, you didn't think I had it in me."

Dranvey's eyes widened. "Oh no, I didn't doubt you. It's just that... well...Kandar says..."

"Kandar says a lot of things. Sometimes I think the old man's made of nothing but piss and wind." He slapped the young man on the shoulder. "Although we'll keep that last remark to ourselves, eh?"

Dranvey snorted then clasped Rovann's hand, forearm to forearm. "It's good to see you whole, Lord First. This will make a fine tale!"

"I hope so," Rovann agreed, grinning. "Let's get back and start telling it, shall we?"

Dranvey nodded to his men who melted into the darkness to scout the way. Rovann walked by Dranvey's side. Before long they reached a deep gully that had once been a river bed. Dropping down into its dusty base, they walked along its course for what seemed like hours until the ground began to rise and they began passing through low hills.

They were challenged by Shinnar guards at the entrance to a fissure that cut through the hill. At a shout from Dranvey, they stood quickly aside. Rovann followed

Dranvey gratefully through the cleft until he emerged into a shallow valley.

A sea of conical tents filled the valley's slopes and at this late hour a few campfires were still burning. Rovann paused for a moment, taking it in. The fighting might of the Shinnar people lay spread out before him. Or at least, those who refused to follow the Songmaker. The Eagle Clan, led by Chief Brennan and shaman Kandar and also the Lynx, the Bear, the Wolf.

As Dranvey's warriors walked into the valley, people hurried over. A barrage of questions was fired at Dranvey which he waved away with a few choice curses. The warrior led Rovann to the north side of the vale where the Eagle Clan had set up camp. Here a group of people were on their feet, waiting.

Brennan, chief of the Eagle Clan, stood with his arms crossed and Kandar by his side. Perala, chief of the powerful Lynx Clan fingered her weapons as she always did, a fierce expression on her face. Halan, chief of the Bear Clan, was chewing on something and as they approached, he turned and spat a stream of brown into the grass.

"Look at this!" barked Kandar. "A bloody welcoming party! Kiss my hairy arse, I bet you didn't realize you were so popular!"

"I never doubted it," Rovann answered with a tired smile.

Kandar was silent for a moment, yanking on a bone in his hair. Then he shook his head. "You did well, boy," he said. "You did well."

"Perhaps you should hear what I have to say before you make that judgment."

Chief Brennan issued instructions. "Bring food and drink for the King's Mage." He turned to Rovann. "Sit down before you fall down, friend. Rest, eat, and then we'll talk."

Rovann wearily seated himself on the grass by the campfire. He felt so tired. Pinching the bridge of his nose, he closed his eyes for a moment, gathering strength, then opened them again, stifling a yawn.

The other clan chiefs folded onto the ground around the fire and, with a rattle of bones, Kandar settled not two paces from his side. A short time later three Shinnar youths brought a big pot of stew and ladled it into bowls for everyone.

Rovann ate mechanically then squeezed his eyes shut, desperately searching for that quiet space inside that would allow him to gather his thoughts. But images of Maegwin and Leo floated on the back of his eyelids like ghosts.

It seemed only moments before the meal was finished and tidied away. One by one, Rovann felt the eyes of the Shinnar leaders fall on him. He sighed. Realms, he just wanted to sleep.

Chief Brennan cleared his throat. He was a big man with thick arms and a long braid hanging over one shoulder. "So. Tell."

Rovann pursed his lips, gathering his thoughts. After a moment he began to speak. "Kandar's trace worked. It took me straight to the Songmaker's hidden base."

There was a murmur of approval and the old shaman looked smug.

"Their numbers are more than we anticipated and they seem to be growing. I risked Walking the astral and saw many thousands in that camp. Trained, disciplined soldiers for the most part."

"So give us their location and we'll go wipe them out!"

growled Perala of the Lynx Clan. "Their presence here is an insult to the World Mother!"

"No, Perala. You must not face them."

The woman bristled. "Are you questioning the strength of the Shinnar?"

"I'm not," Rovann said soothingly. "Only your numbers. The enemy are too many. So far your tactics have worked because you have attacked in small parties, hitting their supply lines and scouting parties. You know this terrain. You can attack quickly and get out again before they can regroup. But an all-out assault? They would dig in and wear you down gradually."

Perala opened her mouth to speak but Kandar barked, "He's right, woman! What good are our horse-archers against heavy infantry?" He turned his raptor's gaze on Rovann. "So what do you suggest? We just let them sit there?"

"Yes, that's exactly what you do. I have a feeling they won't be bothering you for much longer. Leo has a second force, one made up of mages, gathering in a place called Near Point. He and Maegwin are leaving to rally the forces there. I suspect the Songmaker was only tarrying in Shinnar lands until his forces in Near Point were ready."

"And now?" Perala asked.

"Now he will march out of Shinnar lands and begin his assault on Amaury."

Silence met his words. He wondered what they were thinking. Pleased that the hostile force was leaving their lands? Angry at how the Songmaker had used the Shinnar people?

A low muttering broke out. Several fingered weapons as though itching to use them. Chief Brennan rubbed his chin and said, "Has it all been for nothing? We have fought, we have died, all to halt the Songmaker's advance. If what you say is true, we have failed."

There was a rumble of agreement.

"Failed?" Rovann asked incredulously. "That's not a word I'd ascribe to the Shinnar people. Each life given has bought us valuable time. Time to decipher the Songmaker's plans. Time to mount a defense. Without your efforts the Songmaker would be rampaging unchecked through both Amaury and Shinnar lands. So no, Brennan, it has not been for nothing."

The chief nodded, conceding the point. "So what now?"

"Isn't it obvious?" snapped Perala. "We divide our forces. Some stay here. Some go north to this Near Point and attack his forces there. The bastard is making fools of us and we cannot allow it!"

Halan of the Bear Clan, a stocky man with a ring through one nostril turned to the fiery woman. "We should let them go. The Songmaker wants to leave our lands? Why don't we let them do it? Once they're gone we can go back to our lives."

Kandar drew himself up and waved a bony finger at the man. "I might have guessed that whiny voice belonged to you, Halan. Are you an idiot as well as a bloody coward?"

The man bristled and one hand moved to the ax hanging at his side. This didn't deter Kandar.

"Scratch my arse with a pointy stick! Have you learned nothing?" the old shaman barked. The Unraveling has begun. The World Mother's final battle is coming. We fight for Her! Do you think the Songmaker will be content with destroying Amaury! Fool! He will wipe us out like insects! By the World Mother's sagging teats, am I surrounded by utter idiots?" He glared around at the gathering, scorching them with his dark gaze.

For a moment the leader of the Bear Clan glared back, but when he received no support from the others, he crossed his arms over his chest and pointedly looked away.

Rovann spoke. "Halan has a right to his doubts. If I could, I would keep the Shinnar out of this. But I can't. You know this. You've seen what the Songmaker is capable of. So Kandar is right: the fight doesn't stop at Amaury's border. Curse it all, it doesn't even stop at the border of our Realm. If the Songmaker isn't stopped, soon there will *be* no borders. The Realms will unravel and Chaos will take us all."

He glanced at each of the faces before him in turn, trying to decipher their expressions. Most looked resigned to the fight, some even eager. "But you still have a choice. There is no shame in giving up the fight. Should you choose to leave and join your kin sheltering at the coast, none here will say a word against you."

He fell silent, allowing his words to sink into the dense atmosphere between them like a stone into a pond. A long, heavy silence stretched out, punctuated only by the crackle of the fire and the scrape of someone sharpening a sword in the distance.

Then finally, Chief Brennan barked a laugh. "A pretty speech! I can see why they made you Lord First, Rovann. Yes, we could run. We have done all you asked of us. No shame in admitting that. But you won't find the Eagle Clan abandoning its friends. We fight on. Who's with us?"

Instantly, Perala of the Lynx Clan said, "The Lynx stand with the Eagle."

A moment later Halan rumbled, "And the Bear."

Jojen, spokesman for the injured leader of the Wolf Clan added, "The Wolf stand with the Eagle. My chief has spoken."

Kandar threw his head back and cackled. "We're all bloody in it! Did you really think it would be otherwise?"

There was a roar of agreement from every throat around the fire and its sound reverberated deep in Rovann's stomach. They thumped their chests with their right fists and began a deep, throbbing chant.

"Shinnar! Shinnar! Shinnar!"

At a campfire nearby, the warriors took up the chant. The sound spread until a sea of men and women were rising to their feet throughout the valley, thumping their chests.

"Shinnar! Shinnar!"

Slowly, deliberately, he bowed to each of the war leaders around the fire. They responded in kind, faces grave.

"Take no risks," he said. "Hold them here for as long as you can but do not spend lives needlessly. Should Amaury fall, the task of opposing the Songmaker will pass to you."

Kandar pulled a bone in his hair. "The World Mother will look after us. She's annoyed at what that goat-faced bastard is doing in Her name. I can feel it in here." He rubbed his belly with one spindly hand. "What about you?"

"As soon as Lady and Tallo get back we're going to Near Point."

"I thought you'd say that."

"Well, I'd hate to disappoint."

The old shaman stared at him for a moment. "You can't take them all on by yourself."

I made a promise, he thought. *I will kill them all.*

"I can try."

Kandar looked about to speak but then thought better of it. "Come. We've set up a tent for you. You can rest there until you're ready to leave."

Rovann allowed himself to be led away to a small conical tent in pride of place next to Brennan's own. He ducked through the flap to discover that his meager belongings had been placed inside.

With a sigh he threw himself down on the pile of furs in one corner. Exhaustion washed through him. His limbs felt weighed down with stones. His thoughts were becoming foggy and slow. But he couldn't let himself sleep. Not yet.

Forcing his aching body into a seated position, he pulled over a faded hessian sack sitting by the door and placed it in his lap. With a sigh he reached inside and took out a small, leather-bound book. Its pages were empty. It was nothing more than a blank notebook but he set it down with reverence on the floor in front of him. Then, closing his eyes, he opened a gate to the Realm of Aethyr. Reaching through the gate, he snagged the item he'd hidden there and pulled it through.

When he opened his eyes the book still sat there. But now, instead of empty pages, a scrawl of scribbled diary entries, snippets of song and rough sketches met his eye.

Turning the pages carefully, Rovann began to read, searching for any reference to the village of Near Point. There was none.

What had Leo been referring to when he'd spoken to Maegwin? What was contained in this book that he'd needed so much? Rovann ground his teeth in frustration. For all he knew, the book was meaningless drivel and this whole charade was just another of Leo's elaborate games. He studied the maps and diagrams, hoping to find a clue there. Still nothing. The pictures seemed to be stylized diagrams that bore no resemblance to anything Rovann recognized. One showed a circle with tall pillars placed at intervals around it. Some sort of pattern of power radiated out from the circle but Rovann had no idea what it was. Another seemed to show a grid of some sort that reminded Rovann of a castle portcullis with a place name scrawled next to it that he didn't recognize.

"Curse him," Rovann growled under his breath. "Curse them both."

Tucking the book protectively beneath his body, Rovann closed his eyes. He would rest his eyes. Just for a while. Perhaps things would make better sense when he was rested.

"My Lord First!" a woman's cry startled him from a deep and dreamless sleep.

He shot upright, already reaching for his power, before he recognized the two familiar faces grinning at him from the tent flap. The first was a dark-haired woman with ringlets piled on top of her head and a gleaming gold torc around her neck. The second was a man with a huge, drooping mustache oiled into points.

"Lady, Tallo," he greeted them, indicating for them to sit then clasping their hands in turn.

The two soldiers had been assigned to him by Captain Tyan back in Tyrlindon. Both were elite fighters and, despite his protestations to the contrary, seemed to consider themselves his body guards. No doubt they'd been apoplectic when he'd left them behind whilst he went after Maegwin.

Absently, Lady took out one of the many knives she kept about her person and began twirling it. Light flashed from the spinning blade.

"You and I need to have a little talk, Lord First," she said with a dangerous edge to her voice. "About how you ran off and left us." Rovann opened his mouth to speak but she talked over him. "However, that can wait. We've been trying to contact Tyrlindon, just as you ordered. We've checked the cotes in this valley and the next. None of our birds have returned. Somehow all our messages are being intercepted although I don't know how."

"Don't know?" Tallo snorted, stroking his mustache nervously. "Of course we know! Someone's betrayed us, that's what!"

"Shut up, Tallo." Lady snapped

"It's true, I tell you. Everyone is against us!"

"You and your bloody conspiracy theories!"

Tallo shook his head. "What if I'm right? The cursed Songmaker has done a thorough job of severing our lines of communication, the shitty little bastard."

Rovann took this news in silence. It was over a week since he'd last had word from Amaury's capital. Due to the risk of being overheard if they communicated by sorcery, Rovann had instructed the Council to communicate by messenger bird only.

"Perhaps I should Walk the astral," Rovann muttered.

Lady narrowed her eyes, thin eyebrows pulling down. "Captain Tyan said none of you mages were to do that."

"I know what he said," Rovann snapped. "I was the one who gave him that order. But what choice do we have?" He sighed. "I'm sorry. I shouldn't snap at you."

"We're used to it, eh, Tallo?" she nudged the soldier. "With Tyan as your captain, you get immune to outbursts of temper."

Tallo narrowed his eyes at Rovann. "So, where've you been? What's so important you had to go running off without us? The Shinnar are rushing around like an ant's nest that someone's just poked a stick into. I'm guessing that's your doing, Lord First?"

Rovann sighed. "I'm afraid so. How do you fancy a bit of scouting?"

Lady raised an eyebrow and Tallo frowned. "What kind of scouting?"

Rovann told them of everything he'd overheard in the Songmaker's tent. When he finished his story Lady let out a stream of colorful curses that any dockworker would have been proud of.

Tallo looked thoughtful. "Near Point, eh? Never heard of the place. So when do we leave?"

"As soon as we can get word to Tyrlindon."

Tallo pulled on his mustache and then leaned back on one hand. "The way I see it is this. This is a war, right? All wars carry risks. It's a damned risk contacting Tyrlindon, that's for sure. But on the other hand, knowledge is power. Or at least, that's what Sergeant Hannel is always saying. So we need knowledge, right? We need to know what's happening back home and they need to know what the Songmaker is planning."

"Thank you for that insight," Lady said. "It's really helpful."

Tallo frowned at her. "What I mean is we have to contact Tyrlindon but can't do so using the Lord First's normal, um, means. Neither can we use message birds. So, we need an alternative."

There was silence for a moment. Then Lady prompted, "And?"

"And what?"

"What do you suggest?"

Tallo shrugged. "I dunno."

Lady rolled her eyes.

Rovann chewed his lip, thinking. "Wait, you may have a point."

Tallo brightened. "I do?"

"Perhaps I'm going about this the wrong way. I don't need to contact the mages in Tyrlindon directly. There's somebody I can contact who can pass a message on for me. Tanyaka."

Rovann had often communicated with the dragon whilst she still dwelt in the Realm of Fire by using Fire as a conduit. Would such methods work now she was in the Realm of Earth? There was only one way to find out.

"Tallo, give me your tinder pouch."

Wearing a puzzled look Tallo handed it over then scrambled after Rovann as he made his way through the flap and sat down a few feet from the tent. He scraped together a few twigs and used Tallo's tinder pouch to make a spark. Soon a small blaze was burning.

Fire. That was the key.

He stared, unblinking into the blaze until its image was burned into his eyes. Gradually, the fabric of the flames began to separate, becoming the whirling lines of energy that made up the living fire. He formed these into a conduit and sent out a summons.

Tanyaka! Hear me!

Somewhere deep within the Realms he felt a vast presence slowly turn toward him, like a giant boulder spinning on its axis.

Two golden eyes looked out at him from the flames. *Warrior?* Tanyaka's voice flowered in his mind. *Is that you?*

Old friend, Rovann replied, *I need your help. Tell the Council that the Songmaker has another force, this one made up of mages massing in a place called Near Point. When this force is ready he is going to march on Tyrlindon and attempt to close the city in a pincer grip. I'm going to Near Point to discover what I can and try to stop him. But I'll need you there, Tanyaka. You're the only one the Song-maker is afraid of. You're the only one who can destroy his mages.*

A wave of satisfaction hit him from the dragon and he remembered her thrill at burning Tyrvanan.

He should fear me. When I meet him again our unfinished business will be concluded. Do not worry, I will find this place called Near Point.

It's not that simple, Rovann replied. *Hounsey's forces must not discover that you have left Tyrlindon. Falwin and the others must keep up the pretense.*

Yes, I will explain to him, she said. *What can be done, will be done.*

Good. Make haste, my friend. Be there by sundown in two days' time.

I'll be there, Warrior of the Realms.

With that her presence faded.

Rovann blinked. He squeezed his eyes shut and waited for the flames to fade from his vision. When he opened them again, he found Brennan and Kandar standing in front of him.

"So," Kandar said. "You're leaving now, I take it?"

Rovann climbed to his feet. "Time is of the essence. The sun will be up soon. I want to get wherever we're going before that happens. Give us some time to have a look around while it's still dark."

Kandar nodded, making the bones in his hair click. "Good idea. Snooping requires darkness. In my youth snooping was a favorite hobby. I got rather good at it." The shaman fell silent for a moment. He pressed his mouth into a tight flat line and fixed his stare on Rovann. "Be careful, boy. Do you reckon you can manage that?"

Rovann nodded then reached out and folded the old

shaman into an embrace. The old man squawked in surprise. Next Rovann and Brennan clasped forearms.

"Peace and honor," the chief said.

"Peace and honor," Rovann replied.

He pulled a pendant from where it was hanging under his shirt and gripped it in one hand. It was shaped like a tear drop and made of amber. Mage Syrie's Eorthic stone.

"Ready?" he asked Tallo and Lady.

Tallo groaned. "No, I'll never be ready. Isn't there another way we can travel? Last time we used that thing it made me as sick as a dog. I had mud in places you wouldn't care to imagine!"

Rovann grinned crookedly. "Sorry, Tallo. This is not your lucky day."

With a pained expression Tallo shuffled forward and grasped Rovann's outstretched hand. Lady took the other.

Rovann closed his eyes and mumbled the chant Syrie had taught him. He fixed the name Near Point in his mind, trusting the Eorthe to find the place. For a second nothing happened. Then a sudden tug yanked Rovann down into darkness. The smell of damp mud enveloped him. The weight of tons of earth threatened to crush him into pulp. He forced his lungs to relax, even though soil filled his mouth, his nose, his ears.

Suddenly there was a sense of rushing upward and he opened his eyes to a bright blue sky above him. With a groan he rolled onto his belly and then climbed unsteadily to his feet. Sticky mud covered him from head to toe. Tallo was retching in the bushes several paces away. To his right, Lady sat blinking, trying to get her bearings.

"Well, that was pleasant," she observed. "Where are we?"

Rovann steadied himself on a nearby tree trunk and

took a look around. He stood on the side of a valley that nestled between the knees of high, white-capped mountains. A settlement sat in the valley below, blue smoke rising from chimneys.

"Exactly where we're supposed to be," he breathed. "Right in the middle of trouble."

Chapter Three

The small, whitewashed house could have been a farmer's cottage in any village throughout the land. A newly-repaired thatched roof hung low over small windows. Sparrows flitted in and out of the eaves. It looked normal. Ordinary.

Maegwin stared at the closed door, suspecting it was neither of those things.

"Well?" asked Leo at her side. "What are you waiting for?"

She glanced at the Songmaker. He seemed inordinately pleased with himself, practically bouncing on his toes with excitement. A wide grin made him look like a mischievous youth.

Maegwin's eyes moved past Leo to the village of Near Point which spread out in the valley between the knees of the Misthorn Mountains. It was a long way from the Shinnar plains. The journey had been quick, but unsettling. Leo used Chaos to rip a hole through the fabric of the Realms so they could step through, but he used it in a rough, almost violent fashion. It had left her nauseous and shaky.

What was Leo up to? What had he found here that he was so pleased about? The valley was dotted with houses like the one she stood before now. Ordered, tilled fields marched off in neat rows around the settlement. On the lower slopes of the mountains herds of sheep grazed. Smoke rose from the chimneys and the settlement itself was full of the hubbub of people going about their day.

What had she expected to find? Certainly not this. Not this sleepy, almost idyllic place. The local folk were farmers who worked the land and had probably not even heard of the trouble in Tyrlindon. The capital of Amaury was far away, of no importance to the people of this quiet valley.

Except, it wasn't quite like that anymore. This house was testament to that.

The only thing that marked it out as a temple was the tiny shrine to one side of the door. A simple stone bowl filled with water, a small figurine of Sho-La rising from the middle. Flowers, coins and other offerings were scattered around the shrine, showing where the townsfolk's allegiance now lay.

"Well? Are we just going to stand here all day?" Leo asked.

Maegwin frowned. "I still don't understand. How can this be a temple of Sho-La? The Holy Mother was killed, along with the rest of my sisters." She bit down on the sudden pain that stabbed her. Even after all this time, the memory remained sharp.

"Yes, and I regret my part in that," Leo answered, the smile vanishing from his face. "Cedric Hounsey was my man, and although he exceeded his orders when he burned your temple, I am partly to blame."

He clasped her hand and Maegwin felt him trembling. She glanced at him in sudden alarm. His eyes were dark and intense as he watched her, all trace of the mischievous youth vanished. "It's time we put that right."

Maegwin swallowed then licked suddenly dry lips. "How?"

"By ordaining a new Holy Mother. You."

She stared at him. He'd finally gone mad. Either that or he was deliberately taunting her. Ignoring the sudden churning of her stomach, she forced a neutral tone into her voice. "Leo, that's impossible. Only a conclave of at least three sisters can elect a new Holy Mother. I am the last. There are no others."

Leo nodded gravely. "We'll see."

He strode forward and rapped on the door three times then stood back and waited. A minute or so passed and Maegwin was afflicted by the sudden urge to flee. A shiver of unease ran down her spine. She opened her mouth to speak but the sound of a key turning in the lock silenced her. The door swung slowly open to reveal a young woman Maegwin didn't recognize. The young woman's eyes widened then she collapsed onto her knees, pressing her head against the stone step.

"Holy Ones," she whimpered. "Command me."

Maegwin stared at the girl in horror. Leo waved a hand impatiently. "Get up. Take us to the Sanctuary."

The girl scrambled up, then turned and shuffled inside. Leo led the way and Maegwin reluctantly followed. She found herself in a low stone room with a fireplace at one end. Two more young women were sat in wooden chairs, reading. Both scrambled to their feet and bowed as Leo and Maegwin passed. They were led to a back room whose door stood closed. The girl took a bunch of keys from her pocket and nervously fumbled with them until she found the one she needed. She unlocked the door and pushed it open, stepping aside to allow Leo and Maegwin to approach.

Leo strode forward but Maegwin found herself frozen. "What is this, Leo?"

He glanced over his shoulder. "A gift, Maegwin. For you. And for all of us."

Her anger flared. She'd had enough of his riddles. She darted forward and grabbed his arm. "Tell me what's going on, curse you!"

He paused and his shoulders seemed to sag in disappointment. His voice was unusually gentle as he said, "Maegwin, I need you to trust me. Come inside and everything will become clear."

She held his gaze for a moment. He gently pulled his arm out of her grip and entered the room. Maegwin hesitated, torn between annoyance, fear, duty and curiosity. With a growl, she strode after him. As she stepped under the lintel, something prickled over her skin. A ward of some sort, she guessed.

The room beyond was bare, with plain walls, a flagstone floor and three raised beds in a line under the window. Morning sunlight poured through the window, the shafts falling on the faces of three women lying on the beds.

Maegwin halted, her hands flying to her mouth in shock. She recognized these women: Miriel, Tarina, and Ashria.

Three of her dead sisters.

"What is this?" Maegwin hissed. "Some sort of joke?"

Leo spread his hands wide. "I thought you'd be—"

Maegwin was across the room in a heartbeat. Her fingers fastened in Leo's garish tunic as she lifted him and thumped him into the wall, pressing her face close to his.

"Do you think this is funny?" she screamed into his face. "How dare you desecrate their graves? You've gone too far this time!"

Leo's eyes flashed. A force picked Maegwin up and threw her across the room. The wall flashed toward her but Leo sang a note and she jerked to a halt then was lowered gently to the floor.

"Maegwin, listen to me," he said softly. "I desecrated no graves. I've guarded these three, the only three I managed to save from your temple, until such time as I could trust you. Then, and only then, could I reveal their presence."

Maegwin swallowed, once, twice. In a voice trembling with a mix of fury, fear and—inexplicably—hope, she said, "What have you done?"

"It's simple, really. I found them in the ruins of your temple, locked in a cellar, on the verge of death. With my powers, I have kept them in a state of suspension, somewhere between life and death. I cannot bring them back all the way." His eyes bored into hers, flashing with intense emotion. "But you can."

A tremor of trepidation ran through Maegwin's body, making her heart flutter. She heard Leo's words, but they made no sense to her. "I don't understand."

Leo moved around the room until he stood by the head of the middle bed. The light from the window enveloped him in a penumbra, making him glow with an almost angelic aura. "Come and see."

Maegwin didn't want to get any closer to those pale, slumbering forms. She didn't want to see what those faces might reveal. But she couldn't help herself. She took first one step, and then another, until she was standing at the foot of the bed, opposite Leo. Her eyes were drawn to Tarina's face, and then Ashria's, and then Miriel's. They seemed to be sleeping and could wake any minute.

And yet... and yet...

"They aren't breathing," Maegwin cried. "They're dead!"

"No," Leo replied. "Look closer, like I taught you."

Maegwin placed one hand atop Tarina's. The other woman's skin was like ice but Maegwin refused the urge to pull away. She stared at Tarina's face, slowing her breathing and expanding her senses. At first she sensed nothing, but gradually the fabric of the Realm of Earth began to reveal its secrets. A faint line began to appear, running from Tarina's ankle, up through the roof and into the sky. It was not golden in color like a life-cord but it pulsed a dusky gray like smoke. The cord was so insubstantial that it kept flickering in an out of existence.

Maegwin sent her senses questing along that cord. It led her from the Realm of Earth and deeper into the fabric between the Realms to...

"The in-between," she gasped, opening her eyes. "They are in the in-between." She didn't know whether to be relieved or horrified. The in-between was that infinitesimal space between Realms. It was nothingness. A limbo existence.

"Yes," Leo said. "Somewhere between life and death as I said. Do you want them back, Maegwin? Do you want your sisters restored to you? You have the power to make them live again if you choose."

"As do you," Maegwin whispered, glaring at the youth. "You're the Songmaker. More powerful than I. More powerful than any, save perhaps Rovann." Leo's eyes flashed at this but she pressed on. "You could bring them back anytime if you chose. So why haven't you?"

He shrugged. "It is not my task. It's yours."

"Why me?"

"So you can take your place as Holy Mother of Sho-La. We all have our tasks in Her service. This is yours."

Maegwin looked down at the three women. Was it possible? Might she have them back? Then she shook her head. "You're asking too much. I've no idea how to do what you ask."

"Yes you do. You have a rare power in you, Maegwin. Think about it."

Once, she had been healed by a power strong enough to drive the Realms themselves, a power that still resided within her. "The Song of a Sentinel?"

Leo said nothing.

"Yes!" she cried in sudden excitement. "You want me to heal them!"

Leo remained silent. He watched her with a steady, unwavering gaze.

Maegwin unslung the bag she carried on her shoulder and took out the *Canticle of Healing*. Thumbing through it, she found the page she needed and ran her hands over the words, mouthing them silently to be sure they were right.

Then, she began to sing. Her voice echoed strangely in the small room, seeming to become amplified so it sounded as though more than one voice spoke from her throat. As she sang, she searched inside herself until she found it: a tiny, golden ember of song that glowed and grew stronger as she stoked it.

Another note entered her singing, one that spoke of growing things and deep roots, and of a consciousness that spanned the Realms. It intertwined with the words of her song until they became one, each an integral part of the other.

Leo's eyes shone and Maegwin couldn't quite place the emotion she saw there. It looked something like greed.

She directed the healing power into the life cords of the three women, sending a summons out into the in-between to call her sisters back. But when it touched the smoky cords, her power died away to nothing. She tried again, singing the words from the *Canticle* more loudly, as if that would give them strength. Just like when she had attempted to heal her burned arm, the power would not obey.

"I can't do it!" she cried in exasperation. "It won't work!"

"No," the Songmaker agreed. "The *Canticle of Healing* uses the power of Aethyr. It will no longer help you. There is a price for serving our mistress."

Maegwin stared at him, unsettled by his words. "Then how?"

He shrugged. "The *Canticle of Healing* is not the only one in your possession."

She closed the book and it made a dull thump in the still room. She knew what he meant: the *Canticle of Darkness*. The forbidden book. The book that no priestess of Sho-La should possess. Could she use it in the way he suggested? Did she want to? The thought made her stomach churn with sudden unease.

Leo watched her, waiting. Her sisters lay there, waiting. What was she if not a priestess of the Dark Goddess? She had chosen her path long ago. No going back.

She nodded then bent and pulled the *Canticle of Darkness* from her scrip. Her hands shook only slightly as she opened its pages. Was it her imagination or did the light in the room dim? Did shadows seem to gather in the corners?

Running her finger down the words on the first page, she began to sing the first verse. The sound was harsher than she expected, as though the words twisted her voice until it sounded like it belonged to someone else. Yet interwoven through it was the golden ember of the Sentinel's Song, a lighter counterpart to the guttural tones.

"Yes!" Leo cried, clapping his hands together. "It's working!"

The power of the song was creeping toward the life cords of the three women. This time, as it touched them, only the golden notes of the Sentinel recoiled but the words of the *Canticle of Darkness* seemed to grab them, twist them, force them to do its bidding.

In her mind's eye she saw the dark power crackle along those life cords, strengthening them as it extended out, into the in-between, sending a summons.

"Come back," Maegwin whispered. "Come back to me."

She reached the end of the song and fell silent. For a long moment, nothing happened. Maegwin watched motes of dust dancing in the shafts of light. Leo watched Maegwin, eyes shrewd and calculating.

A gasp of indrawn breath startled Maegwin. Tarina suddenly arched her back, her mouth opening as she drew in a second breath and then a third. Maegwin threw herself to the woman's side.

She moved her tongue in her mouth, working up enough saliva to speak before gasping out, "Tarina?"

The other woman's eyes opened and fixed on Maegwin. She looked stunned. Her eyes went wide, her mouth moving but no sound coming out. Finally, she croaked, "Maegwin? Maegwin?"

Maegwin nodded dumbly, unable to take her gaze from the small, slight woman.

"Lady be praised!" Tarina whispered.

She pushed herself upright and wrapped her arms so tight around Maegwin that for a moment, she struggled to breathe. Maegwin stood rigid with shock. It was like being touched by a ghost. Tarina looked the same, sounded the same, even smelled the same. But it couldn't be her. She was dead. She'd burned with all the others.

No, she thought. *I brought her back. Lady, what does that mean? What does it mean?*

A sudden wave of emotion brought tears to her eyes. She wrapped her arms around Tarina, enjoying the reassuring warmth of the other woman's embrace.

"Maegwin," Leo's voice was low and insistent, demanding her attention. "Look."

Maegwin glanced enquiringly at him then followed the line of his gaze to the other two beds. Ashria and Miriel were breathing now too.

"The Lady works through you," breathed Tarina with wonder in her voice. "How may we serve you, Holy Mother?"

Maegwin glanced at her sharply. "Holy Mother? But I'm not—" She trailed off mid-sentence. Leo's eyes were like drills boring into her. She swallowed. How could she deny it?

Laying a hand in benediction on Tarina's head she said, "We have work to do, Tarina. We're going to found a new order. One that serves the Dark Goddess."

———

Something wasn't right. He sensed it. Yet, looking down on the sleepy backwater from his hiding place on the hillside, Rovann couldn't put his finger on the source of his unease.

The small settlement seemed peaceful. Smoke curled from the chimneys. Sheep bleated in the fields.

He closed his eyes and propelled his senses outward. Nothing. No matter how many times he tried, he detected no hint of sorcery. With a gathering sense of dread, he wondered if he'd been sent on some wild goose chase. Was this another elaborate trick of the Songmaker's? Where were his mages and this second army he had spoken of?

Rovann crawled backward from behind the bush, scrambled to his feet then quickly ran back through the thin screen of woodland until he reached camp. The small clearing was empty, no sign of Lady or Tallo, but as Rovann stepped into the clearing, a knife pressed suddenly against his neck. He froze.

"Move and you die."

Rovann turned his eyes to look at the wielder. "It's me!"

Lady stepped out of the bushes. She pursed her lips and shrugged. "So it is. Sorry."

She flicked her knife into the air where it spun a few times before she caught it and returned the blade to her scabbard.

Rovann massaged the skin of his neck. "I'm very glad we aren't enemies, Lady."

She grinned at the compliment, flashing her white teeth. "Well, I think that's the nicest thing anyone has ever said to me."

Rovann snorted then took a seat on a fallen log on the edge of the clearing. "Any sign of Tallo?"

She shook her head. "No, but I found something interesting. Come take a look at this."

Rovann trailed the soldier as she led him north, into the thicker woodland that coated the knees of the mountains.

Oak, alder and ash trees soared into the sky and lush grass carpeted the ground. Lady wound through the undergrowth without making a sound. Rovann followed, keeping his senses thrown wide, alert for danger. All he saw were the shimmering auras of woodland animals as they went about their lives.

Lady stopped so suddenly Rovann walked into the back of her. She pointed. "There."

Maybe ten paces distant a pillar rose out of the forest floor. It was thin, perhaps three paces in diameter, but soared into the air almost to the height of the nearest trees. Cautiously, Rovann approached. It was cylindrical and appeared to be made of stone but its surface was so covered with moss that he couldn't be sure. Halting an arm's span from the pillar, Rovann craned his head back, his gaze wandering up its length.

"What do you suppose it is?" Lady asked, coming up behind him.

Rovann turned in a slow circle, scanning the surrounding area. The trees were large, old, meaning that if this was the remnant of some building it must have been put here before the trees grew. Yet the ground was smooth with no humps or ridges that might indicate buried masonry.

With a frown he stepped forward and pressed one palm against the mossy surface. It felt warm to his touch. "Lady, give me a knife."

She plucked a knife from her scabbard, reversed it and offered it to him hilt-first. Taking the weapon, Rovann leaned closer and began scraping away the moss until he'd cleared a small patch. He revealed a stone surface pitted with indentations in a pattern of swirling lines. The swirls were arranged in square blocks, six patterns to a block. As Rovann scraped more of the moss away, he discovered that the patterned blocks marched all the way around the pillar.

"I think it's an alphabet," he said. "But one I don't recognize."

"It's writing?" Lady said, looking up at the pillar doubt-fully. "Saying what?"

"I've no idea. And I don't like not knowing. Is this the only one?"

Lady shook her head, making her black ringlets bounce. "No, there's more. Follow me."

A hundred paces distant they came upon a second pillar, identical to the first. A hundred paces beyond that, another. Calling a halt, he sat down on a large boulder to think. From here he could see the settlement twinkling in the valley below and the three pillars in a curving line on the valley's side. The angle of their alignment suggested they were part of a huge circle.

"I'd wager these things encircle the whole settlement," he said.

Lady slumped down on the boulder next to him. She took a knife from her belt and began rolling it across her palm. "They look old to me. Harmless."

"Perhaps," Rovann murmured although he wasn't convinced. When it came to the Songmaker, he'd learned to be suspicious of coincidences. "Let's get back to the clear-ing. I want to hear Tallo's report."

They retraced their steps, careful to keep to the deep undergrowth, avoiding open ground, and found Tallo waiting for them. He jumped to his feet, sword snaking out in an instant, only to relax when he recognized them.

He patted his chest dramatically. "Don't do that! You nearly gave me a heart attack!"

Tallo was dressed as a farmer. He and Lady had stolen

clothes from some unsuspecting peasant's washing line and donned a disguise of simple homespun tunic and leggings.

"Tallo," Rovann said, approaching the soldier. "Did you discover anything?"

Tallo returned his sword to its scabbard with a metallic ring. "She's here. They're both here."

Rovann nodded slowly. "Good. Tell me everything you found."

Twirling one side of his mustaches, Tallo folded into a sitting position on the grass. "I have to admit, boss, the Songmaker's one sneaky bastard. At first glance the place seems just a village, like any other. The people here work the land, keep livestock and don't seem to know about anything outside their borders. I'd wager my best boots that until recently they'd never even heard of the Songmaker, or even of you, boss. But I got talking to a couple of lads minding sheep. Pretended I was coming to trade some livestock. I suppose they must have been pretty bored because they gossiped like fish wives." He looked around as though to check nobody was watching and then leaned forward. "A few weeks ago a minstrel showed up. I bet you can guess what his name was? Well, this minstrel bought a house here. Except he's dedicated that house as a temple of Sho-La."

Rovann straightened. "What? Are you sure?"

Tallo nodded. "That's where Maegwin is now. And that's not the only thing. Seems he's been spreading the word of this goddess. Now everyone in the village worships Her. All in only a few weeks." He glanced in the direction of the village and his face suddenly became troubled. "Except I'm not sure the word 'worship' is accurate. It's more like fanaticism. I happened to ask what made them accept the temple so easily and they got pretty mad. I think if I hadn't beaten a hasty retreat, they'd have jumped me."

"Wonderful," Lady growled. "Religious lunatics. All we need."

Rovann sat very still, allowing Tallo's words to sink in. None of this made any sense. What was the Songmaker up to? Why set up a religious community here? How did it serve his plans?

"And the Songmaker's invasion force?" he asked. "Any sign of that?"

Tallo shook his head. "None. Do you want me to scout through the pass? Could be they're waiting in the mountains on the other side?"

"No. I have a hunch we won't find what we're looking for. There's something we're not seeing." He picked up a dry stick and began furiously pulling it apart. Frustration boiled inside him.

"We'd better make camp," Lady said. "There's a cave in the hills that gives us a good view of the village."

"You go on ahead. I want to scout the village's perimeter, see if there's any more of those pillars."

Lady frowned. "Then we'll come with you. Captain Tyan said not to leave you unprotected. We can't disobey orders can we now?"

Rovann smiled crookedly. "No, we couldn't have that. Right. Let's go."

Maegwin could barely see through the steam. The scent of lavender and lemon tickled her nostrils. She struggled to remember the last time she'd had a proper soak like this. It felt...wonderful. Tired muscles relaxed as she sank deeper, laying her head back against the bath's metal rim. Her cares drifted away with the steam. For a moment, just for a moment, she was only Maegwin. Enjoying a simple bath.

The door suddenly opened and a voice said, "Shall I wash your hair now, Holy Mother?"

Maegwin opened her eyes to find a white-robed acolyte standing demurely by the side of the bath. Maegwin cursed and sat up, belatedly trying to cover her nakedness. Her withered arm was uncovered for all to see, the blackness of the broken skin a startling contrast the paleness of her body. Self-consciously, she tucked the arm behind her.

"Who are you?"

If the girl noticed Maegwin's discomfort, she didn't show it. "Isabelle, Holy Mother. Sister Tarina has sent me to help you prepare for your investiture."

"My...investiture?"

Oh. Of course. She'd been doing her best not to think about that. She didn't want to be the Holy Mother. The Holy Mother should be calm, wise, serene. Maegwin was none of those things

She forced a smile. "Yes. Thank you."

The girl smiled in return, obviously delighted. "Lean forward a little, Holy Mother, and we'll begin."

Maegwin did as she was bid. This ought to be enjoyable, she reminded herself as Isabelle began to scrub her hair, but rather than feeling pampered, Maegwin felt more like some sacrificial lamb being prepared for slaughter. The last time she had been fussed over like this was when she and Rovann were disguised as Shinnar so they could sneak into Tyrvanan.

Rovann.

He was the wrong thing to think about. She hugged her arms across her chest at the sudden, sharp stab of regret. Where was he now? In Tyrlindon? Did he ever think of her?

Sometimes she hated herself. Sometimes she hated Rovann. Sometimes she hated the whole damned lot of them and wished they would leave her alone. Yet she always found herself hoping she might see Rovann again. If only for a moment.

"I'll rinse it now, Holy Mother," Isabelle said.

Maegwin nodded, tipping her head back to allow the girl to rinse the foam from her hair.

"If you'd like to get out, Holy Mother, we'll get you oiled and perfumed."

Maegwin looked at the girl sharply. Oiled? Perfumed? With a sigh, she climbed out of the bath and stood dripping whilst Isabelle wrapped a soft towel around her and led her over to a rickety chair sitting in front of a chipped mirror.

Isabelle took a bone comb and began brushing out Maegwin's red-gold tresses. The face staring back at Maegwin from the mirror seemed older. Wearier. There were dark circles under her eyes where they'd been none before. Tiny lines radiated from the corners of her eyes and bracketed her mouth. It was a face that had seen much. Done much. Full of regret.

At Maegwin's sudden sigh, Isabelle started.

"I'm sorry, Holy Mother. Did I hurt you?"

"No," she replied, raising a reassuring hand. "Carry on."

Isabelle finished combing Maegwin's hair then fetched her clothing from the wardrobe. When the girl finally stepped back and announced she was done, Maegwin stifled a sigh of relief. Looking at herself in the mirror, she examined the gown she'd donned— a simple white dress, plainer than any acolyte's robe. A smile of satisfaction curled her lips. Good. She would come before her goddess unadorned, as it should be.

Isabelle shook her head in wonderment. "You look radiant, Holy Mother."

"Radiant is it?" Maegwin replied, raising an eyebrow. "Well, that's a new one on me. I've been called many things in my life but radiant certainly wasn't one of them." Seeing the embarrassment that crossed the girl's face, Maegwin chided herself for her insensitivity. She would need to learn to hold her tongue if she was to be Holy Mother. Gently, she took hold of the girl's hands and forced a smile onto her face.

"Thank you, Isabelle. You've done well."

She was rewarded by a beaming smile that curled the corners of the acolyte's mouth.

"Now go," Maegwin instructed. "I need time to prepare myself."

Isabelle dropped a deep curtsey and then scurried out. Maegwin was, to her relief, finally left alone. She looked around the small space. It reminded her of the room she'd occupied in Tamya's inn in Tyrlindon. She'd been waiting for others to decide her fate then as well, only that time it had been King William rather than the Songmaker.

She doubled over as a sudden claustrophobia came upon her. Needing fresh air, she bolted from the room, down the stairs and out into the small garden at the back of the house. She was relieved to find it empty. Sending a prayer of thanks to Sho-La, she sank onto a bench by the pond. The season was turning and many of the leaves had become vivid shades of red and gold. Yet it remained warm, clinging to the last of the summer heat, and the sun was gentle where it touched her cheek.

Maegwin sat quietly, trying to be still. Trying to find peace. Trying to find anything but the thousand questions that seemed insistent on swirling round and round in her head.

"May I join you?"

Leo stepped out of the house. He'd found some new clothes from somewhere and now he sported a bright red cloak and a mustard colored jacket. The contrasting colors, along with his orange hair and freckled skin, made him look more like a court jester than a minstrel.

Maegwin nodded and Leo slid onto the bench beside her.

"Ah! A beautiful day is it not? The sun is shining, the birds are singing, what more could we ask for, eh?"

Maegwin was reminded suddenly of the first time she'd met Leo. He'd looked like this then too: young, naive, full of the wonders of life. Sometimes she struggled to figure out who the real Leo was. The carefree minstrel or the Song-maker? Were they one and the same? Who was the man she had pledged her service to?

"Is everything ready?" she asked.

Leo nodded, red curls bouncing. "We await only the sunset. In the light of the dying sun you will be reborn, Maegwin!"

She wasn't sure she liked the sound of that. She'd never heard of all this pomp and ceremony surrounding the investiture of a new holy mother. As far as she knew they were always simple affairs with only the priestesses in attendance: little fuss and over quickly. But Leo had invited the whole settlement to attend. The ceremony would take place in the village square, the only area big enough to house so many people. The temple acolytes had been busy all day setting out seats, attaching garlands and banners to poles, building a stage on one side of the square.

No, Maegwin didn't like it one bit. This was supposed to be a solemn, holy occasion. If Leo had his way, it would be more like a carnival.

She opened her mouth to voice her complaints but then thought better of it. Instead, she asked a question that had been bothering her. "Leo, tell me something."

He turned a bright green gaze on her. "Yes?"

"Why do your mages fight for you? They broke from the Council to follow you. Why?"

Leo shrugged. "It's very simple, my dear: power. They broke from the king because he restricts what they can do. Imposes rules. They don't like that. In their eyes, the powerful should control the weak. It's the natural order of things."

"And they think you'll give them the power they seek?"

He smiled. "Yes. Amongst other things."

Maegwin paused. Phrasing her next question carefully she said, "They're right, aren't they? About the natural order, I mean. The strong ruling the weak. So I wonder: why do the mages of Amaury serve? Why do they swear a vow to do as their king commands?"

Leo raised his eyebrows at her. "Are we talking about anyone in particular here?"

Maegwin frowned. "Oh, all right, I mean Rovann. You saw the power he revealed in Tyrvanan. He is far more powerful than King William. He's far more powerful than any of us. Why doesn't he just take the kingdom for himself?"

A look flashed across Leo's features. Maegwin struggled to decipher it. Then she recognized the expression and her unease deepened. Envy.

"Because he's weak."

"But it's not only Rovann is it?" Maegwin persisted. "Throughout the history of Amaury, no mage has ever taken the throne. Why is that?"

Leo watched her with a guarded expression. Then he broke into a smile and wagged his finger at her. "I knew I was right to choose you, my dear. Your wit is matched only by your beauty. You stumbled on the biggest question of our time. And perhaps one day you'll discover the answer."

Maegwin frowned. Despite Leo's cocky grin he seemed a little unsettled by her probing. What was he hiding? She longed to quiz him further but was wary about pushing him too far.

Instead, she changed the subject. "Are you sure your mages can be trusted? If they want only power how do you know they won't stab you in the back?"

"Trust?" Leo rolled the word around in his mouth as though it had a sour taste. "Trust is a luxury, Maegwin. One that I learned long ago I cannot afford to indulge. So no, I don't trust the mages at all. They walk in step with me because it suits their purpose and for the time being that's enough."

"And if they betray you?"

Leo snorted as if the very idea was preposterous. "Don't you worry about that. I have my ways of keeping them in line."

He grinned at her as though he was some schoolboy withholding a secret. The sight of his delighted grin raised the hairs on the back of her neck. She looked away, concentrating instead on the view of the rolling green countryside spreading toward the mountains.

Leo clapped his hands together and rubbed them eagerly. "Are you getting excited yet? In only a few short hours you'll become high priestess of the Order of Sho-La. Now that is a cause for celebration is it not?"

Maegwin glanced at him but didn't answer. Instead, she watched the birds flitting in and out of the trees and listened to the bleating of the sheep up on the hills.

Where are you, Rovann? she thought. *Where are you right now?*

Chapter Four

Rovann glanced at the sky. The sun was past its midday zenith and had begun falling toward evening, turning the sky into a mosaic of red and yellow streamers. Overhead, a phalanx of geese flew, honking. In the village below, all was quiet, peaceful.

He had asked Tanyaka to arrive by sunset tonight and to keep out of sight in the peaks to the west until he called her. When he'd enlisted her aid, pulling her away from the defense of Tyrlindon in the process, he'd envisioned an army of mages waiting in Near Point, an army that he'd need Tanyaka's help to defeat. Instead he'd found this sleepy backwater that seemed to be populated by simple farmers.

It was a mystery he had to solve before the dragon arrived. With a sigh, he leaned against the tall stone obelisk rising from the turf in front of him. A hundred paces to his left, Lady waved at him from where she leaned against another. The stone pillars encircled the whole of Near Point, some almost completely hidden by vegetation, others standing stark against the sky.

Putting two fingers to his lips he whistled a short sharp burst that imitated the song of a piper bird and waited. A few seconds later, Lady and Tallo arrived, and threw themselves to the ground at the pillar's base, chests heaving.

"Well, that's it then," Tallo announced when he'd got his breath back. "Lots of the buggers all around the valley. Exactly the same distance apart, exactly the same height."

"And with exactly the same markings on them," Lady added.

Rovann laid his head back against the pillar. Except for its heat, he could detect no residual power. Perhaps the pillars were some kind of religious artifact left behind by some long forgotten culture. In truth, he had no idea, and that bothered him.

He closed his eyes for a moment, thinking. There had to be a reason Leo had wanted to find this place so badly. Something was here. Something Leo needed. Could these pillars be part of it?

Then a thought struck Rovann and he went suddenly cold. Quickly he pulled his pack from his shoulders and fumbled inside for Leo's book. Thumbing swiftly through the pages, Rovann scanned each one, searching. There. He came to a halt at a page covered by two sketches, one on each leaf. On the right hand side was a geometric design that looked like a portcullis but on the left page was a diagram: tall obelisks arranged in a circle.

Looking over Rovann's shoulder, Tallo whistled under his breath. "Whew! You reckon that's what this is?"

"I don't know," Rovann murmured. "Perhaps."

His unease deepened. For Leo to have sketched this in his book—a book he had gone to extraordinary lengths to recover—meant it had to be important. Somehow, it was connected to his plans. Trouble was, Rovann had exactly no idea what those were.

"So what shall we do, boss?" Tallo asked.

Rovann leaned forward, resting his elbows on his knees, the book dangling from one hand. This skulking and scouting was getting them nowhere. They needed answers.

He looked at the soldiers in turn. "We, my friends, are going to do a little bit of interrogation."

Tallo stroked his mustache in satisfaction. Lady pulled out a knife and grinned.

"Action! It's about bloody time!"

Lady chose the target: a lonely crofter's cottage on the outskirts of the settlement. The three of them watched the cottage from behind a low stone wall until finally Lady seemed satisfied.

"Right. Let's go."

They jumped over the wall and crossed the open ground, keeping low so to avoid being spotted from the windows. Lady moved around the back, leaving Rovann and Tallo to approach the front door.

They stepped onto the verandah and Rovann raised his hand to knock just as Tallo kicked the door open and burst through, drawing his sword with a grate of steel. A bald, middle-aged man, sitting on a bench slurping a mug of soup, yelped in surprise as Tallo dragged him to his feet and shoved him against one wall, sword blade pressed against his throat.

"That's right, Tallo," said Lady, entering from the back. "Nice and subtle, like we agreed."

Tallo frowned. "It's effective isn't it? Why tiptoe around?"

The man watched the trio with wide, frightened eyes. He still held his mug, soup slowly dripping onto the floor.

"We need to ask you some questions," Rovann said, moving to stand before the man. "Answer honestly and you'll not be hurt. Understand?"

The man swallowed thickly, his throat bobbing dangerously close to Tallo's blade. "I understand."

Rovann nodded to Tallo who let the man go, backing up a few steps but still holding his weapon ready. The man kneaded his neck. Sweat covered his brow.

"Sit." Rovann sank into a chair and indicated for the man to resume the one he'd just vacated.

The man shot wary looks at Lady and Tallo and then slid into the seat opposite Rovann, clasping his hands in front of him on the table.

"What's your name?" Rovann asked.

"Melachy," he replied. "I'm just a simple farmer. I don't have nothing worth stealing, I promise."

"We're not here to steal anything," Rovann reassured him. "We want information. How long have you farmed the valley?"

"Not that long, sir, if I'm honest. I had a place about twenty miles from here but it got flooded out with last year's rains. When the call went out, I thought 'why not?' So I came here, well… I'm not sure I can remember when. But I've never looked back. It's a wonderful place to live, sir."

Rovann frowned. "Call? What call?"

"From Lord Leo, sir. He said anyone who came here would be given a parcel of land with no questions asked. All we had to do was swear ourselves to the Lady and we could build a new life for ourselves. I'm glad I did. One of the best

66

decisions I ever made. Our Lady watches over all of us, sir. And Lord Leo has been good to his word." The man leaned forward. "Why? Do you want to live here too? If so there's no need to go about it this way. Lord Leo doesn't like thieves but he'll welcome any hard-working folk who promise to live in Our Lady's light."

Rovann hesitated. The man looked earnest but something wasn't right, that much was clear. "And you are alone here? No family?"

The man's brows pulled down in a puzzled frown. "I... um..." He shook his head as though trying to remember. "There was once, I think. A lady with brown hair. Two children. It's... hazy."

"What are you talking about, man?" Tallo demanded. "It's a simple enough question. Do you have a family or not?"

"I...I..." the man muttered, pressing his palms against his temples as though he had a sudden headache.

Rovann straightened. He picked his next words with care. "Melachy, did anyone else come here from your village?"

Melachy nodded, seeming eager to change the subject. "Some, yes. About twelve of us in total."

"And you all came at the same time? Following a flood?"

"That's right. A chance to start anew and all that."

Rovann fell silent. Tallo and Lacy regarded him quizzically. "And your Lady? Your new goddess? Does She have a name?"

"Sho-La, sir. The World Mother. We have a new temple in the village and tonight we'll have a new holy mother."

Rovann blinked. "A new holy mother? Her name wouldn't be Maegwin by any chance would it?"

Melachy nodded eagerly. "At sundown. I'm sure you'd

be made welcome should you wish to attend. Everyone's invited. It'll be a grand affair!"

The man had become more animated as he talked and there was a light in his eyes that made Rovann uneasy. He'd encountered fanaticism before. And yet, there was something else about this man. Something that didn't fit. The pallor of his skin, the jerkiness of his movements, the very aura about him. It reminded Rovann of something else he'd seen…

Hounsey! he thought suddenly. *He reminds me of Cedric Hounsey.*

Dread pooled in Rovann's stomach. The man had come here after his farm was flooded out…

"Hold him still," Rovann ordered.

Lady and Tallo stepped forward, each gripping one of the man's arms and holding him fast. Melachy's eyes widened. "Don't hurt me! Please don't hurt me!"

"Lady, give me one of your knives."

She hesitated only a moment before pulling a slim silver blade from the brace around her hips and handing it to him, hilt first. "What are you planning, boss?"

Rovann held the knife up in front of him, watching how the light played across the metal.

The man eyed the blade, licking his lips nervously. "Look, there's no need for—"

His words cut off with a gurgle as Rovann plunged the knife into his chest, right up to the hilt. With a gasp, Lady and Tallo sprang back as the man convulsed, his back arching and his eyes and mouth stretching wide. He clawed at the blade sticking out of his chest but the strength was leaving him and he couldn't pull it out. He raised a shaking finger and pointed it at Rovann before slumping back with a groan, his suddenly sightless eyes staring accusingly at the King's Mage.

Shocked silence descended. Rovann didn't take his eyes off the dead man but he could feel the gazes of Tallo and Lady boring into him.

"What?" Lady stammered. "Why? I thought we were just—"

"He was an enemy," Tallo growled. "That's reason enough."

"An enemy?" Lady retorted. "He was a farmer! I don't understand!"

She leaned forward to yank the knife from the man's chest but Rovann grabbed her wrist. When she turned her dark eyes on him he said, "Look at the wound. Do you see any blood?"

She bent to examine the dead man. "No," she said at last. "That's strange."

Rovann nodded. He wrapped his fingers around the knife's hilt and pulled. The blade slid noiselessly out. "And now?"

Lady peered more closely and Tallo crowded behind her, trying to get a look.

"What the—?" Tallo began.

"Still no blood," Lady said. "How can that be?"

"Step away from him," Rovann commanded.

He joined them as they moved to stand against the far wall, leaving the dead man slumped in his chair. They waited. The only sound in the room was the hiss of their breathing. Outside a pheasant squawked and was answered by another further off. A bee droned by the window, bumping against the glass before meandering away. They waited.

Finally, Tallo said, "Look, I don't know what it is you're

expecting to see but we'd better do something about the body. If he's found the Songmaker will know we're here—"

A noise stopped him mid-sentence. It was coming from the dead man. Lady's hand flew to her knives. Tallo drew his sword.

A low moan, like wind through branches, was issuing from the corpse's mouth. In its wake a sudden gale blew through the room, whipping up ash from the fireplace. Rovann screwed his eyes shut against the stinging particles.

When he opened them again, the dead man was sitting upright in his chair, staring at them. There was no sign of a knife-wound in his chest.

"Hello?" the man said. "May I help you? If you're lost I can give you directions to Near Point." Then the man's eyes fell on Lady and Tallo's weapons and he spluttered. "I promise you I've nothing worth stealing!"

Rovann held out a hand to halt the two soldiers as they started toward the man. He made his voice neutral as he said, "We're not robbers, good sir. We're travelers looking for Near Point. We've heard honest folk can make a fresh start there."

At this the man seemed to relax. "Well, you heard right, friend. Lord Leo welcomes any who want to live a peaceful life."

Rovann listened politely as the man gave them directions to the village then led Tallo and Lady from the cottage. They walked away quickly, the two soldiers matching him stride for stride. Nobody spoke. Rovann tried not to run, even though a sick dread added urgency to his steps. When they finally reached the clearing, he threw himself to the ground and put his head in his hands.

His heart pounded against his ribs. A sick, lurching fear sent his thoughts spinning. *No. No. Not again.*

Tallo cleared his throat. "Um, boss? Would you mind telling us what's going on here? Because it looked to me as though you killed that man back there and he came back alive. Now, I know that sounds ridiculous but that's what it looked like to me. I was imagining it, wasn't I? Tell me I was imagining it!"

Rovann sighed, glancing up at the sky as though he might find inspiration there. "No, you didn't imagine it. I'll warrant that if you were to question other villagers you'd find similar stories to Melachy's. All survivors of fires, floods, accidents, murder even." He fixed first Lady than Tallo with a stare. "Except they didn't survive."

Lady's eyes narrowed. Then she let out a low whistle. "Revenants?"

Rovann nodded. "The man was dead. No heartbeat. No pulse. No air filling his lungs. That's why he didn't bleed. I suspect everyone here is the same."

Tallo stared at him, wide-eyed and made the sign to ward off evil.

"What are we going to do?" asked Lady. "Can we be sure they're all revenants?"

"We can't," Rovann said, watching smoke curl from the chimneys in the settlement below. It looked so peaceful. Who would guess that it was a place of death? "But we can't take the risk. They will all have to be destroyed."

The two soldiers took this in silence. Then Lady nodded tightly. "How? There are only three of us."

Rovann looked up at the sky. "Tanyaka. She'll burn Near Point. Even revenants die when they're reduced to ash."

Lady's lips tightened. This did not sit well with her. Realms, it didn't sit well with him. There was every chance innocent farmers and crofters would be caught up in this. Rovann's hands curled into fists. An image suddenly flared in his mind's eye: screaming. Wailing. The terrified cry of people and horses. The smell of burned flesh.

Sandford Moor. Where he'd killed the innocent. Now he was going to do the same again.

"And Maegwin?" Lady asked. "What of her?"

"What of her? She dies with the rest."

Before they could reply, he climbed to his feet and stalked away. Out of sight of the others, he leaned against a tree trunk, breathing heavily. His thoughts spun in dizzying circles. Was this all he was now? A killer?

He straightened, pulling in deep breaths to calm his thumping heart, then closed his eyes and sent a mental summons out onto the astral plane.

Tanyaka! Can you hear me?

Warrior! she replied instantly. *I am coming!*

Where are you?

Close. I will be there by sundown!

Good. Circle into the mountains and keep out of sight. Wait for my signal. There's more happening here than meets the eye.

You do surprise me, came her sardonic reply. *Isn't that always the case with that blasted little man?*

Rovann smiled wryly. *Always. I'll call you when I need you. And, Tanyaka? Answer quickly if I call. I'm uneasy about all this.*

You have my word.

"We'll need disguises," he said when he returned to the clearing where Lady and Tallo waited.

Lady arched an eyebrow. "We're going in?"

He nodded. "I have to know what's happening down there and what the Songmaker is planning. I feel like we're fumbling around in the dark."

"You do realize this might be a trap?"

"Maybe. But I don't think so. I've no reason to suspect the Songmaker knows we're here."

"And if we get caught?"

Rovann sucked in a breath. "Then we'll die."

Lady shrugged. "As long as I know."

Tallo threw up his hands. "Wonderful. A suicide mission. Just perfect."

Lady frowned down at him. "Shut up, Tallo."

"We'll dress as locals," Rovann said, "mingle with the crowd during this ceremony and gather as much information as we can. Once we've confirmed that Leo, Maegwin and his mages are in one place, we'll get out of there and call in Tanyaka."

"And then: boom!" Tallo said, spreading his hands wide to signal an explosion. "Everything goes up in flames." He grinned at them both.

Lady frowned. "Shut up, Tallo."

It didn't take long to prepare. Tallo and Lady already had their disguise and Tallo had stolen enough clothes to provide Rovann with the same. They hid their weapons under wide smocks and set off.

They wove in silence through the woods on the valley side, alert for scouts, but they met nobody. Soon the trees thinned and cultivated plots began to appear instead. Eventually these opened out to pastures, lanes and the occasional cottage like the one Melachy occupied. Finally, the three companions stepped out onto a lane between two dry-stone walls and Rovann tensed. A man was leading a donkey laden with vegetable baskets toward them.

Lady stepped forward confidently and hailed the man. "Afternoon, sir! A fine one ain't it?"

The man smiled warmly. "That it is. Are you here for the ceremony?"

"We are. Are we going the right way?"

He waved vaguely down the road. "Keep going and you'll reach the square. This place ain't big enough to get lost. I'm off to put on my best suit and then I'll be joining you. It's not every day we get our very own holy mother is it? Praise be to Sho-La!"

"Praise be to Sho-La," Lady intoned.

The man ducked his head and continued down the road. Lady raised a questioning eyebrow. Rovann stared after the man and then turned to Lady. "Yes. Dead. Just like Melachy."

Tallo rubbed his arms as though suddenly cold. "How can he be dead? He spoke to us! I tell you, if I'd been told that I'd have to deal with animated corpses at the start I would never have joined up. I should've become a smuggler like my ma wanted."

"Shut up, Tallo."

"There's something we're missing," Rovann muttered, trying to find the right words to express his unease. "There was more. Something about him..." He shook his head. "Let's go."

The sun was a red orb low in the sky. Bars of light shone through gray clouds that had gathered along the horizon and Rovann squinted as they made their way down the lane. It would soon be sunset.

The closer to the center they got, the more people they encountered. Farmers, shepherds, crofters and craftspeople all wore garishly colored tunics and dresses that reminded Rovann of Garn and Etta, the gypsies he and Maegwin had met on the road.

Pleasantries were traded, jokes were made, and nobody seemed to take any heed of Rovann, Lady and Tallo as they joined the people heading toward the center of the village. Rovann smiled and made small talk along with the rest but he was surreptitiously scanning everyone around him. He sent tendrils of Aethyr probing toward all of them and found no trace of life. All dead. All revenants given life by the power of Chaos.

They arrived at the village square to find it already crammed with excited villagers. Crude benches filled the cobbled space and a raised dais had been set at one end. The place hummed with eager conversation. It was like a carnival day.

The three of them took seats at the back. Rovann pulled his hood forward to hide his face and studied the square. Eyes flicking everywhere, he noted the position of every building, every window, every exit. He made a mental note of any group gathered near those exits and any glances aimed their way and who made them. He even scoured the sky and hillsides, trying to detect hidden enemies. There were none. The deception, if deception it was, was a subtle one.

Suddenly a ripple went through the crowd and the talking subsided into silence. A bell began to toll, a heavy, ponderous sound in the evening air. At the far end of the square a line of white-robed women slowly filed in from one of the side streets. Their heads were bowed, their hands clasped demurely in front of them. They made not a sound as they climbed the steps onto the dais and waited. Rovann craned his neck, searching, but there was no sign of the Songmaker. Where was he?

The bell fell silent for a moment but then clanged once, twice, and two other women emerged, walking hand in hand. One was another white-robed woman but she had a gold sash around her waist, perhaps marking her as someone important. The other wore a plain linen shift and a veil covered her head. From beneath the veil, Rovann caught sight of strands of red-gold hair that had worked loose.

"Maegwin," he breathed. "I'm going close," he whispered to the others. "Stand up quietly and take positions near the exits. Make sure you can see me at all times. If I give the signal, run."

Lady and Tallo exchanged a glance and then nodded tightly. Lady rose and sauntered over to the wall of a nearby house, lounging against it as though she had not a care in the world. Tallo sidled off in the other direction, taking up position beside one of the poles that had been decorated with flowers. Rovann was left alone. He fussed with his tunic for a moment, pretending to be fastening the ties. Then, pulling in a breath, he climbed to his feet and began weaving through the benches. As he neared the dais he bowed his head, making sure nobody could see his face.

He shuffled through the press of people around the dais and moved into the shadows of a large building that might have been a workshop. Once there, he looked around, caught Lady and Tallo's eyes, and gave a motion of his hand to tell them to hold their positions.

From this vantage point he watched the activity on the stage. The white-robed women, Maegwin in their midst, were not more than thirty paces away. They hadn't noticed him. Rovann shifted uneasily. Where was Leo? Surely he would be here to watch Maegwin become his creature? Closing his eyes, Rovann gently sent Aethyr probing outwards, trying to detect any hint of sorcery that would give away Leo's position. He found nothing.

He opened his eyes and warily watched the women on the dais. They moved with almost mechanical precision as they led Maegwin onto the stage and then stood in a ring around her, facing out toward the crowd.

They began to chant. A low, rhythmic murmuring floated out from beneath their cowls, a cadence so deep it was surprising to hear it coming from female throats. The sound rang out over the crowd who gasped, watching the spectacle with expressions of awe.

The notes prickled over Rovann's skin like an army of biting ants. He'd heard Maegwin sing once. Whilst he'd lain injured during their journey to the Highhold of Lord Cedric Hounsey she had sung to him. Her voice had been beautiful: high, melodic, full of life and vigor. Nothing like his chant. This was dark, echoing, and conjured in his mind images of deep places where no light shone and of an abyss that fell away into eternity.

After a few moments the women fell silent and Rovann let out a sigh of relief as the awful sound fell from the air. Slowly, the women reached up and withdrew their hoods. Most looked to be in their late teens, obviously novices or acolytes. But three of the women, those standing closest to Maegwin, were older. As Rovann's eyes fell on the three he stiffened in shock.

The sense of wrongness that emanated from the three women was so palpable he could almost taste it. The three stood close to Maegwin, smiling, and to the naked eye they looked like any other priestesses. But to Rovann's senses they stank of the corruption of the Outer Darkness, of Chaos. The air around them seemed to shimmer and ooze.

They were revenants, Rovann realized immediately. Maegwin's order had been destroyed by Lord Cedric Hounsey. Maegwin had been the only survivor. So who were these women?

One of them, the oldest, Rovann guessed by the touch of gray in her hair, stepped to the front of the dais and raised her arms.

"Friends! Brothers and sisters! Children of Sho-La!" she cried in a clear, ringing voice. "Today is a special day. Today is the day we walk into a new age, led by our holy mother who we have come to invest with Our Lady's holy power."

She clasped her hands together and slowly turned in a semicircle so that she could take in the whole of the crowd. She held herself proudly. This was a woman used to public speaking, used to having a crowd eating out of her hand.

"Some of you may not know me. My name is Tarina. Through the grace of Our Lady I have returned to you. Now it is my solemn duty and my honor to invest the one who will lead us all to glory. Our new holy mother!"

Right on cue, the other priestesses took Maegwin by the hand and led her to the front of the platform where everyone in the crowd could see her. Slowly Maegwin lifted her veil.

Rovann went rigid. Maegwin was pale with dark rings under her eyes. She looked weary and sad. Yet the sight of her caused his heart to soar. Images of her smile flashed through his mind. Memories of the touch of her skin against his. Of the warmth of her kiss. He forced them mercilessly aside.

Rovann lifted his chin and caught Tallo's eye. He made a small signal with his hands, sweeping one against the other. *Create a diversion.*

Tallo nodded minutely and pushed off from the pole, hands in pockets. He sauntered slowly through the crowd and then bumped into a burly farmer being flanked by his two sons. Tallo snapped something at the man, who squared up to him, growling. People turned to look at the commotion. Tallo pulled his arm back and punched the man in the face. The man howled with rage as he staggered back. The man's sons waded in and soon a brawl broke out.

Rovann saw his chance. He darted from his hiding place, keeping low to avoid being seen, and stepped up onto the dais from the back. None of the women paid him any heed. They were watching the fight with hands over their mouths in horror, as though they'd never witnessed any kind of violence before. Rovann cast out a tiny bit of Aetheric power to cover his approach and keep them from noticing him as he snuck up behind Maegwin, put one hand over her mouth, the other round her waist. Flaring Aetheric power to stop her struggling, he yanked her backward, dragged her down the steps and then round to the back of a big barn-like building out of sight of the square.

She suddenly bit his hand and he snatched it away, cursing. Maegwin spun, dropping into a fighting crouch. Then her eyes settled on him and widened with shock.

"Rovann?"

"Hello, Maegwin."

She took a step toward him then halted. "What are you doing here?"

"What do you think?"

She looked no different. Warier, yes. More tired, yes. But still the Maegwin he'd once known. Not a monster. Not the terrible creature she'd become in his mind. She looked like the woman who'd saved his life when the Songmaker attacked Angard. She looked like the woman who gave her life energy to allow him to banish the demon outside the village of Threeways. She looked like the woman who'd cradled him whilst he was injured, dressed his wounds and sang vigor back into his body with her Song Spells.

Why did you do it? he wanted to shout at her. *Why did you betray me?* But the words wouldn't come. Instead he took one step forward, arm outstretched as if pleading.

"Maegwin?"

Chapter Five

Maegwin went rigid, shock raising the hairs along her arms. It was Rovann. *Rovann.* But that wasn't possible. He was miles away in Tyrlindon.

She began to say his name but found it suddenly impossible to speak. Instead, her eyes roamed over him, hardly daring to believe he was real. His blond hair was tousled, slightly longer maybe, and curling onto his shoulders where it glinted in the light from the fading sun. His eyes were as blue and deep as she remembered, like still pools she could fall into. He held his body tense, ready to bolt or fight. She was all too aware of how his breath hissed in and out, his chest heaving.

"What—?" She cleared her throat and tried again. "What are you doing here?"

"Maegwin, I—" His hand moved toward her then stopped. "Not here." He grabbed her wrist and yanked her down a narrow alley before kicking in the door of a storehouse and pulling her inside.

The place was gloomy and filled with sacks of grain

waiting to be taken for milling. A musty smell hung in the air and the call of pigeons drifted from the rafters above.

"What are you doing here?" she asked again, glancing nervously at the door where Leo might appear any minute. "Do you know what he'll do if he finds you?"

Rovann regarded her. She couldn't tell what he was thinking.

Ask me, she thought, shocked by a sudden intense yearning. *Is that why you've come? Is it? Then ask. Ask me to leave with you. I'll do it. For you.* She suddenly, desperately longed to touch him.

"I wanted to——" He shook his head as though clearing unwanted thoughts. "I shouldn't have done this. It was a mistake."

"Was it?" she took a step closer.

He stepped back, keeping the distance between them. "I...I..." He scrubbed a hand through his hair in that familiar gesture.

She took another step. This time he didn't move back. Another step. He was only an arm's length away from her now. Oh, how she ached to reach out and touch him. Oh how she longed to feel his arms circling round her, pressing her close.

"Rovann, there's——"

"Holy Mother!" Tarina suddenly burst through the doorway.

The moment shattered. Maegwin shook her head. Rovann whirled to face the newcomers. Miriel and Ashria followed Tarina into the room. Tarina shot a venomous glance at Rovann then took Maegwin's face between her hands.

"Are you all right? Are you hurt? What happened?"

"I'm fine," Maegwin murmured.

She turned and the scene before her made her go cold. Miriel and Ashria were crouching ten paces in front of him and both wore expressions of utter hatred. For his part, Rovann had backed away and his lip had curled in revulsion. For one insane instant the tableau reminded her of a stag being circled by hungry wolves.

"Rovann?"

His eyes flicked briefly to meet hers. "Maegwin, listen to me. You need to step away from that woman. She's not what you think. None of them are."

She moved to take a step toward him but Tarina held her shoulders in a vice-like grip. "What are you talking about?"

"Curse you, Maegwin! Are you blind? The Songmaker is manipulating you. Look at them. Look closely. Can't you see it? They're dead. Revenants, just like Cedric Hounsey."

His words pelted against her like chips of ice. She shook her head. "No, you're wrong. They *were* dead. I brought them back."

His eyes blazed. "You did *what*?"

"Do you still underestimate the power of my mistress? She gave my sisters back to me. Everything I thought lost has been returned to me."

Except you.

"Open your eyes," he snapped. "I don't know what he's made you believe but they're revenants. This whole place is a trap. He's using you!"

A penumbra flared into life around him. Flickering colors rippled across its surface: the silver of Aethyr, the blue of Water, the red of Fire, the yellow of Air, the green of Earth. All the Realms, bar the black touch of Chaos.

She took a step back. What had he become? How could he command such power?

"Look at them!" he hissed.

Maegwin's gaze slid to the two women. She saw nothing amiss. They were her sisters, pure and simple. "You're lying! Why are you trying to trick me?"

"I taught you better than that, Maegwin."

She backed away, pushing the others behind her. She was suddenly very afraid. There was something different about him. Colder. More distant. "What are you going to do?"

He scrubbed a hand through his hair again. "I don't have a choice. You know what I have to do."

So cold. So emotionless. Where had her Rovann gone? Her anger melted into fear. He'd already beaten her once, back in the tower of Tyrvanan. She knew with icy certainty that he could do so again.

"Don't do this," she whispered. "Don't."

Rovann grimaced and his gaze faltered. His voice was surprisingly gentle as he said. "They're already gone, Maegwin. You cannot bring back the dead, despite what the Songmaker might tell you."

Before she could answer, a screech tore through the air, making Maegwin whirl. Ashria and Miriel launched themselves at Rovann. Their hands were curled like claws, reaching for his face, and their expressions burned with hatred.

Time seemed to slow. The two women leapt at him. Rovann's arm rose. His aura flared, Fire exploding around him and boiling toward Miriel and Ashria. A silent scream erupted from Maegwin's chest and on instinct she threw power at Rovann. She expected it to be Air but it was Chaos that answered her, slamming into Rovann's Fire before it could consume her sisters and holding it there, creating a wall between them.

"Go! All of you!" she shouted. "Get out of here!"

Tarina darted forward, grabbed the two younger women by the wrist and, with a last vengeful glare at Rovann, dragged them through the doorway.

Maegwin's wall of Chaos was weakening. Rovann was too strong for her. With a gasp she staggered and the power fizzled out. Rovann strode toward her, fury etching his face.

For one terrifying moment she was sure he was going to kill her. She held out a hand and cried, "How could you? You would have killed them if I hadn't stopped you! They're innocent!"

"You act as if you're surprised," said a voice from behind her. "It's hardly the first time, is it?"

Maegwin spun to see Leo leaning against the doorframe, arms folded. Rovann growled at the sight of him.

"Hello, King's Mage," Leo said jovially. "It's good to see you again. Oh all right, I'm lying. It's not good to see you. But we have to keep up our manners don't we? *Politeness makes the world go round.* That's what my old mother used to say." He frowned and then scratched his head. "Hang on, that's not right. Oh, never mind. She was an evil old witch anyway."

From the square, the chanting began again. Its deep, resonant sound seemed to shake the very air beneath Maegwin's feet.

Leo held up a hand. "Ah, it appears they've got your little distraction under control, King's Mage. Would you care to join us? There are spare seats down the front. I'm sure you'd enjoy the show."

Rovann's eyes darted from Leo to Maegwin. He seemed wary but not frightened. "I'll have to regretfully decline your offer. As gracious as it is."

Leo waved a hand languidly. "I thought you'd say that.

However, I'm going to have to insist that you stay. I've come to realize it's better to keep you close. Has anyone ever told you you're like some kind of terrier? Always nipping at my heels? You are one total pain in the backside."

Rovann smiled but there was no humor in it. "I aim to please. What are you doing here, Leo? I don't suppose you'd care to tell me your plans?"

"I'd love to!" Leo cried, clapping his hands together. "Or then again, maybe I wouldn't." He tapped the side of his nose, appearing inordinately pleased with himself. "Wheels within wheels, my friend. Plots within plans within plots. I'll make you a deal: I'll tell you what I'm up to if you give me back my book."

"What makes you think I have it?"

"Oh, come on! How else would you have found this place? You obviously figured out my messages." He leaned forward suddenly, peering at Rovann as though inspecting an insect. "Wait a minute! You haven't figured it out, have you?" He threw his hands in the air and crowed like a delighted child. "Oh this is just priceless! The King's Mage of Amaury walking right into my hands without a clue what he's doing!"

Rovann took a step closer. His eyes were cold. "Tell me what you're planning or you'll die here along with all your people."

"Oh, threats, threats, threats! That's all I ever get from you these days."

Leo seemed not to be bothered by Rovann's tone at all but it chilled Maegwin to the core.

"Leo—" she said, voice low in warning. "There's something…"

A presence was growing in her mind. Something

approaching. Something powerful that burned with a consuming hunger. It bore the essence of Fire...

"Tanyaka!" she gasped, just as the terrified cry of "Dragon!" went up outside.

You'll die here along with all your people.

Oh, Lady. He was going to burn them! Just like at Tyrvanan. She staggered back as sudden fear swept through her. Her ruined arm flared with pain. The memory of flame filled her vision. Stone burning. Walls tumbling. Leo's screams mingling with hers as they burned in Tanyaka's fire.

She looked at Leo. A spasm of emotion flashed briefly across his face but was soon replaced by a grinning mask.

"Yes," he said. "She's here."

Suddenly he threw out his hands and a wave of power flew at Rovann. But the King's Mage was ready for him. He let forth a blast of Eorthic power into the ground which opened and swallowed him.

The Eorthe spewed Rovann out just meters from the building where he'd confronted Leo and Maegwin. He bolted into the village square and skidded to a halt, looking around wildly. They had to get out. It had been a mistake coming here at all. They must flee and let Tanyaka burn the place to the ground.

Tallo and Lady spotted him and pelted to his side, weapons drawn. Tallo sported a black-eye and bloody lip.

Rovann glanced up to see the great dragon slowly circling the settlement. Her enormous shadow passed over him as she flew, dirt and debris whipped up by her passage.

Warrior! Her voice echoed in Rovann's head. *I came at*

your call! Where is the puny little man? I will burn him to ashes this time!

Hold on, Rovann sent to her. *Wait for my word.*

"Look," Lady said, pointing at the people in the square. "What are they doing?"

Rather than fleeing at the sight of Tanyaka as Rovann had expected, the townspeople had arranged themselves into a pattern that resembled the spokes of a wheel with the three white-robed priestesses who'd confronted Rovann standing in the central hub. On the stage, the acolytes had formed a circle, and they were singing. Like before, the chant sounded ancient, primordial. It lifted and fell in a cadence so deep it should not come from any human throat.

"What's going on?" Tallo asked.

Yes. She's here.

Leo's soft words echoed in Rovann's head. When Maegwin had realized Tanyaka was coming, Leo had seemed at ease. Pleased, even. As if...

"He was expecting her," Rovann breathed, eyes going wide. "Tanyaka!" he bellowed in sudden panic. "It's a trap! Get out of here!"

Her answer was full of disdain. *No trap can hold me! Have no fear, warrior.*

Before he could reply, Maegwin and Leo stepped up onto the stage, ducked through the linked arms of the acolytes and stood within the circle, holding hands. Then they too joined the chant.

Blood red lightning suddenly lit the space between them. The jagged bolts spread from person to person, filling the spokes of the wheel, rippling ever closer to where he and his companions hid. The power soaked into the towns-people, filling them up as though they were empty vessels before moving onto the next.

Rovann staggered, bracing himself on Tallo's arm as a terrible realization hit him. Battle mages. They were being turned into battle mages. He'd read about this but never seen it done. Nevertheless, instinct told him he was right. They were becoming automatons who wielded power at their master's behest. The Songmaker had created revenants, empty, soulless people and now he was filling them with power. Ready to turn them against the people of Amaury.

The crackling energy reached the edge of the circle and carried on expanding, billowing up and out to encompass Near Point like a giant mushroom, spreading up the sides of the valley until it reached...

"The pillars!" Lady cried. "Look at the pillars!"

Rovann had time to bellow, "Tanyaka!" then a penumbra of force exploded out of the ancient pillars surrounding the settlement. Darkness boiled upwards in a coruscating black cloud like roiling smoke. It enveloped Tanyaka.

The dragon bellowed in outrage. She thrashed her great wings, lashed her tail, slashed with her claws. Yet she couldn't escape. The darkness tightened around her, trapping her in a web of black coils which slowly began to squeeze.

"Get out!" Rovann barked at Tallo and Lady. "Wait for me by the camp. If I don't join you within the hour, leave. Get word to Tyrlindon."

For a wonder, they didn't argue, just nodded tightly with eyes wide with fear or revulsion or both. Rovann counted twenty heartbeats, enough to ensure they were safely away before he closed his eyes and swung open the gate that resided inside him. The Aethyr answered first, as it always did.

His thoughts suddenly became crystalline. Tanyaka was a creature of Fire, one of the few things able to destroy revenants. And Leo already had cause to hate and fear her after what she'd done to Tyrvanan. Small wonder he'd gone to such lengths to lure her here, to this place where he could use the ancient, forgotten artifact to trap her.

The power that shimmered around Tanyaka had the feel of the Eorthe to it but was primitive, as though it had formed when the world was young. Veins of Chaos ran through it, making it a power unlike anything he'd seen before. How did you fight something you didn't understand?

He blinked, pushing away the panic that fought at the edges of his Aethyr-induced calm. *Think.*

Fifty heartbeats passed with Rovann trapped in indecision. The Songmaker's followers still chanted. In the square, the Songmaker's battle mages still channeled the power out into the pillars like some giant conductor.

And in the sky above, Tanyaka writhed and howled in pain.

Rovann scrubbed his hand through his hair. Pushing Aethyr to the side, he allowed the fury of Fire and the wildness of Air to rip through him instead. The air ignited. It churned, wrapping him in a whipping maelstrom of sorcery. His cloak and hair billowed; dust and debris whirled around him.

"Leo!" he bellowed, his voice booming like a thunder crack, "Let her go!"

"Never!" Leo's voice said in his ear. "Do you know what she did to me?"

Rovann spun to find Leo standing right beside him. The youth's face, normally so smooth and young-looking, had become a burnt, twisted mess of ruined flesh. One eye was completely gone and his left arm was cradled against his body, the hand curled like a claw.

Leo backhanded Rovann across the face. There was an explosion of light and Rovann was hurled across the square. He collided with a bench that shattered beneath him. He struggled to a sitting position, waves of dizziness making his head spin. Leo stood over him menacingly. All trace of the jovial young minstrel was gone.

"Look at me!" he shrieked. "Look at what she did to me!"

Rovann wiped a hand over his face, trying to clear his vision. He found a soft laugh escaping his lips. "You're afraid."

Leo straightened. His good eye—still the vivid green Rovann remembered— narrowed. "Afraid? Of that stinking creature? Hardly."

But from the way his gaze involuntarily flicked toward Tanyaka, Rovann knew he was right. Tanyaka had taught the Songmaker he was not invincible and now he was terrified of her. For that reason he had constructed this elaborate trap.

And Rovann had fallen for it.

Fool. He is always a step ahead of you. When will you learn?

With a flick of his wrist, he sent an explosion of Eorthic power ripping through the earth. The ground heaved and bucked. With cries of terror the people in the square went sprawling. Leo staggered to his knees then rolled out of the way as a crack appeared beneath him. Rovann seized his chance. Hauling himself to his feet, he ran, dodging between the buildings and out of sight of the square.

Leo's voice rang out behind him. "You can't hide, Rovann! You and your pet will die here! I swear it!"

"We'll see," he murmured under his breath.

He channeled Aetheric power into his body and pelted through the dirt streets with unnatural speed. After several turns he threw himself down in the gloom behind a barn and carefully peered around the corner. The street was empty but it wouldn't remain so for long. He didn't have much time.

Almost directly above him Tanyaka hung suspended in her smoky prison. Her struggles had weakened and she snapped ineffectually at her bonds.

Tanyaka! He sent. *Are you all right?*

Her response was weak. *Warrior? I… I feel strange.*

Tanyaka's body suddenly pulsed a bright red. The pulse of color was sucked out of her and shimmered across the surface of the black cloud and down into the pillars which seemed to hungrily devour it. A moment later a second red pulse followed and then a third. The pillars began to glow crimson, like blood.

"No," Rovann whispered, as understanding sent a sick jolt through his body. "No."

Slowly, excruciatingly, Tanyaka's life force was being drained from her. Drained into the pillars to be stored until…

"Until the Songmaker needs it," Rovann breathed.

A weapon. A power unlike any Amaury had ever seen. The sheer scope of such a plan left Rovann breathless. He had once witnessed Tanyaka's life force devour a demon of the Outer Darkness. What could the Songmaker do with such power?

What are you going to do? Tanyaka had once asked as she carried him from the ruins of Tyrvanan.

I'm going to kill them all, he'd answered.

And now, it seemed, Tanyaka herself would be included in that count.

No. Not while I have breath left.

He slowly stood. He raised his arms and a maelstrom of energies erupted around him, whipping his hair into his face and churning the dust into an inferno.

I am the King's Mage, he said to himself.

You are the Slayer of Sandford Moor, another voice accused him. It sounded suspiciously like Maegwin's.

He nodded. So be it.

Throwing back his head, he howled an incoherent wail and then spread his hands wide as though he would embrace the sky. He relaxed all control. The power of the Seven Realms hurtled through him, wild enough and bright enough to burn him to cinders. But it didn't. It exploded upward and slammed into Tanyaka's oily prison. A concussion rocked the atmosphere, hurling Rovann back against the wall of the barn and sending flocks of birds hurtling from the trees.

When he looked again the smoky darkness was gone and the great red dragon was plummeting from the sky.

"Tanyaka!" Rovann bellowed, flinging himself to his feet. "Fight!"

She didn't hear him. He could see from the way her aura flickered in and out of existence that she was close to death. For one, two heartbeats, he stood frozen by horror. Then he closed his eyes, opened his senses to the astral plane and quickly sketched a gate in the air. It burned with molten symbols. Speaking a word of Eorthic power, he forced the gate open and staggered back as he was buffeted by the ferocious, tearing power of the Realm of Fire.

Next he wielded Air, wrapping the dragon in thick bands to slow her descent. Something dripped onto his lips and he tasted the iron tang of blood. Irritably, he wiped it away. Pressure built in his skull but he ignored it. Gritting his teeth and letting out a wordless howl, he pressed on the bands of air, pushing, pushing, pushing Tanyaka toward the gate. As she felt the pull of her own Realm, Tanyaka's eyes flickered open.

Warrior? What are you doing?

You must return to Fire, my friend, he answered. *I cannot save you. Only your own Realm can do that.*

No! I vowed to fight with you.

And you shall, he reassured her. *But not like this. I won't allow you to die for me.*

The dragon fixed her eyes on him and even from this distance Rovann could see the light beginning to return to them.

We'll meet again, Warrior of the Realms.

With that, she flapped her giant wings and disappeared through the gate into the Realm of Fire. The gate flared brightly and then winked out of existence.

Rovann collapsed to his knees, lungs pumping, heart racing, blood streaming from his nose and ears. The muscles in his arms and legs twitched. He could barely hold his head up

Get up! He told himself. *The Songmaker will be coming. Get up, curse you!*

His body wouldn't obey. He closed his eyes as he heard footsteps converging on his position. He had no energy left to fight. Rough hands grabbed him by the armpits and yanked him to his feet.

"Come on, boss! We gotta go!"

Rovann's eyes flew open. Tallo had wrapped an arm around his waist whilst Lady looked around warily, holding a loaded crossbow.

"I told you to wait for me at the camp." They half carried, half dragged him through the streets. "I'm going to have to report you to Captain Tyan for disobeying orders."

Tallo grinned. "Well, we've never been great at the old obeying orders thing. Why do you think the captain sent us with you?"

Rovann managed a weak smile. The three of them staggered on.

"This way!" Lady shouted, waving them toward an intersection.

They paused for a moment while Lady checked for danger then hurried across the open space and into a narrow street hemmed in on both sides by whitewashed cottages.

"There!" a voice bellowed behind them.

Glancing over Tallo's shoulder, Rovann saw a fat, bearded man watching them. Energy crackled around his raised hand. A mage.

Tallo yanked him around a corner just as the ground where they'd stood exploded in a shower of dirt and stones.

"Well, this is fun," Tallo observed dryly.

Lady took a quick peek around the corner. "Curse it! Two of them coming this way."

She shared a long look with Tallo. They both straightened, forcing Rovann to stand on his own.

Tallo nodded. "On my mark. One, two, three."

In unison, they sprang from their hiding place. Rovann heard the thwack of Lady's crossbow and the thunk of Tallo's throwing knife and then they were back, grabbing him under the armpits and dragging him into the street.

A quick glance showed the two mages sprawled like dolls. One had a crossbow bolt jutting from his neck, the other a knife buried hilt-deep in his eye-socket.

Lady went ahead, scouting for danger whilst he and

Tallo darted from hiding place to hiding place. The streets began to turn steeply uphill and Rovann found his breath beginning to labor in his chest.

"Wait!" he hissed as the aura of a mage intruded on his senses. "Someone's coming."

They pressed themselves against the base of a wall. A haystack sat against it, affording them a little cover whilst giving them a good view of the street. A tall, red-headed woman stepped around the corner and paused. Her eyes narrowed, head cocked to one side as though listening.

"She knows we're here," Lady whispered.

Tallo nodded. "Nothing for it. We'll have to deal with her."

"Be careful, she's a mage!" Rovann hissed.

Tallo gave him a mocking salute. "Always, boss. Always."

The pair threw themselves from their hiding place and into the street. The red-head spun at the sudden noise, eyes going wide, even as Tallo's knife and Lady's crossbow bolt flew at her. The missiles thudded into an invisible barrier two paces from the woman and clattered to the ground, twisted out of shape.

Rovann cursed to himself. How had the woman raised a shield so quickly? She must be an adept. Wonderful. Just what they needed.

With a snarl, the woman flung out her hand and an explosion of Air hurled Lady and Tallo into the wall. They slid to the ground and lay groaning.

Rovann gritted his teeth and pushed himself to his feet. He took two tottering steps forward. "You shouldn't have done that."

The woman's eyes widened as she recognized him. Rovann heard her mental summons. *He's here! Come quickly!*

He raised his arm and the woman involuntarily took a step back. She didn't realize he was spent. Good. Better keep it that way.

"Leave now and live," he hissed.

He felt a sudden intrusion as her senses swept over him, probing his strength. Then a slow smile slid across her face.

"Nice try, Lord First. But I'm not some child to be intimidated by your lofty title. When I last taught at the college you were a cocky novice who just couldn't help getting himself into trouble. We all thought you'd get thrown out within a year. Look how far you've come."

Recognition flashed over Rovann. "Thylse," he breathed. "I'd hoped you were dead. I should have known better. Where else would a snake like you go but into the bosom of the Council's enemy?"

She smirked. "Where else indeed? It's nice to know I've not been forgotten."

"Forgotten?" Rovann hissed, taking a step toward her. "You killed three of your own students! No, Thylse, you've not been forgotten."

She held out her hands mockingly. "Are you going to arrest me? No? I thought not. Well, shall we get this over with?"

Chaotic power hurtled toward him. He wove a shield of Aethyr which deflected Thylse's blast into the wall which exploded in a shower of stones.

Gathering what remained of his strength, Rovann sent a shockwave through the Eorthe beneath her feet. The ground rippled and she staggered back. Rovann followed with a blast of Fire that burned against her shield. Thylse jabbed at him with her hand. A frigid blast of wind slapped him aside and he landed with a thump next to Tallo, all the breath knocked out of him.

Adepts of Air were usually excellent battle mages as, along with Fire, it was one of the Realms that leant itself most readily to fighting. And it seemed that Thylse had not been idle during her long banishment from the college.

With a groan, Rovann rolled over, got his hands underneath him and pushed himself onto his hands and knees. A boot connected with his cheek, snapping him onto his back again.

"Get up," Thylse hissed, standing over him. Against the sky her silhouette seemed black, as though she was a Sluargh of Darkness. "Get up and fight me!"

She tangled her fingers in Rovann's hair and yanked him roughly to his feet then pulled her hand back to deal him another blow.

With a snarl, Rovann caught her wrist and yanked her forward. He closed his free hand around her throat. Thylse's eyes bulged, her tongue protruded. She battered at him with weakening waves of Chaos but he swatted them aside.

"You won't do it," she gasped. "You don't have what it takes."

Rovann cocked his head to one side, regarding her as she slowly choked. Stooping, he grasped one of Lady's knives where it had fallen to the ground and then stabbed it through Thylse's throat. She vomited a gout of blood down his tunic then sagged in his grip. He tossed her lifeless body aside.

Rovann staggered, catching himself against what remained of the wall. Black dots danced in front of his eyes. His vision swung in and out of focus. Curling his hands into fists, he dug his nails into his palms to keep from passing out.

Lady and Tallo climbed groggily to their feet.

"Are you hurt?" he asked.

Lady shook her head and Tallo said, "Well my pride's a bit injured, truth to tell. Never been thrown like that in all my soldiering days. Never want to again, I can tell you."

Lady raced to the end of the street and peered out. She returned with a grim expression on her face. "They're coming."

"Ah, curse the bastards," Tallo growled. "Don't they ever give up? What do we do?"

"We run."

They staggered through the streets as quickly as Rovann's weakened state would allow. Glancing up at the black, featureless sky, Rovann's neck prickled. It was the dark of the moon. He should have known. The night Sho-La was at her most powerful.

They moved furtively, dashing from one hiding place to another and in this manner, they made it to the edge of the village and into the cover of the trees. Tallo let out a sigh of relief and helped Rovann to lean against a tree-trunk whilst Lady scouted back down their path

"They're close," she said as she returned. "Maybe a hundred paces behind. We have to keep moving."

They staggered into the woods. Darkness swallowed them and Rovann found himself having to duck under branches and weave through vegetation, trying his best to keep silent. An owl hooted. Ahead, the bushes rustled and a striped badger stuck its head out and regarded them with dark eyes before silently turning back into the undergrowth.

Rovann's breath sounded loud in his ears. His heart thumped painfully against his ribs. This helplessness was new and unfamiliar. He didn't like it one bit.

Finally they reached the clearing where they'd made camp. Tallo helped Rovann to a seat on the fallen log where he sat with this elbows on his knees, head hanging down.

"We'll rest for a moment and then go on," Lady said.

"We can't outrun them forever," Tallo replied.

"We can bloody well try!"

"Too late for that," said a new voice.

Dark figures emerged from the trees, forming a ring around the clearing. Lady drew her knives and dropped into a fighting crouch. Tallo raised his crossbow, trying to aim at all of them at once. Rovann rose to his feet, searching for a means of escape. There was none.

They were surrounded.

Chapter Six

The din of the hunt echoed in the distance but inside the temple, all was still. Maegwin was alone. An advantage of being holy mother was that others obeyed when you told them to leave. Images of the day's events flashed through her mind in quick succession leaving her with a strange sense of dislocation. The ceremony. Rovann's face. Tanyaka's terrible screams.

With a sigh, she brushed a palm across the soft white fabric of her dress, wiping away imaginary dust. An acolyte's robe. Simple. Unsullied. The irony wasn't lost on her.

Outside, a cry went up. "This way!" Shouts answered from further off. The whole settlement seethed with activity.

They were after Rovann. *Rovann.*

And she sat in here, doing nothing.

None of it made any sense. Rovann had known she was here. And Leo had known Rovann would come, bringing Tanyaka with him. It was all an elaborate trap, one designed to capture Rovann and the dragon both. The only thing she couldn't quite figure out was her part in this.

He's using you! Rovann had told her.

Maegwin suspected he was right. From the moment Leo had given her the *Canticle of Darkness* she'd felt like a puppet dancing on his strings. It was all tangled up in his plans—giving her the book, making her holy mother, activating the ancient artifact that almost trapped Tanyaka, luring Rovann here.

Answers. She wanted answers and she'd get them from Leo when he returned. His reticence was part of the reason she was sitting here right now, neither helping Leo nor helping Rovann. A wry smile twisted her lips. The two men who'd become the axis of her life. It was as though she sat on the edge of a precipice with Leo on one side, Rovann on the other, waiting for her to decide which way to jump. But she'd already made her choice back in Tyrvanan. Hadn't she?

She gazed through the window at the dark landscape beyond. It was the dark of the moon. Within the room everything was still. Black. Suddenly, the shadows began to thicken, gathering like dark pools in the corners. The air was heavy. A presence touched her senses and she folded onto her knees on the dusty floor, her heart suddenly pounding in her chest.

"Mistress," Maegwin whispered.

A pale face with hair of midnight formed in the bowl of water set on the low shrine. Sho-La. The goddess's face was stern as she regarded Maegwin.

"What do you wish of me, Mistress?" Maegwin asked, pressing her forehead against the rough floorboards.

The goddess watched her silently.

"You've displeased Her." Leo stepped out of the shadows, flanked by Tarina, Miriel and Ashria.

Leo's boyish features were unusually serious. "She doubts your resolve."

A shiver slowly slid down Maegwin's spine. "Why?"

Leo's eyes narrowed. "Do you think you can hide your thoughts and feelings from Her? She knows your mind. She knows your heart. You almost betrayed us today."

Maegwin stared at him. "No," she insisted, shaking her head. "I didn't." Yet her words sounded hollow even to herself.

Leo narrowed his eyes. "Don't lie to me, Maegwin. We've come too far for that. You would have gone back to Rovann, had he asked you."

She licked her lips. Swallowed. Glanced at the stern face of her goddess. The shadows swirled around her, reaching out with soft fingers.

Where does your true loyalty lie? they seemed to whisper. *Give yourself to us.*

She faced Leo squarely. "A moment of weakness. It has passed."

"Prove it."

"Prove it? How?"

"Finish the ceremony. Become our holy mother."

She watched him silently and he looked back, unblinking. She felt the stares of Tarina, Ashria and Miriel on her as well. But most of all she felt the weight of the Dark Goddess's will. She'd given herself to the Dark Goddess, pledged her soul to serve Her and by extension, Leo, Her general. It was too late for doubts now.

"All right. But I want something in return."

"Oh?"

"A promise. A promise that if I do this, you'll finally

trust me. That you'll stop keeping things from me and explain your plans."

A sense of satisfaction oozed from the youth. "As you wish."

"Then we're agreed."

Leo grinned suddenly and clapped his hands together. "Excellent!"

He gestured to Tarina and the others who moved to stand before the altar, outstretched hands clasped. Closing their eyes they began to chant. The deep cadence seemed to make the very earth shake. Tiny ripples moved over the surface of the water in the silver bowl, obscuring the face of Sho-La.

Maegwin closed her eyes. The will of the Dark Goddess bore down on her like a weight strung around her neck. The air smelled charged, as though a thunderstorm was brewing. She sucked a deep breath through her nose, allowing the still, heavy air to fill her lungs.

Then, she started to sing. The words were from the *Canticle of Darkness.* Words of sundering and of new beginnings and Maegwin's devotion. It was a promise.

After a moment, Leo joined in. The minstrel's voice added the last part, the perfect balance between the chant and Maegwin's song. As he sang, power began to bleed out of him. A dark light filled his eyes and seeped out of his mouth with his words. Maegwin felt it enter her, fusing the promise into her very bones.

Making it unbreakable.

Abruptly Leo and her sisters fell silent. Maegwin's voice stumbled and then faded away to nothing. She straightened, turning toward the Dark Goddess, meeting Her unwavering midnight stare. Then a deep voice spoke in Maegwin's mind.

It is done.

"Well," Tallo said conversationally, "I think we've got this covered."

The man's wry humor brought a smile to Rovann's lips, despite their dire situation. He, Tallo and Lady had taken stances back to back, trying to keep each of their attackers in view. The figures around the clearing hadn't moved. They just waited silently, blocking all escape.

Suddenly a deep voice spoke from the night. "We'll have to stop meeting like this, Rovann."

A figure stepped closer and in the gloom Rovann suddenly recognized the rough, bearded face.

"Thaldan?" he asked incredulously.

The man swept an arm round and made a mocking bow. "At your service, oh mighty King's Mage."

Rovann worked his jaw a few times before demanding, "What are you doing here, Thaldan?" His brother-in-law was the last person he'd expected to see.

"Saving your sorry backside by the looks of things," the bearded man snapped.

Tallo hefted his sword, taking a step closer to Thaldan. In response, the figures around the glade shifted and Rovann caught the glint of weapons.

"It's all right," he said, raising a hand. "I know this man. Lower your blades."

Tallo eyed him but did as instructed. After a moment, Lady did the same but the two soldiers didn't relax their stance. Rovann straightened and regarded his dead wife's brother. How, by all the Realms, had he showed up here?

"What do you want?" he demanded.

His voice sounded harsher than he intended but there wasn't time for niceties. And he didn't trust Thaldan. Who could say which side he was on?

"We'll discuss that later," Thaldan replied. "Right now, I suggest we run."

Rovann glanced toward the lights of Near Point twinkling in the valley. The Songmaker's hunters would be on them any second. "Mages are after us. We can't outrun them."

In the darkness, he thought he saw Thaldan smile. "Do you think? Follow me."

He moved off and his men followed, shepherding Rovann, Lady and Tallo into a tight circle. They reached the edge of the clearing just as a man burst out of the undergrowth behind them. He raised his arm aloft, red power beginning to flare.

A bow twanged and the man toppled from view with a strangled cry.

"Quickly!" Thaldan growled. "The rest will be close behind!"

They scattered into the cover of the night-shrouded woods. Thaldan's men spread out, forming a scouting perimeter whilst a smaller group stayed with Rovann and the others. Rovann gritted his teeth, cursing his own weakness. A scream cut through the night and everyone paused, looking back.

"Who?" Thaldan growled.

"Tiery was walking point," one of his men answered.

Thaldan hesitated, as though considering going back, but then spun and marched off. "Come on."

"Where are we going?" Rovann asked, coming abreast of him.

The big man didn't answer. Rovann grabbed him by the sleeve.

"Damn you, Thaldan! Answer me!"

"There isn't time to explain!" Thaldan hissed, yanking his arm from Rovann's grip. "You want to face them? Go ahead. You want to live? Then do as I say and keep your mouth shut!"

One of Thaldan's men suddenly loomed out of the night and spoke to his chief in a low, urgent voice. "Three of them coming east. They've picked up our trail. If we continue in this direction, they'll intercept us."

Thaldan cursed. "This way."

They turned south and hurried down the bank of a dry riverbed. Sand and gravel crunched under Rovann's feet as they scurried like spiders, hunched almost double to allow the river banks to hide them. Rovann's pulse quickened. It was as though the night was hunting him. He was prey. They would find him soon. He could sense them getting closer, a dark threat creeping ever nearer.

They moved in silence for maybe half an hour before Rovann realized they were heading toward the mountains. Was Thaldan hoping to lose their pursuers in the high passes? It wouldn't work. There was no cover on the bald flanks of those peaks. They would be easily picked off.

He opened his mouth to tell Thaldan so but snapped it shut again when he saw that up ahead Thaldan's men had halted and were crowding together under a rocky overhang. Above and behind, the mountains rose in ragged ranks.

"Shern, lead the way," Thaldan instructed.

A man stepped forward, carrying a stout branch with a bundle of cloth wrapped round one end. The man muttered a word and the cloth suddenly burst into flame.

Rovann shuddered as sorcery made his skin prickle. A mage.

The torchlight seemed shockingly bright in the darkness. It illuminated the faces of his companions, taught with tension. And it would lead their pursuers straight to them.

He opened his mouth to speak but the man with the torch—Shern, Thaldan had called him—suddenly ducked down, took two steps and…disappeared.

"Quickly!" Thaldan hissed. "Follow him!"

He grabbed Rovann by the shoulder and shoved him. Rovann stumbled then moved forward cautiously, arms outstretched. In a few paces his fingers brushed the rough stone surface of the cliff. Puzzled, he ran his hands over the surface and quickly found an opening a little over waist high. He had to bend almost double to fit. Beyond lay a tunnel with muted yellow torchlight disappearing into the darkness ahead. Almost on his hands and knees, Rovann edged along, feeling the hard stone ceiling scrape along his back. Twenty or so paces further on the ceiling disappeared and Rovann found himself stepping out into a large space.

Shern stood waiting for him, holding the torch aloft to illuminate a cavern of unworked stone. Other openings that might have been tunnels opened off the cavern. Rovann's breath misted in front of him. It was bitterly cold.

"My thanks," Rovann muttered.

The mage inclined his head but didn't reply.

"Get out of the way, Tallo!" came Lady's muffled voice. "Don't stop in the middle of the tunnel you damned fool, I nearly knocked myself out on your bloody sword hilt!"

Tallo emerged, closely followed by Lady. "I was just checking the way was safe!"

Lady straightened and shot the soldier a withering look.

"Well, don't." She gazed around the cavern and whistled under her breath. "Well would you look at that?"

Tallo hunkered down on a boulder and hunched his shoulders, peering around suspiciously. "I don't like small spaces. When can we get out of here?"

Rovann didn't answer. He had no answers. He was acutely aware that he'd placed all three of them at Thaldan's mercy. A man who hated him. Perhaps they should have taken their chances with the enemy mages.

One by one Thaldan's men emerged from the tunnel until finally the big man himself stepped through. He straightened, looked them all over then nodded, satisfied.

"Shern, lead on."

The mage nodded once and set off deeper into the cave system. The party walked in near silence. The only sound was the scuff of their boots on the dusty rock and the drip of water from somewhere nearby. They moved into another tunnel, this one high and wide, as though it had been sliced straight through the bedrock of the mountains.

The mage seemed confident of the way. The pace he set quickly ate up the distance and he didn't hesitate when other tunnels crossed their path. Thaldan marched at the rear of the group carrying a torch. Risking a quick glance back, Rovann caught the torchlight glinting off his drawn sword. There was no sound of pursuit but Rovann knew if Leo's mages found the entrance to these underground passages they could easily be tracked.

No wonder Thaldan looked worried.

He considered dropping back to talk to his brother-in-law but decided against it. He got the feeling his words wouldn't be welcome. So he walked in silence following Shern's bobbing torch as if it was the only thing that might save him.

The neat, straight paths indicated that these caverns were not a natural feature of the mountains. Yet he could see no sign of tool marks or other indicators that humans might have worked down here. In some places the rock walls were wet, with rivulets of water dripping from the darkness above. In other places the walls were bone-dry and gave off a faint smell of rust. In these caves large white spiders scuttled away from the light of the torches. Sometimes the path Shern chose passed through large caverns where stalagmites reared up from the floor like tiny mountains. Some of them oozed strangely colored mineral deposits and Shern instructed the company not to touch them.

Rovann felt the awe of the others. They looked around wide-eyed but their hands never strayed too far from their weapons. Only Tallo seemed unaffected. The soldier's mustached face was folded into a scowl and his hands clenched and unclenched at his sides.

An indeterminate amount of time later, Thaldan called a halt. The company huddled together under the ominous hang of glittering stalactites and took some rest. Thaldan handed around hunks of hard bread and strips of dried meat which Rovann took gratefully and slumped to the ground beside Lady and Tallo, chewing mechanically.

Now they'd stopped moving, he found his thoughts racing. Like some fresh-faced novice who didn't know any better, he'd walked right into the Songmaker's trap. Leo had known all along that Rovann would come and bring Tanyaka with him. And now the great dragon was gone. Her presence had been the only thing keeping Cedric Hounsey's besieging army from storming Tyrlindon. Were his troops pouring into the capital right now?

Fool, he chided himself. *You shouldn't have spoken to*

Maegwin. You shouldn't have gone down into the village. You should have just burned it.

Why didn't I? he asked himself bitterly.

Because I needed information. I needed to know what the Song-maker was planning. We couldn't have discovered that if we'd burned Near Point.

But his excuses sounded hollow even to himself. The truth was he'd gone to Near Point because of Maegwin. Because he couldn't accept that she'd betrayed him. Because he'd deluded himself into thinking she'd return to him.

Fool, he told himself again. *Will you never learn?*

He glanced up as someone slumped down next to him. It was the mage, Shern, noisily munching on an apple. Rovann didn't speak, waiting for the man to explain himself.

"Don't look at me like that," Shern said suddenly.

"Like what?" Rovann replied, taken aback.

"Like I'm some naughty child. It reminds me of being back at the college."

Rovann looked at him, startled. "You were at the college?"

Shern took another bite of his apple and chewed it slowly. He swallowed the mouthful and then nodded to Rovann's question. "Seems a long time ago now. I didn't graduate. I left after the third year."

"Left? Why?"

"To join the Songmaker."

"*What?*"

Rovann was halfway to his feet before Shern waved a hand, "Don't worry, I'm not with him anymore. I work for Thaldan now."

Rovann channeled a tiny amount of Aethyr and held it ready. "Explain yourself."

Shern shrugged then rubbed the end of his long nose. "What's to explain? I left the college because it didn't suit me. Turns out, neither did the Songmaker so I left him too."

"And Thaldan?"

"We're getting along just fine. Seems working with smugglers and criminals might be my path in life." He smiled wryly.

Rovann watched him warily. Was he a spy of the Songmaker's? But if so, why was he helping them escape? And why had he revealed his connection to Leo? Rovann shook his head. Could he trust any of them?

"I saw what you did," Shern said quietly. "To the dragon, I mean."

Rovann grunted. He didn't want to talk about it. He'd failed. He'd been lured into a trap and been unable to save Tanyaka.

"I've never witnessed anything like it," Shern went on. "The Songmaker is powerful. I've seen it. But you...." He leaned into Rovann's line of sight so he had no choice but to look at him. "Nobody should have been able to break those bindings. The whole valley is one big trap. Those pillars channel Chaos and some bastard form of the Eorthe. To my knowledge, nothing has ever escaped them. Until now. How did you manage it?"

Rovann didn't answer. He didn't like the way Shern was looking at him. Since his confrontation with Leo and Maegwin in the tower atop Tyrvanan, Rovann was aware that something had subtly changed within him. During that clash he'd somehow accessed more power than he ever had before. Normally a mage, although accomplished in all, had a particular strength in one discipline. Syrie was an adept of the Eorthe, Earth magic. Falwin was skilled with Air.

Rovann himself was an adept of Aethyr and a servant of the angels.

But in Tyrvanan something had snapped inside him. Now all the Realms answered him as Aethyr did. He understood the rippling, wild energies of Air. He could manipulate the rage of Fire and the quiet touch of Water. The Eorthe called to him, giving up its secrets.

And yes, even the Chaos of the Outer Darkness did his bidding.

That scared him more than anything. Now, if he closed his eyes and concentrated hard enough, he could hear distant voices, demonic voices, calling him from beyond the in-between, from inside the Outer Darkness itself. So when Tanyaka had been trapped, he'd acted without thinking, using his new-found powers to cut her free. He didn't understand how he'd done it. Manipulation of the Realms had become instinctive, as normal to him as breathing.

When the time comes, you will lead us into battle, an angel had once said to him.

He pushed the thoughts away and focused on Shern. "How did you know about the pillars?"

The man shrugged. "Like I said, I worked for the Songmaker. For a while. He never trusted me with his plans but I overheard him discussing it with his advisors once. He didn't know where the pillars were, though. He had some drawings in a book and was looking at old maps to try to find them. Seems even he has no idea who created the place. It's old. Very old. Some reckon it was built during the last great Realm War, when the barriers were torn down. The builders used it as a way to kill powerful wights that had crossed over from other Realms."

"I don't understand how the Council of Mages couldn't

have heard of this place. There's no knowledge of it within the college."

Shern tapped the side of his nose. "Isn't there? There is always knowledge, if you know where to look."

"What's that supposed to mean?"

"Mages are arrogant. I don't mean to offend, but there it is. We think we understand all there is to know about the power of the Realms. But we don't. There's much we have yet to discover and there are people and creatures in the world who comprehend far more than we do."

Rovann smiled wryly. He was beginning to realize that. What other little surprises did Leo have in store for him? His mind went back to Leo's journal. The pillars had been sketched in that book and Rovann guessed that other things he'd seen on those brittle pages were important too. His lack of understanding frustrated him. It was clear they meant something to Leo. Something crucial. Rovann just couldn't work out what. A chill crawled its way down his spine.

The Unraveling has begun, Tanyaka had told him.

The Unraveling. The thought of it left Rovann giddy with dread. For eons the seven Realms had existed separately from each other, their competing powers kept in balance by the One Light and the Outer Darkness. They were separated by barriers that only those with the skill to open gates could cross. But all that was changing. The delicate balance of the universe was eroding and with it the barriers that kept the Realms apart. The Sluargh of the Outer Darkness were desperately seeking a way through, eager to rampage through the Realms.

And somehow the Songmaker was connected to it all.

"Up!" Thaldan barked suddenly, jarring Rovann from his thoughts. "Time to get moving you lazy pigs!"

Rovann allowed himself to be pulled to his feet by Tallo

then took his place in the center of the line as Shern once again led them deeper into the caverns.

The food and rest had done Rovann good. His limbs felt stronger and his power was returning. He slowed his breathing and sent his senses questing back the way they had come. At the cavern's mouth he sensed a wary presence. Then something slowly crept into the passages behind them.

"Curse it all!" he growled. He pulled out of the line and waited for Thaldan to catch up with him.

"They're coming," Rovann said quietly, falling into step beside him.

Thaldan shot him a black look. "You think I don't realize that?"

"What are you planning to do about it?"

"Run, that's what."

Rovann remained silent. Perhaps it was possible to lose their pursuers in this underground darkness. Perhaps not. Rovann suspected the twisting maze of passages and galleries would prove no obstacle to Leo and his mages. He didn't like it. He was at Shern's mercy. At Thaldan's mercy.

"Why are you here?" he asked quietly. "You still haven't explained."

The big man glanced at him, his dark curls falling over his forehead. "Would you rather I hadn't saved your scrawny neck?"

Rovann smiled wryly. "I can honestly say I've never been so glad to see you."

Thaldan snorted. "You see. I knew you'd missed me."

"You still haven't answered my question."

Thaldan sighed and halted, facing Rovann with hands on hips. "You don't give up do you? Why can't you just do as you're told for once in your life?"

"I'm not good at taking orders."

"Then learn. I'll not say a thing until we're safely out of here. Who knows who might be listening?"

Rovann hesitated. Thaldan had a point. "Then at least tell me where we are."

Thaldan began walking again and Rovann hurried to keep up. "Under the mountains. They're riddled with tunnels and caverns. Shern hid out in these caverns when he fled the Songmaker. That's how my men found him."

"You mean you've used this place before?"

Thaldan nodded. "I'm a smuggler, Rovann. Work it out."

Rovann narrowed his eyes, calling up the local geography of this area. He'd visited this part of Amaury only once and that was when…

"Sheshna," he said suddenly. "Sheshna lies beyond these mountains. You've been smuggling things over the border."

Thaldan raised an eyebrow. "Give the boy an apple. Are you going to arrest me?"

"That depends on what you've been smuggling."

Thaldan pressed his lips into a tight, flat line.

"Thaldan?"

"Don't ask, Rovann. That way you can't be disappointed with the answer."

Rovann didn't respond and they walked along in silence for a while. It seemed that the Realms were trying to tell Rovann something. *Use what you have. Worry about consequences later.*

"Tell me about Shern."

"What about him?"

"Do you trust him?"

Thaldan hesitated for a second and then shrugged. "As much as any man."

"He worked for the Songmaker. You really think he's switched sides?"

"Look at it this way," Thaldan said, scratching his beard. "If you were a spy, would you freely admit that you used to be on the enemy's side?"

Rovann nodded, conceding the point. Footsteps suddenly echoed behind them. In a flash, Thaldan spun and lifted his sword. Rovann dropped into a crouch, calling Fire to his fingertips. In the darkness of the tunnel a light appeared, bobbing toward them.

"It's me, Rallson," called a voice.

Thaldan relaxed slightly but didn't put his weapon away as a young man jogged up to them, no doubt the scout sent to guard their trail. The man's face was red and he was out of breath as if he'd been running.

"They're coming, sir," he panted. "Maybe twenty men. They have mages with them. They're fast, unnaturally fast like, and they're following our trail as easy as anything."

Thaldan cursed under his breath. "Damn them. Damn them to the Darkness."

Rovann grabbed Thaldan's wrist. "How can they follow us so easily? These caves are like a maze."

He didn't say it aloud but from the dark look Thaldan gave him, Rovann knew he understood his unspoken question. *Has Shern betrayed us?*

"Go join the others," Thaldan barked to the scout. "Tell them to keep moving. I'll catch you up."

As the scout jogged off into the darkness, Rovann watched Thaldan as he took three steps back the way they'd come. "What are you doing?"

He turned. "You'd better go too."

"You can't stop them all, Thaldan."

"Do you have any better ideas? I'll hold them here for as long as I can."

Rovann stared at him. "The Thaldan I used to know would never stay behind to save his men."

"You're wasting time," Thaldan growled. "Go!"

"No," Rovann stood his ground. "I can stop them. I'll need a large space, a cavern where all the men can gather at once."

Thaldan watched him. In the gloom, Rovann couldn't make out the expression on his face. Was it suspicion? Or hope?

After a long moment the big man nodded. "This way."

They took off at a jog and soon caught up with the rest of the group, struggling through the darkness.

"Get moving!" Thaldan bellowed at them. "Get to Keeper's Cavern you lazy scum! Run like there are wolves snapping at your heels!"

Ahead, the tunnel branched. Sheer rock walls rose on either side of them and the ceiling was so far above that even Shern's light didn't reach.

"Follow me!" shouted the ex-renegade.

He took off down a tunnel, sprinting as fast as the uneven ground would allow. The others followed, Rovann and Thaldan bringing up the rear. Soon the stamp of boots and the pant of labored breathing filled the air. Rovann strained his ears. Was that sounds of pursuit he could hear behind them?

After what seemed like hours of struggling through the winding tunnels the company emerged into a wide cave. A maze of yellow stalactites hung from the ceiling, looking like fangs. The company skidded to a halt, doubled over with hands on knees and gasping for breath.

"This is Keeper's Cavern," Shern panted. "What now?"

"Keep going," Thaldan replied, pointing at the ragged slit in the far wall that appeared to be the only exit from the place. "Lead the others out."

Thaldan's men grumbled at that until he bellowed. "Do as I say or I'll skin the lot of you!"

Reluctantly, Shern moved off, the others following. Lady and Tallo didn't move.

"Go with them," Rovann instructed. "I'll catch you up."

Tallo pulled on his mustache. "Captain Tyan will have our hides if he finds out we left you. If it's all the same to you, we'd rather stay."

There wasn't time to argue. "Fine." Rovann waved at two humped rock formations that sat at the back of the cavern. "Hide behind those. Cover my back but make sure you stay behind me, is that clear?"

They nodded and jogged over to their hiding places, Tallo taking out his crossbow, Lady drawing her throwing knives.

"Extinguish the light," Rovann instructed Thaldan. "We want them to think we've moved on."

"An ambush?" Thaldan asked. "With just four of us? Are you mad?"

"We'll soon find out won't we? Come on."

He and Thaldan ducked behind a large boulder then Thaldan extinguished the torch, plunging them into darkness. With the absence of sight all sounds seemed suddenly amplified: the whisper of breathing, the slow drip of water somewhere nearby.

Rovann closed his eyes and sent his senses outward. He found their pursuers immediately: a large group of men and women approaching quickly along the path, perhaps a hundred paces from the cavern. A moment of apprehension twisted his stomach. How had they caught up so quickly?

Rovann pushed such concerns away. There was nothing he could do about it now. Channeling a tiny amount of Aetheric power, he probed the group, trying to determine its make up without alerting them to his presence. It was a waste of time. Some kind of barrier stopped his senses from penetrating them, rendering him blind to his enemy.

He ground his teeth in frustration. Pushing his senses outward once more, he gently scanned the cavern, searching. Yes, there it was. There were tiny cracks and fissures in the rock, the result of eons of pressure from the weight above. They would serve well.

Something suddenly moved in the tunnel mouth and he froze. It was a light, dim as a candle flame. It paused at the cavern mouth as though deciding whether to enter. In the dim light, Rovann saw shadows beyond, crowding the entrance.

"I can sense him, I tell you," a man's voice suddenly said. "He's close."

"So? That's what we want isn't it?" a woman's voice answered.

The man didn't reply and the light moved slowly into the cave, casting eerie silhouettes on the wall and making the stalactites sparkle. Behind the candle bearer a group of around twenty people moved into the open. Rovann tensed as he recognized some of them from the village. Leo's battle mages—revenants with the power to channel Chaos.

The group fanned out through the space, moving warily as if sensing a trap. The man in the lead sniffed the air like a dog.

"I don't like this. He's here, I tell you."

Rovann narrowed his eyes. *It's me,* he thought. *They're following me somehow. It wasn't Shern leading them at all. It was me.*

He closed his eyes and opened the gate in his mind that

led to the Eorthe. Down here, in the bowels of the earth, the power was strong. It answered him immediately. He focused his concentration on the tunnel opening. An almighty groaning filled the air and, with a crack that echoed through the cavern like a thunderclap, the tunnel roof suddenly collapsed in a shower of rock and dust.

The mages began shouting, spinning in every direction, power flaring as they sought the source of the attack.

"Curse you, Maraid!" one of the mages shouted. "You said these tunnels were safe!"

"It's not the tunnels," the man with the candle yelled. "It's him! He's here! Look—"

The thwack of a crossbow sounded and the man dropped silently. The mages spun in the direction of the bolt but could see nothing in the dim light.

Thaldan dug his fingers into Rovann's shoulder. "Whatever you're going to do, do it now!"

Rovann nodded. He fixed his senses to the Eorthe once more. This time, he used it to find the tiny cracks in the ceiling. One, by one, he fixed his attention on them, choosing those that best suited his purpose. Then, when he had mapped the ones he needed, he gathered the Eorthe and pushed.

The affect was instantaneous. The back portion of the cavern's roof came crashing down. As tons of rubble, rock, dust and dirt thundered down, Rovann yelled, "Run!"

He and Thaldan darted from their hiding place and threw themselves to the tunnel at the rear of the cavern. Dust and rock chips suddenly filled the air, making it difficult to breathe. Tallo and Lady met them by the exit.

"Go!" Rovann growled. "The whole thing might come down!"

The soldiers nodded, their faces pale. Even Thaldan

looked unsettled as they pressed themselves into the narrow slit and edged their way along the twisting passageway. Rovann listened for pursuit as they fled. There was none. An adept of the Eorthe would probably be able to survive such a collapse and protect those around them as well, so Rovann fervently hoped the Songmaker didn't have any of those. If he did they were all in trouble.

"Wait!" Thaldan hissed suddenly. "A light up ahead."

The four of them halted on the narrow path. Thaldan slowly drew his sword. In the gloom, Rovann saw the gleam of Lady's knives as she held them ready. The light grew steadily closer and Rovann found himself holding his breath. Had the enemy somehow got ahead of them?

Then a figure rounded the corner and Thaldan straightened, letting out his breath. "Don't you know how to follow a bloody order, Shern? I told you to get out of here."

Seeing them, Shern broke into a grin. "I was never very good at taking orders, boss."

"Where are the others?"

"Not far. We're almost out." The mage craned his neck to glance past them. "And our pursuers?"

"Dealt with," Thaldan growled. "Lead the way, mage."

Shern inclined his head and, holding his torch high, led the way. Further on the passage became even narrower and the ceiling descended so that the company was forced to squeeze on hands and knees through the narrow gap.

"I don't like this," Tallo grumbled. "We might get stuck."

"Which is exactly why I'm going ahead of you," Lady replied.

"What? You mean you'd leave me behind?"

"In a heartbeat, my friend. In a heartbeat."

A breeze suddenly tickled Rovann's face. It was clean

and smelled of grass. After a moment, he found himself entering a tall gash in the rock and was able to straighten. Sunlight spilled through the gap, so bright and pure that Rovann felt like weeping. Shern extinguished his torch and grinned.

"See?" he said. "Told you I knew the way, didn't I?"

Rovann grinned in turn and then clapped the mage on the shoulder. "You certainly did, Shern. I'm sorry I doubted you."

Shern looked suddenly embarrassed. "Thanks."

The others emerged from the narrow tunnel and one by one they left the darkness behind and stepped out into a bright morning.

Chapter Seven

"Would you look at that?" Tallo breathed. "We made it! We only bloody made it!"

A green valley spread between the knees of the mountains, twinkling in the early-morning light. The rest of Thaldan's crew was sprawled in the grass, resting and repairing weapons.

"Boss! You're alive!" one of them cried, flashing a grin at the shaggy-haired man.

"Did you ever doubt it?" Thaldan replied, throwing himself down amongst them and stretching out his legs.

"Are we safe?" Shern asked Rovann. "Will they follow us?"

There was real fear in the mage's eyes and Rovann found his gaze being drawn to the scars that ran up the man's arms and twisted one side of his face. He'd not noticed them in the darkness of the tunnels but they were more obvious now it was daylight. How much courage must it have taken Shern to lead them through those tunnels, knowing his torturers were so close behind? Rovann's respect for the man grew.

"No, Shern. They can't follow us. We're safe. For now, at least."

Shern nodded in relief then wandered off to join the rest of his crew. Rovann craned his head back, looking up at the rocky peaks. Shern had led them through the mountains and now Leo and Maegwin were somewhere on the other side. So yes, they were safe for now. But that presented another problem. Rovann was no longer entirely sure where they were. Were they still within Amaury's borders? Or was this region part of Sheshna? And if so, would they be welcomed here?

Thaldan let his men rest for only a few moments before he ordered them to their feet. The big man glanced uneasily at Rovann before leading the company off at a brisk march south. For some reason he seemed worried, even more than he had in the tunnels. More than once, Thaldan a shared a look with Shern. Rovann chose not to question them but merely walked in silence as they followed a goat track that hugged the flanks of the mountains, passing through sunlit valleys covered with wildflowers and stands of pines.

It was a beautiful day. The sun rose high in a blue sky and the valleys were filled with the sound of rushing streams and bird song. And yet...something wasn't right.

Rovann was reminded of the time he and Maegwin had been traveling in the eastern provinces of Amaury on their way to Roamsford Edge. A similar feeling had assailed him then, a sense of wrongness that carried on the breeze like a poison. Later that night, the source of the wrongness was revealed: a Sluargh of the Outer Darkness. It had almost killed them both.

His uneasiness increased. The others seemed to feel it

too. Despite their miraculous escape, despite the apparent safety of the valleys, despite the beautiful day, nobody spoke. Nobody made jokes or small-talk. Instead, the company marched in morose silence, eyes scanning the surrounding terrain, fingers brushing the handles of weapons.

They trudged this way for perhaps three hours when Thaldan finally called a halt. They were in a small, circular valley, almost like a bowl within the mountains. Steep, rock walls rose on all sides and the high walls meant that little light penetrated the bowl, leaving it in gloomy shadow.

Thaldan ordered seven of his men to take picket duty around the camp, two others to scout back along their trail and a further two to scout ahead. Rovann frowned. Such precautions would suggest he expected trouble.

Tallo crouched on the rocky ground and began clearing away rocks and pebbles to make space for a fire but Thaldan grabbed his hand as he made to get out his tinder pouch.

"No fire," he said.

Tallo frowned. "I don't know about you, but I could do with some hot food. How long do you reckon it is since I had my last hot meal?" The soldier pursed his lips as he thought. "More than twenty four hours, that's how long!"

"No fires," Thaldan repeated. "If you want to be useful, go and refill the water skins."

Tallo looked at Rovann with one eyebrow raised in a question. Rovann nodded. With a sigh Lady grabbed the water skins then she and Tallo moved down the valley toward the stream.

Rovann bent his knees and lowered himself to the ground, sitting with his legs crossed. Thaldan and Shern joined him. He fixed them with an expectant stare.

"Well?" he asked.

Thaldan ran his fingers through his beard. He looked more uncomfortable than Rovann had ever seen him. "I said that once we were free of those tunnels I'd explain our purpose here." He glanced at Shern. "Tell him."

The mage licked his lips. His face was pale and sweaty. Terrified, Rovann realized. A worm of fear suddenly wriggled down Rovann's spine. What was going on here?

The mage drew in a deep breath as though steeling his courage. "I told you the truth about how I used to work for the Songmaker but chose to leave his employment. When he caught me, he did this." Shern held up his arms so that Rovann could see the puckered scars that marked them. "The Songmaker doesn't like deserters. But he likes thieves even less."

Rovann clasped his hands and leaned forward. "You stole from him?"

Shern nodded. He reached into his pack and pulled out a scroll. "I had no idea what I was taking. I steal things. I can't help it. Most of the time I don't understand why I do it. I took this from the Songmaker's tent one night. His fury was like nothing I've ever seen. I ran. He caught me. Tortured me. But I'd hidden this and he never found it. When I escaped I came back for it. You see, his reaction told me this was important. Very important. So of course, I had to know why." He gestured at the valley. "It led me here. I wasn't sure what to make of what I found here but in my wanderings I fell in with Thaldan's crew. Like I said, I'm good at thieving."

"I caught him poring over this scroll one night," Thaldan took up the tale. "Staring at an old map when he should have been out scouting for me. When I saw what he was looking at I knew I'd been embroiled in mage politics again whether I liked it or not." He fixed his dark gaze on Rovann. "Seems I can't escape your plots, no matter what I do."

"What has this got to do with me?" Rovann demanded.

"You'll see. I realized straight away we must bring this to you. Near Point lies close to one of our smuggling routes. We'd seen strange things going on down there for a while and then a few days ago, the bloody Songmaker showed up. It was only a matter of time before you did the same. So we laid low, watched and waited. And lo and behold, here we are!" His voice was heavy with sarcasm and more than a little annoyance. Rovann opened his mouth to speak but Thaldan silenced him with a wave of his hand. "Show him what you stole, Shern."

Nodding, Shern unrolled the piece of parchment and spread it flat on the ground. It was a map. Yet, unlike any map Rovann had ever seen. It showed the whole of Amaury, and a little of the lands beyond its borders, but no towns or settlements were marked. Instead, strange names marked certain places, all in different colors.

Running his fingers over the map, Rovann found the spot where Near Point ought to be. No village was marked on the map.

But the circle of stone pillars was.

And above it, written in an ancient dialect that Rovann struggled to read were the words, *Ashen Mount, Realm of Chaos*.

Rovann's heartbeat quickened. His eyes roved to the west, into Shinnar lands and sure enough he soon found the place where Tyrvanan should be. Instead, seven concentric circles had been drawn on the map and a label which read, *Tyrvanan, the Seven Realms*.

Heart thumping now, Rovann knelt and leaned closer.

All over the land were places marked with strange labels. Where Silverport should be, a label said, *Vas Karda, Realm of Water.* To the south, near Mallyn another read, *Sho-la-na, Realm of the One Light.*

"By the Seven Realms," Rovann breathed. "Do you know what this is?"

Shern's blue eyes met his. He nodded. "It shows all the places where the Realms touch Amaury. All the places where their power can be harnessed."

"No wonder the Songmaker was furious when you stole it," Rovann said. "But where would he find such a map?"

Shern shrugged. "Who knows? Stole it himself perhaps?"

Rovann frowned as a sudden thought struck him. When Leo had been traveling with him and Maegwin he'd been very fond of telling them how he wandered the length and breadth of the land in his role as a minstrel. How he stayed with lords and ladies and learned old songs and tales as he went. Was it possible he'd found this map during that time? Leo's logbook, from the time before he became the Songmaker, showed a young, eager scholar.

Something nagged at Rovann. There were clues here somewhere. He needed to figure them out.

Rovann raised his head, gazed around the valley, then looked down at the map. He traced his fingers over the mountain range but couldn't find the area they sat in.

"Why have you brought us here?"

"After I escaped the Songmaker I wanted to find out what so interested him about this map. I visited some of the locations marked on here. Many of them are dead, their powers long since vanished. But there are others that still hold power, the stone circle at Near Point being one of them." He looked away for a moment and his gaze settled on the southern horizon, as if he could see something there. Then he tapped the map with his right index finger. "Here."

Rovann leaned forward, squinting to make out the small, spiky script. In black ink something like a portcullis had been drawn and below it read the words: *Arka Cahn.*

His breath caught in his throat. He'd seen that diagram somewhere before.

Urgently, he grabbed his pack. Rummaging quickly through the contents, he pulled out Leo's notebook and leafed through the pages. On the very last page Leo had sketched a stylized portcullis, just like the one on the map. Below it was a diary entry.

I have found it. The map was accurate. Would you believe it? Most think it's a legend but all the best legends are founded in at least a fragment of truth. Arka Cahn. What is it really? Tomorrow I'll find out. Tomorrow I'm going in. I can already see the glory that awaits me! People will be falling over themselves to hear my tales and songs of this quest!

There was nothing more. This was the last entry in Leo's diary.

Rovann stared at it and then at the map showing the location of Arka Cahn. Why the portcullis? What did it symbolize? And what had Leo found there?

"It's here, isn't it?" he asked Shern suddenly. "You followed the map just like Leo did and it led you to this valley."

Shern nodded, wide-eyed.

"Show me."

Shern shared a long look with Thaldan. The big man nodded. "Show him. He'll be able to make more sense of it than we can. The rest of us will keep watch."

Rovann snapped Leo's diary closed then rolled up the map, tucking both beneath his arm as he scrambled up.

Shern rose slowly, reluctance evident in every movement of his body. He pulled in a deep breath and then set off.

"This way."

It was not far. Shern led him down the valley, following the meandering path of the stream until it disappeared among what looked to be a mound of large boulders that had fallen from the mountain side. Shern approached the small gap through which the stream passed. Rovann watched him disappear into the gloom then sucked in a breath, climbed down into the icy water, and followed.

In just a few paces he found himself in a dark, narrow tunnel with barely enough headroom above the rushing water to allow him to breathe. His hands and knees scraped sharp stones on the streambed and the water's chill threatened to steal his strength. He could see light ahead and Shern's shadowed form moved just in front of him.

After a few more paces the ceiling vanished and he saw open sky above him. Shern straightened and clambered out of the stream, moving to stand on a rock shelf that ringed the circular space. Rovann followed, grateful to be out of the frigid water.

The sense of wrongness was so strong here it staggered him. The air felt heavy and thick. It was difficult to breathe. Rovann lurched, pressing his back against the rough rock wall.

Shern laid a hand on his shoulder. "It will pass in a moment."

But it didn't. Blackness flooded Rovann's vision. He seemed to be falling. Down, down, down he went, into nothingness.

Free us! A voice suddenly whispered in the darkness. *Free us! We can give you back your wife if you only free us!*

Shern's face appeared, inches from Rovann's own, looking pale and worried. "Lord First? Are you all right?"

Rovann grabbed the man's arm and slowly straightened, leaning back against the rock wall for support. Above him the sky glittered with stars.

Rovann started. Stars? But it was mid-morning. What the—?

The rock walls of the circular space were even, smooth, clearly man-made. The stream emptied into the space to form a pond. Except that in the middle of this pond was a hole. Rovann squinted, trying to make out what he was seeing.

The water seemed to lap against an invisible barrier that shimmered like heat haze. So instead of pouring down the hole as water normally would, it frothed around it, creating a whirlpool. Then he noticed that something was covering the hole. Bars. A grid work of metal bars like a...

"Portcullis," he breathed.

It was exactly the same as the picture on Shern's map and the sketch Leo had made in his diary. Arka Cahn.

The bars were twisted, broken. As if something had escaped.

"It was like this when you found it?" Rovann breathed, not wanting to hear the answer.

Shern licked his lips and nodded. "Do you know what Arka Cahn means in the old language?"

Rovann shook his head.

"It means First Prison of Night."

He pointed a shaking finger at the far wall. Words were carved into the rock. They were covered in moss in places, weathered by time, but Rovann could still make them out. Some of the words were in pictograms. They showed some kind of creature being imprisoned in the pit. Next to it was a name: *Prison of Night.*

Below it, was a second pictogram showing another of the creatures being confined. Next to this was another name. *Tear of Life.*

"Something was imprisoned here," Rovann breathed. "But there were two of them. The other was held somewhere else."

Shern nodded. "Tear of Life, in the modern tongue."

Rovann looked at him sharply, alerted by the strange tone of his voice. Almost in a whisper, he asked, "And what is Tear of Life in the old tongue?"

Shern swallowed thickly. "It translates as…Tyrlindon."

The word seemed to hang in the heavy air between them. For a long time Rovann stared at Shern, hardly daring to breathe, hardly daring to think.

Tyrlindon. Realms save us, Tyrlindon.

Slowly, everything began to make sense. In this place a creature had been imprisoned that time had forgotten. Leo the minstrel came here, but walked out as the Songmaker. Had he freed the creature? Or been claimed by it? Was that the catalyst that changed a harmless minstrel into such a dangerous renegade mage?

But that was not all. There was a second prison and it lay somewhere in Tyrlindon. *In Tyrlindon.* Rovann's hands curled into fists. All along he'd thought Tyrlindon had been targeted merely because it was the capital of Amaury, the seat of the Council's power. Yet if the Songmaker wanted to destroy the Realms, why bother to take Tyrlindon? He realized with a sickening sense of dread that Leo had never wanted Tyrlindon for itself. He wanted it for the creature imprisoned there.

Realms, what a fool he'd been! He'd left Tyrlindon's

defense, believing he could better serve Amaury elsewhere. And worse, he'd fallen into Leo's trap and brought Tanyaka with him. Tanyaka, a dragon of Fire who might be able to stop Leo's revenants in their march on the capital.

He scrubbed a hand through his hair then dug the heels of his palms into his eyes. The Songmaker was always one step ahead. Why did he never remember that?

"Come on," he said to Shern, sucking in a breath and straightening. "Let's return to the others.

They crawled back through the stream and emerged once again into the mid-morning sunlight of the valley. Rovann paused, eyes roving over the rocky outcrop enclosing the prison. Holding out a hand, Rovann focused the Eorthe on the rocks. They groaned as cracks webbed their surface. After a moment the rocks above the stream collapsed into a pile of dusty rubble, blocking access to the pit beyond.

"The stream will eventually flood the area around the entrance," Rovann explained. "Discouraging anyone from exploring further."

Shern nodded tightly. "I hope you're right, Lord First. The whole place felt wrong, like it shouldn't have been part of our world at all."

"That's because it wasn't," Rovann replied. "It was a fragment of the Outer Darkness, the Realm of Chaos. Whatever was imprisoned there was so powerful its jailers felt the only way to contain it was to trap it outside the Realms."

And there is another in Tyrlindon. Realms help us all!

When they reached the others Rovann didn't bother with explanations. "Gather everyone together," he instructed. "We leave for Tyrlindon immediately."

Chapter Eight

Maegwin stood by the window, watching the fevered preparations in the square below. She'd dismissed her attendants—which usually buzzed around her like a swarm of bees—so that she could get some solitude. Below her window pack animals were being prepared, supplies were being loaded onto carts, belongings and traveling goods were being sorted. Most of the people were Leo's battle mages, identified now by the silver pin they wore in their lapels. They had once been ordinary folk but now they'd given themselves to Sho-La and become soldiers dedicated to Her name.

They were Maegwin's people now. She wasn't sure how she felt about that. She ought to feel proud of what she and Leo had achieved here. The faith of Sho-La had been reborn and it was spreading.

There was a knock on the door and Tarina entered. The older woman bobbed a curtsey. It was another affectation that annoyed Maegwin, but no matter how many times she'd asked Tarina and the others not to do it, they seemed to think it was required.

"Holy Mother," Tarina said. "We're ready."

Maegwin nodded. She gave one last glance at the village where so much had changed and then followed Tarina downstairs and into the courtyard.

Leo was mounted and waiting. He wore a garish red and black outfit finished with a wide-brimmed hat sporting a peacock feather. His lute-case was slung over one shoulder. He looked every bit the court dandy. But Maegwin wasn't fooled. Not anymore.

"Are you ready, my dear?" he asked as Maegwin approached, a toothy grin splitting his face.

He seemed in a better mood. He'd been apoplectic when his trackers had returned empty-handed. They reported that they'd tracked Rovann into a cave system beneath the mountains where he'd brought a rock-fall down on them. Only three had survived.

Maegwin glanced at a large oak standing on the hillside. The distance was too far to make out details but she could clearly see the three bodies hanging there, gently twisting to and fro. Leo's renegade mages had paid the price for failure.

Where are you now, Rovann? she thought. *Plotting other ways to kill Leo? To kill me?*

Glancing at Leo, she asked, "Is everything ready?"

Leo waved a hand. "As you can see, we merely await your command."

Two nervous acolytes were holding Maegwin's horse, a magnificent golden mare who wore trappings rich enough for any queen. Maegwin approached and took the horse's reins, murmuring thanks to the two acolytes. She reached up, clucking to the horse and stroking her nose. Then she set her feet in the stirrups and swung into the saddle.

Tarina, from her side-saddle position atop her own mount, frowned slightly. They'd had an argument about Maegwin's dress: Tarina wanting her to wear the ornate gowns Leo had ordered and Maegwin content to keep to her simple leggings and tunic. They'd compromised by Maegwin wearing a dress with a split down the middle to allow for riding but they still felt cumbersome and awkward.

Maegwin stood in her stirrups. Channeling Air, she projected her voice so everyone in the square could hear her. "Children of Sho-La! Today we march toward our new dawn! Today we march to bring the light of Our Lady to the world! She has given us a task and we will fulfill it or die trying. Who's with me?"

The crowd roared, calling out affirmation of their faith.

Maegwin lowered herself into the saddle and raised an eyebrow at the grinning Leo. "Shall we?"

He bowed grandly. "Of course, my lady."

Together, she and Leo turned their horses and led their people from the village, beginning their long trip south to Tyrlindon.

It quickly became apparent that the journey was going to be very different to what she was used to. The huge column of people and animals shuffled at a snail's pace. When she had first traveled with Rovann then later with the soldiers on the way to the Highhold, they'd moved quickly and with stealth. Not this time. There was no way of hiding the movement of such a large group of people. King William, if he hadn't already, would soon hear of their advance.

"Can't you do something?" Maegwin asked Leo as mid-morning approached and they'd barely covered any ground. "You're the bloody Songmaker aren't you? Can't you take us through the Eorthe or something?"

ELIZABETH BAXTER

Leo smiled at her crabbiness. "My, my, do I detect a hint of frustration, my lady?" He shrugged. "Whilst I'm thrilled by your estimation of my powers, I'm afraid you flatter me too much. It's impossible to move so many through the Eorthe at once. It would kill us all. Besides," he added in a quieter tone. "The Eorthe does not obey me anymore, just as the Aethyr no longer obeys you. There are prices to be paid for serving our mistress." He looked around at the undulating landscape: a patchwork of fields and rivers. In the distance, smoke rose from the chimneys of a farmstead. "We mustn't reach Tyrlindon too quickly in any case. Word of our coming will spread. Panic and fear will spread. I want King William and his people to know despair before they die."

Maegwin looked at Leo sharply. There it was again: that dark glint in the minstrel's eyes. He kept it carefully hidden but just occasionally Maegwin caught a glimpse. There was darkness and hunger inside Leo, just like there was inside her. Small wonder then that they'd found each other.

"You make it sound so simple, but it's not," she said. "Do you think we'll just turn up and the capital will fall to us? Tyrlindon has never been taken."

"We shall see," Leo replied. "History, remember, is written by the victors and aid can come from unexpected sources."

Maegwin got the impression he was keeping things from her again. He'd hinted on several occasions of something important waiting for them in Tyrlindon but every time she asked directly he skirted the issue. "Even when we meet up with Hounsey's besieging army we won't have enough soldiers," Maegwin persisted. "You've been to Tyrlindon; you know what it's like. Built for defense. Each level will be a battle ground."

Leo regarded her in silence for a time. Then he nodded. "You're right." He pulled his horse to a halt suddenly and held up a hand for the rest of the column to do the same. He turned to one of his mages. "Selwyn, you will continue on this course with the column. Lady Maegwin and I are going ahead. There's something I have to show her. You should catch up to us by this afternoon."

Selwyn, a hugely fat man with a beard like a bird's nest, nodded then turned and bellowed orders to the rest of the mages.

Leo turned to Maegwin. "Fancy a little ride?"

She frowned. "What are you up to, Leo?"

"You'll find out soon enough. Shall we?"

Without waiting for an answer, Leo put his heels to his horse's flanks and sent it galloping off down the trail. Maegwin did the same, leaving a concerned Tarina calling out behind. Maegwin caught Leo and pulled her horse abreast, keeping low in the saddle as the two animals pounded along the dusty, tightly packed dirt of the road.

"Where are we going?"

Leo grinned at her. "Somewhere you can find a little faith!"

He edged ahead and Maegwin was forced to follow behind as they pounded down the road, up a steep hill and into the next valley. Maegwin's hair streamed out behind her and her horse's hooves kicked up dust as they went. It felt good to ride. A grin tugged at the corners of her mouth as she urged her horse to overtake Leo's. She lost herself in the thrill of the ride and the beauty of the sunny day. But, as they galloped across the length of a windy upland ridge, Leo slowed his horse to a trot and then finally pulled it to a halt. Maegwin followed his example, patting her blowing horse on the neck.

Leo pointed at the wide valley that opened out below. "Faith, Maegwin. There it is."

White tents, in neat, ordered rows filled the valley. They stretched as far as the eye could see, like some miniature city. Tiny people moved among the tents. Maegwin's eyes widened at the sight.

Leo dismounted and led his horse down the slope. After another moment of stunned gaping, Maegwin followed. They'd not gone ten paces when five men materialized out of the heather. Pickets. They were heavily armed and well-equipped.

"Halt," one of the men said, leveling a spear in their direction. "Who are you?"

Leo smiled at the man. "This is Maegwin de Romily, Holy Mother of the order of Sho-La. My name is Leo March but you might know me better as the Songmaker."

The man paled. "My lord, lady," he stammered. "If we had but known you were coming we could have organized an honor guard—"

"No need," Leo said, magnanimously. "Just lead us to General Shallon."

The man bowed. "At once, my lord."

Whilst two of the men led their horses away, Maegwin and Leo followed the leader down the valley's side and into camp. Word of their arrival had gone ahead and at the perimeter of the camp they found General Shallon and his staff waiting. Shallon's armor, as always, was polished to a silver sheen that seemed to glow in the sunlight. He went down on one knee as she and Leo approached.

"My lord. My lady. Welcome back."

Maegwin watched the general warily. "What happened?" she asked. "How come you're here? I thought you were still in Shinnar territory."

When she'd left the Shinnar plains with Leo, the rest of his forces were bogged down in a guerilla war against the Shinnar and the wights of Roamsford Edge.

The corners of Shallon's lips quirked slightly—the closest he would come to smiling. "We marched. Day and night without stopping. When Lord Leo called us, we came."

"And the Shinnar? The Wights?"

A frown passed across Shallon's features. "They harried us every step of the way. We lost many."

Maegwin cast an eye over the encampment. It still looked vast. "How many?"

"Thousands, my lady."

Leo stepped forward, clasping the man on the shoulder. "Your men were the first casualties in this war. They will not be the last. Our priestesses will pray for their souls and ask Our Lady to guide them into the One Light."

General Shallon smiled. "I know it. Now, you must be weary after your ride. Will you take refreshments with me?"

Leo inclined his head graciously and they walked with Shallon through the encampment toward the general's tent. Soldiers stopped to salute them as they passed and Maegwin was careful to acknowledge them all with either a nod or a salute of her own, even though such gestures felt awkward. Many bore injuries and she wondered how fiercely the Shinnar and the wights had fought to keep this army out of Amaury.

They reached a large white pavilion and stepped inside. The command tent was sparsely furnished and had a transitory look. It reflected the man who occupied it: austere, no-nonsense. Except for the small cot in one corner, the only other decoration was a low table bearing an arrangement of twisted holly branches and flowers. Amongst the flowers sat a bowl of dark clay filled with water. A shrine to Sho-La.

Shallon indicated for them to take seats and Maegwin gratefully sank into a camp chair beside Leo.

"Report, General," Leo said.

Shallon inclined his head. "We did as you requested, lord. We waited a full day after you and Lady Maegwin left and then I opened the packet of orders you gave me. I was surprised and somewhat relieved to be honest, sir."

He flicked a glance at Maegwin and then focused his attention on Leo once more. "I'm glad we were ordered out of Shinnar territory. Morale was getting low. The men were beginning to mutter that it was not the Lady's will that we should enter Amaury. Therefore, I was glad when you told us to march for the border. We broke camp that night and set out in three separate companies, better able to divide our enemy's forces that way. I led the first company myself and we headed west and a little south to come at Amaury's border just north of Roamsford Edge. There was fierce resistance to our march. Our train was attacked by Shinnar raiders, our supplies decimated."

He shrugged and his gray eyebrows climbed his forehead. "I must give this to the Shinnar: in their own lands, in terrain they know, I have never experienced such ruthless and efficient fighters. They would come out of nowhere, attack strategic targets in a lightning strike and then melt into the prairie as though they had never existed. Despite the patrols, despite the scouts I set around the perimeter of our marching columns, we kept losing men.

It took us three days to reach Amaury's border and when we did the Shinnar set fire to the prairie. I think I lost more of my company to fire then I did to the raids. Yet we fought through it and once we crossed the border into Amaury they dropped back."

Shallon fell silent for a moment, hands clasped in his lap. "Second company faced much the same ordeal. I'd sent them north and once within Amaury's borders they angled south and met up with us." He raised his hands to indicate the surrounding space. "We've assembled here as instructed. Of third company there has been no sign."

"No sign?" Leo asked. "How so?"

Shallon turned troubled eyes on Leo. "Third company I sent east."

"Toward Roamsford Edge?"

The general nodded. "None returned."

Maegwin drew in a sharp breath. She understood only too well the destructive power that lived within the vast forest. When she had traveled through it with Rovann on their way to Tyrvanan, she had experienced first-hand what the wights of Roamsford Edge were capable of. She and Rovann had been saved only by the intervention of Fenris, an Earth elemental who commanded the forest. To send a whole company into that immense darkness, that twisted, tangled mass of branches and clinging vines... A shiver walked down her spine.

"They're dead," she said. "Every one of them."

General Shallon nodded. "I know."

Leo leaned back, steepling his fingers and regarding Shallon with narrowed eyes. "Much must be risked in war. When this is over I will expel the wights that live in Roamsford Edge and burn the forest to the ground."

Maegwin nodded. Deep inside, she felt a stab of satisfaction from her goddess. Her mistress feared and hated the Edge.

Bring my men hope, the Dark Goddess whispered suddenly in her mind. *Bring them my blessings.*

Maegwin stood abruptly. "By your leave, gentlemen, I'll inspect the army now."

Leo nodded and General Shallon stood. "I'll accompany you, my lady."

"No. I'll go alone."

She ducked under the tent flap and stood blinking in the sunlight. Nearby, two soldiers were struggling to lift a cart to allow a third man to fit a new wheel. She strode over and silently crouched beside them, wedging her shoulder beneath the cart.

"On my count," she instructed them. "One, two, three."

They glanced at her, surprised, but obeyed her order, digging their feet into the ground and bracing their legs until the back of the cart lifted just enough for the third soldier to slip the wheel onto the axle. With a grunt, they released the cart and straightened. The soldiers' eyes went wide when they realized who had helped them. They made as if to kneel but Maegwin quickly stopped them with a curt gesture.

"Thank you, my lady," one of them stammered.

Maegwin smiled. "Good work. Our Lady is pleased."

Leaving them staring after her, she moved on. She came across a group of soldiers sitting in a circle, listening to a woman reading from *The Book of Sho-La*. Maegwin paused for a moment then cleared her throat. The one who'd been speaking fell silent, looking up at her approach.

"May I join you?"

The woman spluttered, suddenly flustered. She held the book out toward Maegwin. "We would be honored, my lady."

With a nod, Maegwin took the book and seated herself

cross-legged amongst the soldiers. They watched her in silence as she leafed through the pages. The woman had been reading from the *Canticle of Beginnings*, which was concerned largely with philosophical questions about the nature of humanity.

Bring them my blessings, the Dark Goddess had instructed her.

These were soldiers walking into battle in the name of their Lady. They needed words that would put fire in their bellies, not moralistic musing. On impulse, she set aside the *Canticle of Beginnings* and reached into her pocket to take out the wrapped bundle she carried everywhere with her these days. Pulling away the wrappings, she revealed a small leather book. *The Canticle of Darkness.*

She leafed through the pages, only stopping when some instinct told her she'd found what she needed. She began reading. "And Sho-La-Na, lady of shadows and darkness said to her followers: there is no holier cause than to fight in my name. No holier justice than the cut of your swords. No holier motivation than your righteous anger. You are my chosen, my brave warriors. You will strike down my enemies and live in glory by my side even unto the ending of the world."

As she spoke, Maegwin's voice began to change, to become more like a song than speech. The notes began to rise and fall with the cadence of the words, emphasizing those parts the soldiers needed to hear. And as she sang, she felt power leaking out of her, bringing her words to life and taking them deep into the hearts of her soldiers.

Those in the circle leaned closer, faces filled with delight and soon more joined them until a large crowd was gathered, listening to her sing.

Once she had finished that chapter of the *Canticle* she

went back to the beginning. This time, she indicated for the soldiers to join in during the congregational parts. Most of them knew it already, perhaps from Leo's teachings before she'd joined him. Maegwin's voice rang high and clear above the tumult but it was not long before the mingled harmony of male and female voices entwined with hers, sending the undulating song echoing out across the camp.

Maegwin closed her eyes, feeling the power of the song rippling outwards, binding the soldiers together, and binding them to her and to their goddess.

Bring them hope, the Dark Goddess had commanded her. Now Maegwin sensed new determination growing in the hearts of the soldiers.

As they reached the end of the *Canticle* the second time, Maegwin opened her eyes and jumped with surprise. She was surrounded by a sea of people. She scrambled to her feet and climbed onto a barrel so the soldiers could see her better.

Channeling a little Air, she amplified her voice. "Please, be seated!"

They settled cross-legged on the ground in all directions. Maegwin felt like she was at the center of a vast ocean. Expectant eyes watched her. Their expectation seemed suddenly heavy.

Is this how the holy mother used to feel? Maegwin wondered as she remembered all the times in the temple when she and her sisters had sat on the floor, listening expectantly as the holy mother preached from a pulpit.

I am their holy mother now, Maegwin thought. *They are my people.*

Steeling her courage, Maegwin called in a strident voice. "Ever victorious army! I am honored to be amongst you. Tomorrow we march to Tyrlindon. Tomorrow we march to

Our Lady's final victory! Join me, my brothers and sisters! Join me in a celebration of Our Lady!"

She turned this time to the second chapter of the *Canticle of Darkness* and began to sing. In the temple she'd been trained to sing in harmony with others but she'd never thought she would do so with so many. Amplified by Air, her voice rang out clear and strong. After only a few words, the soldiers joined in until the sound echoed across the valley in a murmuring susurration that raised the hair on the back of her neck. She'd never heard anything like it. She'd never felt anything like it. Power. Power that bound the army with chains of devotion.

The faces of the soldiers were transported with rapture. Maegwin saw shining adoration in their eyes as they sang. In that instant she knew that these men and women would never falter, would never retreat, and would never question their motivation.

Maegwin's eyes roved over the crowd. Beyond them, outside the command tent, Leo and General Shallon were watching. General Shallon was singing along with the rest although Leo remained silent. Across the distance, Leo met her gaze and she sought approval in it. He slowly nodded.

Yes, that look said. *You've done well*

Finally, she closed the *Canticle*. She bowed her head, clasping her hands to her chest, and led the congregation in a final prayer to their goddess.

"Sho-La, my light, my guide, my strength. Show us the path to Your wisdom. Show us the way to Your light. We are Yours always."

"Always," the congregation repeated.

With that, the crowd began to disperse, moving off in small groups of three or four, talking in hushed whispers.

Maegwin was left alone, sitting on the barrel, staring down at the *Canticle* in her hand.

"Oh, nicely played," said a voice.

Leo was standing before her. "I couldn't have done better myself. Yes, I definitely chose well in you." These last words were almost spoken to himself.

This statement bothered her a little although she wasn't sure why. Surely it was Sho-La who had chosen her, not Leo? It was a subtle difference yet it seemed important.

"When will the others arrive?"

Leo pursed his lips, pressing a finger to his chin as he thought. "Do you know what? I think they might be arriving just about...now." With a grin he pointed to the head of the valley where a column of horses, wagons and people were slowly making their way down the slope. Soldiers ran to meet them, helping them to tents and places to stow their gear.

Leo hopped onto the barrel beside her and together they kept vigil as night fell. Campfires sprang to life. A hum of excited conversation filled the air. Leo took her hand and squeezed. The valley looked as though it was filled with countless tiny fireflies. Maegwin swallowed as she thought about what tomorrow would bring. Tomorrow they would march. Tomorrow they would begin the final stage of this campaign. The army looked endless.

It looked unstoppable.

Chapter Nine

"You're absolutely sure there's no other way?" Tallo asked plaintively. "We ought to find the nearest river, build rafts and float our way home. Or buy horses and keep swapping them each day so they don't get tired. That would work, wouldn't it?"

Rovann smiled wryly. "Sorry, Tallo. We must reach Tyrlindon quickly and the only way to do that is through the Eorthe."

Tallo groaned, rolling his eyes. "I was afraid you'd say that."

"It'll be over in a few seconds and then we'll be home," Lady said, obviously trying to be comforting. "Isn't that worth a little discomfort?"

Tallo shot her a look that said exactly what he thought of that question. Rovann couldn't blame the soldier for his misgivings. Rovann even shared them. Tyrlindon was a long way off. He didn't have Syrie's skill with the Eorthe and even with the aid of her focus stone, he still might not be able to find the way. They might all die, suffocating in earth before they reached their destination.

Thaldan's crew had assembled a little ways off and Thaldan and Shern had walked with Rovann, Lady and Tallo to the edge of the valley.

Thaldan watched Rovann steadily. There was an unreadable expression on his bluff face. "You really think you can make a difference with what Shern showed you?"

"Perhaps," he replied. "At least now we know what the Songmaker's goal is. That has to count for something."

Thaldan nodded and regarded Rovann in silence. Finally, he stuck out his hand. "I wish you luck. If we both survive this maybe one day you can buy me a tankard of ale and we can talk. My sister would have liked that."

Rovann raised his eyebrows in surprise. Then he reached out and shook his brother-in-law's hand. "Yes, she would. Thank you, Thaldan. For everything."

The big man stepped back and Shern approached. The mage looked tired. Rovann gripped his shoulder.

"Amaury owes you a debt, Shern. Should you ever wish to return to the college and finish your training you'd be most welcome."

A small smile quirked Shern's lips. "Maybe one day. When I get bored with smuggling or do something idiotic and get thrown out of Thaldan's band, maybe I'll take you up on your offer."

Rovann nodded. "As you wish. It has been an honor, Shern. Now stand back, both of you."

He turned to face Lady and Tallo, the three of them standing close in a circle. They joined hands. Closing his eyes, Rovann sent his senses questing down into the Eorthe, trying to find the path to Tyrlindon. In his mind he built a picture of the capital, of the upland plateau on which the city sat, and of the bedrock that formed its foundations. Slowly he began to detect the vibrations of that bedrock as it hummed on the Eorthe with its own distinct signature. It was frighteningly far away.

There, he said silently. *Take us there.*

Tapping into the power of Syrie's focus stone where it rested against the skin of his chest, Rovann opened a gate that burned with Eorthic symbols. A rumble shook the ground and it suddenly opened and swallowed them.

The stink of wet soil filled Rovann's nostrils. Blackness crowded his vision. The tumble of rocks and the roaring of subterranean rivers echoed in his ears. Mud filled his lungs, choking him and yet... and yet... he could still breathe. He forced himself to relax, to allow the energies of the Eorthe to cradle him. The vibration of Tyrlindon was still there but it was muted and he couldn't pinpoint the direction. Instead, he felt as though he was being pulled further down, down into the dark depths of the earth, down where no light reached and nothing living drew breath.

Panic gripped him and he reached desperately toward the vibrations he'd sensed from Tyrlindon. But this time there was nothing. Just dark, suffocating earth and the swirling energies of the Eorthe.

Syrie! He bellowed in the silence of his mind. *I need your help!*

A familiar presence suddenly blossomed around him. He felt the Eorthe focus and contract, holding him tight in bands of force. A voice spoke in his mind, *what are you doing, you fool?*

He was yanked upwards suddenly and the Eorthe flashed by in a swirl of tastes and sensations. Then suddenly he was looking up at blue sky and air once again filled his lungs. He rolled onto his side, retching into warm, sweet smelling grass.

Strong fingers grabbed his chin, lifting his head. His vision swung in and out of focus for a moment before he realized the deep brown eyes of Syrie, Earth adept and Fourth of the Council of Mages were staring down at him.

"If you were a student, you would have detention for a week for the stunt you just pulled," she said, her voice low and menacing. "Do you have any idea how dangerous it is to travel that kind of distance through the Eorthe?"

Rovann rose to a sitting position and folded the small, dark-haired woman into an embrace. "It's good to see you, Syrie."

Syrie shook her head at him but she seemed to be hiding a smile. "You have the angels' own luck, Lord First. I was scanning the Eorthe, watching the enemy's movements outside, when I heard your call. If I hadn't been…" She left the sentence hanging between them.

Rovann placed his palms flat on the ground then levered himself unsteadily to his feet. A few meters away, Tallo was on his knees being violently sick into the grass whilst Lady patted his back reassuringly.

Syrie put her finger to her lips and whistled. A soldier came running. "Fetch Captain Tyan and Sergeant Hannel immediately. And have baths drawn and food prepared." The soldier nodded and dashed off.

Leaning heavily on Syrie's shoulder, Rovann looked around. Syrie had brought them out in the middle of the palace gardens, on the highest level of Tyrlindon. Forty or fifty paces away loomed the long, low buildings of the College of Mages, and beyond that, the palace's twisting turrets rose into the sky. Tall trees dotted the parkland in which the royal enclave sat and the whole thing was guarded by a high wall.

"Thank you, Syrie," he whispered. "Remind me to buy you dinner when this is all over."

She raised a curved eyebrow at him. "I will. Don't you worry."

A moment later two men appeared around the corner of the college and came sprinting toward them. As they drew closer, Rovann recognized Captain Tyan, one of the leaders of the city's defense and his sergeant, Hannel. Both men looked older, wearier. Captain Tyan's hard, angular face was tense and drawn. Hannel's shaggy blond hair was matted with sweat and he seemed more somber than Rovann remembered. He'd never recovered from the death of his sister, Hesha, at Carrow Crossing. The men saluted crisply but Rovann waved them down and then shook their hands warmly.

"How goes the defense?" he asked.

"No change, Lord First," Tyan replied. "A few skirmishes to test our strength but they haven't yet launched a full-scale attack. They don't have nearly enough men to cover all the gates. They've dug in to the east, blocking our supply lines in that direction. They've also set snipers in the countryside around all the other roads."

"Show me," Rovann muttered.

Tyan nodded and they walked quickly through the parkland until they reached the curtain wall. Tyan led them up a set of wide stone steps to the walkway that ran along the top.

As Rovann emerged a cold wind snatched at him, sending his hair billowing out and squeezing tears from the corners of his eyes. At this height it seemed almost as if he stood on the summit of a mountain. The sprawling metropolis of Tyrlindon fell away below him, it's seven levels—built to mirror the Seven Realms themselves—dropping away in a series of concentric circles, each guarded by its own high wall.

In the distance, below the first level, the plain stretched away to a hazy horizon. To the east, the plain was covered by a dark shadow—the besieging army. Lord Cedric Hounsey, the traitor who had led the army here, was dead, but his youngest son now commanded the army in his father's place. The young man was reported to be a brilliant strategist who had sworn vengeance against Rovann personally for the death of his father.

It didn't matter that it had been Maegwin, not Rovann, who had killed Cedric Hounsey. The Songmaker's lies could make anything seem like truth.

Tyan handed Rovann a spyglass. "They're well disciplined," the captain said. "The commanders have a tight control over their men and morale seems to be high. When Tanyaka left I thought they might have a go at one of the gates but they haven't. I don't know why."

"I do," said Syrie with a scowl. "They're waiting. Something's coming, I can feel it." She looked at Rovann sharply but he pressed the spyglass to his eye, ignoring her enquiring gaze. "And now Tanyaka is gone: called away by your orders. I notice she hasn't returned with you. Where is she, Lord First?"

Rovann winced. The thought of the events in Near Point made his guts twist. How had he been so stupid to fall into the Songmaker's trap? "It's a long story," he said. "Tanyaka has returned to her own Realm. We're on our own."

They digested this in silence for a moment.

Sergeant Hannel frowned. "They can't know this. Otherwise they'd have attacked."

Rovann shook his head. "Oh, they know, Sergeant."

"Then why do they just sit there? Surely they realize they can't starve us out? Any fool who's read a history book knows Tyrlindon has never been taken."

"Not by mundane means, anyways," put in Tallo.

Sergeant Hannel looked sharply at Tallo. "What's that supposed to mean?"

Tallo looked meaningfully at Rovann. *Tell them*, that look said.

Rovann sighed. "I'm afraid Syrie's right. They haven't attacked because they're waiting." He stared out at the black mass of Hounsey's army. There were so many of them. "Another army is on the way. The Songmaker is bringing his main force south to join the siege. And he has battle mages with him. Lots of them."

"Realms!" Syrie growled under her breath.

"Wonderful," Hannel muttered. "This is going to be fun."

"How long until this second force arrives?" Captain Tyan asked.

"Two, three days at the most."

"And numbers? Infantry? Cavalry? Siege weapons? Baggage train?"

"Lady and Tallo have the reports. They'll tell you everything we discovered."

Tyan nodded then gave a salute. With a barked command he strode away, Sergeant Hannel, Tallo and Lady a step behind.

Rovann was left with Syrie. "Where is King William?"

"There's something else isn't there?" she replied. "Something you're not telling us."

"Isn't there always?" He sighed, suddenly exhausted. "I'll call a Council meeting later and tell you everything but I must see the king first."

"He's with his advisors in the Rose Room."

Rovann nodded then whirled away, jumped down the steps two at a time, and ran across the parkland to the palace. At the gates the guards crossed their halberds, blocking his way.

"Who are you?" one demanded.

Rovann realized belatedly that he was covered in mud. To the guards he must seem like some kind of disheveled underworld creature. Fumbling in his pocket, he found the ruby ring of the Lord First, jammed it on his finger and waved it in the guard's face.

"Step aside."

The guards, recognising the ring, saluted and moved apart, allowing Rovann to dart between them.

The interior of the palace was alive with hustle and bustle but instead of the usual courtiers and servants rushing around, now soldiers, messengers and couriers scurried through the elegant corridors. Rovann wove his way through them, waving away queries and greetings, until he reached the ornate door to the Rose Room, King William's private audience chamber. Rovann waved his ring at the guards who stepped aside at his barked command. With a blast of Air, he shoved the doors open and strode through.

The king was seated at a polished mahogany table covered with maps, letters and other documents. Several men and women in military uniforms were also seated at the table. They looked up as Rovann burst in.

King William frowned at his abrupt entrance but didn't

seem surprised to see Rovann. His dark eyes narrowed, assessing what his presence might mean. Beside him sat a young man with a white cloth tied around his eyes: Prince Owen, the king's son and heir. Although Rovann had managed to rescue him from the Songmaker's clutches in Tyrvanan, by that time he'd already been tortured into blindness. The city's healers had been unable to save the prince's sight. Nevertheless, Prince Owen seemed to see things more clearly than most people. Even now, the prince's gaze seemed fixed on him, as though he was studying Rovann from behind his blindfold.

Rovann cleared his throat then dropped an awkward bow. "Your Majesty, Your Highness. I must speak with you alone."

King William nodded then gestured to his staff. "Leave us."

Everyone but Prince Owen rose from the table and filed out. King William slowly stood. His lean, weathered face was troubled as he studied his King's Mage.

"I'd like to say it's good to see you back but I suspect from your entrance that you don't bring good news. Am I right?"

"Questions," Prince Owen said suddenly. "He brings questions."

"Yes, my prince," Rovann replied. "I need to know what's imprisoned beneath Tyrlindon."

To his credit, King William didn't flinch. Instead, he turned away, hands clasped behind his back and moved to the table, studying a map of the city. "I'll need more to go on than that, Rovann. We have many dungeons."

"You know what I'm talking about," Rovann snapped, sudden anger making his voice sharp. "I always wondered why the Songmaker wanted Tyrlindon so much. He already had Tyrvanan, a city as great as this one. It makes sense now. I have risked much to discover this information. Tell me."

King William turned to face him, dark eyes flashing. "Some things are better left unspoken. I advise you not to ask me this, Rovann."

"You know I must."

The king stared at him for a moment, hands clenching and unclenching at his sides. Then he sighed. "This is a secret that my line has guarded since Tyrlindon was first built, thousands of years ago. Would you ask me to betray it now?"

"How can you speak to me of betrayal?" Rovann hissed. "You have information that might have helped me against the Songmaker and you kept it from me! Do not speak to me of betrayal!"

"I had good reasons for doing so."

"Really? Such as?"

The king regarded him levelly. "You really need to ask that question?"

Wiping a hand over his face, Rovann turned to the window. From here he couldn't see the besieging army but he felt their presence around his neck like a lead weight. And coming closer was another presence, one that would claim the power in Tyrlindon if it was able.

"Because if a corrupt mage discovered such power they could take it for themselves," he said at last.

"Exactly," the king confirmed. "Have you never wondered why the Amaury royal line has never had a mage among it? In all the years my blood-line has sat on this throne, by the law of averages, at least one should have been born with the spark of magecraft. But none ever has. Does that not strike you as odd?"

Now that Rovann thought about it he realized King William had a point. It *was* odd. The potential for magecraft was a random gift and no one understood why some were born with it and others not. Mage parents might give birth to non-mage offspring and non-mage parents might just as easily have a mage child, as had been the case with Rovann. But the Amaury royal line had never given rise to a mage. Never.

There was something here, something important. Understanding flickered like a candle flame, just out of reach.

King William smiled wryly. "I find it strangely reassuring that there are some things you don't know, Rovann. Is a king not allowed his secrets?" He shook his head. "Tell me what happened in the east and perhaps we can piece this together."

He clapped his hands and a servant entered, bowing low. "Bring refreshment for Lord Rovann," the king instructed. Then, after eyeing Rovann's mud-covered apparel he added, "And bring something to clean him up with as well."

"Yes, Your Majesty," the servant bowed and left.

The king pointed to a chair. "Sit down, Rovann. You look as though you're about to collapse."

Rovann sank gratefully into a cushioned seat by Prince Owen. King William sat down opposite, his raptor's gaze boring into Rovann.

"What happened, King's Mage? Where is Tanyaka?"

Rovann sighed and leaned forward, resting his elbows on his knees. Where to start? How to find the words? Memories flashed through his head, one after the other. Taking a deep breath, he began to speak, telling of everything that had happened since he'd left Tyrlindon all those weeks ago. He was deliberately vague about Thaldan and Shern's involvement but he held nothing back about Maegwin and Leo or what had happened to Tanyaka. When he reached the part about the prison he found himself faltering.

The king's gaze had gone as hard as pebbles. Prince Owen's head was cocked to one side as he listened.

"So that's where it is," the prince said to his father. "We never knew the location of the first one. It will have to be destroyed, of course."

The king nodded. "Although it's a bit like shutting the stable door after the horse has bolted."

"It can't be helped now. This answers many questions, father. We know the Songmaker's plans at last." He shook his head. "All these years we thought him just a rebel mage."

"We were wrong," the king grated. "About so many things." The king's gaze snapped to Rovann. "It's time to show you, King's Mage."

Rovann straightened. "Show me?"

"The heart of Tyrlindon. The Tear of Life."

A shiver rippled across Rovann's skin. That was the name written on the wall of the prison in the mountains. The prison beneath Tyrlindon. So. The king had known about it all along. Fighting down a squirming apprehension, he rose to his feet.

The king crossed to the door and poked his head out. To the guards on the other side he said, "Nobody is to enter this room until I or Prince Owen emerge. Is that clear? Nobody."

"Yes, Your Majesty," came the reply.

King William shut the door and locked it with a small golden key. He shared a long look with Prince Owen then drew in a deep breath as though steeling his courage. "Lead the way."

The prince rose to his feet, then, as though he could see as clearly as any man, he strode over to a tapestry, reached behind it and pulled something. There was a grinding noise and a section of the floor suddenly slid to one side, revealing stone steps leading down into darkness. The king took three torches from the walls and handed one each to Rovann and Owen.

"Shall we?" the king asked.

Rovann's skin prickled. He felt something on the air, something wafting up from the darkness. As Prince Owen started down the steps, Rovann forced himself to follow. King William brought up the rear. After a moment Rovann heard the opening above sliding closed behind them.

"Would you?" King William asked, pointing at the torches.

Rovann channeled Fire and the torches sprang into life, throwing wavering yellow light across the roughly hewn staircase. The walls and steps were carved from the basalt that made up the plateau's bedrock. The Eorthe echoed strongly down here, warring with the taste of wrongness that seeped through the air.

Prince Owen moved at a steady pace down the steps, holding his torch high to light the way. There was no railing and as the tightly coiled steps spiraled ever downward, Rovann found himself becoming dizzy and disorientated. In the blackness it seemed the only living thing was the yellow light of Owen's torch bobbing always out of reach.

A hand gripped his shoulder suddenly. "Easy. Breathe," said King William. "Clear your head. The atmosphere of this place can take you if you're not careful."

Rovann blinked, shaking his head as though to clear it

of cobwebs. With a jolt, he realized they'd reached the bottom of the steps. They stood in a small stone antechamber facing an archway carved with strange symbols. Beyond the archway lay impenetrable darkness. Even the light of the torches couldn't breach it.

"Where are we?"

"Beneath the city," Owen replied. "A long way beneath the city, deep within the plateau's bedrock."

"How long were we walking?" It had seemed like only a few minutes. King William shared a look with the prince. "Time moves a little differently down here."

"What is this place?" Rovann asked, eyeing the archway suspiciously. He took a step closer, peering up at the symbols. They were written in a strange alphabet Rovann didn't recognize. He gasped, straightening. He *did* recognize that script. He'd seen this language once before, on the wall of the broken prison Shern had shown him. Slowly, he reached out a hand.

"Don't touch anything!" the king snapped. "It will know we're here!"

Rovann snatched back his hand. He could see nothing beyond the archway. But he could feel…

"Wards," he breathed. "Wards spun from the Realms. All of them."

Closing his eyes, he sensed the heavy enchantment that guarded this place. Power so old and so strong he'd never encountered its like. It was at once both alien and familiar, as though it was woven of an older, wilder form of the magic that drove the Realms. The touch of it spoke to Rovann of beginningless time. Of the birth and death of stars. Of the passing of uncounted eons.

"The Tear of Life," King William murmured in a voice barely above a whisper. "Beyond this door lies the thing my line has guarded for centuries. Are you sure you want to pass?"

No, he thought. *But what choice is there?* He nodded tightly.

"Then you must pay the price of passage," King William said.

Rovann looked at him sharply. "What price?"

"You must give up your magecraft."

"*What?*"

King William held out a placating hand. "I told you before that my line has never produced a mage. The reason lies here. Only a mage could free what waits beyond so those that built the prison ensured no mage ever had the chance. Only non-mages may pass. And to ensure there would always be somebody to guard this secret, the ability for magecraft was expunged from my line. So has it always been. I suspect, so it will ever be. Should you wish to pass here, you must leave your magecraft behind."

"And if I try to pass anyway?"

"You will die."

Rovann stared at his king. He felt like an untried novice taking his first lesson. He'd thought himself so wise.

"I don't know how to do what you ask," he said finally. "How do I give up something that's a part of me?"

"It's a borrowed part only," King William replied. His dark eyes were like pools of shadow. "Your power comes from the Realms. They can take it back again. Don't worry, it will return to you once you leave this place."

Rovann hesitated, looking from the king to the prince. They waited in silence. "What do I do?"

A faint smile curled the king's lips. He clapped Rovann on the shoulder. "Did I not say I'd chosen well in my King's Mage, Owen?"

Keeping one hand on Rovann's shoulder, King William

steered him forward, halting in front of the archway. The portal loomed over him like a hungry mouth. The king stepped back.

"Keep your intention to give up your power uppermost in your mind. Let the wards sense it. Walk forward, Rovann. The Realms will do the rest."

The instruction sent a chill of unease sliding down Rovann's spine. He ground his teeth and forced his legs to move, striding up to stand directly beneath the interlocking stones of the arch. Cold slammed into him, seeming to still his heart and freeze his blood. Rovann gasped and doubled over. It was like being thrown into a vat of icy water. No, it was worse than that. The cold plunged down his throat, into his lungs, spread along his nerves and through his veins, filling him as if he was an empty vessel.

He recognized the combined power of the Seven Realms. The Aethyr, as always, was the strongest but the others were there as well: the solid presence of the Eorthe, the volatility of Fire, the capriciousness of Air, the slippery touch of Water, and yes, even the dark, cloying touch of Chaos, the power that drove the Outer Darkness. He felt these forces probe him, and then withdraw taking his powers with them.

Rovann stumbled, his legs suddenly unsteady. He caught himself on the wall and leaned on it heavily. He felt... empty. He reached inside himself and found nothing. His senses were truncated and he could no longer sense the world around him as he once had. Everything seemed dull, muted.

But, after all, it seemed he was not empty. Something remained, after the rest was gone. At the core of his being pulsed a tiny sliver of energy. To Rovann's mind it appeared like a golden ball burning in the center of his chest. From it,

waves of warm peace washed through him. With it came...
nothingness. Stillness.

"The One Light," he breathed in awe.

For a moment he stood immobile, marveling at the
sensation. He had never guessed, never imagined. Was this
how non-mages experienced the world? Unblinded by
magecraft, did they feel this power inside them? Were they
somehow more connected to the One Light than he was?

He shook his head. So many questions. The possibilities
for study and exploration left him reeling.

The king moved up beside him. "We must be quick. If
we linger it will sense us and awaken."

He strode away into the darkness, Rovann and Prince
Owen following. Around them, Rovann sensed the vastness
of an empty space but he could discern no shapes in the
darkness beyond the torchlight. However, as they traveled
further, a sickly green illumination sprang up from the
ground, bathing everything in an eerie light. King William
walked with an unerring stride, as if he'd been this way
many times. Rovann saw hard determination in the stiff set
of the man's shoulders.

Then suddenly the blackness overhead vanished and
Rovann found himself looking up at the jagged ceiling of a
cavern. Yellowed stalactites hung down like teeth, slowly
dripping liquid onto the floor. The walls were carved from a
shiny black rock like flint and were made up of sharp,
ragged angles as if they'd been worked by tools but left half
finished. The strange illumination grew bright enough for
him to look around, taking in the cavern. The weight of all
that earth and rock above suddenly felt oppressive. He'd
had his fill of deep places.

The king pointed. "There. The Tear of Life."

In the center of the cavern, maybe thirty paces from

where they stood was a circular pit with a metal grille like a portcullis across the top. Unlike the one at the first prison, this one was intact.

Rovann glanced at the king and then the prince. Both watched him in silence. Neither offered any explanation. He pulled in a deep breath and let it out slowly. Cautiously, he edged forward, step by hesitant step, until he stood by the low wall that ringed the pit. He looked down.

And saw nothing. Only darkness. A void.

Suddenly something moved within and for the briefest of moments Rovann was blasted by a presence that tore through his mind like a screaming gale. Slumbering darkness. Hatred. Unquenchable hunger. Terrible rage.

Rovann staggered, crashing onto his knees and bracing himself against the rock floor. Then the sensation passed, as though the creature had turned over in its sleep.

"We cannot allow the Songmaker to ever find this place," said King William, moving up to stand by Rovann's side. "Should he succeed, all is lost."

Rovann straightened, climbed to his feet, and swallowed a few times. Clinging terror still threatened to overwhelm him. "He's a mage," Rovann gasped. "The Songmaker can't enter here."

"No, he can't," the king agreed. "At least, not without giving up his magecraft, and then he wouldn't have the power to release what's trapped within."

Rovann frowned, shaking his head. "But Shern and I managed to get into the first prison. Surely the same powers guard that too?"

King William shook his head. "From what you told me, when the Songmaker went there he was not the Songmaker. Just a minstrel, a boy really. Somehow he released the prisoner from its prison and with it the warding magic."

Rovann blew his cheeks out. "Then we keep this place secret. We never speak of it. The Songmaker knows it's in Tyrlindon but not exactly where. He cannot get in here. He cannot release whatever is imprisoned in the pit."

The king gazed at Rovann steadily. "I don't think he ever intended to come here himself. Have you forgotten how cunning our enemy is? I suspect his plan was years in the making. He knew he would not be able to enter the cavern so he found someone who could."

Rovann frowned, struggling to follow the king's line of reasoning. Then his eyes went wide. "Maegwin?"

Prince Owen stepped forward. "During my captivity in Tyrvanan I learned much. More, I think, than the Songmaker wanted me to. Maegwin is something else. Something new. A fusion of powers. Creation and Destruction. A mage and yet not a mage. We believe she will use those powers to break this prison."

Despite himself, Rovann's eyes traveled once more to the pit. The darkness beyond the grille seemed absolute, as though it swallowed all light, all life.

Oh, Maegwin, he thought. *What have you done? What are you going to do?*

"So you see," King William said, "this place must not be breached. Whatever the cost."

His eyes bored into Rovann's. *Whatever the cost.* He saw a message in the king's eyes. Should the Songmaker breach the city, there was only one way they could guarantee the Songmaker would never find this place. Rovann nodded.

"It will not be breached. I won't allow it."

King William nodded. "Should things go ill, at the end it may fall to you. Will you do what needs to be done?"

I am the Slayer of Sandford Moor, Rovann thought. *Now you ask me to become the slayer of cities.*

In Tyrvanan when the powers of the Seven Realms had answered him, something within him had snapped. He'd become an adept of all of them. Something new. Something *other.* He was perhaps the only one with the power to do what was necessary should the city be breached.

Finally, he nodded. "You have my word. If it comes to it, I will destroy Tyrlindon."

Chapter Ten

Maegwin looked down at the group of kneeling people. A mixture of men and women, most stared at the ground, avoiding her gaze, but a few met her scrutiny with hostile glares. She'd have to keep an eye on those. At her back, Tarina, Miriel and Ashria waited in silence. Around the village square her soldiers kept watch.

"You are the village elders?" she asked.

One of the defiant ones, a middle-aged man, nodded. Welldon was a small settlement, barely big enough to be called a village, but it sat at an important crossroads so boasted an inn, a cobbled square and a well, despite its diminutive size.

And it stood right in the path of Leo's marching army.

Unusually, most of the villagers had remained in their homes rather than fleeing. An act of bravery? Defiance? Or were they reluctant to abandon the obvious wealth of this way-station?

"Your name?" she asked the man.

He moved his lips a little before answering. Maegwin

wondered if he was going to spit at her. Finally he muttered, "Albrec."

"Do you know who I am, Albrec?"

"Does it matter who you are?" he answered, staring up at her. "Raider, bandit, invader. You're all the same. Take what you want and go."

Maegwin arched an eyebrow. "As it happens, I'm none of those things. I'm you're liberator. I've come to bring you into the light of Sho-La."

The man said nothing but the look on his face betrayed exactly what he thought of that. She looked up and addressed the others instead.

"Listen to me! Would a bandit give you the chance to join us? Would an invader respect your customs, asking only that you allow our army to pass? Would a raider take only what provisions you can spare and leave the rest?" This last bit wasn't strictly true. Her soldiers had stripped the village almost bare but these people weren't to know that. "My name is Maegwin, high priestess of the goddess Sho-La. You're Her chosen people. Will you join us?"

In all the towns and villages the army sacked on its long march to Tyrlindon, Maegwin had made the same offer. Many joined her. Many didn't.

"We want no part of your cursed religion," Albrec growled. "Do you think we don't know where you're going? Do you think we don't know you're here to make war on our king? We're loyal subjects. We won't betray our vows!"

"Very admirable," Maegwin said, "if a little idiotic. Change is coming, you damned fools. You can either embrace that change or be left behind. Many of your coun-trymen have joined us. Many have embraced Sho-La. She welcomes all. She'll welcome you too, if you let her."

There was a low muttering among the gathering and many shared long glances.

"Go," Albrec growled. "We won't join you."

"Does this fool speak for all of you?" Maegwin asked.

"No!" somebody cried suddenly. "He doesn't speak for me!"

A small, mousy-haired woman slowly rose to her feet. She looked frightened but forced herself to meet Maegwin's gaze. "I'll join you. If you'll have me, my lady."

Maegwin smiled warmly. "Any others?"

Two women and a man shakily stood. Maegwin held out her arms, beckoning them closer.

"Welcome to the order of Sho-La," she said. "Don't worry. You'll be well looked after."

She nodded to Miriel and Ashria who stepped forward and led the group from the square. The newcomers would be taken away and baptized into the religion of the Dark Goddess. That baptism would open them to Chaos and they would become battle mages. What better way to serve their new goddess?

The other villagers watched her in silence. Maegwin could sense their unease.

"What shall we do with these?" Tarina asked.

Maegwin regarded them for a moment. Then she waved a hand dismissively. "Have the soldiers tie them up and leave them in the woods."

"Without food or water? They'd be unlikely to survive."

"That's for Sho-La to decide, isn't it?"

Tarina smiled. "Yes, mistress."

As Maegwin strode away, she heard the desperate pleas of the villagers as her soldiers waded among them. So be it. She'd offered them salvation and they'd refused it. She would leave their fate in the hands of her mistress. The Dark Goddess would accept no less.

Maegwin smiled to herself. Everything was starting to come together. Soon, Leo's army would assault Tyrlindon. Amaury's capital would become the center of Sho-La's religion and from there it would spread to the whole of the Seven Realms. Yes, it was all coming together nicely.

At the edge of the square a groom was holding her horse. She swung into the saddle and booted the beast into motion down the southern road. She crested a ridge and joined the tail-end of Leo's honor guard. They moved aside to let her pass and she quickly caught up with him and General Shallon at the head of the column.

"Ah, Maegwin," Leo said, turning to grin at her. "The village has been pacified?"

Pacified. It was a strange term for what they did. She nodded.

"Excellent. We can't afford to leave hostiles at our backs."

"No," she agreed. "Which reminds me: how fares our rear-guard?"

Was that a grimace that passed briefly across General Shallon's face? He cleared his throat before answering. "Reports come in daily, my lady. All say the same. The Shinnar have left their homeland and followed us. They harry the tail end of our army night and day. We have lost many soldiers and even more supplies to their lightning raids."

Maegwin cursed. "Will that bastard Kandar never give up? What will it take to cow these people?"

General Shallon shrugged. "They believe we follow a false goddess. They believe we are corrupting the faith of their World Mother. Religious zeal is a powerful motivator."

Maegwin frowned then turned to look back the way they'd come as if she could see her Shinnar enemies.

"A logical explanation, Shallon," Leo said, waving a hand. "But an incorrect one. The real explanation is much simpler. To the Shinnar, betrayal is the worst kind of sin. Maegwin betrayed them. By doing that she insulted their entire way of life. They will not forget that." His green eyes found Maegwin's. "They swore an oath to the King's Mage. He has won their loyalty." Anger glinted in his eyes now. Maegwin knew he was still furious about losing Rovann in the tunnels. "Curse that man to the lowest level of Hell! I should have killed him the first time I met him! How many times has he thwarted my plans now? I'm beginning to lose count!"

"And yet, here we are," answered General Shallon. "Despite his efforts we're marching on Tyrlindon. The King's Mage doesn't have the power to stop us."

Leo narrowed his eyes at the general. His expression suggested he thought Shallon a damned fool. "Doesn't he?" Leo asked quietly. "We'll see."

Maegwin shifted uncomfortably. Leo's dislike of Rovann had become something all-consuming. It seemed he'd gambled everything on capturing both Rovann and Tanyaka at Near Point. Although Tanyaka had been banished—a victory in itself—this wasn't enough for Leo.

"Ah," the minstrel said, regaining his joviality as he looked up. Two riders came thundering toward them, pulling up in a spray of mud. "Here they are, right on time. Maegwin, Sacha and Belle are messengers from Lord Hounsey's army."

Maegwin started. She hadn't realized they were so close to Tyrlindon. Hounsey's army had been besieging the capital for weeks now, waiting for Leo's forces to join them.

She fixed the two women with a stare. They gazed back with unreadable expressions. Maegwin wondered how they felt about facing the woman who'd killed their lord and commander. "So. What news?"

One of the women inclined her head. "Much the same, my lady. Lord Hounsey has held back from all-out attack. We've led a few surprise attacks on strategic points throughout the city. Their defenses hold. They're well trained and well organized. Until a few days ago, a dragon guarded the city. My Lord Songmaker informs me that threat has been eliminated. In the interim we've been building siege engines and digging in. We await only the command to attack."

Leo smiled at the two women. "Good work." He waved a soldier forward. "Brialle will see that you're given food and rest. Go."

As the scouts followed the soldier from the hilltop, Leo turned to Maegwin. "Well? Are you ready?" He seemed as excited as a little boy, barely able to keep the grin off his face.

"Ready for what?"

Leo rolled his eyes. Pointing, he said, "Our goal. We're almost there. Come on."

He kicked his horse to a canter. After a moment, Maegwin and General Shallon did the same, Leo's honor guard falling into formation around them.

Looking around at the sleepy farmsteads of Tyrlinshire as she rode, Maegwin wondered if she'd passed this way when she, Rovann and the soldiers had left for the Highhold to arrest Lord Cedric Hounsey. Was that copse the place they'd made camp that first night? Was that the clearing where Hesha had taught her to play nine bobs?

A strange feeling stole over her. It took a moment before

she recognized it as loneliness. Back then, traveling with Rovann and the soldiers from Tyrlindon, she'd been simply Maegwin, another member of the band. Hesha, Hannel, Lady, Tallo and the others had accepted her as such. As had Rovann. Now she was someone else: Maegwin, holy mother and high priestess of the dark aspect of Sho-La. Thousands did her bidding.

And yet, she felt more alone than ever.

A sharp tug in her gut made her gasp. *You will not indulge in self-pity*, a voice said in her head. *Remember your place.*

She bowed her head. *Yes, my mistress.*

The countryside was eerily quiet. Most of the fields had been burned by Tyrlindon's defenders, the wells poisoned. The farmsteads and villages were empty, with only slat-ribbed dogs watching them dolefully as they rode through. The farmers and village folk had taken refuge in Tyrlindon, leaving behind nothing that might be used by the invading army.

As they traveled Leo remained silent. Maegwin wondered if he too was remembering. He had journeyed the King's Road with Maegwin and Rovann after they met him in the beleaguered town of Angard. It seemed a lifetime ago, like some hazy memory from childhood or a distant dream she couldn't quite catch. A mage storm had been called down on the town and she and Rovann had rescued Leo from an angry mob of townsfolk who believed he was the culprit. As it turned out, they'd been right. Maegwin shook her head. So much had changed. Back then Leo hadn't been the Songmaker, or at least, they hadn't known he was. He was just a minstrel. A jovial youth with too much optimism. Now what was he? Realms, what was *she*?

Ahead, Leo slowed his horse to a trot as the ground

began to rise. The farmland retreated to be replaced by heather and scraggly brush. The wind picked up, grabbing at Maegwin's hair and clothing. It was cold enough to raise goose bumps across her skin. The road skirted a gnarled outcrop of boulders then the countryside suddenly peeled back to reveal a wide open plain stretching ahead. And out of that plain rose the vast edifice of Tyrlindon.

Maegwin and Leo pulled their horses to a halt.

"Finally," Leo breathed, satisfaction in his tone. "Last time we were here, I was worried the guards wouldn't let me in. This time, I'll enter as its conqueror."

Tyrlindon was bigger, grander, more imposing, than any place Maegwin had seen. Its twin, Tyrvanan, out in the Shinnar plains, paled in comparison. Amaury's capital rose in ever tightening circles like some shining monolith set there by giants. Its walls and spires shone in the sunlight.

And a dark tide of humanity seethed outside those walls.

"Hounsey's army," Maegwin breathed.

The army didn't encircle the capital completely. It would take numbers beyond counting to surround a city of such size. Instead, it had broken into companies and each company was encamped outside one of the city's seven gates, trapping those within.

Despite herself, Maegwin had to admit that Leo had chosen his commanders well. Lord Cedric Hounsey, who Maegwin had killed after he'd burned her temple, had been a competent commander. He'd obviously passed those skills onto his younger son.

Leo stood in his stirrups and raised his arms toward the heavens as though embracing the sky. With a voice enhanced by Air, he bellowed. "I'm coming! You hear me? I'm coming for you, Rovann! You can't escape!"

There was something raw in his voice. Fury. Violence. But something else. Desperation?

Maegwin didn't move. She'd learned better than to disturb the Songmaker when he was in this kind of mood. After several moments in which he stared intently at the city, muttering under his breath, Leo dropped back into his saddle. He nudged his horse into a canter and Maegwin followed.

They hadn't gone far when a group of soldiers materialized out of the scrubby plain and spilled out across their path.

"Halt!" the commander cried.

Leo was in no mood for delays. He waved a hand and the ground at the man's feet exploded, sending him stumbling onto his backside. "Escort us to your commander. Quickly, before I lose my patience!"

The soldier scrambled to his feet and shared a nervous glance with his comrades. No doubt they'd been given a description of Leo. He licked his lips then bowed. "Yes, my lord. My lady. This way."

They followed the soldiers past the first lines of tents and into the seething mass of humanity that was Hounsey's army. The command tent—a large three-peaked pavilion— appeared ahead with a group of people gathered outside to greet them. A groom rushed forward to take the horses' reins as she and Leo dismounted and the officers went down on one knee.

Maegwin scowled, disliking such subservience, but Leo seemed to enjoy it. A boyish smile lit his face and he waved magnanimously. "You may rise."

A young man, not much older than Leo himself, stepped forward. He had white-blond hair cut short, and sharp, angular features.

"My lord, lady," he said. "We're honored."

"Of course you are, Maldric," Leo said. He waved at a sergeant. "Run along, my dear man. Send word to all the division commanders and ranking officers. I want a council of war convened by dusk."

Maegwin watched the young commander warily. Maldric Hounsey. Lord Cedric Hounsey's youngest son. If he was uncomfortable being in the presence of the woman who'd killed both his father and elder brother, he didn't show it.

In less than half an hour, all the military commanders had been assembled. Most were grizzled veterans with scars to prove it. They gathered in Maldric Hounsey's command tent. Maegwin took a seat next to Leo at the large polished table as he listened to their reports.

This close to the city she could almost feel her mistress's presence, as though she waited for her within the capital. A turmoil of emotions whirled inside her. The Dark Goddess was mistress of death, of hatred, of anger. All of these things rolled across Maegwin's consciousness in waves. But there was something else as well. Maegwin strained to identify it. Anticipation?

She glanced at Leo where he was hunched over a map of the city whilst one of his commanders pointed out the army's deployment. He was as bent on sacking the city as the Dark Goddess was. They both wanted it so badly. Maegwin struggled to understand why the city was so important. Many lives would be lost in this attack: an attack that had no guarantee of success. Why were they willing to pay so high a price? Why not just starve the defenders out? They possessed the resources to lay siege for months. Tyrlindon could not hold out indefinitely. Eventually they would have to negotiate terms.

Maegwin shook her head. What right did she have to question her mistress? None at all. It was hypocritical of her in the extreme. Focusing her attention on the map, she forced herself to listen and take note of every bit of information that the commanders could give her. You never knew when something might prove useful.

The evening wore away and servants brought food. Somewhere close to midnight, a bugle sounded and a ripple of disturbance went through the camp. In the distance, she heard the tramp of many feet.

"The rest of the army has arrived!" she said, grinning.

Leo nodded. "Shall we go address them, my dear?"

With the command staff trailing after, she and Leo ducked out into the night. A sea of blazing fires met Maegwin's gaze. It stretched away into the darkness of the plateau, seemingly forever.

"A magnificent sight!" Leo crowed. "Ah! The beauty of it! Why, it's almost moved me to tears!"

Speak to them as you did before, the Dark Goddess said in her mind. *Fill them with my fury.*

Maegwin nodded. She spotted a cart lying off to one side. She climbed into the back of it and then channeled Air to project her voice over the seething mass of the camp.

"Welcome, comrades!" she called. "Our Lady is pleased! Tonight is very special. It's the last night of your old lives. Tomorrow we begin the assault on Tyrlindon! Tomorrow you'll be reborn as soldiers of Sho-La! Tomorrow you'll earn your place at Her side! Pray with me!"

A ripple went through the ranks as soldiers bowed their heads and clasped hands at their breasts.

"Bright Lady," Maegwin began, fuelling her words with Chaos so they settled into the minds of her listeners like a drug. "Bright Lady, hear our appeal! Make our arms strong.

179

Make our hearts brave. Make our mind clear. Fill us with Your wrath. Fill us with Your might. Fill us with Your righteousness. Tomorrow we fight! Tomorrow we go to war!"

She bellowed the last line with all her might and it echoed into the night like a lion's roar. As it faded, the soldiers took up the chant. "Sho-La! Sho-La! Sho-La!"

But it soon morphed into something else. It took Maegwin a moment to recognize the word. A name. Her name.

"Maegwin! Maegwin! Maegwin!"

The noise rang out in the night and washed up against the wall of Tyrlindon. Maegwin felt euphoric. She felt unstoppable. These people were hers.

I'm coming, Rovann, she thought. *Are you ready for me?*

Chapter Eleven

Rovann stood on the battlements of the lowest level of the city, gazing out into the night. The city appeared to float on a sea of flames. In some ways it was beautiful. In others it was utterly terrifying.

How did it come to this? he thought. *How did I let it come to this?*

He wondered briefly if Maegwin was out there asking the same thing. For such a long time now Rovann had felt like a game piece on the Songmaker's board. Now all those pieces were in place and the endgame would begin at first light. So be it.

Footsteps clattered up the steps behind him and a soldier loomed out of the night. He saluted crisply. "Message, my Lord First. The Council request your instructions."

Rovann nodded wearily. "Tell them to gather in two hours. I'll be there by then."

The messenger saluted and dashed off.

"Well," Rovann said, straightening. "I knew I couldn't put it off forever. Coming?"

Lady and Tallo rose from where they'd been lounging against the parapet. Lady finished cleaning her nails with the tip of her knife.

"Wouldn't miss it for the world."

Tallo frowned. "We don't actually have to enter the college do we? All that magery makes my skin itch." He shuddered to emphasize his point.

"Idiot," Lady hissed, slapping him on the shoulder. "Of course we do. You heard Captain Tyan. Where the Lord First goes, we go. Even to the privy."

Rovann smiled weakly. He wasn't sure she was joking. The three of them descended the steps to street level where a groom waited with their horses. They mounted quickly and trotted through wide streets that were eerily empty. Normally the lowest level of the city was the most crowded, but not tonight. Closest to the gates, it was a place of busy commerce where markets and shops vied for the attention of harassed shoppers. Now the shops were closed, the market stalls boarded shut and the inhabitants evacuated to the upper levels of the city. Only soldiers walked this level now. They moved in grim silence, hands never far from their weapons.

As he rode, Rovann tried to calm his whirling thoughts. The city was well prepared. Trebuchets and mangonels had been assembled, ready to repel any attackers that attempted to breach the walls. Each of the seven gates was guarded by a division of soldiers led by an Eorthic mage under the supervision of Syrie. When the attack on the gates came, the earth mages would use the Eorthe to strengthen the metal, making them unbreakable. Well, that was the theory anyway.

Yes, Tyrlindon was well defended. So why did he have a

gnawing fear in the pit of his stomach? No matter what he did, he couldn't shake it.

They turned a corner and approached the heavily guarded gates that led to the second level of the city. *The Realm of Air*, the inscription above the lintel read. The guards let them through without comment and Rovann detected the tell-tale tickle of the ward within the gate. It would trigger an explosion that would block the gate with rubble should an enemy mage try to pass through. Crude but effective.

Sweeping his gaze upward he peered at the sky, examining the primary ward the Council had woven over the whole city. It had taken thirty mages three days to construct it. It was invisible to the naked eye but to Rovann's senses it shimmered like a vast golden net, encompassing the city within. It would repel attack from the Songmaker's mages as long as the Council had strength to maintain it. Turning in a slow circle, he examined where the ward was anchored into the outer wall at strategic points around the city's perimeter. He'd been very specific about that and was satisfied with the results.

He booted his horse into a trot. They arrived at the topmost level at some point in the early hours of the morning. From the position of the moon, Rovann guessed dawn was still some way off.

Soldiers called out greetings as he and his companions cantered into the heavily guarded royal enclave. Here, mages as well as soldiers patrolled the walls, keeping an eye in all directions. Rovann swung down from the saddle, his feet crunching on the gravel, and handed his reins to a waiting soldier. He sucked in a deep breath, gathering his resolve, then led Lady and Tallo through a tall, ornate entryway into the College of Mages.

Despite the hour, torches blazed inside and people buzzed around everywhere. The strongest students had been drafted into the defense of the city and the weaker ones would act as messengers and sources of strength for the ward. Nobody had been spared.

As he stepped into the echoing halls, a sudden swell of pride filled Rovann. There was no panic in the air. Despite the hubbub, despite the messengers rushing to and fro, there was an air of control. Some called out greetings and made obeisance as he passed which he responded to graciously.

"The Lord First," he heard people whisper, as though his title was some kind of benediction. As if it would save them.

Don't put your hopes in me, he thought desperately. *You have no idea what I might have to do.*

Ahead, the doors to the meeting chamber yawned open like a great mouth. A low murmur of conversation came from within. Rovann strode through without announcing himself and took the seat saved for him at the huge oak table. Lady and Tallo positioned themselves behind his chair. Even here they glared around with suspicion in their eyes. They had learned Maegwin's lesson of betrayal well.

Every chair at the table was filled by either a mage or one of the king's military advisors. Rovann sat by the king's right hand, Prince Owen on the king's left. A few seats away was General Mishrall, commander of the king's army and Captain Tyan, his second. Both men looked weary to the bone. Rovann wondered when they'd last slept. Standing around the table were all the students who'd be helping in Tyrlindon's defense. The room boiled with nervous tension.

Rovann clasped his hands on the table in front of him and forced a look of calm authority onto his face. They needed to see him strong.

King William raised a hand and the room fell silent. "Now the Lord First has arrived, we'll begin. Commanders, please report to the Council."

General Mishrall opened his mouth and then closed it again. Irritably, he gestured for Tyan to speak instead. The younger man pushed the chair back and stood. He wiped the back of his hand across his eyes, drew a deep breath and began to speak, pressing both hands against the table to support himself.

"Earlier this evening a second army arrived to reinforce that of Maldric Hounsey's. That force was the one the Lord First had warned us about and had attempted to trap beyond Roamsford Edge in Shinnar lands. At best guess the army numbers perhaps thirty thousand, bringing the total of the enemy forces to around forty thousand. However, many of that number are made up of the renegade mages that follow the Songmaker. Leo March, the Songmaker, leads those forces along with his second-in-command, a General Shallon. They're supported by their high priestess, Maegwin de Romily."

Fevered whispering ran around the room and Tyan raised his voice to carry over the hubbub. "From what we can tell, much of the army consists of warrior priests and priestesses—battle-mages as the Lord First describes them. They're fanatical, tied to the Songmaker in a way we don't quite understand. Expect them to be vicious fighters."

The king leaned forward, sweeping the gathering with his raptor's gaze, "And their tactics? Will they attempt to storm the walls now they have greater numbers?"

Tyan shrugged. "We can't be sure, but I think it unlikely. Storming the walls would be costly in terms of both time and lives. They're likely to focus on where our defenses are weakest."

"The gates?"

"The gates," Tyan confirmed with a nod. "We expect they'll attack all seven gates simultaneously in order to stretch our forces as thinly as possible. As we speak, squads are stationed to defend the gates. They will be supported by covering fire from the archers and siege engines on the wall. In addition, we have a squad of earth mages working with our soldiers. Taking the gates will not be an easy task."

Prince Owen cleared his throat then asked the question that Rovann guessed must be on everyone's minds. "And if somehow they do breach the gates?"

Captain Tyan shrugged. "Then we fall back to the second level and go through the process all over again."

Owen shared a look with his father and then nodded. The king glanced at Rovann and he could see the thoughts churning behind the king's eyes. If they lost the first level... Rovann shook his head. They must not lose the first level.

"Supplies?" he barked, shaking off his stupor. "How long can the city hold?"

Administrator Sindra cleared her throat. "My Lord First, Tyrlindon was built for defense. Each level has its own well system for clean water and his Majesty's store houses are well stocked. We have already begun rationing food. This way we can hold out for months."

Falwin, the bald-headed, bad-tempered Second of the Council, snorted, crossing his arms over his chest. "There we are then," he declared with a scowl. "We defend the gates, keep the bastards out and let them slowly starve themselves. We've ensured there's no forage for miles around. They'll be eating each other before the year's out."

"We have to assume the Songmaker knows of our supply situation," Rovann said. *After all, he knows everything else.* "He needs this battle over with. He'll attack in force, hoping to crack the city like an egg. The attack will come on two fronts: from his army on the ground and from his mages with sorcery. We must defend against both."

He turned to gaze at Syrie. The Earth adept looked small and thin, too delicate to bear the weight of what was asked of her.

Nevertheless, her voice cracked like a whip as she snapped, "If the gates can be held, they'll be held. The Eorthe is a powerful ally. However," she frowned at Rovann, "we have no idea what the Songmaker might throw at us. If we could send out a scouting party—"

"Unnecessary," Rovann interrupted her. He turned to Tiria, Third of the Council, who had sat quietly until now, watching proceedings with a small frown marring the skin between her eyebrows. "Lady Third?"

Tiria sighed and shook her head, making her brown ringlets bounce. "I must be mad for agreeing to this," she muttered as she pushed herself to her feet. She sucked in a deep breath as though gathering her courage. "Last night, at the request of the Lord First, myself and Rallack, our adept of Chaos, traveled the astral and spied on the Songmaker's camp."

"Are you insane?" Falwin barked. "If you were caught you would give away our defenses, you damned fools!"

She held up a hand to stall the Second's tirade. "We were well aware of the risks, Lord Second," her voice crackled with authority. "And Rallack and I are not children. We know how to keep ourselves safe." She shared a long look with the lank-haired Chaotic mage who watched the proceedings in silence. Rallack smiled tightly and bowed his head at the compliment.

"What we discovered troubles me," Tiria continued. "We scouted beyond the ward and as close to the Songmaker's encampment as we could. Our mission was to discover how many mages the Songmaker has in his ranks, what their strengths are and if he has many adepts with him. What we found was strange. The auras of his followers are corrupted, seeming to comprise of conflicting energies. They disturbed the astral plane, making it almost impossible to get an idea of numbers. But I can tell you this," she glared around at the assembly, fixing them all with an intent stare. "These are mages unlike any we've yet seen."

Falwin ran a hand over his bald scalp. "Might the disturbance on the astral be some sort of ward or cloak? Something designed to keep away prying eyes?"

Chaotic Adept Rallack shook his head, drumming his fingers on the table top. "No," he asserted in his sibilant voice, "what I sensed was some perverted form of the Realms. Yet the dominant power was Chaos. I'm sure of it. That's why the auras felt so corrupted."

"What the bloody hell are you talking about?" Falwin asked. "Are you saying they're all Chaotic adepts like you?"

Rallack shook his head. "No, that's not what I mean. They don't just work with Chaos, they *are* Chaos. It's part of them."

"That makes no sense. How can Chaos be part of them? They're human—from the Realm of Earth. They can't manifest the power of the Outer Darkness without it killing them."

"It did kill them," Rovann said quietly.

In the silence that followed this statement, all eyes turned to regard him. Images of Lord Cedric Hounsey's corpse flashed into his head. Maegwin had stabbed the man through the heart but he'd only laughed at her.

"They're revenants," he said. "By some bastard amalgamation of powers, the Songmaker has found a way to make them undead. Perhaps he promised them immortality. All I know for sure is that they can channel Chaos and cannot be killed by normal means."

Stunned silence followed his words. Then Tiria asked, "Then how are we supposed to fight them? How can we kill those who are already dead?"

"There's only one way I know of," Rovann replied. "Fire will consume them. I suspect this is why the Songmaker was so desperate to lure Tanyaka away from the defense of Tyrlindon. He knew she had the power to destroy his battle mages."

Falwin whistled under his breath. "You've got to hand it to the little shit. He's one cunning bastard. In one fell swoop he stripped us of our best defense and almost cost us our Lord First into the bargain."

"But he failed," Syrie grated fiercely. "We may have lost the aid of Fire but we still have the Lord First. That proves the Songmaker's plans can be thwarted."

Rovann closed his eyes. *You don't know the half of it*, he thought. *If you knew what I knew and what I might have to do, you would probably hand me over to the Songmaker yourself.* When he opened his eyes, he found them all staring at him. Waiting. Expecting him to save them. He sat up straighter and put as much authority into his voice as possible.

"Tanyaka showed us what we need to do. It's up to us now. Anyone with any skill with Fire will report to Tiria straight after this meeting. You will be formed into fighting units and join Syrie's squads of Earth mages at the gates. You will engage any enemy mages that might break through. One unit will be held in reserve to aid the others as and when needed."

They nodded, seeming to gain strength from his calm

assurance. *There is a way,* he was telling them. *Follow my lead and we'll prevail.*

He only wished he had such faith in his own words.

Rallack was watching him. The Chaotic mage's eyes were narrowed. "May I ask a question, my Lord First?"

Rovann nodded. "Yes, Rallack?"

"Why did you have us anchor the ward into the foundations of the walls?"

Out of the corner of his eye Rovann saw Prince Owen suddenly sit up straight and King William look sharply at the dark mage. Rovann forced himself not to look at them. "A precaution, Rallack. Nothing more."

The ward isn't anchored into the walls, he thought. *I extended it down through the walls and into the plateau. It runs beneath the city. So that I can use it to destroy Tyrlindon's foundations. So that I can kill all of us.*

King William cleared his throat and climbed to his feet, forestalling any further questions. His raven-black hair and eyes shone in the lamplight. He didn't speak for a moment, merely stood, gazing over his Council. "I could stand here and make bold statements. I could claim we have right on our side. I could claim we fight with honor and integrity. But those would be empty words. The simple truth is that if we lose, it's all over. The Songmaker will destroy Amaury. Somehow, we must find a way to endure. We must win."

He glanced at his son who gazed steadily at his father from behind his blindfold. "Over recent months I've learned that feats we think are impossible, often aren't. My son was returned to me. The Lord First held the Songmaker's army in Shinnar lands and gave us time to prepare for siege. A dragon of Fire aided us in the defense of our city." He shook his head. "I wouldn't have believed such things were possible if I had not seen them with my own eyes. So I say to you: we *can* win. We *will* win. Because we have no choice." He smiled suddenly. "I'm honored to have such people by my side. Now, we all know our tasks. Let's get started."

His words hung in the air for a moment. Then someone at the back began to clap. Others took it up and the sound rippled around the room. Everyone surged to their feet and soon a thunderous applause filled the meeting hall. Rovann climbed to his feet, feeling as though he was being carried on the wave of noise.

You hear this, Leo? he thought. *You hear this, Maegwin? I'm going to kill you all, I promised Tanyaka. I meant it. I'm coming for you. For both of you.*

————————

The chambers of the Lord First stood dark and empty. A servant had been in to lay a fire which now smoldered in the hearth, sending dim flickers of red light through the room. Rovann closed the door behind him and leaned on it. He was so weary he could barely keep his eyelids from drooping. The moon had set and he guessed there were maybe four hours before dawn. Four hours before it all began.

With a sigh he crossed the room to one of the chairs before the fire. Sinking into it gratefully, he laid his head back and stretched his feet toward the fire. For a second, he lost himself in the simple joy of feeling the warmth on his toes and the softness of the cushions beneath him.

He glanced toward his bedroom. The battle ahead would be long and stressful. He really ought to sleep while he had the chance. Yet, he knew it would be futile. Instead, he dug into his pocket and pulled out a small block of unseasoned wood and his whittling knife. Staring into the embers, he let his hands work as his mind wandered. Shavings flew off to land unheeded on his lap and the floor. The familiar routine was strangely calming. He didn't have to think; only let his hands carve what they wished.

He heard the tramp of feet pass by his door. Someone called a name and was answered from further off. Like him, Tyrlindon did not sleep.

He worked in silence, barely paying attention, letting his thoughts go blank. An owl hooted outside, startling him, and he looked down at his creation. A low moan escaped his throat. The half-finished face of a woman stared back at him from the wood. Rovann grimaced. Why did he always do this to himself? Why could he not just let it go?

"Istra."

He whispered the name of his dead wife as though it was a prayer but he didn't know whether the carving was Istra's face or Maegwin's. With a jolt, he realized he could no longer tell the difference. What did it matter? Both were gone. Both had left him, through death or betrayal.

With a wordless howl, he flung the carving into the fire.

"Why do you torment yourself?" a melodic voice whispered suddenly.

He spun, but his apartment was empty. Throwing his senses wide, he detected the tiniest echo of the Realm of Aethyr.

"Angels!" he cried. "Where are you?"

There was no answer. It had been the same each time he'd tried to contact them. The Realm of Aethyr was closed, as was the Realm of Fire. He'd had no answer from either the angels or Tanyaka. It had left him feeling as though his allies had abandoned him.

It was the angels who had enlisted his help, the angels who had insisted he trust Maegwin, the angels who had sent him on his quest against the Songmaker. And now they didn't answer him.

A sudden fury quickened his pulse. He kicked over the chair and swept a decanter of wine from a shelf. It smashed against the floor with a satisfying tinkling of glass.

"Answer me!" he yelled. "Help me!"

Silence. There was the pounding of his heart. Nothing else.

The anger seeped out of him and he slid down the wall to sit hugging his knees. He pressed his forehead to his knees and let out a sigh.

Something stirred his hair. A breeze gently raised the hairs along his arms and he heard the faint tinkling of bells and softly singing voices. The peace of the Aethyr suddenly washed through him, wiping away his fatigue.

"You are the Warrior of the Realms," the voices of angels said. "You cannot be other than what you are. Remember, there is always hope."

Chapter Twelve

The red disk of the sun slowly rose over the edge of the plateau. Its rays bathed the walls of Tyrlindon in blood.

"How fitting," murmured Leo by Maegwin's side.

He sat astride a large black destrier that Maldric Hounsey had given him. The beast was caparisoned in the finest trappings and Leo himself wore an expensive black velvet outfit and had a slim circlet of silver holding back his unruly red hair.

As if he's king already, Maegwin thought.

She had to admit, he looked the part. He sat with his back straight, eyes intense as he stared at the walls of Tyrlindon shining in the sunlight. There was no trace of mirth on his face this morning. He was more serious and focused than Maegwin had ever seen him. An aura surrounded him. It prickled on her senses like a lightning storm. It spoke of hunger, desire.

Her horse snorted and tossed its head. She brought it under control with a jerk of the reins and glanced behind. Leo's forces had formed up in orderly columns that stretched across the plain in a dark tide. Weapons and armor glinted in the sun. The snap of banners echoed in the light breeze.

Then suddenly the atmosphere changed. Hairs rose along the back of her neck. Her skin tingled. It seemed as though the air pressure had increased. It felt charged, as though a thunder storm was approaching.

Now, said the Dark Goddess's voice in her head.

She shared a look first with General Shallon and Maldric Hounsey, then with Leo. Slowly, she nodded. Leo grinned in response.

Maldric Hounsey bowed to Leo and cantered off to the east where his forces waited.

"Shall we, my lady?" asked General Shallon.

Maegwin inclined her head and followed as he peeled his horse away from the group and rode toward their division on the west flank, leaving Leo to lead the middle. Leo had nominally put her in charge of Shallon's forces but she was no military strategist. The general would command, do what was necessary. She just wanted to get into that city.

She and Shallon reached their lines and pulled up their horses. The time for grand speeches was over. The general arched a questioning eyebrow at her and she raised her hand.

"Advance!" General Shallon yelled.

The drummers struck up a marching beat: *doom-boom-doom, doom-boom-doom* and the troops began their march forward. To the east, Leo and Maldric Hounsey's forces had done the same. The plan was simple: breach the gates. They were Tyrlindon's only weakness. With seven entrances to the city, the defenders could not hold them all indefinitely. They would crack eventually. Maegwin intended to be the first to enter the city.

As she rode slowly beside the marching troops, she was reminded of another time she had walked this same route. That day Rovann and Leo had been by her side. It had been her first sight of the great city and it had filled her with awe. This time it filled her only with a burning hunger.

When they were just beyond arrow range Shallon called a halt. A ripple went through the soldiers as the army settled like a great beast. A wide tree-trunk capped with iron was suddenly disgorged from the front ranks of the soldiers and carried forward by a group of twelve men protected by heavy, interlocking shields. In the front rank the drummer took up a slow, ponderous beat. The battering ram inched toward the imposing edifice of the locked gate.

There was movement on the walls of Tyrlindon and a volley of arrows hissed into the air. The sky was black with them. She watched them arc over the advancing ram and then descend in a deadly hail. A few found their mark, either thudding into the ram itself or skittering off the metal shields the soldiers held over their heads. But most fell beyond the attacking soldiers, slamming into the ground in the no-man's land between the forward party and the front ranks of the waiting army.

Maegwin frowned. The defenders would have to do better if they hoped to stop her. Her eyes scanned the walls, searching for Rovann, or Syrie, or Falwin or any of the mages, but from this distance she couldn't make out features.

The battering ram had almost reached the gates. Volleys of arrows continued to rain down, some at the ram but most thudding into the dirt a few meters behind it. What was the commander doing? Why let them waste arrows like this? Were they panicking already?

"My lady! General!" a lieutenant suddenly called.

She followed the man's pointing finger and gasped. Under cover of arrow fire, a small sally port at the side of the main gate had opened and a group of soldiers came running out. They caught the startled men around the battering ram unawares.

"Fall back!" bellowed General Shallon. "Fall back, curse you!"

The officers began calling out orders but to no avail. The soldiers' shields were heavy and they couldn't bring them around quick enough to form a defensive wall. Tyrlindon's defenders swept up, swords drawn, and cut the soldiers down with ruthless efficiency. The ram fell to the ground. One of the defenders smashed a small earthenware pot against the ram, shouted a word, and the ram burst into flames. Then, with a bellowed command, the defenders wheeled about and fled back through the sally port.

It was over in minutes.

Maegwin's hands tightened on the reins. Soldiers lay in a hacked mess on the King's Road, the battering ram was a burning ruin. *That's why they fired arrows at us,* she thought. *Not to hit our lines, but to keep us at a distance while they destroyed the ram.*

A sound suddenly reached her ears. She looked up at the walls and saw they were lined with people waving and making rude gestures. They were jeering at her.

A sudden wave of fury made her dizzy. *They were jeering at her!*

Laugh while you can, she thought. *I'm coming for you all.*

"General Shallon," she barked. "Get those bloody gates open!"

The general's mouth tightened and he bowed stiffly. "As my lady commands." He whirled to his men, shouting orders. "Fetch another ram. Lay down covering fire then advance behind. Send word to the engineers to bring up the siege engines. Break those gates!"

Rovann pressed the spy glass to his eye. He felt like he was being pulled in all directions, trying to see everything at once. He stood atop the tallest spire of the palace, trying his best to watch the battle unfolding. Lady and Tallo paced behind him, both chafing at being unable to join the defense. They stalked across the small round space on the tower top like caged wolves.

Rovann shared their frustration. He needed to see. He needed to know what was going on. True to Tyan's prediction, the Songmaker's forces were attacking all gates at the same time, trying to stretch the city's defenders as thin as possible.

Squinting against the glare of the rising sun, Rovann peered out toward Northgate where the trebuchets were firing balls of burning pitch down onto the advancing army. Turning, he looked toward Watergate where Syrie had earlier ordered two more mages down to bolster its defense from a particularly virulent attack from one of the Songmaker's Fire adepts. Round he went, studying every gate, every section of wall. But still he couldn't see enough.

"I'm going onto the astral," he said, making a decision. "Guard my body while I'm gone."

Without waiting for their response he slumped onto the floor, back resting against the cool stone of the parapet wall. Closing his eyes, he sucked in a deep breath and let it out slowly. His breathing deepened. His mind cleared. Then he was suddenly looking down at his body with Lady and Tallo standing watch over it.

He soared up onto the astral and looked around. The sight staggered him, sending a jolt of fear through him that nearly sent him spinning back into his body. On the astral plane the ward that protected the city shimmered a burnished gold. But beyond the ward, the air was filled with oily black auras.

They were human, that much was clear, but these were twisted. Tiria had reported seeing corrupted auras when she and Rallack had spied on the Songmaker's camp. At that time the enemy mages had been hiding themselves, conserving their power. Now, it seemed, they'd decided to reveal themselves.

The revenant mages hung in the astral on the other side of the ward like tattered black crows. They were silent, unmoving.

What have you done? Rovann wanted to ask them. *What have you allowed to be done to you? Is this the price you paid for immortality? Was it worth it?*

As long as the ward held, Tyrlindon was safe from them, they couldn't cross the ward. But if it was breached... He dropped into his body and opened his eyes, the familiar lethargy washing through his limbs. Unsteadily, he pushed himself to his feet, stretching out the cramped muscles of his legs and back.

Lady held out a hand to steady him. "Did you find anything—"

Her words were cut off as a massive boom suddenly echoed through the city. Rovann spun toward the sound just as a voice blossomed in his mind.

Rovann! Come quickly!

Tiria! Where are you?

Merchant's Row. They're trying to blow the wall!

Rovann dashed toward the steps. "Lady, Tallo, quickly! This way!"

The two soldiers followed, wearing expressions that announced they would be glad to join the fighting. Rovann jumped down the tightly spiraling stairs inside the tower three at a time and burst into a small stone courtyard. A groom had three horses saddled and ready. Rovann climbed into the saddle and nudged the beast into motion, Tallo and Lady a step behind. They galloped through the gate that led down into the city.

"Make way!" Rovann bellowed at the guards.

Once free of the palace grounds they were forced to slow to an infuriating trot. The higher levels of the city were crowded. The populations of the lower levels had been evacuated here and the streets were full of people. Rovann bit down on his impatience. Raising a hand, he shot a bolt of Fire at the flagstones ahead of him. The crowd yelped in surprise and scurried to a safe distance. With a grim smile, Rovann rode on.

Sweat dripped down his face and soaked into the neck of his robe. His heart was thundering. He had no idea what he might find in Merchant's Row. If the enemy had somehow breached the wall... But as he finally turned into the long street that backed right up against the outer wall he found an orderly defense being mustered under the direction of one of Captain Tyan's lieutenants. The man saluted as Rovann dismounted.

"What happened?" Rovann asked.

"Enemy engineers, sir," the officer replied. He signaled for Rovann to follow him up the set of stone steps that led up onto the wall walk. "A squadron laid charges right by the wall. Normally those kinds of blasts don't do too much damage but they're using some kind of powder I've not seen before. We killed the bastards but more keep coming."

Bracing his palms flat on the wall's top, Rovann leaned out. A dizzying distance below, he saw a vast crater at the wall's base. Within the crater soldiers scurried like ants. They were under a barrage of attack from the defenders but the arrows merely bounced off interlocking shields held over their heads.

Rovann cursed under his breath.

"They're laying more charges, sir. This time, with the foundations already undermined, they could bring down a section of the wall."

Rovann thought furiously. They had to clear those charges. A sudden idea came to him. "Where is Tiria?"

"This way, my lord."

They found the Third of the Council on her hands and knees in the dirt by the wall's base. She was surrounded by seven of her students. The Third's eyes were closed. She seemed to be listening to the vibrations from the enemy sappers beyond the wall.

"Seventeen," she murmured. "They've laid seventeen charges."

"Tiria," Rovann said, touching her shoulder.

Her eyes popped open. "Mallor has filled you in? Good. Any ideas?"

Instead of answering, Rovann turned to lieutenant Mallor. "Get some sappers down here and send word to the builder's guild. We need as much rubble as they can give us and we need it quickly. Commandeer any barrows and carts you require. We have to plug that hole."

Mallor saluted and dashed off.

Rovann addressed Lady and Tallo. "Gather a squad of mounted troops. We'll drive the sappers from the crater, you'll ride out and keep them away whilst our engineers make repairs. Take as many men as you need. Assemble by the sally port and be ready to ride on my signal."

Tallo grinned. "Aye, sir! At last a chance to kill some of the bastards!"

He whirled away, shouting orders. Lady hesitated as if deciding if she should leave Rovann's side and then followed Tallo.

Rovann knelt beside Tiria. The hard-packed earth dug into his knees and the smell of disturbed soil and brimstone filled his nostrils. Placing his palms flat against the ground, he sent his senses out through the dirt. There. A gaping void met his questing. Within it were alien devices that were anathema to the Eorthe. The sappers' charges.

"Quickly," Rovann said, raising his voice so that Tiria's students would hear him. "On your knees. We're going to drive those sappers from the crater to give our engineers enough time to fill the hole."

"What are you planning?" Tiria asked.

"Just follow my lead."

"How, Lord First?" one of the students asked. "What do we do?" The young man's eyes were round with fear and a thin sheen of sweat covered his face.

Rovann smiled reassuringly. "What's your name?"

"Ashni, Lord First."

"Ashni, a good solid name. You will channel the Eorthe for me. Strengthen it below the crater. If you feel something strange within it, don't flinch. I'm going to spice it up a little. I'll weave Fire into your Eorthic streams. Let's see if they can withstand burning ground."

Ashni swallowed thickly then nodded.

Tiria smiled tightly. "Yes, let's see."

Closing his eyes, Rovann placed his palms on the

ground once more. After a moment the vibrations of
Eorthic power surrounded him as Tiria and her students
began to work it. None of the mages here were Earth
adepts so it wasn't as strong as if Syrie had been present,
but Rovann hoped it would be enough. When he was
satisfied the power had built sufficiently, he drew a
burning gate in his mind and opened himself to the
Realm of Fire.

Immediately a torrent of energy burned through him.
He directed it into the Eorthic channels the others had
woven within the plain. He used it to find the rocks and
fissures, the pockets of soil beneath the crater and then let it
loose. Almost instantaneously, the rock of the plateau
turned white-hot. A great blast of heat rose through the
ground. Rovann was rewarded by the bellows of pain and
surprise that came from beyond the wall. He heard the
tramp of many feet as the sappers within the crater
scattered.

"Now!" he yelled at Tallo and Lady.

Tallo bellowed a command and Rovann heard the creak
of the winch that opened the sally port. A moment later the
clatter of hooves and the thunder of horses sounded on the
paving stones before disappearing into the hubbub beyond
the wall.

"Hold the heat in the ground until I give you the
signal," Rovann instructed Tiria. "When I give the word, let
it dissipate to let our own engineers work inside the crater."

Tiria nodded. The Third's expression was tight with
strain. "Don't take too long, will you?"

Rovann squeezed her shoulder then straightened and
headed toward the sally port. Lieutenant Mallor was overseeing the arrival of the supplies Rovann had ordered. A
score or more hand-carts had arrived filled with rubble,

rocks and other building detritus. They were being overseen by a squad of grumpy looking sappers.

They saluted haphazardly as Rovann approached. He returned the gesture then moved toward the man who he assumed was the leader. "You know what to do?"

The man scratched his stubbly beard. "Aye. We know. Risk our bloody necks, that's what we have to do. Same as bloody always."

Rovann smiled. "Good. As long as we're agreed. Tallo's squad will give you as much cover as they can. Work as quickly as possible. Remove those charges and secure the wall's foundations."

The man nodded.

"Good luck," Rovann said.

He spun away and climbed the steps to the parapet along the wall. At the top the wind brought tears to his eyes, forcing him to squint at what was happening below. The crater by the wall was empty and the enemy sappers were fleeing back toward the lines of the Songmaker's army. Tallo and Lady's squad harried them, cutting them down from behind. When they got within bowshot, the defenders wheeled their horses and formed a defensive line around the crater, keeping it clear for their own sappers. The sappers didn't have long. A concerted attack would destroy Tallo and Lady's soldiers. They had to move fast.

Even from here Rovann could feel the heat emanating from the crater. He realized suddenly that the heat might blow the charges so he quickly sent a mental communication to Tiria.

Now! Stop!

The Eorthe began to calm. The heat dissipated like smoke. Tyrlindon's sappers started to appear through the sally port pulling the hand-carts which they arranged around the crater's rim. Four or five descended into the crater with all sorts of apparatus strapped to their backs.

Rovann's attention was pulled to the east of the enemy lines where a squadron of longbow men was forming up. A scything hail of arrows launched into the air. Tallo issued instructions for his squadron to fall back out of bow range but as the missiles sailed closer, Rovann realized that the bows they were using seemed to have a longer range. The arrows would fall amongst Tallo's soldiers and the sappers in the crater.

Cursing, Rovann threw up his hands and let forth a blast of Fire that burned the arrows out of the air. The longbow men pulled back and a line of cavalry replaced them. The commander obviously thought the chance to undermine the walls was worth the risk of losing cavalry to the arrows of those on the wall. The cavalry formed into a line. A bugle called from somewhere within the enemy lines and the horses leapt into a gallop.

"About! Form up! Draw weapons!" Tallo bellowed.

His soldiers spun their horses toward the new threat, drawn swords glinting in the sunlight.

"Let's meet these bastards head on!" Tallo roared. "Charge!"

The thunder of hooves shook the ground as the two lines hurtled toward each other. Five heartbeats later they collided with a boom like a thunderclap. Rovann held his breath as the line disappeared in a wall of dust and churning beasts. Then the dust cleared to show the two forces engaged in deadly combat. Tallo's line appeared to be holding. Already ten or more of the enemy had gone down under the onslaught.

Grinding his teeth in frustration, he gazed down at the sappers working in the crater. *Come on!* he thought. *Come on!*

One of the sappers was carrying a black canvas bag out of the crater. He cradled it carefully against his chest as he climbed the crater's uneven slope and handed it to a rider waiting on the crater's lip. Rovann frowned as he recognized the rider. Lady! Words passed between Lady and the sapper then suddenly Lady whirled her horse and went galloping off to the north, away from the fight and directly into the teeth of the Songmaker's waiting army.

"What is she doing?" Rovann cried. "Is the fool woman trying to get herself killed?"

The front lines had spotted Lady careening toward them. A hail of arrows fell around her like rain. Cursing, Rovann threw out Fire to protect her and summoned Air to sweep away a barrage of cross-bow bolts aimed in her direction. Seeing that their aerial attacks weren't working, the front line knelt whilst the second line braced long spears on the shoulders of those in front, presenting Lady with a thicket of razor-sharp spear-tips.

Lady didn't slow. Her horse was in full gallop, speeding toward the thicket as though she meant to impale herself on it. Then, at the last minute, Lady yanked on the reins, dragging her mount into a skidding stop. She stood in her stirrups, whirled the canvas bag over her head and hurled it with all her might over the heads of the first lines of soldiers. Then she wheeled her mount and galloped back toward the city, kicking the beast to as much speed as it could muster.

For a moment, nothing happened. Then, several paces behind the front line, something exploded. A boom shook the ground. Flame and broken earth fountained into the air. A few seconds later there was a second detonation, this one deeper into camp, then a third, a fourth.

The enemy ranks descended into chaos. Those in the

first few lines milled around, waiting for orders that didn't come.

Tallo, Lady and the engineers in the crater took advantage of the confusion. They worked quickly, Tallo forming his defensive perimeter once more, the engineers climbing out of the crater and then upending their carts of rubble into it. Lastly they poured several vats of pitch into the crater. It would set hard, holding the rubble in place and effectively plugging the gap.

Rovann watched with one eye on the works below and one eye on the enemy lines. They were already regrouping. The areas where the detonations had gone off had been cleared. The lines were being rearranged to accommodate for the gaps.

And still the engineers worked. Several had moved to the base of the wall and were busy measuring it with all sorts of arcane equipment. Some even had their ears pressed to the hard stone as if listening.

"Hurry!" Rovann bellowed. "Fall back to the city! Fall back!"

He heard a shout and looked out to see Tallo whirling his sword over his head and then using it to point at the enemy ranks. The front line parted to allow a line of light cavalry access to the center. Even from this distance Rovann could see that they were heavily armored. Each carried a javelin and mace.

"Are you bastards done yet?" Tallo bellowed at the sappers. "Get your arses moving! We can't stand against that lot!"

For a wonder, the sappers followed his orders. They slung their packs over their shoulders and sprinted for the sally port, leaving the empty wagons behind. Tallo and

Lady, flanked by their own soldiers, followed, pulling back their line in an orderly retreat.

Seeing their quarry escaping, the Songmaker's light cavalry broke into an urgent gallop, throwing away all caution. For a second Tallo held the line as though gauging how much time the engineers needed. Then, seemingly satisfied, he kicked his mount in the ribs.

"Run!" he bellowed.

Together the soldiers wheeled their mounts and went galloping back toward the gate, all thought of an orderly retreat forgotten. That was enough for Rovann. He whirled away from the parapet, rushed down the steps to the sally port. The last of Tallo's riders was thundering through. Through the open gap Rovann got a startling, up-close glimpse of the Songmaker's soldiers bearing down on them before the sally port was closed with a thud and the four thick iron bars that secured it dropped into place.

The sappers were huddled in a group by the gate. As before, they had their ears pressed against the wall, apparently listening. Rovann strode over.

"Will it hold?" he demanded. "Are we safe?"

They didn't look up from their inspection for several moments. Then, with a collective sigh, they straightened.

"Aye," said the foreman. "It'll bloody hold all right." He grinned. "Good job, lads!"

Rovann felt a smile quirk the corners of his mouth. "A bloody good job, I'd say." He held out his hand. The man took it with a slightly surprised look on his face. "To the health of engineers everywhere."

"Aye," he agreed. "Unless they work for the bloody Songmaker of course." He raised his chin and called over Rovann's shoulder. "You're either insane or a hero, lass. I'm still trying to make up my mind which."

Lady joined them. She had a tiny smirk on her face. "Well, I'd hate to be predictable."

"What, by the Realms, was that?" Tallo demanded, storming over with a look like thunder on his face. "You nearly got yourself killed!"

Lady pouted, raising her eyebrows in mock surprise. "My, my, were you worried about me? How touching. And here's me thinking you didn't like me."

Tallo frowned. "I'm serious, Lady. You went way too close to their line. You're lucky you're not lying out there like some human pincushion!"

"It was not luck," Lady said haughtily. "I knew exactly what I was doing. And it worked. Right, Stryle?"

The sappers' foreman nodded. "Aye. Blind my eyes, but it bloody well worked all right."

"What worked?" Rovann asked. "What did you throw into their lines, Lady?"

"The charges, Lord First," she replied with a smug smile. "The things they'd planted to blow up our wall. I used them to blow them up instead, along with their stockpiles of similar munitions. They won't be making any big bangs any time soon."

Rovann felt a stupid grin spreading over his face. They'd done it! They'd repelled the Songmaker's first attack.

But his satisfaction was short lived. A tremble suddenly shot through the Eorthe beneath his feet, as though the earth was in pain. A heartbeat later a mental summons cried, "Lord First! Come quickly! The cloth district burns!"

"Lieutenant Mallor," he snapped. "Bring our horses."

Tallo and Lady mounted without a word then spun around and followed as he led them to their next battle.

Chapter Thirteen

The sun was a burning yellow ball high in the sky. No wind stirred the grass under her feet or raised dust from the plain. Maegwin wiped sweat from her brow and scowled. A breeze would be welcome. A rain shower even more so. A headache clung to the back of her eyes and her throat was parched.

Hours had passed. All morning the soldiers had assailed the gates and wall and all morning the defenders had repelled them. An hour ago word had reached her of an attempt to undermine the wall by blowing a hole in its foundations. An attack, so the report said, that had gone spectacularly wrong. The defenders had led a sortie, scattering the engineers and destroying their stockpile of explosive munitions in the process. Leo would be apoplectic.

Her horse stamped and shifted. A loud 'thwack' sounded as one of General Shallon's trebuchets fired another boulder at the wall. She watched as the huge gray rock arched through the air and then heard the dull boom as it struck the wall several meters below the parapet. A small plume of dust rose from the impact but the wall remained unharmed.

So it had been all morning. Shallon had tried a second battering ram but this time, as the soldiers had approached the gate, the ground had collapsed beneath them, tossing them into a pit filled with razor-sharp rocks. One of Syrie's little creations, no doubt. The impaled men had taken a long time to die. Even now, faint groans and screams came from that crater. The sound made her skin crawl.

After that they'd sent squads with scaling ladders against the walls but the walls were so high and so heavily defended that they'd been easily repelled. The siege engines were doing little damage at this distance and they couldn't bring them any closer as Rovann's mages would no doubt burn them to the ground if they came in range of their sorcery. Yes, she could see why Tyrlindon had never been taken.

She chewed her lip in frustration. The gate. They had to break the gate. It was the only way in. General Shallon's tactics were getting them nowhere. They needed help.

"Lieutenant!" she barked, turning in her saddle.

A tall, skinny man trotted over. "Yes, my lady?"

"Where are those mages I sent for? I've been waiting an age."

The lieutenant's eyes flicked to General Shallon where he sat his horse a few paces away. "Word has been sent, my lady. We await a reply—"

"Send another message. And tell the bloody Songmaker if he expects us to take the gates he better give me the mages I asked for!"

The officer saluted and rode off. She wondered whether Leo would heed her request. He'd deployed his renegade mages himself and Maegwin suspected most patrolled the astral plane, trying to find a way to breach Tyrlindon's ward.

"My lady?" General Shallon asked. His tone was clipped. He didn't like her ordering his soldiers about like this. Couldn't the fool man see his tactics weren't working? Did he just expect her to sit here and watch them fail?

"Who's in charge of the siege engines?" she asked.

"Eleventh, ninth and fifteenth squads, my lady."

"But who's overseeing their maintenance? Their positioning? Their design?"

The general rubbed at his bristled chin. "That would be the engineers. Why?"

"I've got an idea. Have the engineers in command brought here."

He watched her steadily for a moment, possibly wondering if he could directly disobey his high priestess. Then he bowed from his saddle. "Aye, my lady."

Maegwin waited with ill grace. Sweat trickled beneath her clothes. The stink of horse and unwashed bodies assailed her. Lady, what she would give for a rain shower. Finally, a small group of mounted people approached led by the lieutenant she'd sent to Leo. Four women and two men, dressed like any common villager. There was nothing to distinguish them as mages except for a silver pin on their lapel.

"You sent for us, my lady?" said a plump-cheeked woman with her long hair tied in a braid over her shoulder.

"Favor the general and I with your advice," Maegwin replied. "How would you advise we breach that gate?"

The woman frowned and flicked a glance at her companions before answering. "My lady, I'm sure you and the general are far more versed in battle strategy than I—"

Maegwin waved a hand. "Indulge me. If you were in command, what would you have them do?"

A look of uncertainty passed across the woman's homely features. She glanced at the high walls of Tyrlindon then back at Maegwin. "I'd tell the soldiers to pull back from attacking the walls, my lady. I'd tell them to stop wasting their lives. I'd tell them to make a concentrated effort on the gates. That's Tyrlindon's weak point."

Maegwin raised an eyebrow. "I agree." She turned to General Shallon whose red cheeks betrayed his annoyance. "General, I believe we've made the mistake of treating our mages and soldiers as two separate forces. Tyrlindon's defenses are strong because they combine the two. Their mages aid their troops, their troops aid their mages. It's time we did the same."

His eyes narrowed. "What do you suggest?"

"We've been using the siege engines to bombard the walls but that's not working. Why don't we use them to bombard the gates instead?"

"That kind of accuracy isn't what they're designed for, my lady," the general replied as though talking to a child.

"Are you sure?"

"Quite sure." His tone said, *I'm the experienced soldier, so why don't you shut up and let me do my job?*

But something was nagging at Maegwin. "General, Our Lady wants those gates broken. Allow me to try my plan. If it doesn't work, we'll go back to your methods. Agreed?"

The grizzled veteran regarded her for a moment. Finally, he nodded. "As you command, I obey, my lady."

She grinned at him as two men came marching up to her. One was middle-aged with hardly a hair left on his head, the other younger with a hatchet nose and large, bulbous eyes. Both had tool belts around their waist filled with all sorts of arcane apparatus.

The elder dropped a hasty bow. "General, my lady. I'm Mallam, head of the engineers, and this is my journeyman, Reny."

"I have a task for you," Maegwin said by way of greeting. "I want every catapult and trebuchet rigged to strike the gates."

Mallam frowned. "All of them? At the same time? My lady, what you ask is impossible. By their very nature catapults and trebuchets are notoriously difficult to aim. We can hit the walls because they're such a big target. But the gates? We'd be lucky to get them one shot in ten."

From the corner of her eye Maegwin caught General Shallon's smug smile. Damn the man!

"I don't want to hear what you can't do," she snapped at Mallam. "You're an engineer aren't you? Then bloody well engineer something! Modify the weapons, come up with new ideas, and use that tiny brain in that thick skull of yours!" Frustration made her tone sharper than she intended.

The younger man, Reny, cleared his throat. "Perhaps the problem isn't our engines but the ammunition we're using."

Maegwin turned her gaze on him. "What do you mean?"

The young man swallowed several times before speaking. "We've been using boulders to try and break the walls. That's not working. As Mallam said, our engines are too inaccurate and the walls of Tyrlindon are too thick. But what if we weren't throwing rocks? What if we didn't need to be one hundred per cent accurate?"

The older engineer rounded on the younger. "What are

you babbling about? Shut up before you embarrass yourself!"

"Wait," Maegwin said, holding out her hand. "I'll hear him out. Explain yourself, journeyman."

The young man glanced at his superior then cleared his throat. "The catapults can be rigged to throw other things —liquid for example. I saw it up in Silverport once. We could fill the cups with pitch and hurl that at the gates. We'd soon have them covered in the stuff. It's worked well in other areas of the city where they've managed to hurl it over the wall. Parts of Tyrlindon are on fire."

Mallam rolled his eyes. "Haven't you been listening? We're trying to break the gates, not set fire to a few houses. How will soaking the gates in pitch make any difference?

Reny shrugged. "Because pitch burns."

"So? Those gates are made of iron. We don't have anything that burns hot enough to set them alight, you cursed idiot!"

The young man shrank from his superior's tirade. "No," he said in a quiet voice then pointed at the group of mages. "But they might."

Maegwin's eyes flicked to the group of men and women. Understanding came on her in a rush. Of course. Fire. That was the key. If the gates were soaked in pitch and set alight using Fire, it was just possible it would burn hot enough to crack the gates.

She fought back a grin. "Reny, you're now chief engineer. Make the arrangements. I want those gates shattered by sundown."

"But...but..." stuttered Mallam. "You can't—"

"Can't?" Maegwin said, turning a cold gaze on the older man. "Are you telling me what to do, engineer?"

The man's face went pale. "No, my lady, of course not."

"Then get to it."

The two engineers bowed awkwardly and scurried away.

Maegwin turned to the group of mages who were watching her warily. "Right, it's time you earned your keep."

The cloth district had become an inferno of searing violence. The shops, the stalls, the houses, had all been engulfed by tongues of angry red flame that roared like a beast. Rovann stared, pulling his horse to a halt before the cordon of soldiers that blocked the way. The heat slammed into him like a wall.

"Don't go any closer, Lord First! It's not safe!" a red-headed woman bearing the sigil of a lieutenant cried.

Rovann paused, scanning the scene. Flames licked through the roofs of many of the buildings and the walls had begun to sag together dangerously. Off to the left in an old courtyard, an emergency hospital had been set up. Healers hurried among the walking wounded, treating burns, cuts and smoke inhalation. Along one wall lay a row of bodies covered with white sheets.

"Who is managing the fire crews?" he demanded.

"Lord Falwin, sir."

Rovann swung down from his horse. "Good. Take me to him."

The cordon of soldiers parted and the lieutenant led Rovann, Tallo and Lady cautiously down the street. They found Falwin shouting orders at a gaggle of students. He'd organized them into teams and they were using currents of Air to lift buckets of water and dump them on the flames. It was hard work but it reduced the risk of them getting burned.

"Good thinking," Rovann said as he strode over to the Second.

Falwin straightened as Rovann approached. He was coated in sweat and soot. His face was almost black and his eyes stood out shockingly white. "Do you reckon?" he growled. "It looks to be making no bloody difference to me."

They needed something more potent than this piece-meal strategy. The last time Rovann had faced a blaze was when Maegwin had torched a tree near Roamsford Edge. That time he had channeled Water...

"Falwin, split up your team. I need mages on each side of the fire. Send squads to the east and west. I'll stay here and anchor the south side. You go north to counter me. We'll build a gate over the fire and pour Water through it."

Falwin scrubbed a hand over his bald pate as he considered Rovann's plan. Then he nodded. "I hope you know what you're doing, you young pup. If this goes wrong we could have a flood rather than a fire on our hands."

"It's a risk we'll have to take. Signal me when you're in position."

Falwin called over his students and quickly split them into teams. They jogged off in various directions, skirting the fire as best they could.

Rovann moved to the edge of the street. The fire raged maybe fifty paces from him. Flames lapped hungrily through broken windows. Smoke and soot filled the air. Rovann coughed and wiped a hand over his brow. This close the heat threatened to crisp his hair and skin. Behind him the fire crews rushed to take the places of Falwin's students, hurriedly forming a line and passing buckets along.

The minutes ticked by. The fire crews kept the fire at bay but had little effect in calming it. The roof of a tailor's shop suddenly sagged.

"Back!" Rovann ordered. "Get back!"

People scurried out of the way just as the roof collapsed with a whoosh of sparks.

Rovann? We're ready, came Falwin's call.

Trusting Lady and Tallo to drag him away should the fire come too close, Rovann sank to his knees and closed his eyes. Slowing his breathing, he left his body and soared onto the astral plane. On this plane the fire writhed in silver and gold. It looked almost like a living entity.

Falwin's astral form hovered several hundred meters to the north and the forms of his students hovered the same distance to east and west. He anchored a beam of power into the Eorthe below then sent it spiraling toward the students. The students caught the beam, anchored it to the Eorthe at their point then passed it to Falwin. The group did this until they'd formed a perimeter of shimmering astral energy around the burning streets. It was rare to make a gate of this size and Rovann knew they would all have to keep their wits about them to ensure they weren't pulled into it. When he was satisfied it was large enough, Rovann drew a gate in the substance of the astral and strengthened it with the strongest of sigils.

A tremor of trepidation ran through him. He had no idea what he'd find within the Realm of Water, or even if it was still accessible. With a flick of mental power, Rovann pushed open the door to the Realm.

Immediately swirling eddies of Watheric power tugged

at him, threatening to pull him through. He clung to his anchor, trusting the Eorthe to keep him in place. Summoning all his strength, he took hold of one of those eddies and tried to yank it through the gate. It resisted him. The powers of Water had always been slippery but now, with the Unraveling begun, it was like trying to clasp hold of oil. The power refused to obey, slipping through his grasp to whip and snap at his astral form.

Rovann gritted his teeth. "I am Warrior of the Realms!" he bellowed. "You will obey me!"

Water suddenly went pliant in his grip, like a raging waterfall abruptly slowing to a trickle. With a surge of triumph, Rovann pulled it through the gate. With a rumble, it manifested on the physical plane: a torrential downpour thundering out of the heavens, falling like a waterfall on the burning city. The rain was so thick it looked like a gray sheet had been thrown over the buildings. In seconds, the fire fizzled and died away to nothing. A ragged cheer rose from the streets.

Satisfied, Rovann slammed the gate shut and the torrent cut off abruptly. He dropped back into his body and opened his eyes. A wave of exhaustion washed through him. He would have sagged onto the wet cobbles had Lady not been holding him up. Her concerned face was inches from his own, her dark eyes boring into his.

"Lord First?" she asked. "Are you back with us?"

He tried to reply but the words came out as a slurred mumble. He moved his tongue in his mouth for a moment and then tried again. "The fire?"

"Extinguished."

"Thank the Realms." All he wanted to do was lie down on the street and go to sleep.

Lady shook him suddenly. "Stay awake! You're needed!"

His eyes snapped open. The sound of fighting reached his ears: the ring of weapons, the roar of combat. It was very close.

Adrenaline surged through him and he staggered to his feet. Tallo stood a few feet away, sword drawn, staring to the south. At the curtain wall.

Following the line of Tallo's gaze, Rovann's blood turned to ice. Attackers were swarming over the battlements like a tide of rats. Scaling ladders and grappling hooks hugged the crenellations.

"Curse them," Rovann growled. "The fire was a distraction. This is their real attack! Come on!"

Fury shot through his veins. He could hardly keep the snarl from his face. At a run he sped toward the wall, not waiting to see if Tallo or Lady followed. He took one of the stone stairwells that led to the parapet and ascended two steps at a time. A raw, primal anger drove him, obliterating all thought.

As he reached the top, he stepped into a scene of utter chaos. A sea of fighting filled the parapet. Soldiers fought in close quarters, stabbing with knives, swinging with swords, chopping with battle axes or just wrestling with bare muscle. The attackers outnumbered the defenders two to one, and more were coming. As the defenders threw back a scaling ladder or dislodged a grappling hook, another clanked into place and hordes of attackers came boiling over the top.

"Realms!" Tallo breathed beside Rovann. "This one is going to be bloody."

Was Rovann imagining it or did he hear a certain satisfaction in the soldier's voice? Lady drew her knives and threw them in quick succession. Two soldiers fell dead, the knives sticking from their eye sockets.

"Yes," she agreed. "Very bloody."

Together, she and Tallo dashed forward, Lady screaming a war cry, Tallo grimly silent. They cut into the nearest knot of attackers, slashing and ducking, pivoting and kicking. In only a few heartbeats a space had cleared around them.

But five paces beyond them Rovann saw a woman wearing the king's colors suddenly grunt as a sword erupted from her chest. She clawed at the blade impaling her, slicing her fingers open in the process, then slowly slid off the weapon and collapsed into a crumpled heap, eyes staring. Her slayer, a big man in leather armor, barely glanced at her before turning to swing his weapon at the unprotected back of a new opponent.

Something shifted inside Rovann. Memories of Sandford Moor and Carrow Crossing played across his mind. Both had been battles not of his choosing and it was happening again.

With a shout of fury, Rovann opened himself to the Realms, relaxing all restraint. A tangled mix of power roared through him, so strong it appeared on the physical plane as an aura of blinding light. He burned like a candle flame. Soldiers scuttled back, yelling in alarm and fear.

With a sweep of one arm he sent energy careening into the enemy soldiers. Some died on the spot, incinerated. Others collapsed to the floor, writhing and clutching at their throats. Still more were swept from the wall to fall screaming to their deaths.

Rovann was careful, precise. He had learned his lesson from Sandford Moor. This would be no indiscriminate slaughter. This would be as exact as a surgeon cutting canker from a wound. He strode along the battlement, swinging Eorthic and Aetheric power around him like a cudgel. Soldiers fell in droves. At first they tried to oppose him. The officers barked orders and the well-disciplined soldiers formed into tight fighting formations that came at him with halberds and axes. But their weapons couldn't penetrate his penumbra so when they got close enough, he simply swatted them away as though they were nothing more than irritating insects.

Tallo and Lady fought by his side. Their eyes shone with battle fever as they finished off the ones Rovann didn't and guarded his back. Together the three of them carved a hole in the attackers, giving the wall's defenders enough time to chop the grappling hooks, throw down the scaling ladders and set them alight with burning arrows.

An enemy officer suddenly straightened in front of Rovann. The man was tall and lean with dark stubble covering his chin. He met Rovann's eyes and then very deliberately threw his sword onto the stone by his feet. It landed with a dull clang.

"We surrender, sir. I give myself and my men into your custody."

Kill them. Kill them all, part of Rovann thought. *What right does he have to ask for clemency? He's your enemy!*

Rovann stooped, picked up the officer's sword and examined the blade. Slowly, deliberately, he pressed its sharp tip against the base of the officer's throat. The man didn't move. He swallowed thickly, forcing himself to meet Rovann's gaze.

"Do you want to die?" Rovann asked softly.

"No, sir. I do not," the officer replied. "But if that is my Lady's will, then so be it."

Rovann cocked his head. "Your lady?" Did he mean Maegwin? Or someone else?

"Sho-La. We're Her servants. We fight in Her name."

"Do you now?" Rovann's voice was a whisper.

The man licked his lips, nervously. Behind him, his men were throwing down their weapons. The defenders surrounded them, swords held ready for Rovann's command. One word. That's all it would take to turn the parapet from a battle-ground into a slaughter.

Rovann pushed lightly. The sword point dug into the man's skin. A trickle of bright blood ran in a line down his neck.

Not a revenant then, Rovann thought. *Just a man. Just a person. Like the rest of us.*

I'm going to kill them all, he'd promised Tanyaka. He'd meant it at the time. Full of rage and betrayal, he'd vowed to destroy his enemies. But now, looking at this man standing in front of him, he found it difficult to tell who his enemies were.

He stepped back, dropping the sword to the ground with a clang. "Take their weapons, bind their hands and throw them in a dungeon."

Soldiers hurried to do his bidding and soon the attackers had been rounded up and marched away. The injured were lifted onto makeshift stretchers to be taken down to the infirmary and blankets were placed over the dead defenders to be collected by the death-carts. The enemy dead were pitched over the wall to become carrion for the crows.

Rovann picked his way through the carnage until he was standing by the parapet and leaned out. Hundreds of meters below, a mess of bodies and broken equipment lay in tangled heaps at the wall's base. This assault had cost the Songmaker dearly.

Sickened by the slaughter, he ground his fingers into the

hard stone of the wall. "Why won't you face me?" he whispered into the wind. "Leo, Maegwin. Let's have this done with."

Soon. Soon he would have to fight them.

And he was going to kill them both.

Chapter Fourteen

Maegwin squinted into the distance. Far away, many miles along Tyrlindon's curtain wall, a speck of light burned like a candle flame. It was indistinct but she was sure it was a person. She didn't need to guess who it was. Rovann, flaunting his power as though that might deter her.

It was a challenge. To her. To Leo. To her mistress. Within, the Dark Goddess stirred in anger.

Soon, Rovann, Maegwin thought. *Can you feel the moment coming closer? It's approaching. The moment when we'll face each other. The moment when one of us will die.*

General Shallon removed his eyeglass and passed it to an aide with a growled curse. "Get those engineers here!" he barked to the aide. "I'll not sit here a moment longer while they taunt us!"

Maegwin shared the man's frustration. The day was trickling away with no progress being made at all. She heeled her horse closer. "They're coming, general."

Shallon's aide returned, bringing Reny with him, the new chief engineer. The young man wore an overall smeared with dirt and grease and his hair was matted into unruly clumps.

"Chief Engineer," General Shallon said, glaring down at him from the saddle. "How go your adaptations to the catapults?"

The young man's face broke into a grin and his bulbous eyes gleamed. "Just finished, general. We're ready to begin testing."

"No testing," Maegwin cut in. "There's no time. Get it in position and await orders. The general and I will be there in a moment."

"But if we don't test—"

"This isn't a discussion!" she snapped. "Just do it!"

The young man paled. Without another word he spun and sprinted back the way he'd come. Maegwin nudged her horse over to where Leo's mages were sitting in a circle holding hands, scouting the Eorthe for clues as to where Rovann had stationed his mages. So far, they'd discovered nothing.

"On your feet! Follow me."

They scrambled up and dusted down their clothes. Yanking her horse around, Maegwin kicked the beast into a trot down the slope, General Shallon riding at her side, until they reached the engineers' enclosure. The catapult loomed over her as she approached the chief engineer and pulled her horse to a halt. Sliding from the saddle she and General Shallon strode over to the man, who was busy shouting instructions to the teams hauling the catapult.

The huge siege engine moved at a ponderous pace that made Maegwin grit her teeth. The great contraption slowly trundled down the King's Road toward Tyrlindon.

"You're sure this will work?" Maegwin asked Reny.

The young man pointed at the throwing arm. "Yes, my

lady. We've altered the angle of the arm. At its maximum reach the mechanism will fire at a flatter trajectory than it did previously." He scratched his head and frowned. "Well, that's the theory at least."

Maegwin stared into the distance. The walls of Tyrlindon still looked impossibly far away. Could this thing throw that far? The young engineer seemed full of confidence. She hoped he knew what he was doing.

"Slow down now," he shouted at the teams pulling the catapult. "Another ten paces should do it. Avoid that hump in the road. No! Not there! Here!"

With a screech of wheels and creak of wood, the great catapult slowly came to a stop. Along the top of the wall, Maegwin saw a long line of faces looking down at her. Shallon's soldiers were still out of bowshot but she knew there would be countless weapons trained on her and the general should they move within range. If their luck held, the defenders wouldn't guess their tactics until it was too late to stop them. The enormous iron gate now lay directly in front of the catapult.

It was time to see if her plan would work. The mages had gathered at her back. Now, at a nod from her, they spread out in a fan-like formation around the catapult.

"Load it," General Shallon instructed.

Men shuffled forward carrying huge vats of pitch. The winch at the base of the throwing arm was turned by two burly men in engineer's aprons. Slowly, the catapult's cup inched downward. When it was level with Maegwin's eye-line the workmen scurried up sets of step-ladders at either side and tipped the pitch into the cup. It took several trips before the cup was filled. The chief engineer strode up, casting a critical eye over the mechanism. Maegwin chewed her lip impatiently as he did his rounds, seeming to inspect every nut and bolt. Finally, he straightened and nodded.

General Shallon raised his arm. "Fire!"

The chief engineer threw a lever and the arm snapped forward with enough force to drive the catapult back on its wheels a few feet. There was an almighty thwack as the arm hammered into its resting spot then the pitch went sailing through the air like a tiny black cloud. There was a faint slap as the pitch struck its target: it splashed right across the gates in a dirty stain. The chief engineer's calculations had been perfect.

"Reload," Shallon snapped. "Keep going until I tell you to stop."

Maegwin closed her eyes and sent her senses outward. As instructed, half her mages had sent Chaotic power burrowing through the earth to attack the Eorthic power Rovann's mages were using to protect the gates. A silent battle was raging in the ground. The two competing energies appeared as colored lines of power: one the brown of soil, the other the oily black of Chaos. The black band was pushing against the brown, trying to break through. Gradually, it began to make ground, pushing back the Eorthe. The brown band retreated inch by slow inch toward the gates.

Then Maegwin sensed what she'd been hoping for. The Eorthe strengthened suddenly, meaning those mages held in reserve had joined the resistance. Just as she'd wagered they would.

"Second attack!" she shouted.

The remaining half of her mages threw forth their power. This time they channeled Fire, not directly at the gates which the ward would stop, but at the pitch that covered them. The ward was designed to protect against direct assault by magecraft only. It was no defense against mundane things such as rocks and pitch. It was a loophole Maegwin hoped to exploit.

An explosion of flames suddenly blossomed into life where the pitch had splashed across the gates. The Fire was mingled with Chaos; a mixture that burned with more violence than Maegwin had ever seen. The mages fed it, stoking the Fire until it glowed white hot. Its jaws bit into the iron and took hold.

Maegwin felt the defending mages transfer their energy to the gates, pouring Eorthic power into the metal in an attempt to strengthen it against the devouring Fire.

A moment later there came the thump of the catapult and a second gout of pitch slapped into the gate. The flames climbed higher. She could hear their roar, even across the distance.

A third thump of the catapult, and all the defending mages transferred their power to the gate. But it was too little, too late. The Fire had taken hold and now it chewed hungrily through the metal. In the center, where the Fire burned brightest, the iron had become molten, slowly trickling down the gate like a miniature lava flow. The flames turned from yellow to a pale blue, burning with unimaginable ferocity. Screams echoed from the city as the defenders pulled back from the heat.

Can you put this one out, Rovann? Maegwin thought. *You can't be everywhere at once, can you, King's Mage?*

The gate suddenly sagged. More and more of the iron began to dribble in molten streams down its surface. Then, as if the structure had finally reached breaking point, it collapsed under its own weight, slumping like some overworked piece of clay.

"Advance!" General Shallon yelled. "Get in there before they can regroup! Take the gates!"

Maegwin grabbed the reins of her horse and clambered into the saddle. Drawing her sword she waved it over her head.

"For Sho-La!"

With an answering roar the soldiers sped forward, thumping across the dusty ground to where the broken gates of Tyrlindon sat like an invitation. Arrows raked through the advancing line. The defenders catapults and trebuchets thumped and cracked, sending deadly missiles through the soldier's ranks. Many fell. But still more rushed on, a tide that would sweep into Tyrlindon and destroy it.

Maegwin leaned low over her horse's neck, exhilarating in the sudden chase after the hours of frustrated waiting. The gates themselves had slumped into a mass of molten rock. Now that there was no longer Fire to drive the heat, it was quickly dissipating. The Eorthe, the metal's natural aspect, was reasserting itself, cooling the broken iron even as she watched.

A thrill of triumph washed over her. This was meant to be. She could feel it.

Then, when the front ranks of the line were perhaps a hundred paces from the gates, mounted soldiers suddenly came spilling out to meet them. So. The defenders would oppose her and Shallon's approach.

Kicking her mount to greater speed, she urged it alongside the general's as he commanded the surrounding cavalry into a gallop. The thunder of hooves and the pounding of her heart filled Maegwin's ears. Dust clogged her throat. Her hair streamed out behind her. The enemy line got closer and closer…

Then slammed into her with a force that nearly ripped her from the saddle.

She flailed her sword, felt it snag something, heard a

man's grunt and a horse's scream and then she burst through the front line. Sawing on the reins, she yanked her horse around to see the headless corpse of a man dangling from its saddle, his foot caught in the stirrup. Blood coated Maegwin's blade.

Are you ready, Mistress? Maegwin thought. *Let's begin.*

A rider bore down on her and Maegwin brought her sword up just in time to catch the swing of his double-headed battle-ax. The weapons clanged together with an impact that sent a jolt of pain up her arm and into her shoulders. The man wore the uniform of the Royal Guard and was so hugely muscled Maegwin was surprised his horse could bear his weight. With a wordless grunt he pulled back the battle-ax and swung a mace at her with his other arm. Maegwin ducked and the mace whizzed through the space her head had occupied.

Cursing, she pulled her horse away, creating a gap between them. He followed immediately and Maegwin had to acknowledge his skill. He guided his horse with only his knees as he aimed another swing of the ax at Maegwin's head. This time, as she blocked the weapon, she was ready for the mace coming at her from the other side. She didn't try to stop it. Instead, she swerved out of the way, allowing it to miss her by the barest inch and then grabbed the mace handle and pulled, letting the weapon's own momentum drag the man forward in his saddle.

As the man overbalanced, Maegwin ripped her sword across his throat then watched as blood sprayed over his mount's shoulders. The man's hands flew to the wound, desperately trying to hold his life-blood in. But it was no good. His eyes widened for a moment before he toppled from the saddle.

I give his life to you, my Lady, Maegwin thought.

She quickly surveyed the battle. She, Shallon, and a number of soldiers had broken through the front ranks of the defenders. The front line had reformed behind them, meaning that Maegwin, Shallon and the tight knot of soldiers that fought with them, were surrounded by the enemy. Through the thrashing of men, horses and weapons, Maegwin could see the gate of Tyrlindon yawning. It was so close. Only a few lives stood between her and her goal.

Howling wordlessly, Maegwin swung around, looking for an opponent. Tyrlindon's defenders fought well, keeping into tightly disciplined lines and quickly closing any gaps. Looking around, Maegwin spotted their commander. Yellow hair spilled from under the man's helmet and he stood high in his stirrups, bellowing orders and dashing here and there wherever his lines threatened to be overrun.

Digging her heels into her mount's flanks, she trotted toward him. The commander saw her coming and pulled his horse around to face her, waiting calmly with hands clasped together on the pommel of his saddle. Maegwin couldn't see his face through the thick cheek guards of his helmet but she felt the weight of his gaze settle on her.

"Surrender!" she yelled. "Surrender and I might let your men live!"

He made no answer. Around her, battle raged but this man seemed an ocean of calm.

"Stand aside," she growled. "Get out of my way and my Lady may leave you your miserable life!"

The commander laughed. "My life? Do you think it means so much to me?"

He swept off his helmet and Maegwin gasped. The man's face had aged and his eyes were dead, devoid of any emotion. Nevertheless, she'd recognize him anywhere.

"Hannel?"

A sardonic smile curled his mouth. "Ah, so you do remember my name. Do you remember the rest of us? Captain Tyan? Lady? Tallo? Ash?" The smile died. "My sister?"

Of course she remembered them. She'd fought beside them at Carrow Crossing. She'd eaten with them, joked with them, bled with them. Hannel's sister, Hesha, had given her life to help Maegwin escape that death-trap.

"Nothing to say?" Hannel demanded. "I'm not surprised. Choking on your betrayal?"

Maegwin opened her mouth to speak but the look on Hannel's face froze the words in her throat. That look was hatred. Pure and simple.

His nonchalant stance invited attack but Maegwin suspected that was deliberate. If he encouraged her to be reckless he'd have that much more chance of killing her. And now, as she met his unwavering gaze, she knew that's why he was here. He wanted to kill her. Wanted to see her die, just as he'd watched his sister die. And why not? Maegwin had betrayed him. Wouldn't she feel the same in his place?

Something burned within her, something she didn't like. Shame? Maybe. In response, sudden anger flared. Who was he to judge her? What right did he have?

Kill him, whispered the Dark Goddess. *Kill them all.*

With a shriek, she raised her sword and charged. Hannel watched her come, a satisfied smile lighting his face. His horse shifted in alarm but he calmed the beast with a few words. Maegwin swung her weapon, aiming the blade to take off his head.

But at the last second, Hannel's sword arm hissed up as quickly as a striking snake and caught her blow on his own weapon. At the same time he flung out his other hand.

Something glinted silver and then Maegwin grunted as pain flared across her cheek. Pressing her hand against her face it came back covered with blood.

Hannel's eyes were cold. "Seems I learned a few tips from Lady after all. She'll be pleased."

The strength leaked out of Maegwin. Numbness spread through her arm. Her sword fell from suddenly nerveless fingers.

Get away! she shouted at herself.

Kill him! screamed the Dark Goddess.

She yanked the knife from her shoulder, ignoring the burst of agony and the blood running from the wound. A snarl curled the corners of her mouth as sudden blood-lust raged through her.

"Retreat!" a sudden shrill cry cut through the air. "Get back to the city!"

A small, dark-haired woman came riding pell-mell at her. Maegwin had time to utter a yelp of surprise then a wave of force slammed into her, lifting her from the saddle and dumping her on the ground several meters away. The breath was knocked from her lungs. Little dots of light danced in front of her eyes. For one, two, three heartbeats she lay stunned, unable to move. Finally her sight cleared. Hannel and the dark-haired woman were galloping away.

Syrie. The Earth adept had smacked Maegwin with a wave of Eorthic power. Curse the woman. Curse her to the Darkness!

Glancing around, Maegwin saw that most of Shallon's soldiers were down. Men and horses rolled on the floor, disorientated.

"On your feet!" General Shallon bellowed, digging his bloody sword into the ground and using it to help him stand. "Regroup! Regroup!"

Maegwin forced herself to her feet and then steadied herself with arms outstretched until the world stopped spinning. Hannel, Syrie and the rest of the sortie were disappearing back inside Tyrlindon. It didn't matter. The gate was broken. The way into Tyrlindon was clear.

"Mount up and reform your lines!" General Shallon yelled. He found four officers and sent them further down the line to relay his orders.

Maegwin staggered over to where her mount stood, head hanging down as the beast ripped up tufts of the sparse grass. He raised his head to look at her as she approached and snorted, ears pressed back in defiance.

"Easy, boy," she said. "I didn't enjoy Syrie's attack much either. But she's gone now."

Perhaps calmed by her voice, the horse waited patiently as she took the reins and climbed into the saddle. Around her, the soldiers were quickly reforming into a square formation. Maegwin assumed her place by General Shallon at the head of the line.

Shallon rose in his stirrups and raised his sword so it glinted in the sunlight. "Forward! Don't stop until you're inside the city! Kill any defenders and make way for our infantry! Secure the gate and immediate area!"

With that, they set heels to their horses and went thundering off down the slope toward the gate. Around her, the soldiers gave vent to their battle-fury by howling their defiance.

Their approach to the gates was not uncontested. A deadly rain of arrows raked them from above. Maegwin kept low against her horse's neck and trusted to the Dark Goddess to protect her.

The gates loomed ahead, maybe only fifty paces away and Maegwin's heart thundered. Battle-fury filled her veins, wiping away all doubt and fatigue. Kicking her mount hard in the ribs, she sent it hurtling out from the front of the line, determined to be the first through that gate. Her eyes scanned the slumped heaps of magma, the broken beams and lumps of metal.

She slowed her horse to a trot to allow the rest to catch up and together she and General Shallon approached Tyrlindon. The huge lintel of the gate loomed over Maegwin's head. Inscribed into the stone she read, *The Realm of Outer Darkness.* A sardonic smile lit her face. How fitting.

She held her weapons ready. As she emerged into the courtyard beyond the gates, she was surprised to find it deserted, no lines of attackers waiting to greet them. Unease squirmed down her spine. What was this? Did they expect her to believe they would abandon the gates so easily?

"Spread out," Shallon barked. "Secure the area."

The soldiers moved to obey, one party swarming up the steps to the battlements, two others fanning out into streets. Something nagged at Maegwin's senses. There was danger…

"Wait!" she shouted.

Too late. As the soldiers stepped out of the courtyard, the streets to either side suddenly collapsed. Soldiers and horses went screaming into a chasm that split the ground. Dust and dirt spewed into the air. Cursing, Maegwin covered her mouth and coughed out the worst of it.

"Get back!" she shouted. "Get back!"

The dust slowly cleared to reveal them stranded on an island. On three sides the ground had collapsed. She dismounted, handed her reins to a soldier, and edged closer to the yawning gap. The pit was deep. At the bottom

Maegwin saw the broken bodies of those that had fallen in. Closing her eyes, she said a quick prayer for the dead to Sho-La.

"What caused this?" General Shallon growled.

"Syrie," Maegwin replied. "Only the Eorthe could do such a thing."

The general nodded. "A delaying tactic. We'll have to build bridges to cross this chasm. That may take a while." He turned to an officer. "Send word to the engineers, they're going to be very busy for the next few hours."

As the man rode off, Maegwin felt a strange mix of frustration and elation. She chafed at the delay. Yet the gate was hers. She'd broken Tyrlindon. Now it was only a matter of time before the city fell.

Chapter Fifteen

Rovann marched purposefully down the street, Lady and Tallo keeping pace to either side. They moved with agitated speed, growling and cursing when people got in their way. Rovann understood all too well the frustration that drove the soldiers' tempers. Despite the defenders' best efforts, the first level of the city had been lost. Even now, an orderly retreat was underway, each unit being pulled back in turn. One company, led by Sergeant Hannel and Mage Syrie was battling to hold the enemy that had breached the west gate, giving the rest of the defenders a chance to make their escape to the second level.

The west gate. He hadn't been able to verify reports of a female commander being involved in the attack but he knew in his bones the reports were correct.

Maegwin.

He gritted his teeth and marched on. He, Lady and Tallo were among the last of the defenders prowling the first level on the southern side of the city, ensuring nobody had been left behind. In truth, he hoped he'd encounter Maegwin and her soldiers. He was itching for a fight.

Rovann shook his head, stunned that things had come to this. Had he underestimated the skill of Leo and his commanders? Maybe. The Songmaker had deployed his forces in organized units at each gate of the city, forcing the defenders into thinner ranks than Rovann would have liked. If the defenders had been able to focus more of their forces on the west gate, perhaps it would have held. If he, Rovann, had been there, perhaps he could have stopped Maegwin.

With a growl he dug his nails into his palms, forcing the thought aside. There was no room for 'what ifs'.

"How many left?" he asked Lady.

"Three," she replied, her dark eyes scanning the area ahead, knives held in each fist.

'Three' referred to the number of streets left to sweep before this section of the first level was clear and they could retreat to the second level. They passed through a bottleneck of closely packed shops before the street widened again. Tallo and Lady moved to the sides, Rovann walking silently down the middle. The shops and houses looked eerily forlorn, doors hanging open, windows broken. Rovann trod warily, eyes scanning every shadow and possible hiding place. Suddenly something intruded on his senses.

"There!" he yelled, spinning toward the gaping doorway of a shop.

Tallo dashed across the street and darted inside. There came the sound of a brief scuffle then Tallo emerged dragging a fat, balding man, his blade pressed to the man's throat.

"Please don't hurt me! I'm on your side!"

Tallo shoved the man away. "What are you doing, you

damned idiot? I nearly skewered you! All citizens were told to evacuate! "

The man went pale. "My shop is my livelihood! You expect me to just leave it to be burned to the ground by the invaders?"

"Would you rather it was your life?" Tallo snapped. "I'll—"

"Peace, Tallo," Rovann said, placing a hand on the soldier's shoulder. To the man he said, "Go to the end of the street and turn left up Baker's Hill. The Merchant's Gate is still open but hurry or they might not let you in."

The man looked from Tallo to Rovann and back again. Then he bobbed his head. "Right away. Um, thank you."

He hurried away and the three resumed their sweep of the street. Except for the squeak of boots and the creak of doors swinging in the breeze, all was silent. To the right, the outer wall rose, casting the street into shadow. On the other side of that wall, Rovann knew, enemies were massed, awaiting their turn to come pouring into Tyrlindon through the broken gate.

He paused suddenly as something caught his attention. Against the glare of the sky, an object poked over the top of the wall. A scaling ladder, Rovann realized. Lady cocked her knives, ready to throw.

"Wait," Rovann stilled her with a gesture.

He glanced around, quickly assessing their options. At either end of the street, two sets of zigzag stone steps led up to the parapet that spanned this section of wall. Attackers coming over the wall would have to use them to get into the city proper.

"There," he said to Lady and Tallo, pointing to the steps. "Take an exit each and conceal yourself nearby. Don't bar their passage down the steps but be prepared to block their retreat."

Lady nodded and Tallo gave a satisfied grin. "What's the plan, boss?"

Rovann shrugged. "We're going to make them remember Tyrlindon is defended still."

Tallo's grin widened. He drew his swords and hefted them, one in each hand. "Yes, sir."

Without another word, he and Lady trotted in opposite directions, ducking behind an overturned cart at one end and some barrels the other.

Rovann glanced up. The tops of the scaling ladders were silhouetted against the sky. Any moment now, soldiers would come pouring over them. And they'd find a surprise waiting for them.

Spinning on his heel, he retreated into a shop across the street and hunkered down by the window. From the scent of yeast Rovann guessed this had been a bakery. Now it was empty, its wares and occupants long gone.

Rovann felt strangely calm. In the dim shop, all was silent but for the cooing of a pigeon on the roof. The usual bustle of the city was still and Rovann wondered how often people had experienced Tyrlindon like this: quiet, peaceful.

His eyes slid closed and he counted his heartbeats: one, two, three, four. Then finally he sensed movement on the wall. He opened his eyes and squinted through the window. A helmeted head peeked cautiously over the top of the scaling ladder. The soldier paused, looking to both left and right then pulled himself up and over, jumping down onto the parapet. He looked tense, crouching low with weapons ready. After several seconds of waiting for an ambush that didn't materialize, he straightened and leaned over the wall to give a signal to those below. In moments more soldiers were swarming over the tops of the battlements.

The first squads spread out along the parapet, securing the area for those that came behind. Nobody approached the stairs leading down onto the street, perhaps awaiting the full squad before they did so.

Rovann smiled grimly. Good. The more, the better.

Minutes ticked past and Rovann's heart began to beat a little quicker. Those men and women, so ordinary looking, had come to invade his home. And yet, as he saw them talking, moving around, working together, he was forced to wonder if they were really that different to himself. Perhaps those men and women had been lured from their homes by the Songmaker's promise of a better life.

The thoughts flashed through Rovann's mind in an instant but he pushed them ruthlessly aside. To think that way invited weakness, and that was something he could not afford.

Instead, he focused his attention on the enemy. The whole length of this section of the wall now seethed with soldiers. A commander—a tall man with a winged helmet—stood bellowing orders at the others. The soldiers formed into two squads at either end and began to carefully descend the stone steps to the street below. Once they reached ground level, they fanned out, weapons drawn and on the lookout for attack.

Rovann tensed as the soldiers passed Lady and Tallo's hiding places, expecting a cry to go up as his companions were discovered but no alarm call came.

"Secure the buildings!" the commander shouted.

The soldiers split into groups and approached the yawning doorways on Rovann's side of the street. He watched as a band trod wearily toward his hiding place. In the gloom of the old bakery, he climbed to his feet and pressed his back to the wall beside the window. Then he waited five heartbeats before emerging from the doorway and casually striding out into the street.

"Hello, friends."

The soldiers jumped, yelling in alarm. A bowstring twanged. Rovann threw out a hand and the arrow ricocheted off a barrier of Air, slamming into the window frame instead. Shouts rang out.

"Careful! He's a mage!"

The soldiers took several steps back, but to their credit, didn't bolt. They fanned out to surround Rovann. He made sure to keep his back straight, his stance relaxed, and forced a smile onto his face as though this was all just some pleasant meeting down the local market. All eyes were fixed on him now. Excellent.

The commander shouldered his way through to the front, pulling off his winged helmet and tucking it under one arm. "Who are you?" he demanded. "What are you doing here?"

Rovann raised his eyebrows. "Shouldn't I be the one asking that question?"

On the far side of the street, behind the soldiers, Rovann saw Lady and Tallo cautiously emerge from their hiding places and climb the first few steps, weapons drawn. Now the invaders' only retreat was blocked and the narrowness of the steps meant they'd only be able to fight Lady and Tallo one at a time. Good.

The commander frowned at Rovann. "This area is under our control now."

"Is it? I disagree."

The commander snorted a laugh. "Really? And how are

243

you going to stop us, mate? Who do you think you are, the bloody King's Mage?"

Rovann allowed a wry smile to curl his mouth. "Well, it's funny you should mention that." Pitching his voice to carry, he said. "You're all under arrest. Throw down your weapons and you'll not be harmed."

Some of the soldiers shifted uncomfortably, unsettled perhaps by the authority in his tone. But the commander merely grunted. "You've had your chance, mate." He waved a hand. "Kill him."

Bows twanged but Rovann threw out his arms and a wave of force tossed the arrows aside before slamming into the knot of soldiers. The commander and those immediately behind were picked up and tossed through the air like sticks, landing on the hard cobbles with a sickening crunch. For a moment the rest of the soldiers stood in stunned silence, unsure what to do with their commander down. Rovann took advantage of their momentary confusion to stride forward, flinging out another wave of force. More soldiers were thrown across the street.

A secondary commander, perhaps a lieutenant, lifted his sword into the air and bellowed, "Crossbows! Bring him down!"

In response, crossbows were unslung from shoulders and aimed in Rovann's direction. But the cumbersome weapons took time to load and by the time they were ready, he'd already thrown up a shield of Air. The weapons made a popping noise as they discharged but the bolts rained harmlessly against his shield.

He strode forward, flung out his arms and another swathe was cut through the attackers. Soldiers lay in crumpled heaps all over the street now, blood pooling under cracked limbs and skulls.

The remaining soldiers banded together, a ragged group with fear in their eyes. Yet they still didn't surrender. They faced him, swords held out defensively.

Grimly, Rovann strode onwards. Some at the back of the group abruptly darted for the steps up to the battlements but found Tallo and Lady waiting for them. Lady dispatched one solider with a swift stab to the neck whilst Tallo dealt another kick to the temple, sending him crashing back down to the street.

"We surrender!" one of the soldiers cried suddenly.

The lad looked barely out of his teens and still had the gangly look of youth. His eyes were wide with terror. He threw his sword to the dirt by Rovann's feet and then backed away. Others did the same. The disciplined fighting unit had become just a group of ordinary men and women, frightened for their lives.

But in the center of the group, a knot of soldiers stood firm, retreating steadily but holding to their formation, swords drawn and shields held high.

Rovann realized they were shielding someone, a man dressed as a soldier but carrying no weapons. A shiver of alarm ran through him.

Letting his power falter, he flung his perception toward the group. The man's aura was masked, made to look like those of the men around him, but it hadn't been done well enough to fool Rovann. Wisps of oily energy escaped, manifesting on the astral like trailers of smoke.

The man was a mage.

Rovann stumbled in sudden confusion. Why wasn't he attacking? Why wasn't he trying to defend the men and women under his command? The answer came to Rovann in a rush: because that wasn't his purpose. He was here for something else. He was here to get inside Tyrlindon's ward so that he could…

An icicle slid down Rovann's back. With a howl of rage, he threw a blast of Air at the group of soldiers and tossed them aside like dry leaves. The mage put up no resistance. He landed with a crunch several meters further down the street. Rovann strode up to him and grabbed him by the front of his tunic.

"What are you doing here?" he hissed. "What is your purpose?"

The man's nose had been crushed but he managed a hacking laugh. "Fool! You're finished! We're already inside!"

Rovann shook the man until his teeth rattled. "Tell me your plan, curse you!"

A smile stretched the man's mouth. "You'll work it out, King's Mage."

With a cry of exasperation, Rovann released him then, as he slumped onto his back, sent a tendril of Aethyr snaking into the man's body. He found no life-force within. So. A revenant. One of Leo's battle mages. Opening himself to the Realm of Fire, Rovann poured white hot force down on the man. He made not a sound as he burned away to ash.

With a thumping heart, Rovann stepped back, scrubbing a hand through his hair and trying to calm his whirling thoughts. A quick glance up and down the street showed that all the attacking soldiers were down. Lady and Tallo still held the steps, scanning the area warily.

"Throw down the scaling ladders," he called to them. "Then get ready to leave. We've done all we can here."

As they moved to do his bidding, Rovann sank onto his knees by the remains of the dead mage. Closing his eyes, he allowed his breathing to deepen then soared out of his body and onto the astral plane.

We're already inside.

Rovann recoiled as his eyes fell on Tyrlindon's ward. The shimmering bubble that cocooned Tyrlindon from mage attack was webbed with a skein of oily tendrils that were slowly eroding it. The mage, by getting inside Tyrlindon, had managed to circumvent the ward and begin an attack from within. How many more had also made it into the city? Right now, how many more revenant mages were attacking the ward from within?

Rovann returned to his body and opened his eyes, forcing his suddenly shaky legs to stand.

"Nobody will be coming over that wall any time soon," Lady informed him, tucking her knives away as she and Tallo jumped down the last few steps. "What should we do now?"

"We have to get to the second level and call the mages together. Come on."

The cobbled road leading to the second level was empty. The citizens had already made their way through the gate and now only soldiers patrolled, stationed at strategic points on the approach to ensure no enemy ambushes made it through. As they approached the gate up the steeply sloping road, Rovann turned to look back the way they'd come. From here, he could see the lowest level of Tyrlindon stretching away into the distance. From perhaps half a mile away came the sound of weapons clashing and the tramping of feet. This marked the path of Syrie and Sergeant Hannel's company that was making an orderly retreat toward the second level whilst delaying the Songmaker's forces. Maegwin's forces, Rovann reminded himself.

Gritting his teeth, he turned back and led Lady and

Tallo through the gate inscribed, *The Realm of Air,* and into the second level of the city. He was not three strides into the street beyond before a boy came pelting up to him. He had messy brown hair and big eyes.

"My lord!" he cried. "I'm glad to see you! Hours I've been waiting, I have. Hours I tell you! Any longer and I think mistress Tamya might have had me flogged!"

Despite himself, Rovann smiled. "You've always been one for exaggeration, Tom. Tamya would have done no such thing."

The lad frowned. "You reckon? I hope you're right because you're the one who can explain where I've been all day."

"And I'll do just that. Are the others ready?"

The boy nodded, making dust fly from his hair. "They've already gone up, my lord." He pointed meaningfully at the sky. "Lord Falwin said it couldn't wait."

Rovann accepted this in silence. Then he turned to Lady and Tallo. "Join the garrison here, help to secure the gates." Lady opened her mouth to protest but he held up his hands to forestall her. "I know you were ordered to guard me, but where I'm going you can't aid me." He fixed her with a hard stare.

After a moment Lady held out her hand and Rovann gripped it, forearm to forearm. "Good luck, my Lord First."

Tallo stepped forward and did the same. "I don't like it. Just make sure you don't get killed, eh? Captain Tyan would never let us hear the end of it."

"I'll do my best," Rovann said, smiling wryly. "If we get out of this alive, I owe the both of you a stiff drink."

Tallo's eyebrows shot up. "Did you hear that, Lady? You heard it didn't you? The Lord First promised to buy us a drink! We'll hold you to that, you know."

"I don't doubt it."

He clapped Tallo on the shoulder then turned and followed Tom down the street. The second level of Tyrlindon was more spacious than the first and filled with townhouses, taverns and small businesses. The streets were crowded with people who'd been evacuated from the first level. They waited in long queues to be directed to their billet by weary looking soldiers. Rovann hunched his shoulders and hurried by, following Tom up the hill to a wide stone inn with a sign hanging outside that proclaimed it as *The Laughing Frog*.

Tom and Rovann pushed through the door and walked into a wall of noise. The common room was crammed with people. Tamya, the stout innkeeper, and her team of serving staff were busily wending through the tables, keeping their guests fed and watered.

Fear filled the room like the reek of stale sweat. Rovann was reminded of another tavern like this one back in Angard all those months ago. Then, he and Maegwin had been waiting for a mage storm to flatten the city. This time the patrons were waiting for an invading force to breach the walls. The outcome would be much the same.

Over by the cold fireplace a minstrel sat on a three-legged stool plucking at a lute disconsolately and singing something nobody could hear over the din. Rovann shuddered at the sight, thinking of how Leo had paraded as the same in this very inn.

"Lead on," he instructed Tom.

"This way," Tom muttered, moving to the stairs at the back of the common room.

They ascended to the top floor which was made up of one large room normally used for storage. Now, as Tom pushed open the door with a creak, Rovann saw that it housed an entirely different type of cargo.

The room was full of mages.

Tamya had provided low cots that filled every available inch of floor space, with only narrow gaps between. On each cot lay a sleeping form. Or, at least they looked to be sleeping but Rovann knew otherwise.

Tom shrugged. "Told you. They've already gone up."

Falwin and Tiria lay next to each other, hands clasped on their breasts, eyes closed. A few other members of the Council were also present. The rest were final year students.

"They wouldn't let me go," Tom announced suddenly. "I tried but Falwin sent me back. He said I wasn't ready."

"And he was right," Rovann replied, raising an eyebrow at the lad's admission. The boy was unusually talented but he was only in his first year. He wouldn't be ready to Walk for a long time yet. "We each serve in our own way, Tom. You served by keeping watch over their bodies and coming to fetch me." He laid a hand on the boy's shoulder. "You see?"

Tom looked doubtful and Rovann was reminded of himself at the same age. He only hoped Tom would be given the opportunity to grow into the powerful mage his potential promised.

A spare cot lay near the door. Rovann slumped wearily and lay down on his back, hands clasped on his chest.

"You know what to do?" he asked Tom.

The boy nodded, eyes suddenly a little too round. "If something goes wrong. I'm to lock the door and seal it with a band of Air."

"Good. And then?"

"Fetch the reserves Captain Tyan has waiting."

Rovann nodded. This was the safe house the Council had agreed to use for their Walking. It was far less conspicuous than the palace and so safer from an attack by the Songmaker. But if it all went wrong and the Council were defeated on the astral plane, there was a chance the enemy could use their severed astral link to gain control of their bodies. In essence, they would become like Lord Cedric Hounsey and half the mages under the Songmaker's command. Revenants. The undead.

Rovann had taken precautions to ensure that didn't happen. He'd left a packet of orders with Captain Tyan, to be opened in the event of the Council being lost on the astral. They would evacuate *The Laughing Frog* and then burn it to the ground, making it a funeral pyre for the Council. It was the only way to be sure.

He closed his eyes and deepened his breathing. In only moments he found the calmness that allowed him to shrug off his body and rise out through the ceiling into the sky above Tyrlindon. Here on the astral plane he appeared as little more than a wraith, a figure of wispy substance that was vaguely man-shaped. From his ankle ran a golden cord that connected him to his body.

Tyrlindon lay spread out below him, its turrets and towers and houses and streets all gleaming in the setting sun. It looked oddly ephemeral, as everything did on the astral plane. Scanning the sky, Rovann spotted the members of the Council. Falwin's astral form floated above the exact center of Tyrlindon and he was bellowing orders. Tiria drifted lower, perhaps scouting what was happening on the physical plane below. Around the edges of the ward, the final year students and the rest of the Council had fanned out, awaiting instructions.

Rovann moved over to Falwin. "How goes it?"

Falwin's astral face scowled. "Badly. We're outnumbered, even with the students. The bastards seem happy to watch. What are they playing at?"

Glancing at the ward, Rovann saw that the skeins of strange energy were pulsating all over its surface, flickering into existence and then out again. As the smoky energy pulsed, an eerie song rose and fell in time with it. There were words but they were so jumbled Rovann couldn't make them out. The sound seemed to be coming from all directions at once although Rovann saw no sign of the singer.

Yet Rovann recognized it instantly. He'd heard it before, in Near Point. It was the Songmaker's song.

And beyond the diseased ward, row upon row of enemy mages waited in silence.

"Falwin," Rovann barked. "Send students toward the first level. Have them find the mages that have infiltrated the city. It's they who are fuelling this attack on the ward from within. They're on the physical plane so once you've found them, contact Syrie and have her dispatch soldiers to kill them. Some of them may be revenants so mages will be needed."

"How do you know this?" Falwin asked. "We've seen no sign of any mages within the city."

"They're disguised as soldiers," Rovann replied, "and have learned to mask their auras. Tell the students to look for the signature of Chaos. It will be faint, but it will be there."

Falwin nodded, seemingly glad to be able to do something. "Right."

His astral from sped off, gathering a large group of students to him. Together, they descended onto the lower astral to begin their hunt.

Rovann called to Tiria. The Third of the Council rose toward him.

"I'm glad you're here," she cried as she approached. "Have you seen what they're doing down there? Syrie's command is getting slaughtered whilst we tarry here! We have to repel this attack on the ward and get back down there!"

Rovann understood her frustration. "Peace, Tiria. Everyone has their designated roles. We can't put all our efforts into saving a level that's already lost."

She glared at him, anger bright in her eyes. But after a moment, it faded. "I know, I know. But if we lose the second level, what then?"

"We retreat to the third. And the fourth after that, and the fifth," he spoke calmly, trying to impart steel into his words.

Tiria ran a spectral hand across her brow. Then she let out a deep sigh. "And there we have one of the many reasons why you are Lord First. You're right, of course. Forgive me, fighting for my life does strange things to my temperament."

Rovann snorted a laugh. "I've sent Falwin to ferret out the enemy mages within the city. They ought to—"

He trailed off as a wave of force suddenly rippled through his astral being, as though a cold wind sprang up before suddenly dissipating again. As it subsided Rovann felt a sudden change in the atmosphere.

"Well done, Falwin," he breathed, recognizing the release of power following the death of a mage. "He did it! Remind me to give that man a big fat kiss when I see him!"

Tiria raised an eyebrow. "Am I to take it he found those enemy mages?"

"Yes. Look." He pointed to the ward. Already, the oily

skein on its surface was beginning to dissipate, leaving a clear, shimmering bubble once more. "They'll have to come at us from outside the ward, now." Raising his voice, he shouted, "Everyone, to your position. They'll attack soon now Falwin's destroyed those inside the city."

The defenders took up pre-arranged places on the edge of a defensive circle, each mage no more than ten meters from the next. In this way, they could combine their strength and aid each other if needed.

Rovann and Tiria took up their positions in the center of the circle, like the hub of a giant wheel. They went still. Waiting.

The astral form of an enemy mage floated closer, stopping just the other side of the shimmering ward. She appeared young, too young to be leading such forces, and she stared at Rovann with emotionless eyes before issuing a curt command to one of the mages gathered behind her. The man nodded then gestured to three others who dropped out of formation and disappeared into the west.

Tiria growled. "I don't like the look of that. Where are they going?"

Rovann shook his head and uneasiness churned in his belly.

"Rovann!" shouted Tiria suddenly. "Look!"

Twenty or so enemy mages had moved wide to take up positions around the defender's circle. Some dropped so low onto the astral they almost touched the ground.

"What are they doing?"

"They know we're strong as long as we can hold this circle. With our power combined we can maintain this ward indefinitely. I'm guessing they'll attack from above and below as well as from the sides. They expect to find our weak points."

Tiria smiled grimly. "Idiots. Do they think us children? Let them come. We'll show them the price of their damned arrogance!"

Rovann dropped out of the center of the circle of defenders and took up position directly below it, hovering just above Tyrlindon's highest tower. In response, Tiria rose higher, halting above Rovann on the upper levels of the astral plane. What resulted was a formation like a spinning top: Rovann at the bottom, Tiria at the top and the students and remaining members of the Council forming a rim around the center.

They took up position just in time. There was no signal. No call to attack. No trumpets blaring. But between one heartbeat and the next, the enemy mages burst into life, calling forth power in a blazing whirl of colors. They bombarded the ward with violent Song-Spells that were designed to tear the ward to shreds. Rovann yelled words of encouragement to his companions as they repelled the attacks, using the Eorthe to strengthen the ward wherever it was struck.

Rovann glanced up and saw, with a juddering shock, that Tiria was not faring well. She had linked herself to the ward to be better able to defend it and the force of the assaults there were rattling her astral form, buffeting her this way and that as though she was a leaf in the breeze, despite her attempts to deflect the blows before they reached the ward. Enemy mages converged on her, like scavengers around a wounded predator.

"Tiria!" Rovann bellowed.

Then the Third's power guttered out and she floated aimlessly, so close to the ward that the shockwave of an attack would likely rip her to pieces. Rovann was too far away to intervene. He could only watch in horror as ten or more enemy mages gathered a wave of Chaos around them, ready to smash through the ward and rend Tiria's astral form.

But then, when the mages were so close they had no time for retreat, Tiria's hand shot out and her astral fingers touched the ward. Energy erupted outwards. She was not an adept of the Eorthe like Syrie but Tiria's grasp of weaving the Realms was second only to Rovann himself. She sent a pulse of Eorthic power tinged with Fire into the ward. It flared out like an erupting volcano, engulfing the astral forms of the enemy mages and shredding them in a maelstrom of Fire. They burned until there was nothing left but wisps of pale smoke.

Tiria glanced down at Rovann and winked.

The students cheered and Rovann allowed himself a small smile of triumph. If everyone could fight like Tiria, they stood a chance. Seeing the Third's success Earth Master Arnulf, supported by two of the stronger fourth year students, launched a counter-attack of his own. He wove a net of twisting golden strands of Eorthe, opened a gate through the ward, and threw it over three enemy mages. The renegades yelped in surprise as the net settled over them and pulled tight, like a fishing net on a catch. With a shouted word, Arnulf set the net afire, engulfing those within.

After a few moments, the young woman who seemed to be the Songmaker's commander bellowed the retreat and the enemy mages moved back, floating several hundred feet away.

"What are they doing?" Tiria called.

Rovann turned slowly around in a circle, taking in the hovering forms. "Waiting."

"For what?"

Below, Falwin and his students appeared from the maze of Tyrlindon's streets and sped toward Rovann.

"What's going on?" The big man growled. "How come they've pulled back? And what the bloody hell is that racket?"

Rovann cocked his head, listening. The Songmaker's singing continued unabated, but that wasn't what Falwin was referring to. Beneath the music was another sound, a set of discordant notes that made his teeth rattle. It was the sound of bells, but nothing like the beautiful harmonies that signaled a manifestation of Aethyr. No, this was wild, dark, a clashing of sound that was utterly terrifying.

Ice filled Rovann's veins. "They're coming," he whispered.

Falwin's mouth formed the word 'who' but before he could speak, the border of the Realm of Earth high above began to glow. The silver arc became bright, like molten metal. It blazed brighter, brighter, brighter …then with a burst of incandescent light and a shockwave that rolled through the sky like thunder, it shattered.

"Realms save us," whispered Falwin, pointing with a shaking hand. "What is that?"

Shadowy shapes came pouring through the broken border. They looked like a flock of birds; carrion crows come to feast on the souls of the living. But they were not birds. Vaguely human in shape, only taller and thinner, they had black tattered wings, a perverse parody of the angels of Aethyr. So many. How could there be so many? They washed the sky with shadow, blocking out the light.

Tiria rushed toward Rovann, her eyes wide with terror. "How is this possible? The Sluargh have come! Demons invade the Realm of Earth! Is the Outer Darkness broken?"

The dark figures drew nearer, spreading across the sky

like some vast, cankerous fungus, encircling Tyrlindon. But they didn't attack. They just waited, slowly rising and falling with the cadence of the Songmaker's song as though controlled by his music.

Then they began to sing, joining with Leo's song.

Rovann stared, mouth hanging open in shock. Their voices were beautiful. A vast, sweeping harmony filled the astral plane, undulating in piercing counter-point to the Songmaker's melody.

The song was a message, a plea...

And something responded. From beneath Tyrlindon a boom rocked the plateau and a voice louder than any thunder clap rolled across the sky.

FREE ME!

The shockwave of the cry slammed into the ward with the force of an explosion. The shimmering bubble flickered and began to dissipate. The enemy mages saw their chance and rushed forward to attack the Council.

Turmoil erupted. Tiria shouted, "To me! To me!" and Falwin bellowed, "Form up! Don't let them break your formation!"

The circle of mages buckled as enemies attacked from all sides. They could not strengthen the ailing ward and defend themselves at the same time.

"Fall back! Fall back!" Rovann called desperately.

The Second and Third of the Council followed his lead as he wove a spell to control the movements of the astral tides. The three of them called in a wild gale, and turned it on the enemy mages. It gathered up their spirit forms and hurled them away like dust blown on a wind. It disrupted their attack just long enough for the students and Council members to drop back to Tyrlindon and the safety of their bodies.

Rovann opened his eyes to the dimness of the attic of *The Laughing Frog*. Dust motes danced in a shaft of light from the window. From nearby came the sounds of fighting and the hubbub of frightened voices. Rubbing his forehead, he pushed himself into a sitting position.

"My lord?" asked Tom, rushing over from his position by the door. "What's happened?" The lad's face was taut with fear. "There's something...I feel..."

Rovann placed his hand on Tom's shoulder. "Peace, all will be explained."

Around the room, the others began to open their eyes.

Rovann addressed them grimly. "We can't hold the ward. Tiria, find Captain Tyan and order a retreat. Get everyone back to the top two levels. Once everyone has retreated, Falwin and I will shrink the ward to cover those two levels only. If it's smaller, it won't take so much power. There's a chance we can hold."

He didn't bother to tell her how slim he thought that chance was. Tiria's expression said it all. The Lord First was ordering a withdrawal, effectively surrendering most of the city. She swallowed thickly and then nodded.

"Everyone else, support Tiria in the evacuation then retreat to the top levels. Guard the palace and ensure King William and Prince Owen are safe."

With empty expressions the others nodded and filed from the room, leaving only Rovann and Falwin behind.

The Second of the Council raised an eyebrow. "Well," he said, running a hand over his bald scalp. "I never thought I'd see this day. Still, look at it this way—it can't get any worse can it?"

Rovann looked at him sharply. *Can't it, Falwin?* he thought. *Are you sure?*

He felt bone-weary. Every muscle in his body ached. His

body longed for sleep but he pushed his fatigue aside ruthlessly. "Right, we've got a ward to secure. Shall we get started?"

Chapter Sixteen

Maegwin marched down the street beside General Shallon. The once-bustling first level of Tyrlindon had become a ghost town. The only living things she saw were stray dogs that slunk off into alleyways when they appeared.

A restless energy made Maegwin's senses tingle. It came from Leo's song which wafted on the air, rising and falling, swirling in a crescendo of notes that seemed to carry some message just beyond understanding. The beauty of the song almost brought her to tears and she knew the troops felt it too. They walked a little taller, marched a little quicker, looked more determined than ever.

Well done, Leo, she thought.

They'd needed this boost to morale. Shallon's forces had paid dearly for breaking into the city. Mage Syrie and Sergeant Hannel had fought for every inch of ground.

A flash of anger shot through Maegwin at the memory of the diminutive Earth adept. Who would have imagined such a fragile creature could be capable of such destruction? Yet, the dark-haired woman had used the Eorthe in ways that left Maegwin staggered. She'd filled soldiers' lungs with sand, ripped holes in the ground that swallowed them up, dragged great granite boulders from the earth that crushed men where they stood.

And then the bitch had escaped.

Syrie's opposition had been a delaying tactic. As soon as the first level had been safely evacuated, Syrie, Hannel and their forces had evaporated into the winding streets of Tyrlindon like a crew of street thieves. It left Maegwin seething with frustration.

"General! My lady!" Maegwin looked up to see a scout running toward them. The young lad skidded to a halt three paces away and sucked breaths through his nose. "Just ahead...they're... they're..."

"What is it, man?" Shallon snapped. "Catch your breath and then speak."

The soldier nodded, stood with his hands on his knees, panting, then continued. "The second level gates are barred but no soldiers man the walls. The defenders are retreating from the second level as well."

"What? How do you know this?"

"The call went up about an hour ago. We didn't realize what it was at first so the captain sent scouts along the base of the wall to east and west. They reported the same thing. All the gates closed but nobody patrolling the walls or the watchtowers. Three scouts scaled the wall and found the second level as deserted as this one. The defenders are pulling back."

Maegwin went still, allowing this news to sink in. Retreating? She could imagine nothing that would make Rovann and the Council of Mages give up. They would die defending Tyrlindon.

"This might be a trap," she said. "Trying to lure us into letting down our guard."

General Shallon nodded. "I agree." He whirled to one of his lieutenants. "Send infantry with battering rams against the second level gates but have each battalion covered by archers. Post crossbowmen at every intersection and have them train their weapons on the wall. Be on the lookout for any nasty surprises they might have prepared for us."

The man nodded, saluted and hurried away. Maegwin took a deep breath and tried to still her churning thoughts. Why? Why would Rovann retreat? She closed her eyes, shutting out all sound, and concentrated. Leo's song hung in the air but beneath it she detected something else, a second, deeper song that had joined with Leo's but was undetectable on the physical plane.

Just as Rovann had once taught her, she left her body and rose onto the astral plain. A gasp of shock ripped from her mouth at what she saw. Shapes filled the sky beyond the shimmering bubble of Tyrlindon's ward. The Sluargh, Maegwin realized, the Unforgiven Dead that dwell in the Outer Darkness.

And they were singing.

Maegwin gazed at them in wonder, feeling their song tugging at her soul. They sang of revenge, retribution, anger. Their hunger spoke of a perfection that she struggled to match. They were the Dark Goddess's soldiers, come to do her bidding. Come to complete the Unraveling. Come to help their high priestess.

She opened her eyes, finding herself once more on the dusty street. "Quickly!" she barked. "We have the advantage. We mustn't squander it. Come on!"

She marched off, and with a curse, General Shallon

hurried to catch up. In several hundred yards they reached the first of the entrances to the second level. The massive iron-studded gates stood closed. Craning her head back, Maegwin looked up at the wall, searching for hidden defenders. Just as the scout had reported, she saw nobody.

Along the street Shallon's units were stationed in tight formations. Archers and crossbowmen knelt in lines, weapons trained on the parapet that spanned the wall, protecting the infantry below. A battering ram had already been brought up from the plain and now a group of heavily shielded men were busy wrestling it into position.

Maegwin watched in tense silence. Any moment she expected defenders to appear atop the wall and rain down magecraft on the soldiers. But they didn't.

With a roar of defiance, those carrying the battering ram surged forward. The iron-shod tip of the ram thumped into the gate with an ear-wrenching crunch. Maegwin scanned the wall, eyes darting right and left. Still no attack came. The men pulled back and readied the ram for another pass. It impacted with a boom. Then another. And another. As the ram struck the gate again, it finally gave way and the wood splintered with an almighty groan. The soldiers sent up a ragged cheer and Maegwin permitted herself a small smile of triumph.

I'm coming, Rovann, she thought. *I'm almost upon you. Can you feel me getting closer?*

"Forward!" General Shallon bellowed. "Get those gates open and secure the area. We're dealing with mages, remember. Expect anything!"

A squad of heavy infantry moved forward. The big men set their shoulders to the broken gate and heaved. The thick timber inched forward, the hinges squealing, until finally it swung wide. Maegwin got her first glimpse of Tyrlindon's second level.

What met her eyes was a narrow street that carried on up the hill toward the next level. It was bordered on each side by rickety buildings with second stories that tilted together crazily. A thin strip of sky showed between the roofs above, casting the street into shadow.

The troops moved in cautiously. Maegwin found her heartbeat quickening, despite the soothing power of Leo's song.

As the first soldier stepped beneath the gate's lintel an explosion turned the world white.

Force slammed into Maegwin, lifting her from her feet and tossing her through the air as though she was made of sticks. There was a crunch and everything went black.

She awoke to roaring pain in her skull. It was like hot knives were being pushed into her brain. She rolled onto her side and retched into the dirt, emptying the contents of her stomach onto the muddy street. Spitting out the acid bile, she gritted her teeth, got her feet under her and, slowly, painstakingly, forced herself to stand. Little dots of light danced in front of her eyes and she staggered, only catching herself from falling by grabbing hold of a jagged piece of wall. With a moan, she squeezed her eyes shut, pressing the heels of her hands against her temples until the dizziness began to ebb.

When she opened them again, she started in shock. For maybe half a mile in all directions, Tyrlindon had been flattened. Broken buildings, toppled towers, cracked streets all met her eye. It was a scene of utter devastation. Except for the wall, she realized. The second level wall stood tall and unmarred.

Mages, she thought. *Why didn't we check for traps?*

Bodies littered the street. Bile rose in Maegwin's throat again and she swallowed thickly. She turned, searching the rubble until she saw the edge of a tell-tale blue cloak fluttering beneath a chunk of masonry.

She staggered over and went to her knees in the mud. General Shallon lay on his back, pinned under a great lump of stone. His eyes were wide, staring upwards. There was a smile on his face.

"General?" Maegwin said. "General?"

Slowly, his gaze swiveled to hers. "Holy Mother," he whispered. The effort sent a stream of blood trickling from his mouth. "I can see Her. I can see Our Lady."

"Hold on," Maegwin replied. "I'll get you out of there."

The general caught her arm. "No. It's too late. I'm leaving. Our Lady is waiting. Can't you hear Her?" His eyes moved upwards to stare into the sky once more. "Listen," he whispered. "Listen."

Then his grip went slack and his breath hissed out of his chest in one final rush.

With a trembling hand, Maegwin reached out and closed the general's eyes. "May Sho-La guide you to the One Light," she murmured.

I can feel you close, my daughter.

Maegwin's head whipped round at the sudden voice. It was so clear it could have been right beside her.

Listen, General Shallon had told her with his dying breath. *Listen.*

Maegwin closed her eyes. *Mistress? Is that you?*

Come to me, Maegwin, said the Dark Goddess. *The time is almost here. Your time is almost here. Free me.*

How? Where are you?

You already know.

She opened her eyes. Her heartbeat quickened. She

gazed down at the general for a moment and then stood. Around her, survivors were dragging themselves from the rubble, climbing to their feet. She spotted Shallon's lieutenant leaning on a wall as he cradled a broken arm against his chest.

"Lieutenant," she said, striding over. "You're in charge now. Send messengers to the Songmaker and to Maldric Hounsey. Warn them to be careful. No doubt there are similar surprises waiting at the other gates.

The man nodded wearily. "But where are you going?"

She raised her eyes, gazing up the hill toward the heart of the city. "Where I should have gone from the start."

Without waiting for his reply she jogged away, through the shattered gate— safe now the ward had been triggered —and up the street. At the end she found an intersection with five streets radiating off like the spokes of a wheel. Without hesitating, she took one of the streets and broke into a run. She was sure of her way. It was like being drawn to a magnet.

As she ran, a smile spread across her face. At last. At last she would free her mistress.

Rovann opened his eyes. His blurred vision sharpened a second before pain shot through this body, so intense it made him arch his back and clench his fists into the bed sheets by his sides.

"Easy," a voice said. "Drink this. It will pass in a moment."

Something was pressed against his mouth and he swallowed reflexively. A bitter taste flooded across his tongue and dribbled down his throat. In only moments, the pain began to ease. He lay back, gasping and then slowly moved his head to the side to take in his surroundings. He was lying on a bed, one of many narrow cots that stretched in ordered lines along the wall. Windows sat high up, letting in early evening sunlight. He realized he was in the college infirmary.

Falwin was struggling out of bed a few paces away, bellowing at a doctor trying to stop him. "Out of my way, man! Don't you know I've got a city to save?"

"I'm grateful I'm not tending Falwin," said a voice.

Rovann was surprised to find King William sitting in a chair by his bedside, holding Rovann's cup.

The king seemed to have aged a lifetime in the last few days. Dark circles ringed his eyes, making them seem like black pits. Already lean, the king had lost weight, and now his skin hung sallow against the lines of his skull.

"Your Majesty?" Rovann croaked. "What happened?"

Memories suddenly exploded on him. Losing the first level. Struggling to hold the ward against enemy mages. The shattering of the border of the Realm of Earth. The arrival of demons of Chaos. Ordering the retreat to the upper levels. He and Falwin flinging power around in a wild maelstrom, holding back the enemy while the retreat was organized. Somebody—Lady and Tallo?—picking him up and carrying him out as *The Laughing Frog* went up in flames.

He struggled onto his elbows "Where are the attackers? Are we holding? Is the ward intact?"

"Peace," King William said in a hoarse voice, worn out by too much shouting. "We're holding. You were evacuated here, along with everyone else at your safe house."

"The evacuation! We had so little time. How many people were lost? What about Syrie and Hannel? Did they make it through?"

The king frowned. "What do you think we've been doing here in Tyrlindon while you were off in the east? Sitting on our behinds, just watching Hounsey's army?" He smiled to soften his words. "We've had a lot of time to prepare. We've had plans in place for many months, should the worst happen." He glanced at the window although nothing could be seen beyond but the slowly darkening sky. "And the worst did happen. Most of the city's citizens were safely brought to the inner levels. Civilians have been billeted in houses, inns, temples—anywhere able to take them. Some have even been sent into the crypts below the city."

"How cozy," Rovann murmured.

"Quite. Still, they may turn out to be the safest of all. If the Songmaker breaks through there's a chance he won't think to search them."

Rovann looked at the king sharply. He didn't like the note of resignation in his sovereign's voice. "And the Council? Are they holding the ward?"

The king nodded. "It now covers only the top two levels, just as you ordered. Is it true, Rovann? Has the Realm of Earth cracked? Do we face demons now as well as the Songmaker and his minions?"

A chill walked down Rovann's spine as he remembered the dark shapes filling the astral plane over Tyrlindon. How could he hope to defeat such creatures? "Yes, it's true."

The king went very still. "You know what they've come for?"

"I know."

"Then you may soon have to do what we discussed."

Rovann held the king's gaze, unable to look away. He knew what the king was referring to. In his mind's eye he saw a city teeming with thousands of lives, bright with promise. Then he saw that same city destroyed, everyone dead, that promise wiped out in an instant.

Duty? Istra's voice suddenly spoke in his memory. *Remember that? You've always done your duty, Rovann. Will you abandon it now? When it is most needed?*

He shook his head, clearing his thoughts. "It won't come to that," he stated with more confidence than he felt. "We'll find another way."

The king held his gaze for a moment, seemed about to say something, and then changed his mind. "Perhaps. Are you strong enough to stand?"

Rovann nodded then clambered out of bed, steadying himself on the king's arm as a wave of dizziness roiled through him. When it passed he followed the king from the infirmary.

They strode purposefully through the college. Most rooms had been turned into makeshift hospitals and the moans of the wounded and dying echoed through the corridors. Rovann steeled himself and hurried on. At length they reached the center of the college and began to climb a set of spiraling steps up the tower.

At the top they stepped onto a large circular space open to the air with only a low parapet around the outside. The tower was normally used for astrological observation. Now it was being used for observation of a different kind. Captain Tyan, Sergeant Hannel, Syrie and Falwin leaned on the wall, gazing out on the city. Prince Owen waited patiently by the stairs. He nodded to his father when he emerged then took Rovann's arm and helped him over to the wall.

Down in Tyrlindon, Rovann saw torches being lit against the encroaching night. It seemed as though he was surrounded by a sea of fire. The dancing flames illuminated the night, making it seem as bright as day. Drums, alarm calls and the noise of fighting echoed from the lower levels. The garrison atop the wall to the sixth level had been tripled so that it bristled with spearmen, crossbowmen and archers. The Songmaker's army would have a hard time getting through.

"Captain Tyan, report," King William said quietly.

The soldier saluted crisply. "The defenses of the sixth and seventh levels are holding. If this was a normal battle without magecraft to contend with, I believe we could hold them out of the inner levels indefinitely. Our supplies are good. We have wells for water. We could let them starve outside the walls." He rubbed his chin. "But we'd all be dead of disease long before then. We have almost the entire population of the city crammed together in the inner levels. It won't take long for sanitation to fail. When that happens, illness will follow."

The king nodded slowly. "We've trebled the capacity of the infirmaries. I have teams of engineers on standby to deal with any sanitation problems. We'll do what we can."

"Begging your pardon, Your Majesty," Captain Tyan continued, "I said if this was normal battle. It's not. When their mages attack I don't know how we'll hold them off."

"The ward," Syrie answered. "It's holding. The Council will counter anything they dare to throw at us."

"For how long?" Tyan persisted. "We've effectively trapped ourselves here. There's nobody coming to lift this siege. If we don't find a way to beat them back, we're finished."

The captain's words were blunt and honest. And he was right. Most of the city had been abandoned to the invaders. Should they break into the inner levels, what was left for the defenders? There was nowhere else to run.

Prince Owen suddenly slammed his fist into the wall. "I won't have it," he growled. "There must be more we can do. I won't wait here like a rat in a trap!"

Before his blinding Prince Owen had been called the Hawk, named for the elite fighting unit he led. Rovann had almost forgotten how fierce the prince could be.

"What do you suggest?" King William asked.

"Ride out," the prince replied, turning to face his father. "Ride out and meet them head on. Make them pay dearly for every inch of Tyrlindon they take."

"To what end?" Falwin barked. "For some vain attempt at glory that will just get you killed?"

Prince Owen's fists clenched at the Second's impertinence. "Falwin, I will make whatever choices I deem necessary."

"And throw your life away?" Falwin persisted, undaunted. "That would achieve precisely nothing!"

"So you would have me cower up here and wait for the end?"

"Yes! Standing by your people. Would you abandon them for your own vanity?"

The two men spun toward each other, Falwin's eyes flashing dangerously, the prince dropping into a fighting crouch. With a growl, King William stepped forward to intervene but before he could speak they all froze as a strange sound suddenly shattered the sky. It was a piercing cry, like that of a diving hawk. Rovann's heart thumped. He recognized that sound. He'd heard it before.

The hunting call of the Shinnar.

He spun to the parapet and stared out. From the horizon a dark stain was spilling across the plain, spreading toward Tyrlindon like ink. Like a tidal wave. Like something unstoppable.

"Give me a spyglass!" he snapped.

Captain Tyan passed over a leather tube and Rovann quickly pressed the glass to his eye. What he saw left him staggered.

A tide of Shinnar warriors, thousands upon thousands of them, were marching in tight, ordered ranks. Some were mounted on small, shaggy ponies. All carried spears, shields and bows. At the head of each company rode a shaman and even from this distance, Rovann could sense the power they had summoned. It was the Eorthe, untamed, primitive and wild. It shook the ground beneath them, making their approach rumble like an avalanche. But this was not the only wonder. On the Shinnar's flank raced another army, this one composed of strange, smoky creatures in numbers beyond counting. At its heard ran a great wolf.

Rovann's breath left him in a rush "Fenris," he breathed in awe. "Roamsford Edge has come. And so have the Shinnar."

"The Eorthe," Syrie said beside him. "It sings to me. I've never sensed it so strongly."

"What did I tell you?" bellowed Falwin with a laugh. "We're not finished yet! Not by a long shot! How do you like that, Songmaker, you bastard?"

A trumpet suddenly blared in the distance and a ripple went through the besieging forces. Like a great, lumbering beast, the Songmaker's army began to move, rearranging their lines to turn about and meet the threat coming upon them from behind.

For a moment there was stunned silence on the tower top. Then King William began bellowing orders. "Tyan, assemble as many men as you think can be spared from the defense. Have them mounted, armed and ready by the sixth level gate within a quarter bell. The Shinnar are giving us a

273

chance and we have to take it. We're going to carve our way through the enemy and retake the first level. We'll hit the Songmaker's forces and make them fight on two fronts."

"Aye, sir," Tyan saluted, a grin splitting his face.

Sergeant Hannel approached the king. "Permission to go with you, Your Majesty."

King William studied the sergeant. Hannel's eyes were flat and dead. He hadn't been the same man since his sister Hesha had been killed at Carrow Crossing. His expression suggested he had no intention of returning from this mission. King William paused for a long moment. Then he nodded.

"Count me in as well," Falwin growled. "You'll need someone to guard against rogue mages."

The king opened his mouth as if to object but then appeared to think better of it. "You'll be an asset, Falwin."

The Second of the Council snorted. "I'll be scared out of my bloody wits is what I'll be. Still, should be fun, eh?"

Syrie suddenly knelt before the king. "Your Majesty, I beg you not to do this. Send another in your stead. Tyrlindon needs its king."

A smile curled King William's mouth, softening the hard lines of his face. He raised Syrie to her feet. "Ah, I chose well in you, Syrie de Montrey. You have repaid my faith ten times over."

Syrie glanced down at the stump of her right hand, a permanent reminder that King William had plucked her from life as a thief on Tyrlindon's streets.

"I must go, Syrie. You will stay here and aid the King's Mage," the king instructed her.

She nodded silently.

King William approached Prince Owen. The two men

regarded each other in silence. Something seemed to pass between them and at length the prince shrugged.

"I know what you're going to say," Prince Owen said. "That I can't ride with you. That I must remain behind."

"Is that such an onerous duty? At the last, everything may come down to you."

Prince Owen cocked his head, regarding his father, despite the blindfold that covered his eyes. "Good hunting."

The two men gripped forearms and Rovann was taken with a sudden sense of foreboding. It looked like a final goodbye.

The king turned to him. "Hold my city. Do whatever you must, King's Mage."

"I will, my lord." *And I'll do what's required, should it come to that.*

King William held out his hand and Rovann clasped it, forearm to forearm. Then the king spun away, leading his party from the tower top.

Rovann sucked in a breath. "My prince, I ask that you retire to the palace. We can't guard you and fight at the same time."

Prince Owen's face folded into a scowl as if he was about to argue but then he nodded. Without a word he turned and disappeared down the steps. Rovann was left alone with Syrie on the tower top.

The Earth adept watched him, her expression grim. "You know the Shinnar and the wights can't save us. Not with what's waiting up there."

Rovann nodded. "I know. Shall we?"

Rovann sank into a sitting position and Syrie followed his lead. With his back pressed against the cool stone of the wall, Rovann closed his eyes and slowed his breathing. A moment passed, then another, then he was rising up from his body onto the astral plane, Syrie beside him.

Hold my city, the king had commanded.

Trouble was, he had no idea how to do that. The ward was now a tiny, shimmering bubble, covering only the top two levels of Tyrlindon. Beyond it, as far as the eye could see, the sky was filled with the Sluargh, the Unforgiven Dead. Creatures of the Outer Darkness, the Realm of Chaos, come to destroy the Realm of Earth. They hovered just outside the ward, their voices filling the astral plain with a beautiful, haunting song. It intertwined with Leo's voice, a song without words. But for their singing, the Sluargh were motionless and Rovann wondered what they were waiting for. Some signal from the Songmaker perhaps?

"I wish they would attack, curse them!" Syrie hissed. "I would rather fight than wait here like a damned idiot!"

"What are you waiting for?" Rovann said, almost to himself.

"They are waiting for us," said a voice by his ear. "They are waiting for the Appointed Time. This time, general."

With a shocked yelp, Rovann spun. Beside him floated a tall, shining figure. It was so bright he couldn't see its face but he had the impression of deep silver eyes, filled with endless compassion. From its shoulders rose white, magnificent wings.

Rovann's eyes widened. The sky was filling with angels.

Time stopped. All thought vanished. The remnants of Rovann's consciousness struggled to put together these events. How had the angels come here? The Realm of Aethyr had been closed...

The Unraveling. Of course.

He swallowed thickly. Closed his eyes. Opened them again.

"How? What?" he gasped, unable to frame a coherent question.

Then a sound rolled over him, cutting off his attempt at speech. It was the sound of laughter. It echoed from below Tyrlindon, from deep within the bedrock on which the city was built.

I knew you would come, a voice boomed across the astral plane. *You must always meddle in things that don't concern you. Go back to the Aethyr and await your slow deaths.*

"It is the Appointed Time," replied the angel by Rovann's side. "Now begins the Ending and we have come to stand against you in defense of the One Light."

I will destroy you if you stay.

The angel nodded. "Perhaps."

You cannot comprehend the passions that move me, the voice grated. *Without me you are nothing. Without me, the universe would be without meaning. My generals are stronger than yours. They will defeat you and free me.*

Generals? Rovann thought. *Leo and Maegwin?*

My generals are stronger than yours. Yours. A shiver ran through him as comprehension dawned. The angel had addressed him as 'general'. Tanyaka of Fire had always called him 'Warrior of the Realms.'

The angel turned shining eyes on him. "Yes," it said as if reading Rovann's thoughts. "It is the Appointed Time. Will you lead us, Warrior of the Realms?"

Rovann looked down at the physical plane where the people of Amaury spent their lives against the enemy. He looked out beyond the tattered border of the Realm of Earth to where Tanyaka and her people battled to save the Realm of Fire, to where Water nymphs and mermaids fought savagely to protect the Realm of Water, to where spirits of wind and cloud struggled to keep demons from devouring the Realm of Air. And if the Sluargh were not stopped, they would begin an assault on the One Light itself.

General. It is time.

Will you always be a slave to duty? Istra used to ask him. He had always thought it was his duty to King William and the people of Amaury that had prevented him from giving himself wholly to her. But perhaps he'd been wrong. Perhaps it had been something else that bound him all along, a duty he could not escape.

King's Mage. First of the Council of Mages. The Slayer of Sandford Moor. They were all names that belonged to him. Warrior of the Realms.

He scrubbed astral fingers through his hair. "Yes," he said. "I will lead you."

The angel nodded. "As it must be." It reached out a shining hand and gripped his forearm in a warrior's handshake. At the touch, Rovann was engulfed in thought and memory.

He saw the creation of the universe. He saw the Realms being born from the One Light. He saw the fall of Shel-Masa the Destroyer, the Dark Goddess of destruction. He saw her and her mate sealed into prisons beyond time, beyond the Realms.

The angels' thoughts were his. Their passions were his. He relaxed all restraint. The power of Aethyr roared through him, obliterating everything but his singular purpose. In an instant he became connected to the multitude of angels filling the sky.

In a million sparkling voices they cried, "We follow you, Warrior of the Realms!"

He turned to Syrie who floated beside him, wide-eyed

with awe. "Lower the ward," he said. "It can do nothing now."

She closed her eyes, relaying commands to those students and mages anchoring the ward below. After a moment, it wavered and vanished. Syrie opened her eyes and swallowed thickly. "It's done."

Rovann nodded then turned to regard the angel at his side. It gazed at him steadily, waiting. He raised a fist. "It is the Appointed Time!" he bellowed in a voice that shook the sky. "We fight!"

The army of angels drew gleaming swords. In one hand each held a trident so bright it could have been forged from lightning. Golden armor encased their glowing bodies and their shining eyes burned with fierce determination.

The air in front of Rovann suddenly shimmered then coalesced into the figure of a man. A lustrous aura burned around him, almost as bright as the angels. Within the shimmering penumbra, Rovann recognized the grinning face of Leo March, the Songmaker. His astral hands clasped a lute which he was playing as he sang.

As he approached Rovann, he fell silent and let the lute dangle from one hand. The sudden silence that filled the astral seemed ghostly. Rovann waited, his army of angels at his back, whilst Leo moved to within a few paces, his own army of demons and renegade mages behind him. Two forces. It would only take a word for carnage to begin.

Leo stared at Rovann for a moment before his face broke into a boyish grin "Well, here we are then. Now we'll see who's the best, won't we?" His voice trembled with excitement.

"Is this a game to you, Leo?" Rovann rasped.

The minstrel pressed a hand to his heart as though wounded. "You do me an injustice, Rovann. Your words cut to the bone!" He grinned again. "Of course it's a game! What else would this be? It's chess, isn't it? All the pieces are in place but who will reach checkmate first?"

A growl escaped Rovann's throat. "Get away from me."

Leo threw back his head and cackled. He backed off and then opened his arms wide. He began to sing again, this time with a hint of command in the sound. Behind him, his demons drew swords of smoky glass and formed into columns.

The sun was setting. It cast crimson rays over the Realm of Earth. The clouds were tall and impossibly white, banked up in great gleaming towers which reflected the sunlight, washing the sky with pink and purple and gold. It was beautiful.

The Songmaker sang a high note and his demons rushed forward.

Rovann didn't speak. Instead, he sent out a wave of Aetheric power, relaying commands to his soldiers as quickly as thought. The angels obeyed, forming into companies led by a lieutenant. They hurtled to intercept the demons and the two armies met with a clash of weapons that rang out across the astral, sending shockwaves through the Realms. Swords of glass and fire, tridents of lightning and thunder crashed against each other. Angels' wings cut the sky. Demon hands rose and fell.

The Songmaker watched the battle with delight. The song dripped from his lips, notes sprang from his lute. Then he raised a hand and curled his fingers into a fist. At this signal, his revenant mages lurched into motion like slaves yanked on a chain.

They moved into a wedge formation and rushed across the astral toward Rovann and Syrie, a wave of Chaotic sorcery boiling ahead of them. Syrie bellowed in fury. The

Eorthe flashed out in a coruscating wave and the Chaotic power was consumed.

"Do you want more?" Syrie shrieked, brandishing the stump of her arm at them. "Come and get it, you traitorous bastards!"

The battle was raging on three fronts now. Below, on the physical plane, Rovann saw King William's forces fighting their way through the city, whilst further out Kandar's Shinnar warriors skirmished with Hounsey's soldiers. On the lower levels of the astral he and Syrie faced the Song-maker's revenant mages.

And on the upper astral tides, where the Realm of Earth bled out into the universe, the angels of the Aethyr fought the Unforgiven Dead of the Outer Darkness.

Rovann spun, trying to keep everything in view. His third company of angels cornered a group of demons. Molten swords flashed and tridents pierced deep into demons' bodies. The Sluargh howled and struggled to escape but were held fast on the barbed tips of the tridents. They fizzed and sizzled until there was nothing left but a faint smoke on the astral.

General, they're moving onto the lower astral, one of his angels thought to him. *They mean to attack you and possibly those on the physical plane below. What are your orders?*

Follow them, he answered. *Take your company into the lower astral and send a second to hide in the clouds. When they come close enough, attack from both sides. I will fight them from below.*

Yes, general.

A company concealed themselves within a bank of cloud whilst another pursued a host of demons who were dropping down through the sky like a flock of black birds, closing in on his and Syrie's position.

One of the demons spotted the angels rushing to intercept and raised its hand to signal a halt. The company slewed around to face them. The two forces met with a rumble that rolled across the sky like thunder. Swords of glass rose and fell. Magnificent wings became red with blood. Silver eyes dimmed with pain.

Then a blaring of trumpets rang out. The reserve company rushed out of the cloud bank and closed on the demons. A thrashing melee blotted out the stars and for a while the sky was dark with carnage and bloodshed. The leader of the first company battled with the demon lieutenant, sword and trident whirling so fast they left mirages in the air. The concussion of their blades as they clashed together sent shockwaves outwards that buffeted Rovann's astral form as though he was a leaf on the breeze.

The angel's trident ripped through the demon's neck in a spurt of black gore and the bulbous head went flying off. But the decapitated corpse raised its smoky sword and punched the blade through the angel's chest. The tinkling of bells rang through the astral and the angel died in a blast of white light.

Rovann pressed his lips together, steeling himself against the pain of the angel's loss.

Return to the upper astral, he commanded his angels. *The battle is heavy there.*

The Songmaker had formed his companies into wedges. Each demon rested its smoky sword on the shoulder of the one in front, focusing their energy to the apex where a lieutenant wielded a massive two-handed great sword with a blade made from red glass.

Angels converged on the wedges, slashing at the demons and stabbing them with their tridents. But to no avail. The demons had used their formation to form a shield that protected them from the angels' attack.

One angel broke off and threw itself in front of a demon lieutenant. It spread its wings to either side, a glittering wall denying the demons' advance. The angel raised its sword and trident to strike but the demon lieutenant swung the massive red sword up to meet it. The great blade sliced through the angel's trident and the arm that held it, carrying on deep into the angel's body. An explosion of force rocked through the upper astral and waves rippled outwards like a stone dropped into a pond as the angel died.

Copy their tactics! Rovann ordered. *Combine your strength. Each company form a wedge. Use your tridents to focus power to your lieutenant.*

The lieutenant of each company took its place at the head of each wedge as they quickly formed up and then took up position, each company of angels rushing to meet a company of the Sluargh. To Rovann the sky looked like some giant game board with black and white pieces moving across it.

Like chess, the Songmaker had said.

Yes, only much more deadly.

"Rovann!" Syrie suddenly screamed. "King William! He's in trouble!"

Cursing, Rovann sped down through the astral toward Tyrlindon. He found King William's forces spilling out of the first level gates onto the plain. They'd managed to fight their way down through the occupied levels and had retaken the gates.

Out on the plain a battle raged: King William's men on one front, the Shinnar on the other and the Songmaker's army caught between. Dead men and horses littered the battlefield like discarded toys. The Songmaker's heavy horse had been annihilated, brought down by the king's cavalry.

Yet the cost had been terrible. Only a handful of the

king's cavalry remained, fighting valiantly through the center of the Songmaker's lines to try and link up with the Shinnar lines on the far side.

Within the knot of churning soldiers, the standard bearer, a young lad no more than fifteen, gripped the king's standard with bloody hands and stared around him with fearful eyes, sticking resolutely the side of King William's black destrier.

Beyond the charging group, a core of the Songmaker's infantryman faced down the approaching cavalry with long spears planted into the ground and interlocking shields to defend them.

A look of pure terror stretched the faces of the Songmaker's soldiers as they watched King William's forces bearing down on them.

Rovann paused. This was not the determined, resigned expression of trained soldiers. Some had soiled themselves. Some had closed their eyes, praying loudly. The halberds shook in terrified grips.

Sudden understanding sent a cold wave of dread rippling through him. These weren't soldiers. They were peasants and camp-followers, held in thrall to the Songmaker's will, forced to do his bidding. Rovann had seen this before, long ago on a bloody day at Sandford Moor. That day he'd not realized his error and he'd killed hundreds as a result. He couldn't let it happen again.

"Stop!" he bellowed at the king. "Break off your attack!"

But of course, they couldn't hear him. He was on the astral plane, they on the physical. His words had no more effect than the wind.

He watched, appalled, as a man threw himself toward a mounted knight armed with nothing more than the broken pole of a halberd. His ruddy face spoke more of working long days in the fields than of any military prowess. His eyes were full of terror, his skin bleached of all color, tears of despair streaming down his face. The man raised the sharp stake over his head and swung it in a wild stab at the knight's horse. The knight caught the pole on his shield and then took the farmer's head off with a mighty swing of his battle-ax.

It was Sanford Moor all over again. And Rovann was powerless to stop it.

Falwin, riding at the king's side, bellowed in fury and rained sorcery down on the soldiers. Great swathes were ripped through their lines but they didn't break and run. They couldn't.

Then, as if at an unheard command, the Songmaker's soldiers surged forward in an undisciplined rush, the pure weight of numbers pushing aside the knights around the king. King William and Falwin were suddenly surrounded by clinging arms that reached up, grasping at bridle, saddle, clothing. Their horses stumbled to their knees and the two men disappeared under a mass of heaving bodies.

A moment later a blast of Eorthic power flung their attackers away and King William and Falwin surged to their feet. Falwin, too exhausted to cast more sorcery, grabbed a morning-star from the bloody ground and smashed it into a soldier's face. His head exploded like a ripe melon.

The remnants of the king's cavalry fought to reach the king's side. Rovann saw Sergeant Hannel swinging his sword desperately, hacking and chopping as he fought. It was no good. The surging mass of humanity between them was too thick.

There was a sudden 'thwack' of a crossbow. The sound seemed unnaturally loud as it echoed in Rovann's ears. The missile whistled as it sped through the air. Rovann turned, seemingly in slow motion, and saw the bolt explode through King William's neck. The king's eyes went wide in shock. His body crumpled forward onto the blood-slicked ground. Falwin roared in fury, just as a sword-blade erupted from his chest. The big man spun and punched his attacker to the ground before collapsing beside the king.

The sounds and sights of battle receded. Rovann froze with mute horror. Filling his vision was the sight of King William and Falwin lying on the hard, blood-soaked ground.

Get up, he willed them. *Get up.*

But they didn't. Rovann watched as the light left their eyes and their chests, rose, fell, rose, fell. Then stilled.

"The king is dead!" the standard bearer cried. "The king is dead!"

"To me!" Sergeant Hannel bellowed. "Regroup!"

The mounted knights charged. The people around King William and Falwin were mercilessly cut down or trampled beneath the iron-shod hooves of the warhorses.

Sergeant Hannel was covered in blood so that he looked like some kind of red specter. When he fought his way through the press, he reined in and jumped from the saddle, kneeling in the bloody mud by Falwin and the king. He felt their necks for any sign of a pulse and then let out a string of curses that almost ignited the air. For a moment he sagged, head bowed. Then he straightened.

"Dresha, Fash, carry Falwin and King William back to Tyrlindon. The rest of you with me."

"What?" a soldier cried. "The king is dead! The battle is lost! We must retreat!"

Hannel waved his bloody sword at the soldier. "We still live and breathe don't we? Then the battle is not lost! The Shinnar are over there fighting their way to us. We'll obey our king's command! Now form up and follow me, curse you!"

He jumped onto his horse and yanked it around to face the enemy lines. With a roar he and his soldiers raced back into battle. Slowly, reverently, Falwin and the king were lifted onto horses and their bodies carried to Tyrlindon.

Rovann watched the soldiers ride away, feeling numb, detached.

General! What are your orders?

Clearing his thoughts, Rovann rose through the air to the upper astral. All across the sky Sluargh and angels were fighting furiously. The power they unleashed was terrifying. It ripped and buffeted Rovann as though it would tear him apart. How long could the Realm of Earth withstand such a cataclysm? How long before it tore?

He closed his eyes and connected his thoughts to his army. Their crystal voices deluged him.

Be careful. They're moving below you.

We see them. Fourth company, can you help us?

We're coming.

General, what do you wish of us?

Rovann gathered his thoughts and then opened his mouth to speak. But before he could utter a word, the Song-maker dropped suddenly from above him, seeming so large and luminescent, he dominated Rovann's sight.

"Did you really think you stood a chance of defeating me? The day will be mine!" he bellowed, moving close enough that Rovann could see the droplets of dark song that shivered in the air around him. "Listen! Can't you hear her?"

Rovann paused as a sound intruded on his senses. Someone was singing, but not Leo this time. It was a female voice, high and lilting, hauntingly beautiful.

When will you come back to me?
The road is long, the trail is cold,
The sun has gone, the day grows old
Oh, when will you come back to me?

The words were simple but the cadences were complex, made up of countless notes woven together. It was a voice trained by many long hours of singing the glory of a goddess, a voice trained to carry to the high, vaulted ceilings of a temple.

Rovann would have recognized the voice anywhere.

The Songmaker crowed. "Hear that, King's Mage? Didn't you wonder where Maegwin was? You poor blind idiot! She's found it! Do you hear me? She's found it!"

Chapter Seventeen

Maegwin peered cautiously around the corner. A long, opulent corridor stretched ahead of her. It was empty, just as she'd hoped. Checking quickly to left and right, she darted from her hiding place, keeping low and close to the wall as she padded along the thick crimson carpet.

"Who are you?"

Maegwin jumped at the authoritative voice that spoke behind her. Curse it! How had she not heard them approaching?

She sagged, letting her sword-point drop to the carpet as though she was giving up but then suddenly spun, swinging her blade around in a two-handed grip.

A tall, thick-set man caught her blade on his, his eyes going wide in surprise. He wore the uniform of the Royal Guard and the scar running across his nose marked him out as a veteran. His surprise lasted less than a heartbeat. Maegwin didn't even see the blow coming before his fist connected with her cheek, sending her staggering. Her face pressed into the carpet and for a moment, her vision went black. When it cleared, fury came with it. Ignoring the ringing in her ears, she levered herself to her hands and knees and glared up at the guard.

He was standing over her, sword pointing at her throat. "One chance. Who are you and why are you here?"

She didn't have time for this. With a snarl, she flung out her hand, singing one high, clear note. Chaos erupted from her outstretched hand. It tossed the guard aside as though he was a piece of wreckage. He collided with a pillar then collapsed to the floor, stunned or dead. Maegwin didn't care either way.

She climbed to her feet, listening for the sound of running feet. It wouldn't be long before others came, alerted by the noise. She had to get moving.

Sheathing her sword, she sprinted down the corridor and skidded round the corner, pelted down the next corridor, ignoring doors that flashed by on either side. She felt the pull of her mistress like a lodestone, drawing her on. She barely noticed the finery of the Royal Palace, just as she'd barely noticed anything around her as she'd made her way up through the city, scaling walls, hiding in alleys, mingling with crowds when she needed to so she wouldn't get noticed.

All the time getting closer, closer to her goal.

Finally she reached a vestibule where two large golden doors were closed. A black and white tile mosaic covered the floor and two guards stood outside the doors. She staggered to a halt, breath coming in ragged gasps.

The guards drew their swords and one of them started toward her menacingly. "State your business!" he bellowed.

Maegwin straightened. From beyond the door she sensed a pulsing of power and she knew she'd found what she was looking for.

"Stand aside," she rasped. "Get out of my way and I'll not hurt you."

The guard didn't even pause. "State your business!" He was only three paces from her now and held his sword as though he planned to run her through.

Maegwin threw her arms wide and sang.

> When will you come back to me?
> The road is cold the day is old,
> When will you come back to me?

A maelstrom whipped into the vestibule. The golden doors burst inwards and the two guards yelped as they were thrown aside, bones cracking as they thumped into the walls and then lay still.

Maegwin didn't even spare them a glance as she strode through the doors into what she assumed was one of the king's council chambers. She moved purposefully over to a tapestry, yanked it aside and pulled the lever hidden behind. A section of the floor slid to one side with a low grating sound and she found herself at the top of a stone staircase, looking down into darkness.

Bracing herself with one hand pressed against each side of the roughly worked walls, she paused. Around her hummed the power of her mistress. It charged the atmosphere like a thunderstorm and made the hairs on the back of her neck stand straight up.

Come, the Dark Goddess's voice whispered in her mind. *We are so close now. So close to victory. Can you not feel it, my child?*

Maegwin closed her eyes, savoring the thumping power that coursed through her as though she was connected to the heartbeat of the world.

Yes, mistress, she answered. *I feel it.*

A slow smile spread across Maegwin's face. Gradually the hum of power began to change. Softly at first but growing stronger with every breath, she started to sing. There were no words this time, just a melody that wove itself into Leo's song, and that of her mistress's dark angels. Spangles of music shimmered in the air around her, filling her with strength, with power.

Almost giddy with exultation, Maegwin lifted her foot to place it on the first step...then shuddered, stumbling as a discordant note rippled through her song. It was like insects crawling across her skin. It rippled through the melody, disrupting its cadence, weakening its power, as though something was resisting, fighting the harmony she was trying to create.

And with a jolt of shock, Maegwin realized it was coming from inside her.

Her song. Her melody. It didn't quite fit with Leo's song or with that of the dark angels, no matter how much she fought it.

"It doesn't matter," she said, her voice echoing off the cold stone walls. "It doesn't matter." So she was flawed? Not yet a perfect vessel for her mistress. So what? That would soon change.

Deliberately, she lifted her foot and placed it on the first step. A crawling sensation flared along her limbs. It wasn't pain exactly but was uncomfortable enough to make her gasp. A ward, she realized. Perhaps set by Rovann himself to ensure nobody came down here who didn't belong.

She pursed her lips and concentrated. After a moment the ward's pattern revealed itself to her senses. The Eorthe, mostly, but with Fire and Air woven into it. If she triggered the ward, it would make the walls collapse and bury her in tons of rubble.

Carefully, she sang again, this time matching her tone exactly to the timbre of the ward, using just the right amount of Fire and Chaos. The song fused with the ward, sinking into it like water into sand. For a moment nothing happened. Then, with a flash of light, the ward vanished. Maegwin smiled. Was this the best Rovann could do? If so, Tyrlindon was utterly doomed.

She jogged down the steps quickly. They spiraled around and around, going deeper and deeper. By the time she spied light ahead her legs were aching and her lungs were burning. Yet she barely felt it. All her thought was fixed on her goal and how close she was. At the bottom of the steps she discovered a small antechamber on the far side of which was an archway that led to darkness. She couldn't see what lay beyond the arch but she could guess.

Her mistress's power was so strong here it filled her lungs with every breath. She edged toward the arch but encountered nothing. A weak light, like the beginnings of dawn lit the antechamber although Maegwin struggled to pinpoint where it was coming from. As far as she could tell, she was surrounded by stone. And yet, the light seemed to move with her, illuminating the area a few meters in front of her feet.

Approaching cautiously, Maegwin placed one hand on the chill stone of the wall and peered through the archway. Her heart began to beat a little faster. A trickle of sweat traced its way down her face, even though the air was cool, like that within a cave.

She could hear nothing, see nothing. After a long moment of stillness, Maegwin shifted her weight forward, ready to take a step.

A soft rustle warned her. The barest hint of a footstep. She whirled, just as a figure stepped out of the darkness behind her. With a cry she threw her hands up, bringing the sword up in a defensive posture. She braced herself for attack, singing a melody that threw a shield of Air around her.

But no attack came.

The figure stood just beyond range of the weak light.

"Who's there?" Maegwin demanded.

"Don't go any further, Maegwin. I beg you."

She'd expected Rovann but the voice didn't belong to him. She recognized the calm authority in that voice, even if she couldn't quite place it. She squinted, taking half a step forward. "Who are you?"

The figure moved into the light and Maegwin gasped in shocked recognition. The man was young, athletic and strong-looking. He was dressed as a warrior although he carried no weapons.

And both his eyes were milky white.

"Owen?" she said. "What are you doing here?" The last time she had seen the prince had been in Leo's throne room in Tyrvanan. She and Rovann had gone there to save the prince, but Maegwin had betrayed them and gone over to Leo's side instead. She didn't like the sudden twist of pain the memory evoked.

The blind prince didn't answer. He cocked his head to one side as though listening, perhaps trying to pinpoint her position. Then those unseeing eyes fixed on her face.

Uneasiness prickled down Maegwin's spine. There was something about that gaze... as though he was looking right at her although she knew it was ridiculous. Owen was blind. A cripple. No threat to her.

"Get out of my way," she snarled.

Kill him! shouted the voice of the Dark Goddess. *Kill him now!*

Prince Owen smiled. "Will you do as she says?"

Maegwin straightened. "What did you say?"

"She told you to kill me. She is your mistress isn't she? What are you waiting for?"

"What?" Maegwin asked in an incredulous voice. "She speaks to you?"

"No. She speaks only to those she's enslaved. But I hear her. I hear lots of things. And I see things, Maegwin. Things others would like to keep hidden."

She snorted, trying for a bravado she didn't feel. "You're stalling, Owen. A blind man sees nothing. Maybe you were the Hawk once. Maybe you would have made a good king one day. But you're useless now. Leo saw to that. A useless cripple who's in my way. Now move or I'll do what my mistress commands!"

Her cruel words had no effect on the prince. A wry smile twisted his lips. "Yes, I'm blind. But that doesn't mean I can't see."

A sneer twisted Maegwin's lips. "Riddles? Metaphors? Is that the best you can do?" She took a step forward, sword raised. "Get out of my way."

He crossed his arms over his chest. "I see the song within you, Maegwin. Most of it is dark and twisted. The words of the Songmaker and that thing you call your mistress. But it's not all like that. There's another song, one that you try your best to ignore. But I hear it. Just as you do. Listen, Maegwin."

She opened her mouth for a retort but shut it again. A faint music intruded on her senses. It was that discordant note she'd noticed earlier, the one that was so out of kilter with the music of Leo and the Dark Goddess. For the briefest of moments she listened and it reminded her suddenly of leaves and roots and growing things, of the sun rising over a green hillside.

Kill him! Kill him! the Dark Goddess screamed in fury.

The strange music evaporated. The power of the Dark Goddess roared in her veins. Fury made her hands shake. How dare this man question her? Who was he to claim he knew her?

She raised the sword in a two-handed grip. "Defend yourself."

"I won't. Do what you must."

Do it! howled the Dark Goddess.

With a scream of fury, Maegwin sprang forward, swinging the sword in an arc aimed at the prince's exposed throat. But another blade suddenly swung out of the gloom somewhere to her left, catching her weapon before it reached the prince. The clash of metal was so loud it hurt her ears. She gaped in shock and pulled back her sword for another blow but something as cold as ice suddenly punched through her shoulder, splattering blood across the wall and the startled prince.

Maegwin staggered then collapsed to her knees as red pain ripped through her body. She looked up, her eyes widening as she recognized her attacker, a bloodied sword clasped in each hand.

It was Rovann.

"Realms!" Rovann hissed in annoyance, yanking the sword out of Maegwin's shoulder and pulling it back for a second blow.

Curse the woman. She'd jerked at the last minute and his aim had gone wide, punching through her shoulder rather than her heart. Intervention by Leo? Or just his rotten luck? He panted, trying to suck in air that was heavy with a dark presence. It scraped at his throat and filled his lungs like treacle.

Maegwin should be dead. He'd thrust with all his might, forcing all his determination into that one stroke. Instead, she staggered to her feet and backed off, holding her sword in front of her. One arm hung limp and useless by her side. Blood trickled from her shoulder. With a grimace, Maegwin shrugged out of her tunic and wadded it into a ball which she pressed against the wound.

Rovann's eyes widened. Below the tunic Maegwin wore only a vest, exposing her arms and shoulders and for the first time Rovann saw that one of her arms was black and shrivelled as though it had been burned. The fingers of that hand curled inward like claws.

"Like what you see?" Maegwin hissed. "Like what you did to me in Tyrvanan? Are you proud?"

Rovann swallowed. "Get behind me," he growled at Prince Owen.

The prince didn't obey. Instead, he regarded Rovann with a knowing look in his white eyes. "My father is dead, isn't he?"

Rovann flinched as a vision of King William's death played across his eyes.

"Yes," he whispered.

"I felt it," Prince Owen said. He tapped his chest. "In here. I hope he died well."

"He did," Rovann replied, wiping sweat from his face with his forearm. "They all did."

Tightening his grip on his sword, he stepped closer to Maegwin. She crouched like a wolf at bay. Her eyes blazed with anger and hatred. And with something else. Hurt?

"Are you here to kill me?" she asked.

"Yes. You knew it would come to this the moment you betrayed me."

She flinched, a spasm of pain crossing her face. "Don't speak to me of betrayal, Rovann. I betrayed my destiny when I sided with you. I merely found my way back."

He wiped sweat from his eyes with the back of his hand. Why did he feel so hot when it was so cold down here? Every muscle in his body ached. His skin burned with a hundred minor wounds.

"Excuses. Is that all you have for me? I thought I knew you once. Perhaps I never truly did." He was irritated by the hurt in his own voice. Where had his calm detachment gone? She was just another enemy. She had to die.

Maegwin smiled wryly. "Leo said that I'd have to fight you. Kill you. But I hoped he was wrong. I have no desire to hurt you, Rovann. Does that surprise you? If you step aside, I'll let you live."

"You think you have that kind of power?" Rovann asked softly. "Is that what you've been promised? Is that what turned you to Leo's path?"

"Power?" she spat, stung to anger. "You think that's what this is about? It's about faith, Rovann! Faith and duty."

He watched her, noticing how her eyes flicked behind him to the chamber beyond. Did she feel the pull of the creature? Was it talking to her? Maegwin radiated power like nothing he'd ever seen before. Waves of Chaos poured off her, swirling in the air like smoke.

"No," he said. "It's about choice. It's always been about choice. You claim to serve Sho-La, but that's a lie. You chose to walk the dark path. You chose vengeance and hatred. Now you'll die for it."

Her eyes widened. A screech escaped her lips and she launched herself at him. He brought his sword up, caught her blow on the bloody steel. A shockwave went up his arm and he staggered back. Her blows were strengthened by Chaos, each strike strong enough to destroy him. Had her attack reached Prince Owen, he would have died instantly. But Rovann was wound with tight bands of Earth and Fire forming a shield. Even so, her strength was enough to stagger him.

"Shut your mouth," she hissed, advancing. "How dare you question me? I serve Sho-La! What do you serve? An idea, that's all. Your duty. Your honor. Just words, Rovann. Meaningless. Isn't that what Istra thought? The wife you allowed to die for your empty service?"

The words were designed to cut and he sensed the Dark Goddess's influence in their cruelty. But they had no power over him. Not anymore. How many times had he told himself the same?

He shook his head. "You know nothing. Don't you understand that service is a choice? I made mine. I live with it every day. But at least it was mine to make. Instead, you've given over your will to a creature that uses you, who dupes you into thinking it's your goddess. And in doing so, you do what it asks without question."

"Is the surrender of choice not a choice in itself?" she asked quietly.

Somehow, he'd been turned around and now Maegwin stood closest to the archway. She spun away from him and Rovann let her go. An ancient power warded the inner chamber, one that would not let anyone with magecraft pass through. It would kill any who tried.

Despite himself, he opened his mouth to warn her. "Maegwin, don't!"

Owen grabbed his arm, shocking him into silence and the two men watched as she edged closer to the archway. In only two strides she was standing directly beneath it. If she took one more step, she would trigger the ward. And she would die.

He bit his lip, steeled himself and remained silent.

Then, at the last moment, Maegwin turned to look at him. She smiled.

And then stepped through the archway.

A flash of light momentarily blinded him. When the light dissipated he saw Maegwin calmly stepping into the chamber. He staggered with a sudden cold, hard fear.

What? How? The ward had failed. Maegwin had reached the Second Prison of Night.

"The Song," Owen was mumbling at his side. "It's the Song that's inside her."

"Yes," Maegwin called to them. "Did you think my mistress didn't know about the ward that guarded this place? Did you think Leo didn't know? No mage may pass. But you see, Rovann, I'm no mage. I'm something else. Something other. Something those who created the ward never imagined."

With a smirk, she turned and walked into the darkness.

"Maegwin!" he bellowed. "Maegwin!"

"It's gone," Owen said, stepping forward, hands reaching out to gently probe the pitted stone of the archway. "She's destroyed it. Come and see."

Warily, Rovann stepped up beside the prince. The arch towered over him but there was no prickle of power, no flaring of any ward. The power that protected the Second Prison of Night was gone which meant he could pass through unharmed. And if he could pass through, anyone could.

Even the Songmaker.

"Light save us," he mumbled. "Come on."

He grabbed the prince's arm and pulled him through into the chamber beyond. The space was lit by a pale greenish light. No brighter than a candle flame, it was enough to show the circular pit in the middle of the chamber and Maegwin crouching at its side. The lattice work of thick iron bars covering the pit was glowing red, as though it had become molten.

Prince Owen tensed, head cocked as if listening. "She's laughing."

Maegwin straightened. "Yes. She finds you both very amusing."

Without warning, she attacked. Her movements were like lightning, so fast, Rovann struggled to track them. She rained blows down on him, each one hammering him with sorcery. He blocked with his sword, using Aethyr to absorb the attack. Beneath his feet, the ground shook. A deep, subterranean rumble grated within the earth as though something was rising from the abyss.

"Rovann!" Owen hissed in warning.

He ducked under Maegwin's swing and sliced his blade across her hamstrings. With a cry she collapsed to her knees.

Grimly he strode forward, lifting his weapon for a killing blow.

I have to do this, he told himself. *I am King's Mage, First of the Council of Mages. I am the Slayer of Sandford Moor.*

Maegwin was on her hands and knees, blood dribbling from where he'd hamstrung her. She looked small, vulnerable.

She was his enemy.

With a cry, he lifted the sword above his head and swung it at the back of her neck.

Maegwin felt the blade coming but couldn't move. Her legs didn't work. She'd lost. Rovann had won. Death was coming. Strangely, there was no fear. Only calmness. Peace washed through her. She'd tried. She'd failed. What more could be asked of her? She closed her eyes, waiting for Rovann to take off her head.

No! bellowed the Dark Goddess. *Get up!*

A wave of power exploded inside her. Vitality like dark vitriol roared through her veins. She rolled away just as Rovann's blade came down and it struck the stone instead. She jumped to her feet, injuries gone, fatigue evaporated. She felt...invincible.

"Fool!" she crowed. "Did you think it would be that easy? Now you see the true might of my mistress!" She felt, giddy, almost drunk with power. It took all her effort to remain aware, to stop herself being swept away on that sweet, sweet tide.

Curling her hands into fists, she backed up three steps. She'd lost her sword but she no longer needed it. Energy crackled at the ends of her fingertips.

Rovann slowly straightened and then threw his own sword to the ground. Perhaps he recognized they were beyond such weapons now.

She cocked her head to one side, regarding him. The man who stood before her now was not the man she had known. He was ruthless in a way that her Rovann never was. Here was the King's Mage. The Slayer of Sandford Moor. His eyes, so bright, so blue, were cold and devoid of emotion. They regarded her with an icy detachment.

And his power was astounding. He used no magecraft but

Maegwin could feel his aura battering at her like the relentless waves of the sea. He'd led angels in battle. The power of all Seven Realms answered him. It flickered around him in a halo of colors. His image seemed to bleed into the air as though he stood not wholly in one Realm but in all of them.

"What are you?" she whispered.

Death, a voice whispered in answer to Maegwin's question. *I am death.*

Sorcery raged inside him. It had become an inferno whipping through his soul. He touched the Eorthe, Air, Fire, Water, Aethyr. All of them. But the strongest was Chaos, the power of the Outer Darkness. It whispered to him seductively, promising an end to doubt, an end to pain. Only let go. Just let go and you'll be free. His control began to slip. He was tired of fighting. It was time to end this. Time to stop battling what he'd become.

"King's Mage!" Prince Owen's voice spoke in warning. "What are you doing?"

Rovann realized that the cavern had begun to shake. Dust and debris fell from the ceiling. Tiny cracks snaked along the walls.

"Rovann!"

He ignored the prince. His focus was fixed on Maegwin. On the woman who'd betrayed him. Something flowered suddenly inside him. It was dark, full of pain. And it clamored for revenge.

In response, Chaos surged inside. *Yes*, it whispered. *Let go. Destroy her. Take your revenge and be free.*

A cry of rage and anguish tore from his lips as he took

another step toward her. Prince Owen placed a restraining hand on his shoulder but he brushed the prince aside.

Maegwin straightened, lifted her chin as she faced him. A small smile curled her lips. Was she mocking him? Even now?

His restraint snapped. Throwing his arms wide he released a torrent of sorcery, no longer caring if it would destroy them all. His rage, his hurt, were ripped out of him, sent cascading in a wave of black force at the woman who'd betrayed him. It would cut her to pieces.

And yet, Maegwin merely stood there. Her smile widened as his sorcery slammed into her. Slammed into her and dissipated to nothing, like mist evaporating under the morning sun.

He staggered forward, collapsing onto his knees. What? How?

A bark of cruel laughter suddenly echoed through the room and a new voice said, "Ha! Excellent! What a performance, Rovann! You ought to think about joining a theater troupe, you really should."

Then the Songmaker stepped through the archway.

The youth was grinning, his eyes shining with mirth. His lute hung from a strap over his shoulder. His hair was freshly combed, his garish clothes clean and pressed. No stain of battle marred him.

Leo gave a flourishing bow. "I thank you, Rovann, for leading us here. For falling for my trap. For making it possible for me to achieve all the things I have. I couldn't have done it without your help." He made a big show of smoothing his hair and brushing imaginary dust from his clothes. "Now, as you can see, I've prepared myself for the greatest performance of my life. This shall be my masterpiece, the performance for which I'm remembered down the ages."

Leo was no longer singing but the notes of his melody still rose and fell, as though somehow it had become part of the very fabric of the air around them. Its discordant cadence set Rovann's teeth on edge. It sounded to him like nails being scraped across slate.

"Is that what you want?" he rasped. "Notoriety? Fame?"

Leo's green eyes snapped to his. "Fame? You do me a disservice, Rovann. Do you really think I'm that shallow?" He pursed his lips as though thinking and then grinned. "Oh, all right, I'll give you that one. Maybe I was that shallow, once. Do you know I once used my last three silvers on a haircut and new waistcoat and then spent the next week slowly starving?" He shook his head as though remembering the folly of youth. "But that was before."

Rovann shifted a step closer, making his movements small and unobtrusive. If he could get closer to Leo...

"That will do, thank you," said Leo, holding out a hand. "No closer, if you please."

Maegwin moved to stand by Leo's side. Her face had gone blank and her gaze distant as though listening to the music. Prince Owen shifted to Rovann's left. Like this, they faced each other.

Leo clapped his hands with glee. "Oh, isn't this nice? Four old friends reunited! This reminds me of when we got together in Tyrvanan. Do you remember that, my prince?"

"I think I recollect," answered the prince, tapping his chin with one finger. "Oh, yes. You mean the time you tortured me into blindness?"

Leo grinned at the prince's sarcasm. He seemed to be enjoying himself immensely. "That's the one. Realms, how you screamed. Bless me, I thought you were going to shatter the windows, it was so loud!"

The prince tensed and Rovann held out a hand to restrain him. "Don't let him goad you."

Owen glanced at Rovann with his white eyes and then looked back at the Songmaker. He smiled suddenly. "Do you remember how that ended? If I recall, Rovann bested you both and then Tanyaka destroyed Tyrvanan. But correct me if I'm wrong, of course."

The smile vanished from Leo's face. "Ah, yes. The dragon. A minor annoyance, I have to admit. But she's not here now, is she? You have no allies down here. Nobody to come to your rescue."

He's afraid of you.

Words flowered suddenly in Rovann's head. He glanced behind him to the pit but there was nothing to be seen except the glowing molten bars.

Who are you? he asked.

You know who I am. He's afraid of you as he should be. He knows what you are. As I do.

Rovann gritted his teeth as he realized what the voice belonged to. *Do not speak to me, Destroyer.*

Quiet laughter echoed in his head. He was reminded suddenly of the time he'd traveled to the in-between that borders the Outer Darkness. The Sluargh had laughed like that.

You know my name, said the creature. *My true name?*

You are Shel-Masa, the Destroyer. You were trapped beyond the Realms by the Lords of the One Light.

Very good. Join me, Rovann. Become my general. Together we will rule all creation.

An image suddenly engulfed him. He sat on a high throne and all the Realms lay at his feet like a map. He turned and saw a woman sitting by his side. She was small, slender and had dark hair in ringlets. She smiled, lighting her eyes.

"Beloved," she said. "You have freed me."

"Istra?" he whispered to his dead wife. "Istra?"

Yes, said Shel-Masa the Destroyer. *You can have her back. Free me and I will have dominion over all things. Even death. I will give her back to you. All you have to do is join me, Warrior of the Realms.*

A terrible, unexpected desire washed through Rovann. After all, why shouldn't he win? Why shouldn't he get what he wanted?

Yes, crooned the creature. *That's it. Give in. Give me what I want and you will have your reward.*

Something connected with the side of Rovann's head and white pain exploded behind his eyes. He straightened to find Prince Owen standing in front of him, hand raised.

"Do not listen!" he hissed. "Her words are poison!"

Shel-Masa's compulsion shattered and Rovann recoiled in revulsion. Deep in his mind he heard the creature bellow in fury but he shut the sound out, refusing to listen.

"Enough of this," he said, taking a step toward Maegwin and the Songmaker. "We all know why we're here. I won't let you do it. I won't let you free the creature in that pit."

"Creature?" Maegwin cried. "How dare you? She is Sho-La!"

"Sho-La? Is that what Leo told you?" It suddenly made sense. Maegwin was a priestess of Sho-La. Perhaps she really believed she followed her goddess. "How many have you killed, Maegwin? How many lives have you destroyed? Would the goddess of light ask that of her followers?"

"You know nothing," she replied. "Sho-La has a darker aspect. It is She who rules me. Perhaps it always was."

Rovann shook his head. He knew too little about her faith to argue. "It doesn't matter. That creature is no goddess. It is a Sluargh, a demon of the Outer Darkness. Look, Maegwin. Look closely."

Maegwin shook her head. "Can you not hear Her song, Rovann? She sings to me. If you listen, you will hear Her."

Perhaps it was the tone of Maegwin's voice that warned him. Or perhaps it was the tiny shift of Leo's stance. He threw up a shield just as a surge of power blasted into him. He and Owen were thrown backward and both went sprawling to the ground at the lip of the pit.

Maegwin and Leo advanced. Rovann pushed himself to his knees, bracing a hand on the low wall that circled the pit. The bars were glowing white now as though any minute they would collapse into magma. He didn't want to think about what that might mean. He averted his gaze, refusing to look into the roiling darkness as he helped Prince Owen to his feet and turned to meet Maegwin and Leo.

They were almost upon him. Both were singing. No words that he understood, but a melody that seemed scraped out of the bowels of the earth. It cracked and spat in his ears and charged the air with a heavy resonance. They were only three paces away now. He flung out a hand, throwing a desperate wall of Aethyr between them. Their song crashed into the wall and shredded it. A wave of force slammed into Rovann, picked him up and flung him against the unforgiving stone of the wall. He crumpled, dazed.

Owen hauled him to his feet and then yanked him to the side as another wave of sorcery smashed into the wall where he'd been standing. The stone exploded in a shower of dust and fragments. Rumbles sounded in the earth below his feet and a second cascade of stone fell from the ceiling. He braced himself against the far wall, gave himself one, two heartbeats to gather himself. Then he sucked in a deep breath and turned to face his enemies.

Angels! he thought, sending the message spiraling outwards and hoping they might hear him. *Give me strength!*

On the edges of his perception he heard the tinkling of bells. The clear peace of the Aethyr suddenly flowed into him as though a gate had been opened. He straightened, threw out both hands and sent a wave of Aethyr roiling through the cavern.

Leo sketched a sign in the air, sang a string of notes, and an explosion of force ricocheted outwards, meeting the Aethyr halfway. The powers of two different Realms met and sizzled, spitting like the sparks of a bonfire. A section of the far wall suddenly collapsed inward, sending boulders careering across the room and filling the air with dust.

"Owen!" Rovann yelled. "Get out now, before it's too late!"

"No!" the prince replied. "I won't!"

"You're the king now," Rovann said. "You must save yourself!"

"To what end? What will I be king of if we fail here? I will stay and do what I can."

Rovann opened his mouth to protest but at that moment the voices of his angels broke into his mind, full of panic.

"General! Look!"

He closed his eyes and in his mind's eye he saw the Realm of Earth. It blazed with the powers being unleashed within it. The battle outside Tyrlindon continued unabated. The cataclysm between the angels and the Sluargh still raged on the astral plane.

Forcing his gaze to move, Rovann saw the Realm of Air,

spinning madly as though enveloped by a tornado, then the Realm of Water boiling, the Realm of Fire, churning in a maelstrom of fury. Deepest of all, so far away he could barely make it out, a ball of white light marked the inner Realm, the One Light.

He could see all of Creation. And it was dying. Reality was bleeding. The borders that separated the Realms had failed and each Realm was losing its substance, beginning to run into the others like dripping paints on an artist's canvas.

The Outer Darkness had spread the furthest. It appeared like a black mist or sea of oil, enveloping the rest, trying to find a way in. If that happened, the Realms would become Chaos where nothing would survive.

Something suddenly slammed into him and he went spinning, spinning through the heavens and landed back in his body within the cavern. He looked up in time to see a wave of sorcery towering over him, ready to come crashing down.

Instinctively, he channeled Fire. It roared through him, so hot and fierce it threatened to rip him to shreds. It burst out of him, enveloping the deadly wave of energy and devouring it.

From across the cavern, Leo and Maegwin waited, watching him steadily. Their song suddenly swelled as they reached out their hands and a second wave of Chaos raced toward him. He threw up a barrier of Aethyr this time and the two powers met with a cataclysmic crash.

Rovann glanced at the pit to see that the bars were beginning to melt. Leo and Maegwin's song was slowly undoing the sorcery that had sealed the prison. Despite his efforts, he was failing. He couldn't stop them.

"No!" he bellowed. "No!"

"Rovann," Prince Owen said calmly. "The time has

come. We've tried to save Tyrlindon and failed. You must do what we agreed."

A wave of horror swamped Rovann as he realized what the prince meant.

"I won't do it," he muttered. "I can't."

You are the Slayer of Sandford Moor, a voice said in his head. *You've killed thousands. What difference will thousands more make?*

I swore to defend Tyrlindon, he answered himself. *How can I now destroy it?*

Because you must. It is your duty.

A sardonic smile bent his lips. Ah, duty. That word again. So. In the end it had come down to this.

Tyrlindon was built on a hub, a gateway to the Seven Realms. It was because of this that they could access the pit which was not part of any Realm but rather a separate dimension of its own. Destroying the hub would trap the creature forever within that dimension with no connection to the Seven Realms.

But to destroy the hub he must destroy Tyrlindon.

Tens of thousands of lives, snuffed out in an instant.

Prince Owen—King Owen—met Rovann's gaze. *You are the King's Mage,* that look said. *You have a duty. Do it.*

Slowly, Rovann nodded.

Chapter Eighteen

The song was everything. It ran through Maegwin like some sweet, seductive drug. No words. No meaning that she could decipher. And yet the beautiful harmonies spoke to her. Of revenge. Of power. Of completion. It was intoxicating. With its strength she was indestructible.

She stared at Rovann. Oh, how she longed to kill him! She wanted it so badly she could almost taste it. She wasn't sure why. Because of what he once was to her? Or because she wanted to prove she was stronger than him?

Die, die, die, the song sang in her soul.

Risking a quick glance across the chamber, she saw that the bars of her mistress's prison were weakening, blazing white hot. The song was destroying the ancient sorcery of Her prison.

With grim satisfaction, she raised her arms, sang a note, and hurled a wave of power at Rovann. He swatted it away as if it were nothing and sent a spear of Fire racing toward her heart. Leo threw out a hand, caught the spear and tossed it nonchalantly to the ground where it dissipated into little flames that sparked uselessly round his feet.

Maegwin wove Fire and Chaos into a deadly whirlwind. It whipped her hair, her clothes. It ripped chunks of rock from the floor and ceiling, churning them into the core of the maelstrom where they ceased to exist, thrown into oblivion by the power of Chaos.

It would do the same to Rovann.

With a grim smile, she set the maelstrom loose, and it went tearing through the cavern toward him.

"I like your thinking, my dear!" Leo cried through the tumult. He clapped his hands together. "What do you think of that, Rovann?"

The King's Mage's eyes widened as he recognized what she had created. The whirlwind was unreality. A tear in the fabric of the universe. It would unmake him.

He threw himself to the side, landing heavily on the ground and rolling from its path. But, with a flick of her wrist, Maegwin turned the vortex to follow him. She wouldn't let him escape. Not when she was this close. She licked her lips. Clenched and unclenched her fists at her sides.

She hadn't felt this exhilarated since she'd killed Lord Cedric Hounsey.

Yes, my child, whispered the Dark Goddess. *Oh yes. I have chosen well in you. You will destroy the universe for me.*

But Rovann was First of the Council of Mages for a reason. The angels of the Aethyr had made him their general for a reason. She should have remembered that.

He staggered to his feet and faced the vortex. He stood tall, chin tilted back. His clothes were torn and bloody, his skin coated with grime and sweat, his hair hung in tangles around his shoulders. He didn't flinch as the maelstrom moved closer.

Die, die, die, went the song inside her.

Suddenly Rovann turned his head and their eyes met. He mouthed something but she couldn't make out the words through the howling of the whirlwind.

Then he threw himself into the vortex.

For a moment his face twisted in agony. Then the whirling energies devoured him and he disappeared.

Raising her hands, Maegwin sang a melody and the power winked out of existence. In its place there was... nothing. Silence descended.

Maegwin stared, stunned. Rovann was gone.

"Dead, dead, dead!" cried Leo. He broke into a jig, capering around the cavern like a jester at some lord's banquet. "He was a worthy opponent wasn't he, my dear? I will compose a funeral dirge in his honor. Oh, how the maidens will weep to hear it! *Rovann's Last Stand.* What do you think? Or how about *The Fall of the King's Mage?* No, no, I've got it: *The End of an Annoying Little Shit.* Yes, that's far more fitting."

Maegwin stared at the spot where Rovann had stood.

There was no elation. No exhilaration. Instead she felt...nothing. Nothing she could put a name to.

Leo went to his knees by the pit and unstrung the lute from his back. He moved slowly, reverently as he positioned the instrument. His face bore an expression Maegwin hadn't seen before. A strange mixture of hope and fear.

"Come, my dear," he said, patting the ground beside him. "It's time. Let's free Her."

Yes, she said to herself. *Let's finish this. Keep moving. Don't think about it.*

She took a step forward but something suddenly

grabbed her shoulder and slammed her against the wall. A strong hand circled her neck, squeezing.

"I won't let you do it."

A face loomed in front of her, handsome once but now with white, staring eyes. Prince Owen. How had she forgotten about him?

She punched and scratched at him but the prince didn't flinch. His grip tightened. She couldn't speak. Dots of white light danced before her eyes.

Prince Owen thumped her against the rock and growled, "I will not allow it, do you hear me? Listen, curse you! Listen!"

Mistress, she cried in the silence of her mind. *Help me!*

There was no answer. She couldn't hear anything but the thundering of her pulse. Her heartbeat seemed unnaturally loud. Thump, thump, thump.

"Leo!" she gasped. "Leo!"

But the Songmaker was staring intently into the pit, oblivious to everything around him.

Gray mist filled her eyes. She was losing consciousness.

"Listen!" Owen snarled into her ear. "Listen!"

What was the fool man talking about?

As awareness faded, so did Leo's song. There was no sound. Just the thump, thump, thump of her heart. But then she noticed something else. There *was* another sound, something deeper, more elusive, running through her body in time with her pulse. It wafted around her like a faint melody heard from far away.

But as she listened it became louder, louder, louder, until it hummed in the air around her, blocking out everything else. She recognized it: the discordant notes she had fought so unsuccessfully to master.

Except, now it didn't sound discordant at all. It sounded

beautiful. The song spoke of crumbling soil and deep roots. Of fragrant grass and the open sky. Of rain on a leaf and wind in the branches.

It was the song of a Sentinel.

She reached out a trembling hand, reached out toward the pearly notes shimmering in her mind, and grasped them.

Suddenly she went spiraling back, back, back, to another time and place where she'd been a different person, a better person. She lay in a dark glade, a Sentinel towering above her. Its golden leaves spilled light and its song shimmered in the air. A song of healing. Of life. It reached out and touched Maegwin, fusing into her heart.

Once touched by a Sentinel a part of it stays with you.

It had always been there, deep inside her. It was still there.

The pressure around her neck eased and she fell to her knees.

The cavern blurred and suddenly she was standing before a still pond in a dark wood. Overhead, the stars blazed but there was no moon. The surface of the pond sparkled. Maegwin recognized this place. These were the woods outside Mallyn where Rovann had brought her after rescuing her from the hangman's noose.

This was the place where she'd taken her first step toward the darkness.

She knelt on the thick grass by the pond's edge and leaned over, staring into its still depths. After only a moment a face appeared in the mirrored surface; a face with midnight hair and fiery eyes without iris or pupil.

You have come, my daughter, the Dark Goddess said. *Serve me and I will give you the vengeance you desire. Remember the murder of your sisters. Remember the anger, remember the hatred.*

The tableau of the day Maegwin's temple was destroyed would remain with her forever. She could still smell the smoke and charred flesh. She could still hear the screaming. Inside, the familiar fury began to build. How dare they? How dare they?

Fury simmered in her belly. It grew, turning her face hot with rage and making her hands tremble. But a song intruded on her thoughts. A golden song. With it came a peace that washed away her wrath. She had a choice. She always had, but in the end she'd made the wrong one.

Will you serve me? asked the Dark Goddess.

Was it too late? Had the touch of the Sentinel come too late to save her?

She bowed her head, feeling the weight of the atrocities she'd committed. She again saw the look of utter horror in Rovann's eyes as, in the tower of Tyrvanan, she moved to stand by the Songmaker's side. As she betrayed him.

She saw the hatred in Kandar's eyes as she waged war against the Shinnar, a people who had befriended her. She saw the rage and distrust in Hannel's face as he tried to kill her, a man she'd once fought beside. She saw herself, a wild, uncontrolled thing as she gave into fury and plunged her sword into Lord Cedric Hounsey's beating heart, feeling nothing but joy as the old man died.

What had she become? How had she wandered so far from Sho-La's path? How had she allowed her hatred to make a monster of her? It felt as though a veil had been lifted from her sight and she was seeing clearly for the first time in months.

Her eyes were suddenly wet with tears.

"Forgive me," she whispered to the angels of the Aethyr, Tanyaka of Fire, Fenris of Earth. To Kandar and Brennan of the Shinnar. To the people of Tyrlindon.

But most of all, to Rovann.

There was no going back. She'd made her choice.

You are wrong. There is always the hope of redemption, said a voice from her past. The face of her Holy Mother floated before her mind's eye. A kind old face, the face of the woman who had taken Maegwin from the streets and given her a home, an identity. *Our Lady is redemption. Love. Hope. Forgiveness. Never forget that, Maegwin.*

Will you serve me? asked the Dark Goddess from the stillness of the forest pool.

Images battered at Maegwin, one after the other. Betraying Rovann. Killing Cedric Hounsey. Fighting the Shinnar. Leading her armies to Tyrlindon.

And finally, finally, sending the vortex of Chaos to destroy Rovann.

He'd looked right at her in those final moments and mouthed something. She'd not heard the words. She'd been too caught up in the throes of power and retribution. But now, those words came to her. She'd caught them after all but chosen not to listen.

I could have loved you.

Slowly, Maegwin clenched her hands into fists. The dark glade surrounded her once more. She pulled in a breath of the cool night air, feeling it fill her lungs. At last she looked down into the still pool and met the blazing eyes of the Dark Goddess.

Sometimes, just sometimes, steps can be retraced.

In a quivering voice she gasped, "No. I will not serve you."

Then a brilliant light gathered at her back, and turning, Maegwin saw a dazzling figure walking toward her through the darkness of the glade.

"Sho-La?" Maegwin asked. "Mistress?"

A glowing hand reached out and gently brushed her cheek. *Welcome home, my child.*

Maegwin opened her eyes. She was lying face down on the floor of the cavern. The dusty smell of stone reached her nostrils. This close she could see minerals reflecting from the rock and a tiny spider that was making its steady way across it. The air that pumped in and out of her lungs tasted deliciously sweet. Even the silence was beautiful.

She flipped onto her back and then levered herself into a sitting position. Leo still knelt by the lip of the pit. His head was cocked to one side as though listening. Closer, crouched Prince Owen, his blind eyes watching her with too much knowledge in them.

Only a heartbeat had passed. Less than the time it takes to breathe. And yet... and yet... everything had changed. She climbed warily to her hands and knees and then stood up, staring at the prince.

"Owen?" she rasped, her voice croaking and sore with emotion. "How did you know?"

"I knew nothing," he replied. "But I hoped."

She looked away, suddenly unable to bear the scrutiny of his blind gaze. It saw too much. "I...I'm sorry."

"Words are meaningless," he grated. "Action is the only way you can redeem yourself. Look."

He pointed to where Leo had suddenly straightened. He was staring intently at the wall of the cavern. Maegwin followed his gaze but could see nothing.

No, wait. Perhaps there was something after all. A faint shimmer disturbed the air, like a heat haze. She felt something pressing against her skin, as though the pressure in the room was increasing. The air suddenly seemed hot and heavy, making it difficult to breathe.

"What is this?" cried Leo in a voice filled with rage. "What is this? You're dead, curse you!"

A silent concussion rocked the chamber. It flung Maegwin onto her back and threw Leo and Owen from their feet. Maegwin scrambled to her knees and saw that a figure now lay on the floor where the heat haze had been. Vapor rose from it like mist. Slowly the figure uncurled and then climbed to its feet.

Maegwin's heart thudded. The breath left her lungs in a whoosh.

Rovann.

Joy and hope flared, making her dizzy.

"My Lord First!" Owen yelled in triumph. The prince took a step forward but Rovann flung out a hand to halt him.

"Stay away. Don't come near me."

His voice sounded odd, strained, although he looked the same. It was Rovann. It had to be. But he'd thrown himself into a vortex of Chaos. How could he survive such a thing?

He shifted, staggered as if in pain. Then as he straightened, he turned in her direction and Maegwin's blood went cold.

Rovann's eyes were completely black.

And then she sensed it, something she'd missed before. A vortex of Chaos swirled nearby, so powerful it could tear them all to shreds. But it wasn't in the room. Oh Lady, it wasn't in the room.

It was inside Rovann.

———————

Rovann snapped back into existence with enough force to rip the breath from his lungs and send blood roaring into his ears. There was pain. Blinding agony. For a second he was sure he couldn't hold it. It would kill him. Surely it must kill him? But eventually, it ebbed.

When he opened his eyes he found himself back in the cavern. The Songmaker was standing by the lip of the pit, eyes wide with disbelief. Prince Owen stood by Maegwin on the other side of the cavern. He couldn't read the expression on her face. Was it relief? Or horror?

She had tried to kill him. She'd sent a vortex of Chaos against him but in doing so had inadvertently given him the means to achieve his goal. All it required was surrendering his soul. So he'd walked into that vortex and fought it until he became its master. Now it obeyed *his* will.

"Rovann!" Maegwin shouted. "I—"

He didn't let her finish. With a flick of his wrist, he unleashed a wave of Chaos that swept her from her feet and she thumped heavily onto her back.

With a cry, Owen knelt at her side, quickly checking her pulse and pressing his ear to her chest to listen for a heartbeat. Rovann frowned. What was going on? Had Owen betrayed him too? Had he joined Maegwin?

A clashing cacophony suddenly filled the cavern.

The Songmaker was playing his lute. The young man's face was white with fear or fury. Sweat matted his red hair to the sides of his head. As his long fingers played across the strings, sorcery gathered around him, responding to the command of each note. When strung together, the song wove powerful sorcery.

"You cannot be here!" the Songmaker shouted. "I saw you taken by the void! You cannot be here!"

Rovann winced. The void. Was that where he'd been? He'd known darkness and suffocating pressure and a feeling of being utterly alone. If that was the void then he had no desire to ever see it again. He'd found his way back only by doing the impossible: by taking the power of Maegwin's vortex into himself. Now the power of Chaos swirled inside him, tingling along every nerve, powering every organ.

It was trying to devour him from the inside. Every breath was pain. Every movement drove agony through his skull. And yet there was a seductive sweetness to the pain. It whispered to him. All he had to do was let go. It would scour his emotion and leave him a vessel of pure power, without the weakness of conscience or sentiment.

Rovann watched the Songmaker. Finally perhaps, he comprehended the young minstrel who'd given into the seduction of Chaos. Rovann understood the impulse. It was easier to let go. To surrender. What would he have done if he'd faced the same choice at Leo's age? Would he have had the strength to withstand it?

"Leo," Rovann said, trying to make his voice sound reasonable. "You can't win, just as I can't win. If you persist, Tyrlindon will die. You will die. I will die. And your mistress will still be imprisoned. Stop this."

The minstrel cocked his head. "You really expect me to give up now? When I've come so close to my goal? I've been working for years for this. I've planned and plotted and waited, all leading to this moment. Do you have any idea of what I've sacrificed to get here?"

Rovann thought of the void. "Yes, I think I do."

The Songmaker pursed his lips. "Perhaps after all you do, at that. I see what's inside you. If you don't surrender, it will destroy you."

Rovann nodded. "I know."

"Then why do you fight it? Surrender is your only choice."

"There is always another choice."

"Ha!" Leo suddenly barked a laugh. "There it is, that stubbornness of yours. Most would call it a weakness but they would be fools. It's that stubbornness that's caused you to be such a pain in the behind."

Rovann shrugged. "You're not the first to say that."

Leo grinned and for a moment, just for a moment, Rovann saw the young minstrel he must have once been.

"No, I would imagine I'm not." He tilted his head suddenly as though listening. A spasm passed across his face and his expression changed to one of determination. His fingers moved effortlessly over the strings of the lute, his Song- Spell forming the background to his words.

Rovann tensed, sensing the change in Leo's demeanor. "I'll try one last time. Will you withdraw?"

"You know I can't."

As the last word left his mouth Leo sang a high-pitched note and a blast of sorcery lashed into Rovann. He spun a wall of Chaos around himself and the blast ricocheted off. So be it.

Do it, Prince Owen had commanded him and he would obey his lord's command.

Rovann closed his eyes and guided his senses out and down, into the bowels of Tyrlindon. He detected the life-forces of the many thousands of people who filled the city, burning like tiny candles. If he was successful, those candles would soon be snuffed out.

Hardening his heart, he flung his senses further out, into the bedrock of Tyrlindon. Deep beneath the city, into the rock of the plateau, he found the hub on which the city had been built. A gateway into the Seven Realms, it hummed on his senses like a vast thunderstorm. From it, Rovann sensed lines of power radiating out into each Realm. Should the Songmaker—or worse, the creature that controlled him—

seize control of the hub; they would rampage through the Realms. Even the One Light would not be safe.

He pushed his perception through the ground to the foundations of the curtain wall. Gently, he probed searching for a tell-tale signature. Yes. There it was. At seven cardinal points around the curtain wall, Rovann had anchored Tyrlindon's ward. Most of the ward itself was already destroyed, but the anchors remained.

They pulsed deep within the earth, a mix of Eorthic and Aetheric power. Rovann relaxed his control slightly, allowing tendrils of Chaotic power to dribble out of him and wrap itself around those anchors. A rumble sounded deep underground as the Eorthe shook itself, bucking against the Chaos that touched it.

The whole of the plateau seemed to shift and all over the city, Rovann sensed cracks appear in walls and roads. A collective wave of anxiety rose from the people within, both defenders and attackers pausing for a moment as the city shook. But as it settled and another did not follow, the anxiety dissipated.

It was only a minor earth tremor. Nothing to worry about.

But they were wrong. Terribly, terribly wrong.

Forgive me, Rovann whispered silently.

Then he relaxed his control and sent Chaotic power blasting through the bedrock of Tyrlindon.

"What are you doing?" screamed the Songmaker.

He pounded Rovann with blast after blast of power. It should have been enough to tear him to shreds. But although

Rovann staggered under each new assault, the shield he'd woven from Chaotic power held, and he stood upright, arms thrown wide and shoulders back, as sorcery poured out of him.

But it didn't attack Maegwin or Leo. Instead, it flowed downwards, into the foundations of the city.

"What are you doing?" Maegwin whispered, echoing Leo's question.

Prince Owen reached out a hand and she allowed him to pull her to her feet. He appeared strangely calm. Maegwin's neck still hurt where he'd grabbed her but the rage he'd showed earlier had faded and now he seemed resigned.

She backed away a few steps and shook her head, trying to clear her thoughts, figure out what she should do now. Leo didn't even look at her. He thought she was still his ally. Rovann thought she was still his enemy.

But what was she now? She glanced at Owen and found him gazing at her steadily. His white eyes seemed to see everything. She shuddered and turned back to watch Rovann.

"What is he doing?"

A tightening of the prince's shoulders betrayed his tension. "What must be done."

"What's that supposed to mean?"

The prince watched her but didn't answer.

"You know, don't you?" She suddenly remembered the prince's words to Rovann. *Do it.*

A shiver walked down her spine. Cold dread seeped into her stomach.

Stepping close to the prince, she demanded, "What is he doing? Tell me!"

Prince Owen watched her for what seemed an age. He

crossed his arms over his chest. "I see the Sentinel in you but that doesn't mean I trust you. Do not interfere."

His words made her hair stand on end. She spun to face Rovann and saw that his eyes were closed, his face almost serene. Then a rumble shook the plateau and she was thrown hard against the wall, smashing her elbow into a rock with enough force to make her scream.

She closed her eyes and flung her percipience outward as Rovann had once taught her. She found it almost immediately. Bands of a dark, roiling power wrapped the city. They were anchored into place at seven points around the city's curtain wall. The bands had dug deep into the foundations of Tyrlindon, running through the bedrock of the plateau like a canker. And they were beginning to squeeze.

Maegwin opened her eyes. "He's going to destroy the city!"

Prince Owen watched her impassively.

"Didn't you hear me?" she cried. "He's going to kill us all!"

Owen shifted his weight. "Yes."

She stared at him. King William was dead. That meant Owen was now ruler of Amaury. And here he was, calmly acknowledging that his capital city was about to be destroyed. What could drive him to such an action?

Even as she thought of the question, the answer came to her. Her eyes strayed toward the pit. She no longer heard the voice of the Dark Goddess but from the darkness she felt the burning hatred. Beyond lay a creature who had been imprisoned beyond the Realms for all eternity. A creature of immense age and immense power. Maegwin herself had tasted a bit of it. She knew what She was capable of. If She was freed, She would destroy the Realms.

What were the lives of thousands against that?

"He has to be stopped," she whispered.

Prince Owen's hand closed around her wrist, jerking her around to face him. "Don't try to interfere."

"I have to!" she hissed. "Do you expect me to just stand here? I can stop him, I know I can."

"You will do the Songmaker's bidding if you do."

She shook her head. "No. I won't. Please, you have to trust me." She gazed at him, willing him to see the truth written in her eyes.

He studied her and she thought for a moment that she saw the light of a Sentinel dancing in his gaze. Then he blinked and the sight vanished. He let go of her wrist.

She spun away, jogging across the chamber to Leo's side. "He's trying to bring down the city," she shouted. "He'll destroy the hub and the link to our mistress's prison! We have to stop him!"

"What? How do you know this?"

"I've seen it! You have to trust me, Leo! There's no time! We have to stop him."

Leo's mouth twisted into a snarl. "Curse him! He'd choose death over what our mistress has offered him? Why did I have to be cursed with such a stubborn enemy?"

It's not stubbornness, Maegwin thought. *It's duty. He's been driven by it. It's what killed Istra. It's what will kill the rest of us if we don't stop him.*

She shook her head. "It's already started! Can't you feel it? If we don't act everything we've worked for will be destroyed."

Everything we've worked for. The words stuck in her throat but she forced them out.

Leo nodded. "We attack in concert. Do you remember the Song Spells I taught you? Use a Fire Song. I will use

Chaos. Follow my lead and add in the counterpoint when I tell you. It will give us a way through his defenses."

She nodded.

Leo's fingers found a new position on the lute and a different tune filled the air. Maegwin recognized its power immediately. It was a summons to the Outer Darkness, pulling the power of Chaos from that dark, distant Realm. After a moment, Leo's voice joined it. He sang in a deep baritone, the words in a language Maegwin had never heard before. It sounded like rocks grinding deep within the earth.

Shadows began to move. From the gloom in the corners of the cavern, darkness slithered across the ground. It pooled around Leo's feet until it seemed he stood within a roiling pond of black water. He raised his voice, the notes becoming louder, deeper, and the darkness rippled across the floor toward where Rovann stood.

From the corner of her eye Maegwin saw Owen start toward them, a grim expression on his face. She glanced at him, throwing out a hand to halt him. She met his gaze and sent an unspoken message.

Trust me. Don't interfere.

For a wonder, he understood. He backed away but remained alert, ready to throw himself to Rovann's aid should he think Maegwin had betrayed him.

Leo's song continued building. The pool of Chaos slithered across the floor to surround Rovann but couldn't find a way through his barrier. Not without Maegwin's help. Leo nodded in her direction.

Maegwin closed her eyes and began to sing. The words tripped easily off her tongue, a Song Spell of Fire that Leo had taught her soon after she'd joined him. Leo himself rarely used Fire—he'd been afraid of it ever since Tanyaka had almost incinerated him in Tyrvanan—so he'd taught them to Maegwin to use in his stead.

Now she sang the words that would access the Realm of Fire and wove its power into Leo's song. Fire and Chaos fused in a swirling mass, fighting each other as they always did.

Maegwin directed the tendrils of Fire at Rovann's ward. She probed gently and then found a weaker spot where Leo's Chaos had begun to corrode it. Singing a higher note, she formed the Fire into a sharp blade which she used to slash at Rovann's defenses.

It didn't work.

She felt a backlash from Rovann, so powerful it almost threw her from her feet. For a moment, her song faltered as she doubled over, coughing. Gasping in a breath, she righted herself and resumed singing.

Leo had concentrated his Chaos on the spot where Maegwin had attacked and the barrier was beginning to weaken. Honing Fire into another blade, she pushed Leo's power away and replaced it with her own, using it like a surgeon's knife to cut through Rovann's defense.

She was braced for the backlash this time. A pulse of Chaos slammed into her but she stood her ground, singing more quickly now, more desperately, pushing power into the knife and sawing at Rovann's defenses.

And then a tiny nick appeared within the wall. Instantly she left her body, throwing her consciousness through the gap before it sealed behind her.

She found herself in a star-filled sky. Below her lay Tyrlindon, shining with lamps against the darkness. Beyond the outer walls, campfires marked the lines of the Shinnar army. The upper levels of the city were still held by the defenders but surrounded by the sea of Leo's army. Her army. She swallowed. Blinked. Drew in a breath to steel her courage and looked around.

There. Rovann stood a few paces away, staring at her with eyes gone dark as a grave.

"What are you doing here?" he rasped.

Her heart fluttered with sudden fear. Power pulsed around him in waves. Lines of oily energy stretched from him in all directions like some giant spider's web of which he was the center. The lines reached down into Tyrlindon, into the hub that lay beneath, forming a vast network of glowing tendrils that ran through the bedrock like veins.

Lady help me, Maegwin thought.

Horror closed her throat, stealing her voice. She stared, uncomprehending, at Rovann and the power he'd unleashed. Was this what the angels had in mind when they made him their general? She doubted it. Even now she imagined them desperately trying to reach Rovann, trying to stop him. But he'd shut them out. Only Maegwin had penetrated his defenses. She was the only one who could stop him.

"Rovann," she croaked. Her voice was barely above a whisper. She cleared her throat and tried again. "Rovann, please. Listen to me."

His eyes narrowed and she was nearly knocked flat by the force of his hatred. "Why are you here? Surely you know you can't kill me? If you want to live then run. Take whatever is left of your army and flee. It's the only chance you'll get."

"That's not why I'm here."

"Leo sent you."

She shrugged. "Does it matter if he did? We share the same goal, but not the one you think. Not anymore. You have every right to hate me, Rovann. I expect no less. But you must listen to me. Don't do what you're planning. There is no need. I'm not what I was, Rovann. If you stop this, we can go back and face Leo together. We can defeat him."

What did she expect? That Rovann would crumble into weeping and welcome her back? What she got was a cruel laugh.

"Ah, Maegwin. Is it any wonder I was taken in by you? You're an accomplished liar. Were you taught that in the temple of Sho-La? Or is that something Leo gave you?"

"Listen to me, damn you!" she snapped. "I'm trying to save you!"

"Save me? From what?"

"From yourself, you cursed fool! What will you become if you do this? If you murder thousands of innocent people?"

His face twisted into anger. "This is what you made me! You and Leo. Don't you like it, Maegwin?"

Fear shivered through her. She saw the darkness that roiled within him. It threatened to destroy him. She could only guess at the struggle going on inside. If he gave in, like she had done all those months ago, they were all lost.

She pulled in a deep breath and held a hand toward him. She had to make him see. Make him understand.

"I'm sorry. I was wrong. I no longer follow the Dark Goddess, Rovann. I'm not Hers anymore. Prince Owen helped me to change the path I was walking. Can't you see? There's no need for this any longer. Leo needs my help to free his mistress, that's why he enlisted me in the first place. But I'm not going to help him. I'm going to fight him. If we work together we can defeat him. Come back with me now. Please."

She watched him, urging him to hear the sincerity in

her words. He stared right back, eyes full of darkness. Then she saw something flicker. Doubt?

For a moment, she dared to hope. But then Rovann's face twisted into a mask of fury and hope vanished.

"Liar!" he raged. "I will kill you for what you've done to me!"

He raised a hand and a wall of darkness shot toward her. Maegwin recognized the stuff of the void and gasped in terror. It would unmake her. Destroy her utterly.

Desperately, she threw up her arms and sang a few notes. White light exploded outwards and slammed into Rovann, making him stagger. Song erupted around her but this was not the voice of the Songmaker. This was high, haunting, otherworldly. Spangles of light danced like droplets of melody.

A song of light and healing. The song of a Sentinel.

Rovann's eyes widened as the song enveloped him. "What are you doing?"

"Saving you," Maegwin replied, tears stinging her eyes.

Something was coming. From deep within the Realms she heard the tinkling of bells. Then voices joined the song of the Sentinel, blasting through her into the in-between.

The angels, she thought in awe. *The angels have come.*

But their power wasn't directed at Rovann. It was directed at her. Her eyes widened in wonder. The Aethyr had never obeyed her, never answered her call. But now, a warm peace suddenly filled her, sweeping away all doubt, all fear.

Save him, tinkling voices trilled. *This is what we chose you for.*

In answer, Maegwin began to sing, sending droplets of Aethyr and Sentinel melody to surround Rovann. His eyes were wide with pain and his face had gone pale. He was fighting. The darkness within him hissed and spat, resisting the touch of Aethyr.

With a strangled cry she realized it might be too late. Had the darkness devoured him already?

"Rovann!" she cried. She threw herself to his side and he turned pain-filled eyes on her.

"Maegwin? What's happening?"

Parts of his essence were beginning to shred. Tiny wisps of substance evaporated into the in-between. Already his form was beginning to waver. In horror, she realized he was being torn apart.

She stopped singing, appalled, but the blackness of Chaos continued to writhe within him. It was going to rip him into pieces.

"No!" she cried. "I won't allow it!"

She threw her arms around Rovann, encompassing him with her aura. Chaos slammed against her but she steeled herself and held it within. Then she summoned the Song of a Sentinel and began to sing. She had no idea if it would work. A Sentinel had once healed her of mortal wounds. Could it not do the same for Rovann? Words fell from her lips, a plea to Sho-La, goddess of light and compassion.

> *Blessed Mother, guide me.*
> *Blessed Mother, heal me.*
> *Blessed Mother, teach me.*
> *Blessed Mother, I am yours.*

How long since she'd last uttered those words? Too long. And yet they felt right, natural. She remembered another time, long ago it seemed, when she'd said those prayers in the darkness of a cell in Mallyn, awaiting her execution.

Rovann had saved her that day. It was time to repay the favor.

She repeated the chant, stronger this time, using its plea to fashion the Sentinel's Song and weave it around Rovann. For a heartbeat, she thought it might work. Rovann went rigid and the glowing power grew brighter. But a heartbeat later Rovann's expression twisted and he sent out a blast of Chaos that made her falter.

"Don't fight it!" she cried. "Please! Listen to me. I know how seductive the darkness is. Don't give in like I did. You're the King's Mage! You're First of the Council! You have a duty!"

Perhaps she thought the words would rouse him, remind him of who he was. But they had the opposite effect. He looked at her with eyes full of darkness.

"That's right, Maegwin. I have a duty. To stop you and the Songmaker. Now step away."

"At what cost?" she barked. "Are the lives of so many a price you are willing to pay?"

"There's no choice. You've driven me to this. The dead will be on your conscience as much as mine."

She flinched but forced herself to meet his gaze. "No, Rovann. Aren't you the one who's always telling me about choice? Don't pretend there is no other way. I've given you a way out. You have to choose to take it."

He shook his head. "Such decisions are the price of power. Nobody else can make them. I do what I must."

A shrill laugh escaped her. "Listen to yourself! This is how Leo justifies his actions. What's the difference between you? At least the Songmaker doesn't lie about what he is!"

Rovann's face twisted in fury, turning him into a man Maegwin didn't recognize. A cruel man, drunk on power. She stepped back a pace. "What do you know about it?

Nothing! Do you have any ideas of the sacrifices I've made?"

"So it's self-pity now, is it?" she hissed. "Have you sacrificed more than those soldiers lying dead on the battlefield? Have you sacrificed more than the mothers who've sent their sons to war? Have you sacrificed more than the Shinnar who've marched from their homeland to aid you?"

"Shut your mouth! You lost the right to speak to me this way when you betrayed me!"

His voice had gone low and cold. It frightened her more than anything. The tendrils of power emanating from him had grown thicker, stronger. Below, an earthquake was shaking Tyrlindon. She heard the cries of terror of the thousands of inhabitants below.

"Hear that? Is that what you want? Haven't you learned your lesson by now, Rovann? This isn't the King's Mage I see before me. It isn't the First of the Council. It's the Slayer of Sandford Moor! Now I know why they gave you that nickname!"

With a snarl he flicked out a hand. A wall of force slammed into her, sent her spinning. For a moment, she feared he had killed her. Glancing down, she saw the cord that attached her to her body. It was frayed but still held. Just.

She fought to remain conscious. A rising tide of despair threatened to drown her. It was too late. Rovann wouldn't listen. He'd gone too far down the path that led to the darkness, a path she knew only too well.

She sent a plea out into the Aethyr, hoping the angels would hear. *You have to help me! There's only one person he might listen to!*

The tinkling of bells sounded on the edge of her awareness. She didn't know if the angels heard her or even if they had the power to act if they did. It was a last, desperate plea.

After what could have been a heartbeat or a hundred years a sound caught her attention. Deep within the fabric of the Realms, so faint as to be almost beyond perception, she heard singing. It was coming closer.

A jolt of terror went through her as she wondered if this was Leo's song. Perhaps he had found a way to penetrate Rovann's defense and come after him. But then she realized this was a woman's voice, singing words she recognized.

> *Copper halls and laughing maids,*
> *The clan is gathered here together,*
> *Sing! Clan Tamarand! Sing we shall!*
> *Tell the tales and write the deeds,*
> *Clan Tamarand we are one!*

Maegwin opened her eyes just as a burst of searing light lit the heavens. From that light stepped a woman. She was small, with olive skin and dark hair. Maegwin's breath caught. She'd never seen this woman before but she'd know her anywhere.

Istra de Lacey. Rovann's dead wife.

Chapter Nineteen

Closing his eyes, Rovann let the rage of Chaos rampage through him. The power of the Outer Darkness was the most seductive of the Seven Realms but also the most difficult to control.

It was already beginning to destroy him.

At first that had frightened him but no more. The darkness promised immortality. Was this why Leo had succumbed? Why Maegwin had?

He channeled the Chaos into the web of dark power that he'd woven beneath Tyrlindon. He pushed and pushed and pushed, letting the web grow. He remembered suddenly the mage storm in Angard. That had taken days to build, gradually layering energy upon energy until it hung poised above the town, ready to be unleashed. He'd done the same to Tyrlindon.

Finally, he sensed it was ready. He had only to unleash his power and Tyrlindon would be destroyed, the gateway to the Second Prison of Night with it. He sighed. Let his shoulders drop and began to relax his restraint...

But a sudden flash of blinding light forced his eyes open. Notes of song shimmered in the air around him. From the light stepped a woman and it was she who was singing. Rovann reeled at the sight of her.

"Istra?"

His dead wife approached him and the light behind her faded as though a door had closed. She stopped an arm's length away and watched him, the song of the Tamarand clan falling from her lips. He'd forgotten how beautiful her voice was. How could he forget such a thing?

She cocked her head, almond-shaped eyes regarding him with an emotion he couldn't recognize. Then she reached out and took his hand.

"Come, beloved. I have something to show you."

The world blurred and Rovann found himself trudging up a hill in Tyrlindon. It was spring. A light wind stirred his hair, bringing the scent of flowers that covered the plain below. The sun was beginning to set and people called out greetings as he walked, Istra by his side.

"What is this?" he asked her. "What's going on?"

She didn't answer, just jerked her chin forward. Rovann followed her gaze to a small townhouse that sat at the joining of two streets. The windows were dark, the porch unswept. A thrill of fear raced through him.

Springtime. An unkempt house. How many times had he seen this image in his nightmares?

"I don't want to see this."

"You must."

Slowly, he walked up to the door. It wasn't locked. Inside the house, all was still. His footsteps echoed on the tiles.

Dust motes danced in a shaft of sunlight and Rovann's eyes were drawn to the staircase. Almost without volition, he found himself placing his foot on the first step. It creaked under his weight, just as it always had. He inched upwards, Istra a silent presence at his back.

At the top, the three doors on the landing stood closed. Somewhere above, a pigeon called. Out in the street a dog barked and someone shouted at it to be quiet.

With a thundering heart, Rovann approached the middle door. The handle felt strangely cool under his hands as he turned it and pushed the door open.

And there she was, just as he had found her. Istra was lying face down, halfway to the door, one arm stretching out. Around her was a black pool of blood.

Anguish made Rovann's sight blur. For a moment he couldn't see, couldn't breathe, couldn't hear. Then arms enveloped him and Istra's familiar scent filled his nostrils.

"Hush, beloved," she whispered. "Hush."

He held her tightly, not daring to let go. "Why have you brought me here?" he gasped. "Why do you show me your death? Don't you know how many times I've seen this in my nightmares?"

She pushed him to arm's length and he saw tears shining in her almond eyes. "I'm sorry, beloved, but I need you to see something. Something you didn't the first time. Look."

Rovann's gaze moved to Istra's body lying on the floor. She was so still. So cold. But as he watched, something began to happen. A light wind blew through the room, swirling Istra's hair and lifting the dust from the floorboards. An object shimmered in the air, it was rectangular, burning with pentagrams at each corner.

A gate.

It swung open and Rovann was enveloped by a warm, comforting wind. Blazing light filled the room.

From deep within the gate a voice spoke. "Come, daughter. Come home."

And Istra's astral form rose from her body, the golden cord that linked them severed, and approached the shining gate. With a look of joy on her face, she stepped through.

"The One Light," Rovann murmured. "It took you."

"Yes," Istra replied. "The Sluargh lied to you. I was not damned. All that guilt, beloved, all that doubt that led you on his path. There was never any need for it. So let it go. Let it go."

She pressed a hand against his chest, a hand shining as brightly as the gate did and golden energy ripped through him. It blasted through his consciousness, obliterating guilt, despair, anger, everything. Instead, it brought peace.

"It's a choice," Istra said. "You must choose to let it go."

Rovann searched inside himself and realized that the maelstrom of Chaos still whirled, still threatened to devour him. The One Light couldn't take it from him. He had to choose to let it go.

But it was hard. Light, it was hard.

Closing his eyes, he concentrated on the swirling power within him. Slowly, oh so slowly, he began to relax his control, loosen the strings that bound Chaos to him. It clung on desperately, sinking claws deep into his soul. His form shuddered, pain tearing along his nerves. Chaos was sweet, like a drug and forcing it out of his system was like ripping part of himself away.

He bared his teeth, grunting against the pain and went down on one knee, bracing his fists on the floor. Istra knelt beside him, pressing her hands against his forehead.

"I know it hurts, beloved. But you must do this."

With a howl, he burst upright, throwing his head back and arms wide as he let it go, finally let it go. He drew a gate in the air and threw it open. Beyond, the Chaos of the Outer Darkness whirled. He took hold of the churning vortex within him and, with searing, burning agony, tore it out of himself and tossed it through the gate, slamming the gate shut.

He collapsed to his knees.

Istra was there, laying her head against his shoulder, putting her arms around him and holding him as he rocked, waiting for the pain, the emptiness, the dislocation to subside.

Centuries, eons, later he finally looked up. Istra watched him with her huge, dark eyes.

"I did as you asked," he said. "But have I doomed us all? I cannot defeat Maegwin and the Songmaker, Istra. They will release the creature and destroy us."

"No, beloved," Istra said, shaking her head. "Things are not as they appear. The angels chose Maegwin. Chose her to save you. And she's fulfilled their faith. Do you remember what the angels said to you when you first met her?"

Yes, he remembered. The day he'd rescued Maegwin he'd been seated alone by the campfire when an angel had come to him.

Now you are two, the angel had said.

Since then he'd wondered how the angels could have made such a grave error. How could they so badly have misjudged her?

But now? Now Istra seemed to be saying... He shook his head, a tumble of confused thoughts and emotions racing through his mind.

"But she betrayed me," he said at last.

"Yes," Istra agreed. "And now she has saved you. The power of a Sentinel resides in her heart, the healing power that drives the Realms. In the end, she found her way, although the path has been crooked."

"Why are you telling me this?"

A wry smile twisted her lips. "Because she's your ally, Rovann, despite everything she's done. Now the choice is yours. Will you continue on this path? Or will you trust Maegwin and turn aside?"

Istra stared at him and he looked back, drinking in her features, trying to imprint every last detail on his memory. Realms, how he'd missed her. And yet, when he probed, the pain inside him didn't flare up like a newly-opened wound. It ached, like a wound beginning to heal.

"You'll never believe what's happened," he said, forcing a smile. "Thaldan and I made up. We might even end up being friends."

She laughed, a bright, clear sound. "You and my brother, friends? Impossible! How did you win him over?"

Rovann shrugged. "Let's just say we had a mutual interest. Actually, he saved my life."

Her curved eyebrows rose. "Then you're honored. You have a debt to clan Tamarand now, Rovann. My brother will ensure you repay it."

"I'm all too aware of that," he muttered. "I dread to think what he'll ask of me."

"If I know my brother, it will be only just this side of legal."

They fell silent. Rovann curled his fingers through hers. On the edges of his perception he could feel the One Light gathering close, a warm glow like a bonfire over his shoulder.

"You have to go so soon?"

"Yes, beloved. I've been here too long already."

"Will I see you again?"

A shadow of sadness passed across her features. "No, not until you pass into the One Light. And I hope that won't be for a very long time yet. The Realms haven't finished with you, King's Mage."

"What am I supposed to do without you?"

She smiled and placed her palms on either side of his face. "You will endure, and live, and love, Rovann. There is another who could take your heart now and she has my blessing." She leaned down and pressed her lips against his and a warm peace spread through Rovann. He closed his eyes, savoring the sensation.

When he opened them again, she was gone.

He pulled in a breath and scrubbed a hand through his hair. "Goodbye, Istra. Goodbye."

Rovann opened his eyes to find himself staring at the cracked and pitted ceiling of the cavern. A ripple of warning passed over his skin and he threw himself aside, just as a bolt of sorcery slammed into the space he'd occupied, sending up fragments of rock and stone. He shook dust from his hair and staggered to his feet.

The Songmaker was standing by the pit, Maegwin at his side. The youth was slowly strumming on his lute, its sad notes echoing off the walls of the chamber. Beyond them, Prince Owen stood in the shadows, watching.

"There he is!" shouted the Songmaker in triumph. "Well done, Maegwin, my dear! I knew you'd bring the King's Mage back." Leo's sparkling green eyes fixed on Rovann. "You can't win! Don't you realize that by now? Maegwin and I are too powerful. I'm going to kill you, you annoying little worm!"

He hummed a tune and a wave of Chaos slammed into Rovann. He collided with the wall with a crunch that made his sight blur. Pain exploded through his body and the iron tang of blood filled his mouth.

A cruel grin spread across Leo's young face. Slowly he held the lute out to arm's length then plucked a string so hard that it snapped with a twang. In response, a wall of Fire sprang into existence around Rovann. Instinctively, he wove a shield of Water and Air. As a result, he was surrounded by scalding steam rather than searing flame. His clothes smoldered and the skin of his hands turned red but he didn't burn.

"Curse you!" The Songmaker shrieked. He bent over his lute, fixing the broken string and the wall of Fire fell away.

Prince Owen ran to Rovann's side. "Lord First?" he asked in a tight, worried voice. "What happened? Why does Tyrlindon still stand?"

Do it, the king had ordered him. *Kill us all if you have to.* Owen's white eyes were harsh and demanding.

"I found another way," Rovann replied. His gaze fell on Maegwin standing almost in a daze by the Songmaker's side. "At least," he added, "I hope I did."

Owen studied him, weighing his words. Finally he said, "What do you want me to do?"

"Stay alive, my lord," Rovann answered. "Amaury needs its king."

Owen nodded. Together they turned to face the Songmaker.

The youth had fixed the broken string and he began softly strumming the instrument once more. Its mournful dirge prickled at Rovann's skin like a winter wind. Some-

344

where beyond the cavern the singing of the Sluargh was getting closer. They were almost here.

He glanced at Maegwin. She was staring at her feet, oblivious to all around her. *Oh Light,* he thought. *Don't let me be wrong about her!*

"Maegwin!" Leo said sharply. "Come stand by me. I need your Song Spells of Fire."

Slowly she lifted her head and then shuffled to stand by the Songmaker. The four combatants faced each other across the cavern, the Second Prison of Night lying between them like a broken promise. Rovann was reminded of another time and place, another tableau like this. It seemed an age ago, in the throne room of Tyrvanan. Then, just as now, Maegwin had stood by the Songmaker's side. She had betrayed him.

Rovann watched her, hoping. But she didn't move.

No, no, no, he thought. *Not again!*

"Maegwin!" he yelled desperately.

Her head jerked up at the sound of his voice. Her eyes were glassy, out of focus as if she was looking inward. She stared at him, her mouth working wordlessly.

"Rovann?" she gasped at last. "Rovann?"

Her sight seemed to clear and she straightened. Then, she slowly walked across the cavern to stand between Rovann and Prince Owen, turning to face the Songmaker with a look of determination on her face.

Rovann held his breath, hardly daring to believe his eyes. The angels had been right. Istra had been right. She'd come back to him.

He reached out and squeezed Maegwin's hand. The smile she turned on him was filled with a strange mix of emotion but her eyes were bright with joy. Light, he'd forgotten how beautiful she was when she smiled.

Leo stared at her with a hate-filled expression. A bitter grin twisted his face. "Ah, I see how it is. Betrayal is becoming something of a habit with you, isn't it, my dear?"

Maegwin's hands clenched into fists at her sides but she didn't answer.

Leo pointed at the pit. "Do you think She will allow this? She does not tolerate betrayal. She will hunt you down and make you suffer for eternity."

Maegwin paled. She swallowed, once, twice, before she answered. "I am protected by Sho-La."

Leo's head dropped and a long sigh escaped him. For a moment he looked just like the youth he was, tired and defeated.

"Why must I do everything myself? My mother used to say that if you want a job doing well, you better do it yourself. Who would have thought the old bitch was right, eh?"

Without warning, he plucked a series of notes on the lute and a wall of force roared through the cavern like a hurricane. Rovann wove a shield of Air but the Song Spell moved harmlessly between him and Owen. With a start, Rovann realized they weren't the target.

Maegwin was.

She screamed as the Song Spell tightened around her. Dark drops of melody clung to her skin like black rain.

"You feckless bitch!" the Songmaker spat. "It's too late to turn back! There is no redemption for you! You're rotten on the inside, Maegwin de Romily. You're my mistress's creature and always will be!"

"No!" Maegwin cried. "I am a priestess of Sho-La! I won't help you! I won't!"

An evil smile crept across Leo's face. "Really? Are you sure about that?"

He plucked a note on his lute, one that sounded

strangely out of key. In response, Maegwin jerked, taking a step forward.

"No," she gasped. "Don't! Please!"

"It's too late, my dear. You are what you are. Just as I am. You were chosen to become our mistress's vessel. You agreed. You can't back out now."

For an instant, Leo's form wavered and Rovann thought he saw something else standing there, something that resembled an angel but whose wings were tattered and ragged, its face twisted with pain and hatred.

Rovann staggered, putting out a hand to steady himself as realization dawned. Leo had released a creature from the First Prison of Night in the mountains by Near Point. Where had that creature gone? Rovann had often wondered. Now he knew. It hadn't gone anywhere. It was right here. Inside Leo.

You were chosen to become our mistress's vessel.

The words sent a chill to the core of Rovann's being. *Oh, Maegwin!* he thought. *What did you agree to?*

Leo plucked a second note and Maegwin took another step toward the pit. Sweat dripped down her face, her teeth were bared at she fought the Songmaker's compulsion. It did no good. She moved woodenly, like a marionette on strings.

"Enough!" Rovann bellowed.

He sent Air howling at Leo but it ricocheted harmlessly off an unseen shield around the minstrel. With a growl of frustration he grabbed Maegwin's arm, trying to drag her back but the power that held her was far stronger than Rovann. He clung on as she tried to pull away but let go when he realized she would tear her arm off before she stopped her inexorable journey toward the pit.

Instead, he closed his eyes. In his mind's eye he saw

roiling black bands enveloping Maegwin. They ran around her like rope but they ran *through* her as well.

"You see!" the Songmaker crowed in triumph. "My mistress's song is woven too tightly through her soul. She cannot be saved, King's Mage! This is who she is!"

He plucked another series of notes. In response Maegwin's mouth opened and she began to sing. Her face was a mask of horror, tears rolling down her cheeks as a high, beautiful melody issued from her throat. It swirled in the air above the pit before falling like rain onto the molten bars.

Then a voice boomed through the cavern, so loud it sliced into Rovann's head like a knife.

Free me! I will devour your soul, my daughter!

A sudden pressure slammed into him and Owen, pinning them both against the cavern wall. Squinting against the crushing pressure, he saw that the bars of the pit were melting, dripping into the darkness.

And from the hole, black smoke was rising.

The dark smoke billowed around Leo. His eyes were wide and staring, a rictus grin twisting his face, arms thrown open as though welcoming the presence of his mistress.

The air suddenly turned white-hot, clawing down Rovann's throat like poison. He doubled over, coughing and gasping.

"King's Mage," Prince Owen rasped. "Do something!"

Rovann concentrated all his power and opened a gate to the Realm of Air. Clear, beautiful wind poured into the chamber and he took a shuddering breath. He struggled, trying desperately to move but the pressure only increased, pressing him against the wall like a struggling insect.

Laughter boomed through the chamber. *See, worm? See*

the price of denying me? I offered you power. I offered you immortality. Instead, you have chosen pain. So be it! Taste your future!

Agony erupted along every nerve in Rovann's body, as though he'd been doused with oil and set alight. His vision went white and his thoughts scattered. He jerked and spasmed, froth flying from his lips. He was burning, burning, burning.

Then abruptly, it ceased. He lay gasping like a landed fish. After a moment the pressure eased and he lifted his head to see Maegwin facing Leo and the dark presence. She was maybe three paces from where they waited.

But she had stopped moving.

The Songmaker frowned. His fingers glided over the strings of his lute, coaxing a melody. "Come, Maegwin," he commanded. "It's time to welcome your mistress."

Maegwin didn't move. She shook her head and Rovann saw the veins standing out in her neck as she fought, fought with all her being. She clamped her mouth shut and her singing ceased abruptly.

"Oh no you don't!" Leo cried. "You're ours! Do your mistress's bidding!"

Maegwin gritted her teeth but the bands of dark melody around her tightened. She gasped and her lips were forced open. A song began issuing from her throat.

But this song was entirely different.

Soft and gentle and full of light, it swept through the cavern like a wave. In Rovann's mind he saw brown earth, seeking roots, the quiet fall of leaves. He experienced the delight of a sprouting seed, the peace of a still pond, the calm sighing of the wind through branches.

"No!" Leo howled.

A bellow of rage from the creature almost flattened Rovann. Leo rained down deadly sorcery on Maegwin, no longer trying to control her, merely trying to stop her. The power evaporated before it hit, becoming notes of sparkling melody that shone in the air like mist.

Suddenly all color left Leo's face. Behind him, the black cloud billowed and a wave of rage rolled through the room.

"Stop it!" the youth shouted. "Stop it!"

Sorcery boiled out of him. It spiraled in all directions, uncontrolled. He recoiled as though he'd been slapped, dropping the lute with a crash and waving his hands as though trying to bat away an insect.

"Leave me alone!" he bellowed. "Get out of my head!"

Maegwin's song sparkled in the air around Leo like fireflies. Rovann remembered another time when he'd seen something like this. It had been in a dark glade near the town of Angard and Maegwin had been gravely injured. He'd begged the Sentinel to heal her and it had acquiesced.

His eyes went wide with awe. Maegwin sang with the power of a Sentinel. The healing power of the Seven Realms.

She was trying to heal the Songmaker.

Leo suddenly straightened. His once bright green eyes had gone utterly black, devoid of iris or pupil. They looked like gateways into the pit.

"No!" he thundered in a voice not his own. "I will not allow it!"

Behind him, the smoky darkness billowed and grew as more of the creature broke free. It spoke through Leo. "He is mine! You are all mine!"

A snarl pulled back his lips and Leo raised his hands. Sorcery gathered at the ends of his fingertips. In that maelstrom Rovann felt the powers of Fire and Air meld with that of Chaos, creating a deadly mix that would destroy them all.

Rovann gritted his teeth and forced himself to take a step forward, then another. He wove symbols in the air, calling the powers of Earth and Aethyr to make a shield, even though he knew it would not be enough.

Leo raised his hands high above his head, ready to release his power and kill them all.

Then suddenly his eyes rolled back and he sagged to a heap on the floor. Owen stepped out of the shadows, clutching a bloodied rock in one hand.

The creature bellowed in outrage, the black smoke shifting and bubbling as though trying to reach the unconscious youth.

"Quickly!" Owen yelled. "Before he comes round!"

Maegwin scrambled across the chamber and threw herself to her knees beside Leo. Pressing a palm to his forehead, she closed her eyes and sang. With a flick of his wrist, Rovann extended his shield around Maegwin, Owen and Leo, shutting out the dark smoke.

But beyond his barrier, the black hurricane writhed. The malevolent presence battered at his shield, sending shockwaves of power rippling through it that made Rovann stagger. All the time it howled—an ear-splitting shriek of fury born from eons of imprisonment. Unbidden, images suddenly flowered in Rovann's head. Rending. Tearing. Spilled organs. The stench of blood. And fury. Fury so deep there was room for nothing else.

Agony! A voice boomed in his head. *An eternity of agony awaits you. I will eviscerate all your loved ones while you watch. I will burn children and feed you their hearts! I will tear down the universe whilst you weep at my side!*

Rovann lurched under the onslaught. Blood dripped from his nose. Pressure began to build behind his eyes so he squeezed them shut. Pain filled his skull, ripping his thoughts to shreds. His organs labored in his body, struggling to keep him alive. Realms! He couldn't survive this. He couldn't hold on.

You must! he told himself. *There is no one else.*

He crashed to his knees, his heart thundering, his breath feeling like acid as it sawed in and out of his straining lungs.

Then the trilling of angels' voices suddenly spoke inside his head. *Hold on, Warrior! Keep Her out! Just a little longer! We will help you!*

Aethyr suddenly flowed into him, as sweet as water in a parched land, and his shield strengthened, the pressure on his body easing slightly.

"Leo?" Maegwin said.

Rovann prised open an eye and saw that the youth was sitting up, staring around with wide, fearful eyes. Owen crouched on his other side, his white eyes glaring at his torturer, shoulders hunched as though holding back from strangling the man.

The Songmaker looked from Maegwin, to Owen, to Rovann. He seemed at a loss for words. Then his gaze strayed to the black winds swirling beyond the shield.

"I feel… strange," he said at last. He patted his chest as though checking he was whole. "What have you done to me?"

Maegwin shook her head, unable to answer. There were tears on her cheeks.

Leo looked younger than Rovann remembered. The mockery was gone from his expression and his eyes had returned to their vivid green. With a start, he realized he was no longer looking at the Songmaker. Instead, he was looking at Leo, the young minstrel as he had been before he'd walked into the darkness.

"Leo," Maegwin said, taking hold of his hand. "We need your help."

The minstrel looked at where Maegwin's fingers curled around his. He seemed surprised at the contact. "I don't know what you did, Maegwin. I don't know how you reached past Him. But I thank you. I had forgotten what freedom feels like."

"Leo," Maegwin said imploringly. "You have a chance now. A chance for redemption. Leo the minstrel was my friend once. Was Rovann's friend once. You can be again. Will you help us?"

The youth stared at her. Conflicting emotions flashed one after the other across his face. "Yes," he whispered at last. "I can feel the Sentinel. It's holding Her at bay. Holding them both at bay. Realms, but I'm tired. Tired of all this. I'll do it. I'll seal the pit for you."

Maegwin let out a breath. "Thank you, Leo. And then we'll help you. We'll find a way to fix all this."

Leo shook his head sadly. "No, Maegwin. You will throw me into the pit with Her."

Maegwin recoiled. "What? No! You can be saved, Leo! Sho-La will forgive you!"

"Of that I have no doubt, my dear," he replied, patting Maegwin's hand. "Unfortunately, it's not as simple as that. Is it, Rovann?"

"What are you talking about?"

Rovann spoke in a voice hoarse with strain. "A creature of the pit was bound beneath Tyrlindon, outside the Seven Realms in an unbreakable prison. But it was not the only one. There was another." Rovann remembered the First Prison of Night he and Shern had found in the valley. He shuddered as he recalled the broken bars and the reek of corruption.

The blood drained from Maegwin's face. "Where is the other one?"

Leo tapped his chest. "In here. He was bound in a prison unbreakable but for one method: if a living being willingly gave themselves as a host. As I did."

"Why?" Rovann rasped. "Why would you do such a thing?"

Leo's eyes snapped to him. "Why do you think? A lust for power? A desire from dominion? Those reasons are a little boring, don't you think? I've always thirsted for knowledge, King's Mage. Even as a child my parents couldn't keep up with my insatiable appetite for learning. They hired a mage to become my tutor. Ah, the things he taught me! I still remember that old man with fondness. It's a pity he caught me experimenting with things I shouldn't. I had to kill him for that. It's a pity my parents caught me burning his body, I had to kill them for that too. That's when I became a minstrel—what better way to wander the land seeking knowledge? I discovered everything I could, became the most powerful mage I could. But it still wasn't enough. There was always *more*. Always something new to learn. I came to realize that a puny human mind could never know everything. If I wanted to understand the infinite I would have to become something else. Something new. That's why I did it, King's Mage. That's why I broke open the First Prison of Night. Does that answer your question?"

Rovann didn't answer. Leo stared at him for a long time before transferring his gaze to Maegwin.

"You cannot trust me, my dear. I would betray you, forever seeking the knowledge and power I crave. I'm broken inside. Corrupt. Not everyone is worth saving."

Maegwin shook her head. "You're wrong, Leo."

He shrugged. "Perhaps. But this is my choice. Just as

you chose to return to the King's Mage's side." There was no bitterness in Leo's voice which surprised Rovann. Leo was still the Songmaker. This was still the man who'd come so close to destroying the Seven Realms themselves. He had to remember that.

Gritting his teeth, Rovann forced himself to stand. The movement made him dizzy and a gush of blood splashed from his nose.

"Rovann!" Maegwin cried. "You're hurt!"

Prince Owen caught Rovann by the elbow to steady him. Rovann wiped the blood away irritably. "I'm all right. We don't have much time. I can't hold Her off forever."

Leo nodded then climbed wearily to his feet. He seemed smaller, younger, more vulnerable now that he was cut off from the source of his power. It was difficult to believe this was the Songmaker of the stories. Rovann steeled himself. There was danger in assumptions. He would not be fooled again.

"Pass me my lute," Leo said, holding out a hand.

Prince Owen reached down and plucked the instrument from where it had fallen on the floor then threw it to Rovann. "I don't think so."

Leo let his arm drop. "Fair enough. In your place I wouldn't let me have it either. It doesn't matter. The prison is almost broken. A Song Spell will suffice to open it the rest of the way." He lifted his chin and met Rovann's gaze. There was a question in that stare.

You know what to do?

Rovann nodded.

Leo climbed onto the low wall that circled the pit. Throwing his arms wide, he began to sing. Quietly at first, but growing in volume as his power flowed. After a moment Rovann realized it was a drinking song, the kind you might hear in any Tyrlindon tavern after dark. It wasn't the words that mattered, the power of the song lay elsewhere. Rovann felt it grow around Leo and he braced himself for an attack, wary of treachery. But none came. A glowing cocoon surrounded Leo, so bright that Rovann could hardly see the man inside. Finally, the youth nodded and Rovann could just make out a smile beyond the shining wall of power.

"Now," Leo said.

Rovann dropped his shield. Howling winds tore at him but he fought to stay on his feet. Leo closed his eyes, crossed his hands over his chest, and then slowly, deliberately, fell backward into the pit. As he fell, Leo's power exploded outward, enveloping the black smoke and dragging it into the pit with him. It slithered into the darkness like millions of writhing black snakes. A howl of rage ripped through the cavern but that too was pulled down until it faded, faded, faded. And fell silent.

The three of them leaned over the pit, staring down. Rovann saw only darkness. Yet he could imagine Leo and the creature falling, falling, falling, through the Realms, into a non-place, a space between realities, so far away as to be beyond comprehension. Until finally they hit the bottom...

A concussion rocked through the chamber and light flashed. Rovann threw his hands over his eyes and when he opened them again the bars covering the pit were whole once more, as if they'd never been disturbed.

With a groan, he collapsed onto his back, breath heaving in and out of his lungs, struggling to remain conscious. Every muscle ached, every organ labored as though it might burst. Yet he allowed himself only a moment's respite before staggering onto hands and knees and then levering himself to his feet.

He looked around. The cavern was almost destroyed.

Half the ceiling had fallen in, filling the space with boulders larger than a man. Cracks had shifted the walls so now they were jagged rents sticking out at acute angles.

But the prison was sealed. He, Maegwin and Owen were alive. The Songmaker was gone.

It was over.

He allowed that thought to wash over him. It was over. Over.

General! came the call of the angels. *The Sluargh are withdrawing! Chaos is pulling them back into the Outer Darkness! We will follow to ensure none escape.*

Be careful, Rovann warned. *Some may try to hide in other Realms.*

We will purge them all, general. A dragon of Fire patrols her borders. She will find any within her Realm and consume them.

Tanyaka, Rovann thought. *Thank you.*

Good hunting, he sent to his angels.

Rovann pulled in a deep, shuddering breath, trying to find strength from somewhere, anywhere. "My king," he said to Owen, who was still staring into the pit. "I suggest we sally, ride out, and retake the lower city. The Songmaker's army will have sensed his death, particularly his mages. We have to take advantage of their confusion and flush them out before they get a chance to regroup."

Owen straightened, a frown creasing his forehead. "I agree. We'll—"

"No," Maegwin said suddenly. "No more killing. Please."

"Tyrlindon is occupied," Owen snapped. "We may have killed the Songmaker but the fight isn't over. There are still thousands of his troops out there."

Maegwin stepped close to Owen, forcing him to look at her. "I was his High Priestess and Holy Mother of Sho-La.

Leo is dead. General Shallon is dead. The army will obey my orders now. Maldric Hounsey will follow my command. I'll order the withdrawal. There need be no more killing."

Owen raised an eyebrow. "You expect us to let you walk out of here? After what you've done?"

She shook her head. "No. Yes." She sucked in a breath. "I know you don't trust me. Realms, in your place I wouldn't trust me either. Yet I give you my word, for what it's worth, that I will order the withdrawal and when Tyrlindon is free I will return to face your judgment." She stared at Owen who gazed silently back.

"She's telling the truth," Rovann said suddenly, surprising himself by speaking. "The angels of the Aethyr trust her." He thought for a moment then looked at Maegwin. "I trust her." It was amazing how easily the words tripped off his tongue.

Owen looked from Rovann to Maegwin and back again. "Very well. I'll follow the advice of my King's Mage. You have three days, Maegwin. Withdraw your army. Those in command will stand trial, yourself included. If you haven't returned within three days, we'll come looking."

Maegwin bowed her head. "Yes, my lord."

She turned to leave but hesitated at the threshold of the cavern. She crossed to Rovann, took his face in her hands and kissed him. Rovann was so startled he didn't have time to react before she spun away and disappeared through the archway.

Owen raised an eyebrow but didn't comment. He let out a long sigh. "What's to be done about this place?"

Rovann looked around the ruined chamber. "We'll seal it. Fill the space with rubble. Nobody must ever come down here again.

"Agreed. Well, King's Mage, shall we go and see what's left of our city?"

Rovann nodded. Leaning on each other, they staggered to the stairs and made their way back toward the light.

The cottage garden was ordered and well kept. Tall foxgloves grew along the borders with bees droning in and out of the long purple flowers. Smoke rose from the chimney of the small, white-washed house, indicating somebody was at home.

Maegwin paused on the path, surveying the scene. It was as peaceful a place as she could imagine. Apt for what she had come to do. She didn't bother to knock on the door. It swung open at her touch, as though the occupant was expecting her. Inside, the flagstone floor had been swept and a vase of freshly-picked flowers sat on the wooden table which dominated the one-roomed space.

A figure sat in a chair by the window and didn't look up as Maegwin entered. The late afternoon light revealed a woman beyond her middle years holding an embroidery hoop as she sewed mechanically.

"I've been waiting for you, Maegwin," she said. "Tea?"

Maegwin glanced at the kettle on the fireplace. It was just beginning to boil. "No. Thank you."

The woman nodded as if she'd expected this answer. She put down the embroidery hoop and clasped her hands in her lap before finally looking at Maegwin. "You look well."

Maegwin smiled wryly. Well? An odd way to describe her. "You know why I've come, Tarina."

The older woman sighed. Regret flared in her eyes. "Yes, I do. Miriel and Ashria?"

"Gone."

Maegwin flinched at the memory. Miriel and Ashria had been her sister priestesses and she had loved them, even though she knew they'd become revenants, soulless shells and no longer the women she had known. In the end, she had done what was necessary. Now only Tarina remained.

She climbed to her feet, brushed down her dress and straightened her hair. "Do it then. I cannot pretend I'm not afraid. Even knowing what I am, I prefer life over death. Who can say if Sho-La will welcome me now, after everything I've done?"

"Of course She will welcome you," Maegwin said hoarsely. "I made you what you are. Everything you've done since I dragged you back from death is my fault, not yours. Sho-La is waiting for you."

Tarina pressed her lips together and nodded once. "I'm ready."

Maegwin stepped close and wrapped her arms around the older woman. "May Sho-La guide and keep you."

Even as the last words left her mouth Maegwin plunged a knife into Tarina's chest. The metal was imbued with Fire and strong enough to kill even a revenant. Tarina jerked in Maegwin's grip.

"It hurts," she whispered. "It hurts."

"Hush," Maegwin soothed, brushing her hair. "It will last only a moment. Hush."

A low groan escaped Tarina and then she sagged. Slowly, Maegwin lowered her to the floor. Tarina's eyes were open and staring, her mouth stretched wide as though in surprise. Maegwin reached out and closed her eyelids before placing a kiss on the older woman's forehead.

"Be at peace," she said. "Priestess of Sho-La."

She stepped back and yanked the knife from Tarina's chest. The ward within the knife flared and Fire erupted around Tarina's body. It burned white-hot for several seconds before winking out of existence. When it died, there was nothing left of Tarina but ash.

Maegwin straightened, pulling in a breath. It was done.

She closed the door behind her and made her way to the lane that ran outside the small cottage. There, she waited. A piper bird landed in a tree and regarded her with its head cocked. A weasel darted out of the undergrowth, caught sight of Maegwin then scurried back into the bushes. A light breeze stirred the trees, sending the first of the autumn leaves cascading to the ground.

Maegwin drank it all in, savoring this last glimpse of freedom.

She heard hoof beats. Plucking her knife from its scabbard she tossed it into the dirt. Let them see she was unarmed.

A group of riders appeared on the road. They thundered toward her, slowing as they reached her and surrounding the spot where she stood. The horses stamped and blew, the riders watched her with hard eyes. Maegwin felt a tremor of trepidation as she realized who'd been sent to fetch her. She recognized all of them. Once, she called them friends.

"Maegwin de Romily," Captain Tyan said, nudging his horse towards her. "We're here to escort you to Tyrlindon."

She nodded at the lean, rangy man. "I know, captain."

"It's 'general' actually," said Tallo, seeming highly offended as he pulled on his mustache. "General Tyan now. And Hannel here is our new captain."

Maegwin's eyes flicked to the blond man who sat his

horse calmly beside Tallo. Hannel glared at her with hatred in his eyes. Who could blame him? The last time they'd met she'd tried to kill him.

"And Lady and me?" Tallo continued brightly. "We're sergeants now. Who would have thought it? Me, a sergeant? If only my old mother could see me now!"

"Shut up, Tallo," Lady, the last of the four, said. The dark-haired woman had drawn a knife and was idly running it over the back of her hands. "So," she said, fixing her eyes on Maegwin. "The Lord First said you'd give no trouble. Was he right?"

"He was right," Maegwin nodded. "I gave my word."

Hannel snorted in disgust. "Tallo, bind her hands."

"Yes, captain," Tallo said, throwing him a salute. He slid to the ground and untied a coil of rope from his saddle.

Maegwin held out her hands obediently. Tallo wrapped the rope around her wrists, tying them together securely. Then he led her to a spare horse and helped her into the saddle.

"We ride for Tyrlindon," General Tyan said. "Let's go."

They kicked their horses into a gallop. Maegwin clung to the high cantle of the saddle as her horse was pulled along by Tallo's. They reached a bend in the road and Maegwin looked back, hoping to catch one last glimpse of her friend's resting place.

But dust obscured the view and she saw nothing.

They passed through countryside alive with activity. Three times they were stopped by patrols of the King's Guard scouring the land for any stragglers from the Songmaker's army. Refugees who'd taken shelter in Tyrlindon were now hurrying home: pulling carts, carrying belongings on their backs, all eager to return to their lives and begin gathering what was left of the harvest.

Then, too soon for Maegwin, they reached the upland plateau and saw Tyrlindon in the distance. She swallowed, her mouth suddenly dry. The plain was littered with the detritus of battle—broken siege weapons, discarded weapons, the remains of tents, pickets and other camp paraphernalia. The dead had been gathered into large funeral pyres which burned steadily all over the plain, wreathing the capital in dark smoke.

Three days ago she'd been attacking this place. Was it only three days? Realms, it felt like a life-time ago.

Maegwin squeezed her eyes shut but the images of that day seemed imprinted on her eyelids. She still heard the screams. She still smelled the fear-sweat. When she opened her eyes she found Hannel watching her with a grim expression on his face. He seemed about to say something but then thought better of it.

"Quickly," General Tyan snapped. "We're late."

He kicked his horse into a canter down the King's Road and the others fell into formation around him. About half a mile from the Water Gate Tyan suddenly led them off the King's Road and into a dry stream bed with high sides. There, they halted.

Maegwin looked around, puzzled. "What are you—?"

She trailed into silence as a woman stepped from the shadows of the gully. She was small, with dark hair and large eyes. One of her wrists ended in a stump.

"Syrie," Maegwin breathed.

Her heart skipped. Was the Earth adept here to kill her? If so, she wouldn't resist.

The dark-eyed woman stared up at her. "It seems the

Lord First was right," she said curtly. "Perhaps your word means something after all." She turned to the soldiers. "Dismount. Varan will take the horses. They don't travel well through the Eorthe."

The soldiers swung out of their saddles as a man came forward to take the reins. Tallo helped Maegwin dismount.

"What's going on?" Maegwin said to Syrie. "I'm to return to Rovann—"

"I'm aware of that! Would you rather ride through the city?" Syrie snapped. "Should anyone recognize you, you would likely be torn to pieces. This way at least you will survive long enough to be sentenced!"

Maegwin bit her lip and nodded.

At Syrie's direction the soldiers gathered around her.

"Hold hands," the Earth adept instructed.

"Oh, Realms," moaned Tallo. "I hoped I'd never have to do this again. Why is it always me?"

"Shut up, Tallo," Lady growled. "It will be over in a heartbeat."

Syrie muttered words under her breath. Something grabbed hold of Maegwin and yanked down, hard. The next thing she knew she was lying on soft grass, looking up at a blue sky. Sitting up, she saw rolling parkland surrounded by tall trees. In the distance, high turrets rose into the sky. She was within the royal enclave in Tyrlindon's highest level.

"I don't believe it!" Tallo cried, scrambling to his feet. "I feel fine. In fact, I feel better than fine! How come it always made me sick before?"

Syrie arched an eyebrow. "Soldier, you have obviously never traveled the Eorthe with a master. When it comes to this, the Lord First is a rank amateur."

"She gave no trouble?" said a voice behind Maegwin.

She spun to find six people seated cross-legged on the ground. The one who had spoken was Prince Owen—King Owen—Maegwin reminded herself. He wore his blindfold but despite this, Maegwin knew he saw as well as any man. Syrie took a seat on King Owen's right. Tiria sat on his left and next to her were two men Maegwin had hoped never to face again—Chief Brennan and Shaman Kandar of the Eagle Clan of the Shinnar. A worm of fear squirmed in her belly under the hard stares of the two men.

Rovann was the last member of the group, sitting a little apart from the others. He glanced at her. He seemed tired. New lines bracketed his mouth and radiated from the corners of his eyes. Maegwin's pulse quickened. She couldn't read the emotion in Rovann's eyes. Was it indifference? Or resignation? After a moment, he turned away, staring at his hands folded in his lap.

Rovann, please look at me! Maegwin thought. *There is so much I need to say.*

But he didn't. It seemed he had nothing to say to her.

"This is the second time you've been brought before a king to face justice," King Owen said in a voice that cracked like a whip. "My father pardoned you for the murder of Lord Meryk Hounsey because you were acting in defense of your temple. What about this time, Maegwin? What reasons will you give for your actions?"

"None," Maegwin answered, tearing her gaze from Rovann and forcing herself to concentrate on the king. "I'm not here to plead for my life or to offer excuses. I'm here to pay for my crimes."

Kandar snorted and then wagged a finger at Maegwin. "Burn my behind, but you still have a smooth tongue, even if it is forked. I can see why so many people followed you, how you tricked them into believing the bloody World Mother wanted a war." The old man yanked on a bone tied to his hair and leaned forward, eyes narrowed. "So you don't want your life, eh? Well maybe that's what we should bloody well give you! No more fitting punishment than life when all you want is death."

Maegwin turned to the old man. "You misunderstand. I don't wish for death. I merely accept the result of my choices. Action and consequence—one of the basic teachings of Sho-La."

Kandar watched her steadily, his eyes as fierce as any hawk's. "So it's Sho-La again now is it?" He tapped his chin. "Tell me, Maegwin of Sho-La, what is the first teaching of the World Mother?"

Maegwin cocked her head, wondering where he was going with this. "You know that as much as I."

"Yes. Indulge me. I'd like to hear you say it."

Maegwin glanced at the others. She sensed she was being led into a trap but couldn't quite figure it out.

"Sho-La forgives all."

Kandar nodded and his gaze softened somewhat. "The World Mother forgives all."

"The World Mother may forgive all, Kandar," King Owen said. "But the people of Amaury do not. I, do not." He turned to look at Maegwin and she flinched under the power of his scrutiny. From behind the blindfold, he seemed to see all. "We have argued long and hard about what to do with you, Maegwin de Romily. Syrie would hang you. Brennan would have you staked out in the sun until you die of thirst. Kandar and Tiria argue for mercy. My King's Mage says nothing."

She glanced at Rovann but he stared at the ground. A faint flicker of hope flared in her chest. Did he want her to live? Was that why he didn't speak to condemn her? Did he still feel something for her, after everything?

Don't be foolish, she chided herself. *Whatever was between you is dead. You killed it, remember?*

Syrie and Brennan's vehemence did not surprise her. She deserved no less. But she was surprised by Kandar arguing for clemency. The old man had never trusted her. What had made him change his mind?

"For myself," King Owen continued. "I'm driven more by pragmatism. You are something new, Maegwin. A new kind of mage, one that any king would be foolish to toss aside. I could lock you up and have my mages study you until they understand your powers and how they can be harnessed. I could have them conduct experiments that would make you howl. But I'm not the Songmaker and will not resort to his methods. So instead I offer you a choice." He leaned forward, clasping his hands together in his lap. "I will spare your life if you swear by your goddess that you will serve me and the Seven Realms until you have paid for your crimes. Even if that takes the rest of your life."

Maegwin stared at the king, hardly daring to believe his words. Was he taunting her? Offering her a chance of life only to snatch it away at the last minute? It was the kind of thing Leo would have done.

Her eyes flicked to Rovann. *What would you have me do?* she thought. *Say you want me to live. Say you forgive me and I'll do whatever they ask.*

He looked up and she gasped. His eyes were intense, full of longing and regret. He opened his mouth as though to speak. "I...I..." Then he snapped his mouth shut and resumed his study of the ground.

Maegwin transferred her gaze to the king. "Yes," she said in a clear, strong voice. "I swear by Sho-La and my hope of attaining the One Light that I will do as you ask. I will serve you, the Seven Realms, the Shinnar and the people of this land until my dying breath." Her voice broke a little and she had to swallow several times before continuing. "I will make recompense for what I've done, if you'll let me."

The World Mother forgives all.

King Owen stared at her so long that Maegwin began to fidget, feeling scoured right down to the bone by that all-seeing gaze. She wanted to look away but found herself unable to move.

Finally he nodded. "It is done then. My first order to you, Maegwin de Romily, is to leave Tyrlindon, leave Amaury and not return until I tell you."

Maegwin stared at him. She resisted the urge to glance at Rovann. "But how can I serve you if you send me away?"

"I've heard tell of a community in a village called Near Point. A religious community, little more than a group of novices and acolytes, rudderless and needing guidance now the Songmaker is gone. You want to make things right? This is where you'll begin. You will go to Near Point and take charge of the temple of Sho-La there. The people of Near Point were sorely used by the Songmaker. You will put that right. A horse will be readied. You'll leave by sundown."

The words sank in slowly. She'd been given a reprieve. Given back her life as a priestess, given back everything she'd once thought lost. It was more than she had any right to wish for. And yet…and yet…

I'll never see him again, she thought, going cold. *I'll never see Rovann again.*

She turned his way and found him staring at her. Maegwin opened her mouth to speak but yelped as Hannel yanked her to her feet. Without a word, he dragged her off. Maegwin looked back over her shoulder.

"Rovann!" she called. "Rovann!"

I need to say goodbye.

But Hannel dragged her away mercilessly. The last thing she saw before vegetation screened them was Rovann staring after her.

The horse tossed his head and Maegwin patted him on the neck. "I'm tired too, boy. Perhaps it's time we made camp."

It was almost dark. Tyrlindon was many leagues behind and the road she was traveling was little more than a goat track, barely wide enough for two horses abreast. Pulling her mount off the road, Maegwin found a clearing amongst the tightly packed trees and tied the horse to a branch, leaving the reins long enough to allow him to crop the thick grass.

She placed the saddlebags at the base of a tree and then folded onto the ground, leaning back against the rough bark. She sucked a deep breath through her nostrils. The cool night air filling her lungs reminded her that she was still alive.

Still alive.

The fact amazed her. With a grunt, she pulled her tunic over her head and began a ritual she'd gone through every night since the burning of Tyrvanan. She screwed her eyes tight shut, expecting the usual sharp pain as her fingers probed her burned arm. It didn't come.

Her eyes flew open and she peered down, gasping in shock. Rather than the blackened, shriveled, painful skin she'd grown used to, her right arm looked different. Better.

Like it was starting to heal. Already, tender pink skin was showing through the puckered blackness.

She slumped forward, tears leaking from her eyes. *The World Mother forgives all.*

"Thank you, Sho-La," she whispered. "Thank you, mistress."

Her horse suddenly lifted its head and whinnied shrilly. Maegwin sprang to her feet, just as a figure stepped out of the shadows. The hairs rose on the back of her neck and she reached instinctively for a weapon only to realize she no longer carried one.

"Your senses are still sharp, Maegwin."

The figure pulled back its hood, revealing a face Maegwin recognized. Her legs nearly gave way and she had to lean on the tree to steady herself. Her tears were so thick she could barely make out the figure but she'd recognize him anywhere.

"Rovann?" she gasped. "Rovann?"

He was so close she could smell him. If she reached out she could curl her fingers through his hair, feel the soft skin of his face. Realms, she wanted to touch him so badly it was an ache in her chest, stealing her breath. But she didn't.

"Are you really here?" she whispered. "Or are my desires haunting me?"

His voice was so soft that when he spoke she barely heard him. "I'm here. I...I couldn't let you go...by the One Light, I'm no good at this." He scrubbed his hand through his hair in that familiar gesture.

She shook her head. "Look at us. Back where we started. This whole thing began with the two of us camped in a wood."

"I remember. You were not a pleasant traveling

companion. Your mood was like a warhorse with a tooth ache."

"Me?" Maegwin replied incredulously. "I don't think you said more than three words to me that first night!"

Rovann smiled. "Neither of us was at our best, I think. That first night out of Mallyn was when the angels first told me they'd chosen you to help me. I never really knew what they meant until the end. As it turns out, they chose well."

Maegwin grimaced. "In the end. But I took a dark, twisty path to get there. Yes, I helped you at the last but will that excuse everything I did before then?"

His eyes were kind. "You sound as though you've spent a lot of time thinking about that."

Maegwin looked away. "Yes," she whispered. "A lot of time."

In her mind's eye she saw images of the Sluargh, the Unforgiven Dead of the Outer Darkness, who'd invaded the Realm of Earth and attacked Tyrlindon. She remembered their rage, their hatred. But above all, she remembered their despair.

Was that what lay in store for her now? The World Mother forgives all, Kandar had told her. Oh, how badly she wanted to believe that! But, try as she might, she couldn't bring herself to accept it. Unless…unless…

"Why are you here, Rovann?" she said.

Do you forgive me? She wanted to ask but she didn't have the courage. She was too afraid of what his answer might be.

He stared at her and his eyes shone like blue lamps in the darkness. "Because, despite everything that's passed between us, despite the fact that we've tried to kill each other more than once, despite the fact we've been on opposing sides all these months, I meant what I said beneath Tyrlindon. I still mean it."

Maegwin's breath caught. *I could have loved you.* That's what he'd said.

She shook her head, refusing to allow that seed of hope to take root. It was impossible. He was King's Mage, tied to Tyrvanan and Amaury. She was a traitor, condemned to banishment.

"You'd better go." She forced the words past a tightness in her throat. "King Owen won't be pleased when he discovers you came after me."

He watched her for a long time. Finally, he said, "King Owen thinks I need a rest. I'm under orders to do nothing until I'm fully healed and back at full strength." He shrugged. "So I thought I'd travel. I hear Near Point is particularly pretty at this time of year."

Maegwin stared at him. As his words sank in she barely dared to breathe. Slowly she crossed the ground between them and stood staring into those blue eyes of his. Realms, how she'd missed him.

"Yes, I heard that too," she whispered.

Rovann reached out and brushed his thumb across her cheek. "How would you feel about a traveling companion?"

Maegwin didn't answer. She grabbed the front of his tunic, pulled his head down and kissed him.

Also by Elizabeth Baxter

vinci-books.com/everwinter

Can science and magic ever exist in harmony?

A skeptical engineer, a cunning ruler, and a banished princess must navigate a realm where magic and science clash. As the Everwinter tightens its icy grip, their choices will shape a world on the brink of ruin.

Turn the page for a free preview…

Everwinter: Prologue

731 AD

The king had gone mad.

Captain Harn Yorgesson had suspected for a long time, but now he was sure. Why else had the king brought them on this trek? Why else would he not tell Harn where they were going? These days, the king consulted only with that accursed monk. The Great Warrior alone knew what poison that man had been pouring into the king's ear.

Harn shook himself. What right did he have to question the king? He was a captain of the Royal Guard of Variss, sworn to obey. He would do his duty even though every step he took up this gods-forsaken mountain intensified his dread.

"Captain," said sergeant Tarl. "When are we going to call a halt? If we don't stop for food and rest, the injured men will die."

Harn cast his eye over the line of soldiers. Many of them carried small injuries: cuts, bruises or torn muscles.

374

But the three worst injured—those caught in the rock-slide two days ago—were being hauled on crude stretchers slung from the exhausted shoulders of the others. Anger twisted Harn's mouth. The king refused to send the injured men back to Variss, leaving only two choices: bring them along or leave them on the mountainside to die.

"I'll consult the king," he said.

Harn waited at the side of the trail until the king's party caught up to him. As always, the king and monk were deep in conversation. For a moment, Harn thought they would walk right past without even noticing him, but as he came abreast of the captain, the king's gray eyes snapped up.

"Captain Yorgesson. Is there a problem?"

Harn bowed. "Sire, we need to make camp for the night. My men are weak and exhausted. Many sustained injuries in the rock-fall. They need food and shelter."

The king stared at him for a time and then shook his head. "No. We don't have time to stop. We must reach our destination before nightfall."

"And what is our destination, sire?"

The king gazed up at the mountain's peak. "The gods." He took the monk's arm and moved on, leaving Harn alone on the trail.

Harn pinched the bridge of his nose, beating back a headache. His gaze wandered along their route, showing him nothing but the endless vista of the Sisters. Although the spring weather had been kind, they'd had plenty of other dangers to contend with. Wolves and bears, creatures normally shy of humans, had become aggressive, plaguing the party through the mountains. And there were other creatures as well. Creatures that stalked just beyond the edge of the firelight. Creatures Harn had no name for. Once, Harn would have scoffed at the stories of ghosts and ghouls that haunted the Sisters. Fairy stories, he would have said. Tales to frighten children. But now he wore a protection charm around his neck like the rest of his men.

So far, Harn had lost nine soldiers. Nine dead and the king did not care.

King Beorl Godwinsson was not the king Harn had once loved. He was no longer the shrewd, brilliant young general who had won Harn's loyalty all those years ago. *That* King Beorl had refused to leave even one injured soldier on the field when he led his army at the battle of Mother's Ridge. *That* King Beorl would have wept at the injuries the men sustained in the rock-slide.

But no longer.

Now a hunger Harn could not comprehend drove the king of Variss. Since the monk had arrived in Variss a little over six months ago, the king had begun to change, gradually becoming somebody Harn no longer recognized.

The princess had seen it. She had done her best to halt the growing influence of the monk over her father. But whatever hold the foreigner had gained seemed unbreakable. The princess had refused to accept her father's new gods and been banished. Harn's guts still twisted at the memory. He remembered standing with the princess and Lidda, her maid, on that last afternoon. He remembered the shock and fear in the princess's eyes. He'd so wanted to go with her, to turn his back on Variss and ride off with her into the south. But he hadn't. He was a king's man and his vows held him chained. Six months had passed with no word. He wondered if the king ever thought about his daughter, ever wondered where she was or what she was doing.

"You all right, captain?" said Sergeant Tarl, frowning at Harn in concern.

Harn shook himself. "I'm fine, Tarl. Come on."

They marched in silence. After a while, the trail ended, and the soldiers halted in confusion. The monk pushed to the front of the group and knelt on the ground, forehead pressed into the dirt, as though praying to his strange gods.

Harn scowled. He disliked any god that put a man on his knees. The Great Warrior taught all men to face him with head high and sword in hand.

The monk took a map from the pocket of his robe and unrolled it on the ground. Leaning close, he studied the map for a long time.

"I knew it," he whispered. "All the searching, all worth it. I've found it!" His bony finger pointed upwards at Black Seza towering above them. "There."

Harn sucked in a breath. Black Seza, the tallest peak of the Sisters, had a dark reputation. Lost souls walked her summit, the tales said, and none who climbed her pitted flanks ever returned.

The king conferred hurriedly with the monk. After a moment, he turned to Harn. "Captain Yorgesson, that is our road."

What would be his punishment if he refused? What would happen if he ordered his men to abandon the king and his mad plans? Would the Great Warrior forgive him? Probably not. A soldier never left a comrade on the field and Harn had sworn oaths to his king that bound him like chains.

"Sergeant Tarl, take four scouts and range ahead. Find us a trail up the mountain. Corporal Mannon, you take the rear. The rest of you form up in marching order. Sire, I suggest you hold your place in the middle of the line."

For a wonder, the king smiled. "As you wish, captain."

Tarl and the scouts moved out. Harn and his men waited in silence and soon heard the call of a white eagle.

Harn nodded. "That's the signal. Let's get moving."

In marching formation, they began to climb. They picked their way through outcroppings of boulders sticking out of the ground like the mountain's bones and clumps of small, scraggly brush. At times, they had to move in single file, which Harn didn't like one bit. Strung out like this, they became the perfect target for an ambush.

But who would set an ambush out here? He thought. *Nothing human, that's for sure.*

He shuddered.

Tarl waited ahead. "The scouts have found a trail of sorts. It's odd, captain. The trail is paved like a road, but who would build a road up here?"

Harn shook his head. He didn't want to guess. "Show me."

The road appeared through the scrub, wide enough for a cart and paved in square-cut stones. It ran straight and true toward the summit of the mountain as if newly laid for their purpose.

Harn made the sign of the Mother at his breast. "What devilry is this?"

The rest of the troop had caught up, and now the monk and king pushed their way to the front. Seeing the road, the monk's eyes widened.

"We've found it, sire!" he cried. "Didn't I tell you we would? We are so close now!"

The king stared at the road and then up toward Black Seza's crown. For the first time since they'd left Variss, Harn saw doubt in the king's face. It flickered across his features for a moment before the mask descended again.

378

"Captain," the king said. "We must hurry. Dark will soon be falling."

They made good speed on the road. It sloped gently upwards along the mountain's flank, and where the ground rose too steeply, the mountainside had been cut away to make the road's passage easier. Harn marveled at the engineering involved. Who had built this? And how had they brought the materials up here, this far into the Sisters? Variss lay many leagues to the south. No other settlement existed in the Sisters. Nothing lived up here, except...

No.

It couldn't be. Could it?

The Quiet Land.

Harn shook himself. A children's story, a name to whisper around a campfire. Nothing more.

The road bent round to the east and Harn saw that a great cliff bisected this part of the mountain, blocking their path. The road ran straight into the cliff.

As Harn reached the scouts, one of them said, "We can't find a way around. The road leads here and stops. If the king wants to go on, we'll have to climb."

The rock face was sheer and high. They'd need climbing gear and would be unable to hoist the injured men up. Black Seza's cloud-wreathed summit towered above them. At this angle, the jagged crags almost looked like a face leering down.

Harn turned to the king. "The road ends here, sire. There is no way around. If you want to continue, we must go up."

The king regarded him. "Up? Why would we want to go up? We've found it."

Harn looked around. What was the king talking about?

They were surrounded by the featureless flanks of the mountain. There was nothing else.

The monk stepped forward. His large hands roved along the cliff face, gently caressing.

"What's he doing?" Harn asked.

"Be silent!" snapped the king.

The monk seemed to be searching for something. After a moment, he stopped and pressed his ear to the stone.

"Here, sire."

The king placed his hand on the stone where the monk indicated. "You're sure?"

"Yes. Close your eyes. Can you not feel it?"

"I can!" whispered the king after a moment. "So much life! So much power! The Lords of Life are close. Let us begin."

The monk bowed, then took a knife from his belt and sliced the blade across his arm. Blood welled from the cut, a sheet of red liquid that spread over his hand and dripped from his wrist. The monk wiped his arm across the face of the cliff, smearing blood across the rock.

Harn watched in fascinated horror. He was in the company of mad men.

The monk's blood gleamed in the sunlight, and to Harn's eyes, looked as though it was spreading along the stone, crawling as if alive. But that was impossible.

Around him, the men began to mutter. They had seen it too. The monk's blood moved upwards and sideways, spreading itself across the stone until it revealed a rough pattern like the outline of a door.

Harn's heart thudded. He had been in many battles and seen things that would cause nightmares for a lifetime. Yet nothing had filled him with the cold fear that drenched him now.

He stepped forward. "Sire, what is going on?"

The king tore his eyes from the door and looked at Harn. The captain stepped back a pace. A shadow danced in the king's eyes, a dark madness that jumped and spun.

"We stand at a crossroads, Captain Yorgesson. You and your men are privileged to witness the dawning of a new age. All my life I have guarded the ancient secret given to my line. Never must this door be opened, lest it release a terrible power from the other side. But Nashir has helped me to see that my ancestors were wrong. The Lords of Life wait beyond. It is my duty to release them."

Harn tried to move. As the king approached the cliff, his every instinct screamed at him to stop this. But he was rooted to the spot. Fear chained him.

The king bared his arm and let Nashir slash the blade across his skin. The king wiped his blood down the rock.

"I open the Rift. Lords of Life, I give you the freedom of this realm! I live to serve you! Bring us all into your loving embrace!"

The king's blood ran across the cliff face, seeping into the pattern of the door.

For a second, all was quiet. Harn dared to hope. Perhaps they were wrong. Perhaps all this drama was just the delusional antics of two mad men.

But then a shaft of light burst from the door. Harn threw his arm across his face and his men yelled in alarm. The light flared brightly and then faded.

When Harn looked again, he saw an opening in the cliff face, a dark tunnel like a hungry mouth.

The king went to his knees. "They are coming! I can feel it!"

Something small and white landed on Harn's shoulder. A snowflake.

Snow began falling all around. The men muttered in fear. It was a warm spring day. What was happening?

The wind rose. It screamed from the tunnel and hit them so hard that Harn stumbled backward. On its heel came a blizzard.

Harn had time to cry out, "Sire!" before he was enveloped in a white blanket.

The world turned to chaos. He heard his men shouting to each other, fearful and lost.

The king, he thought desperately. *I must reach the king!*

He took a tottering step forward but was driven to his knees. His clothes were sodden, his hair plastered to his head. He dashed snow from his eyes and peered into the storm. Ahead, he saw the shadow of the tunnel. Something moved by the tunnel entrance. A scream cut through the air.

"Retreat!" Harn bellowed to his men, not knowing if any of them heard.

But he was a captain of the Royal Guard of Variss and must save his king. He placed his hands on the ground and began to edge forward. Inch by slow inch, he moved into the heart of the blizzard, crawling like a blind man.

A shape reared up before him. Then a talon the length of his arm erupted from his chest.

Who will warn Variss? he thought as pain flooded him and his thoughts spun down into darkness.

Everwinter: Chapter One

RAL TORA

Three years later

Bramwell Thornley was not and had never been, a religious man. But now, as he hung three hundred paces from the ground, he was beginning to reassess that stance. Squeezing his eyes shut, he sent a prayer to any god, goddess, demigod or friendly spirit that might be listening.

Let me get down in one piece and I promise to never do anything this stupid again. Please!

Above him, the spire of First Storm Tower soared into the gray sky. Clouds had gathered, ready to throw their anger at anyone stupid enough to enter their domain. A freezing wind blew from the north, howling around the tower and lifting the ends of Bram's sweat-sodden hair. He clung to the metal ladder so tightly his fingers were cramping. His nose, lips, and ears felt like frozen slabs of meat. To top it all, he'd strapped his pack on too tightly and now it was digging into the skin beneath his armpits.

All in all, Bram wished he were somewhere else.

The wind dropped, and Bram seized his chance to squint upwards. The tower's pinnacle rose only a few paces above him, but it could have been a hundred miles away.

If only he'd kept his mouth shut! If his stupid pride hadn't goaded, him he'd be safely on the ground right now. It was always the same with him—his mouth always ten seconds ahead of his brain. This morning, when Chief Engineer Rassus had asked for a volunteer to repair Old Rosella, why had he raised his hand? He should have stared at the ground and pretended he hadn't heard like Romy had.

Fool! Think before you open your mouth! He told himself. *You're an engineer, not a steeplejack!*

Shaking his head to clear the clinging threads of hair from his face, he reached for the next rung and pulled himself up. As he climbed, his world shrank to a pinprick; only the ladder and his next handhold mattered. Nothing else.

Despite the freezing temperature, sweat beaded on Bram's forehead and dripped into his eyes, making his vision blur. He settled his boot on the next rung and felt the grips on his boots catch on the icy metal for a second—then slide out from under him. Desperately he threw up his arms, trying to find a handhold, but his gloves slid off uselessly and the weight of his body ripped him from the ladder.

With a strangled cry, Bram fell.

Panic flashed through his body. Blood roared in his ears. Then, with a grunt, the breath was punched from his lungs as the safety harness jerked him to a halt. He'd only fallen about five paces.

Bram hung there, winded, desperately trying to pull in a breath. Dots of silver light danced in front of his eyes. Unbidden, Bram's eyes swiveled downwards and he caught a glimpse of the patchwork of Ral Tora's streets, far, far below.

Gorge rose in Bram's throat. Waves of dizziness swamped him. He closed his eyes and sucked in deep breaths, then forced himself to grab the ladder and haul himself upright. His boots scrabbled against the rungs and eventually found purchase. Bram pressed his forehead to the cold metal, allowing the fear to leak out of him like water from a burst skin. It felt as though his thudding heart would shatter his ribs.

You're all right. You didn't fall, he told himself over and over.

The wind howled, sounding like cruel laughter in Bram's ears.

You're not up to this job, the wind seemed to whisper. *Go back to the menial tasks you can cope with. Only real engineers should be up here.*

Bram almost gave in. *You can't do this,* he told himself. *Go down before you kill yourself.* But a louder voice answered, *what, and prove you can't cut it as an engineer? That you should still be an apprentice?*

Sudden anger flared in Bram's chest.

I will not give up!

Gritting his teeth, he narrowed his eyes at the ledge and climbed.

One rung.

Two rungs.

Three rungs.

Four.

At last, Bram scrambled onto the ledge and lay on his back, gasping. Triumph surged through him. He'd done it!

In front of him, the pointed top of First Storm Tower rose up, a narrow spire that ended in a weather vane shaped like a cockerel. Several tiles had slipped from the roof, leaving gaps through which Bram could see Old Rosella, the great bell, hanging in the chamber below. If she hadn't commanded such affection from the citizens of Ral Tora, Chief Engineer Rassus would not have spared the labor to conduct repairs. The engineers were busy enough already.

But Old Rosella was one of Ral Tora's oldest landmarks and people measured their day by her hourly peals. So when she had failed to chime this morning, the chief engineer had sent Bram to investigate. But while the bell chamber itself was accessible from inside the tower, the roof above was too narrow and could only be reached from the metal ladder on the outside of the spire.

Bram saw the problem immediately. The hole had been letting in snow that seized up Old Rosella's striking hammer. Bram shrugged the pack of tools from his shoulders and took out what he needed. None of the tiles had fallen from the roof and smashed on the street below, so all he had to do was re-position them and then nail them into place. He worked as quickly as he could, before his hands became too cold to use the hammer, doing his best to ignore the wind that tried to tear him from his precarious perch.

At last, Bram nailed the last tile into place. He put his tools away and slung the pack over his shoulder. The wind dropped and the clouds broke to let through the midday sun. The effect was startling. The dull, lifeless day suddenly came alive with beauty. Ice glistened on the roofs of Ral Tora, glittering like thousands of tiny crystals.

Holding the safety line, Bram edged forward and looked out over Ral Tora. The city spread out below like a giant's map. In the far distance, Bram could see the curtain wall that protected the city, and the twelve watchtowers rising along it. Directly below Bram's perch the four quarters of the city fanned out in perfect symmetry around First Storm Tower's central courtyard. It reminded Bram of a wheel, with First Storm Tower as the hub and the streets radiating outwards like spokes.

Home, he thought.

Pride swelled in his chest. This was Ral Tora, the greatest place in the world.

Tugging on the safety line to check it was secure, Bram turned around, lowered his foot onto the first rung of the ladder, and began his descent. Although Bram wouldn't have thought it possible, going down was worse than going up. Agonizingly slowly, Bram crawled downwards. Each time he moved he had to pause and make sure his grip was secure before moving on.

At length, he reached a door in the spire's side. Bram gratefully took his feet from the ladder, pushed his way through the door, and lay panting on the landing inside. The smell of old wood replaced the icy odor of the wind.

He'd reached the bell chamber and the great bell, Old Rosella, hung above him, the iron turned green with verdigris. With the roof fixed, he just had to free the mechanism and then he could get back to the ground. He unclipped himself from the safety harness and with cloths, brushes and oil, set about cleaning the cogs and springs that controlled the bell's striking apparatus. Finally, he greased the whole thing so the icy air wouldn't cause the machinery to freeze.

With tired arms, Bram slung the pack onto his back and climbed to his feet. A hefty staircase spiraled around the inside of the tower. As he tottered down it, the reassuring feel of the banister helped to steady the thumping of his heart.

A voice suddenly called from somewhere below, "Hoi! Bram! What took you so long?"

Bram saw a familiar figure standing at the bottom of the stairs. He smiled. "Next time I volunteer for this, Romy, will you please give me a whack on the head?"

Romy barked a laugh and then rushed to take Bram's pack as he reached the bottom and sat down on the smooth flagstone floor.

Romy leant over him. "You all right? You look a bit pale."

Bram waved his friend's words away. He needed to gather himself.

But before he could catch his breath, another voice spoke. "Engineer Thornley, report!"

Chief Engineer Rassus stood in the doorway, hands planted on his hips. He was a bear of a man, with bushy eyebrows and a glare to melt lead.

"Well?" he demanded. "Did you complete the repairs?"

"Yes, sir," Bram replied. "I found a hole in the roof and the mechanism had seized. It should be fine now."

"Then why hasn't Old Rosella chimed this hour?"

Bram opened his mouth and closed it again. He'd been so focused on his descent that he hadn't been listening for the bell's chimes.

Oh no! He thought. *Don't make me go back up there!*

A loud peal suddenly rang out. The clonking cacophony echoed through the tower, rattling Bram's teeth. As the last strains died into silence, Bram sighed in relief.

Rassus glanced at the tower and back to Bram. "Good work, engineer." He strode off without a backward glance.

Romy blew out a breath. "What a day for surprises! A climb that would have the best of us soiling our breeches, then a compliment from Rassus. This must be your lucky day, Bram!"

Bram raised an eyebrow but didn't reply to his friend's

sarcasm. Romy's yellow hair was matted with grime, his face a patchwork of mud and soil.

"What happened to you?" Bram asked. "You look like a street urchin who's been scrapping in the dirt."

"Charming! I trudge all the way across town to see how you're doing—without even stopping to have a bath—and all I get is insults! I've been at the north wall all day. Again."

"How's it going?" Bram asked, kneeling to tie his bootlace.

"It's the last section of tunnels that's giving us the trouble." Romy shrugged. "I suppose when they built the wall, they didn't think that one day we might need to lay pipes underneath. Rassus has given me the honor of overseeing one of the digging teams. Gods, those boys can moan! Three times they had me in the tunnels, checking the measurements. Three bloody times! They reckoned the wall was going to collapse. Of course, it wasn't. I've never met such a superstitious bunch of old women in my life!"

"I'll swap you then," said Bram, straightening. "Next time Old Rosella needs repairs you can go up, and I'll look after your digging team. What do you say?"

Romy craned his head back and looked up at First Storm Tower. "No chance."

Bram laughed and they left the tower, locked the door behind them, and headed toward the center of town. They found themselves on a busy thoroughfare. People scurried back and forth, heads bent against the blustery weather. Wind-blasted olive and fig trees lined the street, black and shrunken.

The street opened out into a large park with a cluster of buildings sitting in the middle. Lamps gleamed in the windows, battling the already fading light. A sign by the gates read:

University of Ral Tora, Engineering Academy. Charter granted by Great Father Toran, year 299.

Had it really been less than a year since his graduation? It felt like forever.

The two friends skirted the length of the university precinct and entered a large square. A fountain shaped like a rearing horse dominated the center. In better days, people had sat round the square, enjoying the warm southern climate and chatting with friends. But now the water in the basin was frozen and there was no warmth to enjoy.

Nevertheless, a large group of people were gathered round the fountain, staring avidly at a man who'd climbed onto the rim and was bellowing at them. The man had a livid scar running through one eye and he'd smeared soot around his eyes, giving his face a skull-like pallor.

Romy whistled under his breath. "Great. It looks as though we've walked into the middle of a Wailer meeting. Shall we go the other way?"

"No, it'll take ages. If we keep our heads down, they shouldn't bother us."

They pulled their collars up and scurried around the outside of the square, heads bowed. As they drew nearer, Bram could make out the man's words.

"Listen! The mighty ones are coming! Already we feel their power! In our pride, we have forgotten the old gods and they are punishing us. If we don't repent, they will send us all to Hell!"

Bram shook his head. The man was talking nonsense. There was a perfectly rational explanation for this unseasonal weather. Old gods had nothing to do with it. Why did the Wailers have to keep stirring things up? Didn't Ral Tora have enough problems already?

"There!"

Bram looked up to find the man's eyes had fixed on him and Romy. He pointed a bony finger at them, a triumphant expression on his face.

"There! Two of the blasphemers! Two of those who ignore the will of the old gods and defile their names!"

The crowd turned toward the two engineers. An angry murmur broke out.

Bram glanced at Romy. His friend's face had gone pale.

"Let's get out of here," Bram whispered.

They turned on their heels and strode back the way they'd come. Once out of the square, Bram wiped his brow and whistled under his breath. "That was close. The crowd was beginning to get ugly."

Romy snorted contemptuously. "Who do they think they are? They have no right to intimidate people, as though they own the city. The city fathers should do something about those scare-mongering lunatics."

Bram nodded his agreement and they made their escape down Merchant's Way, a roundabout route that would take them twice as long.

At last, they turned into White Road and reached their destination. The headquarters of The Honorable Guild of City Engineers was a three-story building made of good Ral Toran brick. It had a gabled roof and a large red door. Warm light spilled from the windows.

"I don't know what you're looking so relieved about," Romy said. "I bet Rassus is waiting for you in his office, wanting a full report."

Bram groaned. "You're right. No doubt he'll find something he can shout at me for."

Romy looked sympathetic. "Tell you what; let's get a few of the lads together later. I might even stretch to a jug of wine or two."

Bram clapped Romy on the shoulder. "I'll hold you to that."

Grinning, they made their way into the guild house.

Grab your copy...
vinci-books.com/everwinter

About the Author

Elizabeth Baxter spent most of her childhood wandering the paths of the Shire, the trails of Narnia, and the sun-speckled glades of the Hundred Acre Wood. She wrote her first book when she was six years old and plans to continue until they nail shut her coffin. When she's not sipping a latte and dreaming up fantastical places for her readers to visit, she enjoys reading, hiking, watching cricket, and cramming as much world travel as she can into one lifetime.